Talanski

TALANSKI

Thomas D. Williams

VANTAGE PRESS
New York

This is a work of fiction. Any similarity between the names, characters, and places in this book and any persons, living or dead, is purely coincidental.

To my children Wanda, Wendy, and Tommy
for sharing my fascination with great white sharks

TALANSKI

Book I

One

Difficult Acceptance

1

It was raining heavily that June 1944 day in Pittsburgh, and the Talanskis' ground floor apartment was taking water. Twenty-two year-old Marie Talanski was crying and cursing while she worked desperately at mopping up the water as it seeped beneath the door and through the many layers of newspapers and rags. Marie had just finished emptying the twelfth bucket when the phone rang.

"Hello, Ma, how're you folks doing over there in all this rain? Yeah, well, little Joey and I are trying to wait for it to let up so we can go to the sitter's and to work. What . . . oh, please, Ma, let's not get into that again! I married Carl because I loved him!"

The general subject of this conversation between Marie and her mother was certainly nothing new. Ever since high-school-drop-out Carl Talanski started dating their only daughter of six children, the Flahertys tried to dissuade Marie from seeing "that *dumbpolski*," as Mr. Flaherty often referred to him. Aside from being handsome and having a muscular build, Carl had very little else in his favor as far as Marie's parents were concerned.

"And just who the hell is this boy, anyway?" asked Mr. Flaherty just three days prior to learning of the elopement. "You've been seeing him against our wishes for about six months now, and you have not even met his people!"

Poor Marie was really in a bind. Her father was right. She knew very little about nineteen-year-old Carl other than the fact that he lived with an aunt who ran a boarding house, and that he owned a new red '39 Buick convertible. Carl was just as flashy as his car, and his wallet always contained at least thirty dollars. He didn't regret dropping out of high school at sixteen, because Vic Stolick, his aunt's star boarder, was a foreman at one of Pittsburgh's leading steel mills.

It didn't take long for Marie to fall head over heels for this handsome rake after her girlfriend introduced her to him at a neighborhood block party. Practically every bobby-soxer between East End and Squirrel Hill yearned to be sitting in a car beside Carl Talanski. Since he worked the night shift and had plenty of time to cruise around many of the high schools, young Talanski always kept his eyes open for girls who didn't mind accepting his offer to drive them home.

Election Day 1940 was a big one in Pittsburgh. Franklin Delano Roosevelt was once again made the choice of the laboring man, and democrats throughout the Golden Triangle were celebrating. Carl's Aunt Madge was working the polls, which meant that there would be no one at home for several hours. Marie finally yielded to her convincing boyfriend. Their intimate interludes became more frequent. However, when Marie missed her monthly in February, she panicked—but, surprisingly, Carl didn't. His demeanor changed. No longer was he the flitting firefly. Now he spoke of their relationship in subdued tones. Carl insisted upon talking to Mr. and Mrs. Flaherty about his desire to marry Marie, but she convinced him that her stubborn father would never consent.

"I know I haven't met all of Carl's family, Papa. He only has his Aunt Madge who he lives with, and . . ."

"Look, my little colleen," interrupted her father in a calm voice, "this boy is only one of many that you'll meet along life's way. You're growing up to be a beautiful woman, and you'll find that laddies from all over, not just the 'burgh, will be seeking after you."

"Your father's right, Marie," said Mrs. Flaherty as she sat down on the sofa beside her visibly distraught daughter. "There'll be plenty of fine, upright young men for you to choose from. Just think of all the good things that'll be happening to you between now and September: eighteenth birthday next month; Mike's going to finish teaching you how to drive; graduation in June; maybe a two-week stay with your Aunt Cora in Atlantic City; business school next September. . . ."

"Yeah," chimed in her father, "and there's a good chance that you might get on at the plant as a full-time secretary up in the business office. If Jim O'Shaughnessy can do it for his two daughters plus a niece, then I'm sure I can do it for you, m'love."

4

The anguish that spread across poor Marie's face was too concentrated to hide. Suddenly, she began to cry uncontrollably. Mr. and Mrs. Flaherty thought they knew what the problem was, namely, Marie's coming to the realization that she must stop seeing Carl Talanski.

"There, there, now, darling," said the mother as she gently hugged her sobbing daughter, "the world's not coming to an end—only the relationship you had with that boy."

The words *that boy* triggered a spontaneous response from Marie that stayed with her for several years. She pulled back from her mother's shoulder, jumped up, quickly wiped her puffy eyes with the back of her hands and loudly proclaimed, *"That boy* you speak of is a man! The man I love—and the man I'm going to marry!"

"Heavens! May the Saints preserve us!" shouted Mrs. Flaherty.

"Ma, oh, Ma. . . ."

Mr. Flaherty slowly stood up, walked over to the glowing fireplace, and with both hands folded behind his back while staring at the burning wood, he said, in a voice that was barely above a whisper, "Marie, I'm gonna ask you a question, and I want you to answer me with the truth."

"Yes, Papa," came the low reply. Marie's knuckles were devoid of blood from clenched fists as though she was expecting the sky to fall.

"Have you 'n that Talanski kid been messin' around?"

Silence. Mrs. Flaherty's eyes grew as big as saucers. Silence. Then all hell broke loose.

"Well?" shouted Marie's father as he spun around and focused his eyes into hers. "Answer me! Are you pregnant?"

"Yes, Papa, yes! But Carl and I love each other, and we want to get married!"

"Oh, Marie, honey," cried her mother, "how could you?"

"I'll kill the sonofabitch!" yelled her father. "No . . . no . . . first, I'll chop off his kielbasa . . . *then* I'll kill the sonofabitch!"

However, Patrick Flaherty did not do either to Carl, but he did refuse to attend the small wedding reception (Mrs. Flaherty, three of Marie's brothers, and Carl's Aunt Madge) that was held in the back room of the Polish Falcons Club.

It became quite clear to Madge that the Flahertys looked upon her nephew as though he was the scum of the earth. Therefore, she

5

set out very early in this relationship to show everyone how the Talanskis take care of their own. She subtly pressurized one of her more prestigious gentlemen boarders, and the newlyweds found themselves able to afford an apartment because of Carl's promotion to that of charging machine operator, the mill's youngest operator of a piece of heavy equipment.

On October 5, 1941, Carl and Marie became the proud parents of Joseph Bernard, a strapping nine-pounder. By then, Mr. Flaherty's anger had all but melted away, and his Irish eyes smiled again, especially when he learned that Marie had persuaded her husband to attend night school.

"Well, my little half-shamrock," said the grandfather as he picked up the squirming bundle of joy, "maybe your old man's not such a *dumbpolski* after all."

2

"Oh, Carl, this is terrible!" cried Marie as she dropped the letter on the floor and sat in his lap. "What are Joey and I supposed to do while you're gone? Oh, God, how can I make it now?"

Carl held on to the crying bundle with one arm and stubbed his cigarette as he replied, "Come on now, baby, stop crying. You know I promised you when we got married that you'd never have any cause to cry again. I'm going to make you and your family proud of me. Besides, by the time I finish basic training at Indiantown Gap, this thing might be over."

The thing to which Carl referred was World War II. And the letter that his wife dropped was a notice for the draft. Most of Carl's friends had volunteered by the end of January 1942, and he would have also, especially after the remark passed by his father-in-law on the occasion of a going-to-serve party for three of Marie's brothers who had signed up and were leaving for Marine Corps boot camp.

Carl's words did very little to soothe the hurt that Marie felt. He wasn't the only one who wanted to prove a point, and just when finances and other matters were beginning to look good, the war interrupted. Joey was only six months old when his father was drafted into the Army on that rainy day in April 1942. Marie, in spite of the protestations leveled by her parents, declined acceptance of their offers for her to move back home until Carl was discharged from the service. For the next two years, Mr. and Mrs. Flaherty always managed to turn practically every conversation around to how terrible it was for Marie and Joey to stay cooped up in that small apartment. And, as usual, her father never refused the opportunity to blame *that dumbpolski* for everything.

Marie was still talking to her mother on the telephone when the doorbell rang.

"Just a minute, Ma, someone's at the door. Don't worry. I'll be sure to find out who's there before I . . . oh, for heaven's sake, Ma, give me at least some credit for breathing!"

As Marie approached the door, she could see the outline of a rather short figure through the curtains; however, she still asked, "Who is it?"

"Telegram," came the reply.

During those dark days of World War II, wives and families of servicemen went through moments of trauma whenever a telegram came. Marie's heart was beating very fast as she opened the door and looked at the rainslicker-clad figure.

"Mrs. Marie Talanski?"

"Yes."

"Telegram for you, Ma'am."

When she reached for it, her fingers seemed to have lost all strength. The envelope fell. Joey, while holding on to his mother's skirt, quickly stooped down to retrieve it.

"Ta-ta, Mommy, ta-ta," he said in a serious tone as he held it up for her to take.

By that time, the delivery boy was on his bicycle. It was as though he knew what was about to happen and didn't want to be part of the scene.

Marie nervously opened the envelope and read the brief message: We are sorry to inform you that your husband, Sgt. Carl H. Talanski, was killed in action.

The funeral took place without the body. Carl and two other volunteers from his platoon were shredded by German machine-gun fire and mortar rounds as they attempted to cut barbed wire during the battle of Cherbourg.

But Marie's father was right. Time does eventually heal all wounds. As a matter of fact, the plant's Christmas party served as

7

the occasion for the young widow to shed all black and other dull colors. Undoubtedly, she was one of the most beautiful women in attendance, and many of the single men, plus several married ones, paid notice to the strawberry blonde wearing the bright green dress. However, it was handsome Bob Callahan, the plant's new thirty-two-year-old bachelor physician, who dominated Marie's time for the evening. Needless to say, that when she took Dr. Callahan to her parents' home for Christmas dinner, Mr. and Mrs. Flaherty liked him immediately.

On Valentine's Day, Bob asked Marie to marry him, but she did not give her answer until a week later. When she told her parents about Bob's proposal, they were ecstatic.

"I think you should accept," said Marie's father. "After all, Dr. Callahan is certainly in a noble profession, and he can provide a comfortable financial base for you and Joey. Also, I like the good family stock—told me his father took part in the 1916 Easter Rebellion in Dublin."

"You should know that, Papa. At the New Year's Eve dinner, you and Bob practically forgot all about Ma and me when the subject was raised."

"Oh, did I now? Well, m'lovely colleen, when home-rule Irishmen talk about the Emerald Isle, just stand back and let the politics flow! Ha, ha, ha!"

"Patrick Henry Flaherty, you are impossible! Our daughter here is trying to get our feelings about Dr. Callahan's marriage proposal and you can do no more than highlight politics!"

"That's okay, Ma," said Marie as she kissed her father on the cheek, "because all of Papa's words tonight mean that he approves and gives us his blessing."

The wedding ceremony was held in one of Pittsburgh's largest Roman Catholic churches. And since the circumstances surrounding Marie's losing her first husband were considered honorable, the whole format (white gown, many attendants, plush reception, and a honeymoon at Niagra Falls) was followed in accordance with etiquette and nuptial protocol. Also, one of the main ingredients missing at Marie's first wedding was certainly present at this one—her father.

3

Madge Talanski, in spite of her brassy appearance, was quite a perceptive woman. For almost a year after Marie's marriage to Dr. Callahan, Carl's aunt would call her at least once a month, and the conversation, after all of the light amenities about housekeeping, fashion, and such, always ended with little Joey's progress, or the lack thereof. At five, Joey was the biggest child in kindergarten but by no means the brightest. Not learning the alphabet was bad; however, not learning to distinguish the basic colors really became a *cause celebre* in the Callahan household. And, although Marie never really pushed the subject, she often wondered when, or if, Bob would ever formally adopt Joey as his son. The child's slowness in school did not help matters at all, and, just before Thanksgiving, Madge focused the entire telephone conversation with Marie on Joey.

"I can understand how Bob feels, Marie. After all, he waited this long to get married, and the man has reasonable expectations in wanting everything to go right, especially having children of his own."

"Really, Aunt Madge, you're so much easier to talk to than my own mother. I hope you'll always be close enough for me to . . ."

"Oh, Marie honey, I forgot to tell you last week, I'm closing down the boarding house and moving to Philadelphia. Now that the war is over, I want to pursue a couple of real estate ventures."

Madge Talanski, at forty-nine, still looked good. If there was one thing she believed in wholeheartedly, it was taking care of the body. She used it most advantageously to get whatever she wanted from men of means who were interested in pursuing a safe and discreet extramarital relationship. No doubt about it, Madge was the best at gaining the confidence of clientele. However, what suffered over the years was the thought of having children, because, at age twenty-one, she had herself medically eliminated from that category. Suffice to say, Madge regretted having gone the route a few times since then. Perhaps this was why when, as a result of one of her girlfriends dying on the dining room table moments after giving birth to Carl, Madge adopted the infant. And now that there was once again a void in her life, she was determined to fill it with the only person whom she considered true kin—Carl's son, Joey.

This was the undisclosed reason why Madge had kept in such close contact with Marie since her husband would be amenable to the idea of at least permitting Joey to live with his aunt for a while.

When Marie broached the subject to Bob, he was somewhat ambivalent about having his wife's child taken over by someone else. Nevertheless, Joey's presence seemed to be an invisible chain that prevented the seven-month-old marriage from moving toward full consummation. And since none of Marie's family had indicated any real closeness to the kid, Bob did not feel obligated to adopt him, especially with there being early signs of low academic ability. After waiting for as long as he did to get married, Bob was a little surprised with himself for selecting a ready-made family. And even though he didn't think it would be fair for him to dwell on this matter, he was eager to discuss it. Besides, Bob remembered the casual, but interesting, remark Marie's father made just before the wedding: "Bobby, m'boy, Marie's going to make a fine wife and mother, but I'm sorry about Joey. You should work on your own real soon." When Marie turned off the radio at the conclusion of Gabril Heater's evening news commentary, Bob did not expect the intensity of the conversation that followed.

"And just what can Madge give your son—I mean *our* son—that we can't or haven't?"

"See there? That's part of the problem, Bob! You feel morally obligated to accept Joey as your son, but deep down you don't—and can't! You waited a long time to give up bachelorhood, and I feel honored to be your choice out of a zillion other women. . . ."

"Darling, I love you. From the moment I saw you at last year's Christmas party, I knew I had to have you for my own."

"But Joey—what about Joey?"

"Marie, honey, if it will make you any happier, I'll have adoption papers processed immediately. It shouldn't be diffi—"

"Madge wants Joey to live with her."

"What?"

"She's moving to Philadelphia in a few weeks, and she asked me to let Joey go with her."

Bob was completely surprised by this latest turn of events. He felt guilty for not being able to muster the kind of negative shock that he thought he should, but, at the same time, Bob felt somewhat relieved as this formerly suppressed topic continued.

"Well," he said, "even though I haven't really had the opportunity to get to know Madge Talanski better, I must assume that she definitely has a great love for Joey since she raised his father."

"Oh, no doubt about it," Marie quickly responded. "Carl's Aunt Madge was very good to him—and to me. She's the only relative here in Pittsburgh. But you know—it's funny—whenever I used to mention contacting any of his people, he would lightly change the subject. I used to think he was trying to hide something terrible from me, and, during the early weeks of our marriage, I felt sorry for myself. Then I found out that Carl's entire world consisted of just three people—Joey, Aunt Madge, and me. And considering the circumstances under which we got married, he really worked hard at being a good husband and a good father."

Bob, noticing the tears welling up in his wife's eyes, said, "Sweetheart, it's not necessary for you to explain that segment of your life to me. . . ."

"On the contrary, Bob, it is, because it serves as a backdrop for the kind of rationale I'm giving myself for the decision I've made to let little Joey go live with his Aunt Madge."

"But, Marie . . . you shouldn't . . ."

"Please, Bob, don't try to be the gallant one by talking against my decision. It's a decision that serves as a solution to the unspoken-of problem that we've been silently thinking about for at least five months now. And, as far as your adopting Joey is concerned, suppose we just hold off on that for a while."

When New Year's 1946 officially came in, it found Joey sound asleep in the little room down the hall from the large lacy bedroom in which his Aunt Madge was entertaining one of Philadelphia's prominent politicians. For the next eight years, while money was not an obstacle, Madge had no problems operating her Germantown parlor house. Although there may have been some neighbors who didn't particularly like the idea of having a bordello in their midst, no one made it an issue of obvious concern. However, in September of 1954, a change in some of the after-working-hours habits of men in high places caused them to decrease their visits to Madge's place. Plus, problems of another kind began to surface when Joey was suspended from school.

11

"I don't care what the kid called you, Joey," said Madge as they left the vice principal's office, "you didn't have to fight! My God, this is only the third day of school! How do you expect to be even considered for Central High next year if you're going to spoil things here in the ninth grade?"

Joey knew that his aunt was more disappointed in him than angry. He thought about all of the encouragement and understanding she had given him while at the same time arguing with school officials who did not want to switch Joey from the general to the academic program.

For the most part, the ride home was punctuated by Joey's efforts to convince his aunt that he was going to do his best to make her proud of him—as soon as he got back from the three-day suspension. Madge shook her head and smiled as she thought about those years gone by when she was raising Joey's father. Devils in short pants, both of them. But she wouldn't trade either one for all the angels in Heaven.

4

Christmas Eve 1954 started out all wrong. In a matter of hours, Joey's thirteen-year-old world came down with a crash. When he first heard the muffled voices coming from Aunt Madge's bedroom at one-thirty in the morning, Joey did not bother to rouse himself. He had certainly stopped believing in Santa Claus several years before, and, besides, it was probably too early to see what Aunt Madge had put under the tree. Therefore, our sleepy little devil just turned over on his stomach and shut his dark brown eyes in a final effort to return to dreamland.

Crash! The shattering sound of glass followed by screams caused Joey to leap out of his bed. When he jerked open the door, horror, as he had never seen it, enveloped the entire second floor. Madge, stark naked, ran screaming from her bedroom. She was completely hysterical. Three pistol shots rang out in rapid succession and the nude woman fell headlong down the stairs.

"Aunt Madge!"

Before Joey could get to her, a huge mountain of a man, clad only in shorts and brandishing a revolver, stumbled drunkenly down the long hall and bellowed, "Where's that whore? I'm gonna blow her fuckin' head off!"

The frightened youngster was between the stairs and the ranting maniac.

"Get outta my way, you snivelling, bastard, before I give it to you, too!"

Pushing Joey aside, the mountain of flesh seemed even bigger as it was viewed through the popping eyes of the frightened little boy. Things were happening so fast that Joey could not think. All he knew was that his Aunt Madge lay at the foot of the steep staircase and now the man was standing at the top looking down at her. With every muscle fibre in his body straining, Joey jumped up from the floor and head-rammed the pistol-toting man right in the buttocks. Perhaps the mountain of flesh was too drunk to react or yell as he tumbled down the stairs.

At sunrise, while other kids his age were eagerly ripping paper off their Christmas gifts and shouting in happy voices, Joey sat in Police Lt. Clayburn's office. Not once had he cried since a couple of officers had forced open the door and found two dead bodies at the foot of the stairs. And sitting on the top step, where he had been for nearly an hour, was Joey. Lt. George Clayburn, upon noticing the arrival of Capt. Albert Napolitano, left the two patrolmen in his office to watch Joey while he talked to the precinct chief.

"No, we haven't been able to get anything out of the kid," responded the lieutenant. "He hasn't said one word since Mason and Kruger found him in the house. But from what a couple of the neighbors told 'em, the woman was his aunt. Too bad. She was hit twice in the back with slugs from a .38. When the lab boys finish their work, we'll have a more detailed report. At any rate, it looks as though the man shot her. He really had a tight grip on the gun. Can you imagine? The guy must've broken his neck in falling down the stairs."

"Yeah, that's too bad. Now what about the kid? Did you follow through on checking for relatives in the Philly area? You mentioned something earlier about a neighbor saying that just the kid and his aunt lived in the house."

"From what I understand, Al, this Madge Talanski used to entertain some pretty high gents 'til about three or four years ago," responded the lieutenant as he pressed the water cooler button.

"Then she must've kinda fallen out of favor with downtown, or something, because we got orders to sort of watch the house for any signs of soliciting."

"Um, I remember that," said the captain. "I also remember that when we tried to make a routine check downtown as to how hard we should lean on the house, no one could pinpoint the origin of the order."

Clayburn laughed as he said, "You mean no one *wanted* to pinpoint it. I heard that if Madge Talanski had blown the whistle, half of the big shots downtown would've run for cover. But when the election brought in some new faces, Madge's dubious popularity sort of faded away. This was probably when the broad started dealing with characters like the one we took out of there last night."

Autopsies were performed on both bodies. Madge Talanski, listed only as a rooming house proprietor, died as a result of gunshot wounds. The man, identified as Lars Swensen, merchant seaman, died as a result of a broken neck. Throughout all of the questioning and investigating, no one bothered to ask the frightened, trauma-laden lad about the circumstances surrounding Swensen's demise. Given the facts that the six-foot-five, two hundred sixty-eight pound mountain had a vise hold on the gun and his blood contained a super-high alcohol content, it was assumed that he accidentally stumbled and fell down the stairs.

5

"No, I'm not angry," Bob Callahan insisted as he tried to avoid gritting his teeth. "I'm just getting a little sick and tired, Marie, of your trying to make me look like the bad guy in this damn scenario!"

"See, see, there you go again, Bob," whimpered his wife, "always unloading on me! All I'm asking is that you have just a little bit of consideration for the position that Joey is in."

Dr. Callahan was practically at wit's end. Ever since Marie's son came to live with them six weeks before, sporadic bickering occurred. Perhaps because of the traumatic experience that Joey had undergone, he was not as spunky and happy-go-lucky as his younger step-sister and brother. Undoubtedly, there were some psychological

scars grooved into Joey's mind that caused him to wake up screaming in the middle of the night. At first, Marie and Bob were united
in their concern and compassion. But the frequency, coupled with
the chronic disturbances to ten-year-old Michael and six-year-old
Susan, eroded away any real understanding. Besides, Joey was the
spitting image of his deceased father, and Marie was finding this
hard to deal with on a rational level. Sometimes she was the loving
mother to Joey, and at other times she acted like she did not want
him around. Actually, Marie and Bob were just beginning to know
Joey as a real person, because those brief periods that he had come
to Pittsburgh during the summer months were spent mostly with
his grandparents.

"Look, what do you want me to do, Marie?" Bob asked as he
looked at the clock, and saw that the hour was getting late—twelve-
thirty A.M., and he was due in surgery at ten. "Just tell me, for Christ's
sake, and I'll do it!"

"Now you're being ridiculous, Bob, and I don't like it! You
know what I've wanted you to do concerning Joey ever since we've
been married. . . ."

"Hey, now wait a minute, sweetheart! Don't even *try* to lay that
guilt thing on me! Damn it all—I told you years ago that I was willing
to adopt the kid, but, no, you and your father thought that maybe
it was too soon! And when Madge, may her soul rest in peace, asked
to have him live with her, I didn't hear any loud protestations coming from his mother! Damn! No wonder the kid's so screwed up!"

As Joey lay curled up in the fetal position, tears trickled across
the bridge of his nose and sank into the brightly colored down-filled
pillow. He had been listening to his parents argue, and it wasn't the
first time since he had come back to live with them. Bob and Marie
were unaware of Joey's deep perceptions. Practically every night,
their voices would penetrate the wall between the two bedrooms.
But, if there was one thing that Joey had learned well, it was to listen
and internalize everything he heard. How often had he lain awake
and listened to voices coming from Aunt Madge's room. Because
of the adult conversations that Joey had heard over the years, he
was mature beyond age fourteen. And it was a burden that he frequently cried about in the darkness of his room. No one, not even
Aunt Madge, could ever detect that Joey was aware of certain things,

15

because he never mentioned any of the things he overheard. However, many were the days that Joey's general demeanor was pensive. He kept everything bottled up inside. Usually, his dark eyes were sad, and he seldom smiled, to say nothing about laughing.

Within the recesses of her subconscious, Marie Callahan detected a faint ringing. Then it became louder. She switched on the light and noticed the time—four A.M. Meanwhile, the persistent telephone kept ringing. Marie reached across her soundly sleeping husband and picked up the receiver. This was certainly not out of the ordinary, because Dr. Callahan frequently received super-early calls from colleagues seeking emergency tips from one of Pittsburgh's leading neurosurgeons. Therefore, regardless of the hour, Marie was programmed to answer in at least a pleasant voice.

"Hello, Mrs. Callahan speaking."

"Hello, Marie?"

"Oh, Papa, how are you? Is Ma all right? Why . . ."

"Whoa, slow down, darling. Holy St. Christopher! You've asked a million questions already! How about giving me a chance to respond to a few?"

"Okay, okay."

"Now, that's more like it. Do you happen to know where your son, Joey, is at this hour?"

"Joey? What kind of a question is that at four o'clock in the morning? He's in bed—asleep!"

"Well, I'm sorry to disappoint you, Marie, but your son is sitting right here with me in the kitchen."

The telephone dropped to the floor as the now wide-awake mother scrambled out of bed and ran to Joey's room.

"What the hell . . . who's on the . . . Marie!" yelled Bob as he tried to pull himself out of a deep sleep. Before he could find out from his father-in-law what was going on, Marie ran back into the bedroom and snatched the telephone receiver from her husband's hand.

"Papa . . . well, how am I supposed to act when . . . never mind. We'll be there in . . . "

Bob was now sitting on the side of the bed listening to Marie screech through a puzzling conversation, but he was unable to put the pieces together.

16

"For Pete's sake, Marie, do you mind taking a second to tell me what the hell's going on around here?"

Bob's request only earned him a stern side-glance from his wife as she was wrapping up her conversation, "Okay, Papa, I think that's a much better idea under the circumstances. . . ."

After hanging up, Marie proceeded to fill Bob in on the matter. "For reasons that he didn't really explain, Joey just got up and left."

"At four o'clock in the morning, Marie, not even Joey would go out in the ten-degree weather. No, he must've had a damn good reason . . . or at least *he* thought so."

6

Even though it was a school day, Joey did not go in. His grandfather deemed this conference to be of great importance. Between the time that Joey appeared at his front door and later fell asleep on his parlor couch, his grandfather and he had talked about several things. Mr. Flaherty's eyes were opened to a grandson whom he was just beginning to know as a thinking person. It was hardly a secret that the old man never forgave Joey's father for soiling his "blushing colleen." The hard feelings that Mr. Flaherty had against Joey's dad were never really erased. Although he tried not to aim those feelings toward his grandson, Mr. Flaherty's general aloofness whenever Joey was around sent a clear non-verbal message to the child that his grandfather did not exactly include him among his favorite grandchildren. And as for Joey's grandmother, she spent all of her time hugging him for seemingly just being alive. When he was younger, the tender expressions were always followed by ice cream and other nice things. However, as Joey grew into the teens, he interpreted his grandmother's feelings toward him as being those of pity, not love.

The youngster also knew the nature of Aunt Madge's prime source of income, but he never questioned her about it nor did he ever knowingly show, either by his words or action, any degree of curiosity or disapproval. All Joey was interested in was the genuine love and concern that she gave him.

So, the parents and grandparents of the sad-eyed, pensive boy, who was viewed as being devoid of many of the intellectual and social qualities that they thought he should possess, were gathered in the living room. Mrs. Flaherty had begun building a defense for her grandson when Mr. Flaherty decided that now was the time for the lad to stand on his own two feet.

"I'm very upset about what you did, Joey," Marie said as she sat down beside him. "Your father and I were. . . ."

"My father's dead," came a rapid response from the boy as he leaned forward with an apparent determination to bring the dormant issue to life. The remark shocked everyone.

"Joey, how could you ever say such a thing? Your father is right here! What's wrong with you?" However, before Joey could answer, Mrs. Flaherty turned to her son-in-law and said, "Bob, you're a doctor. Don't you think the poor child needs to be looked at by . . . er . . . you know. . . ."

"A psychologist, Grandma?" came the quick, unsolicited reply from Joey. "Or better yet, just to make sure that I'm examined all the way, maybe a psychiatrist should look inside my head."

"Hey, now just wait a minute, mister!" Marie yelled. "Don't you dare speak to. . . ."

"Whoa, let's not lose our heads here this morning, folks," said Mr. Flaherty. "I don't think we're gonna get very far by not being patient, Marie. I also don't think we're gonna get very far by being fresh, Joey."

"I'm sorry, Mom. It's just that nothing seems to go right with anything I do."

Bob gave Marie a quick glance and then he said to Joey, "We all know what you've been going through for the past couple of months. But your mother and I are here to help you with any and all problems, Joey. Don't close us out."

"Go on . . . tell him what we decided this morning, Bob," urged Marie smilingly. "I'm sure he'll be happy to hear it."

"Well . . . (ahem) . . . Joey, as you know, your sister and brother are Callahans . . . and . . . er . . . ," Bob struggled while trying to overcome apparent difficulty in framing the right words, ". . . . well . . . I . . . I mean, *we* would like for you to become a Callahan, too."

Mrs. Flaherty was the first reactor. "Oh, Bob, thank you so much for doing this! You don't know how long I've wished for Joey to be taken *all* the way into the family."

"You did it, sweetheart." Marie smiled as she kissed Bob on the cheek. "I'm so happy I could cry." And she began to do just that.

Mr. Flaherty, maintaining complete composure, never took his eyes off Joey while asking, "Well, Joey, what do you think about *that*? I told you your stepfather was okay."

Finally, the room quieted down enough for Joey to speak, and he addressed his remarks to the doctor.

"Sir . . . I mean, *Dad* . . . I certainly appreciate what you're saying. You don't know how long I've wanted to be legally adopted by you so I could *really* be a Callahan. Aunt Madge used to tell me all the time that all of you loved me. I don't know . . . I used to get all mixed up inside, and she would tell me about how brave I should be . . . like my real father."

Marie, sensing something about to go awry, said, "Joey, your real father was brave, and he died in the service of his country. No one here would ever want to take those thoughts from you, but . . . he is dead, and . . . "

"Mom, I want my name to be Talanski for the rest of my life."

Silence. The hush that enveloped the room was electrifying. Surprise registered on everyone's face, except Mr. Flaherty's.

"Marie, Bob, now you know why it was so necessary for me to insist that you come over this morning. My grandson here and I talked until daybreak about many things. And I want to tell you something," continued the old man as he gave Joey a hug, "this lad is a deep thinker. I learned more about him during the few hours that just the two of us sat drinking coffee and talking at the kitchen table than I ever imagined. This kid's gonna be somebody one of these days! Mark my word! And as for the name? I say if anybody can make Talanski as big as Callahan or Flaherty—Joey can!"

Two

Can't Win for Losing

1

Joe's mind was not thoroughly focused on that afternoon's program, even though it was a milestone in his seventeen years. Speakers addressed George School's graduating class of 1959 with much dignity and well wishes, but Joe could care less. His head was still throbbing from all the beer that he had consumed the night before. Besides, it was just through the good graces of the swimming team's coach that Joe was not expelled from school back in January.

Young Talanski had become one of the best butterfly and freestyle swimmers in the history of George School. Several colleges were hoping to land him, but he finally decided to accept a four-year swimming scholarship to Penn State University. However, during the height of the season, Joe and a couple of buddies tried to sneak into the girls' dormitory. Talanski was the only one caught by security personnel. As a result, he was dropped from the swimming team. Of course, this embarrassment caused even his step-father to stop making proud remarks to friends. It wasn't until Joe's junior year at George School that Dr. Callahan started visiting his step-son, and that was only after Joe had begun doing so well on the swimming team.

In spite of his father's efforts to pull some strings in trying to get Penn State to let Joe hold the scholarship, things did not work out well at all. Not only did he lose three-quarters of his senior swim season but the headmaster placed him on probation for the remainder of the year. Now everything was all over, including no more having to feel sad because of weekend loneliness. In four years, Joe's parents visited him three times. Graduation day was not one of them.

"Joseph Bernard Talanski," came the name over the microphone.

Suddenly, Joe perked up. He felt good as he proudly approached the stage. Hearing that name resound throughout the auditorium caused him to reflect momentarily on his determination to make *Talanski* really mean something one day.

"Hey, Joe," the voice yelled from across the parking lot, "wait a minute!"

Cliff Westerbrook, the person to whom the cracking voice belonged, was Joe's best friend at George School. The two of them used to pal around and ease into and out of situations together. What a contrast! Here was Joe, tall, muscular, and athletically inclined, compared to Westerbrook, also tall but pitifully thin, and in possession of absolutely no athletic ability. However, they found many other mutual interests, such as photography, chess, beer, girls, and oceanography. Strangely enough, it was this last area that really brought these boys close together. They were both "A" students in the class, and the teacher tried unsuccessfully to get them to generate further interest in oceanography. Since Cliff's father, an uncle, grandfather, and a great-uncle were lawyers, Cliff's destiny appeared clearly defined. He was supposed to follow in their tracks—Yale.

"Where're you going, big guy?" asked the blond-haired, blue-eyed scarecrow. The question was almost rhetorical, because Cliff knew that his friend was completely bent out of shape over the fact that none of his family was there to see him graduate. Westerbrook was standing by the day before when Mrs. Callahan called from Pittsburgh to tell her son that the circumstances at the hospital prevented them from leaving as planned. But then again, since this was nothing new, especially since Dr. Callahan had become chief surgeon. However, Joe did expect them to arrive in time to see him receive his diploma.

Without even turning around or slowing his long gait, Joe replied, "You know damn well where I'm going! Wanna go?"

"Far out, man! We really hung one on last night," Cliff answered as he stepped in front of his friend, "and that was more than enough for me—and you, too."

Cliff's arms were definitely not strong enough to hold Joe's shoulders from moving forward on the mile walk to Newton. The scarecrow just kept bouncing backward several steps as the determined hulk continued unimpeded.

21

Even though the boys were not of drinking age, they knew several reliable "townies" who, for a small fee, would make purchases at the state store. Every George School student was at least aware of beer sources. Joe was heading for his.

"Look, Cliff, maybe you should stick around and talk to your folks. I'll see you later this afternoon at the headmaster's reception—that is, if my folks are here by then."

To Cliff, Joe's words conveyed one message but his demeanor another. "No, man, that's all right. We'll go into town together," the perceptive scarecrow replied. "If you think I'm going to leave you out here to get wasted by yourself, you have another thought coming. Just like last night, we can chug-a-lug one more time, right?"

For a moment, Joe stopped walking and placed a big arm around the slight shoulders of his friend as he laughingly said, "Okay, you win again. Let's put our last blast on hold until I see you this summer."

Unfortunately, Joe and his buddy did not see each other that summer of '59. As a matter of fact, they didn't meet again until many years later.

2

"Up your nose, bonehead!" yelled one of the demonstrators. "If you're not with us, then you're against us!"

"Yeah!" shouted another, "why don't you take off that goddamn uniform right now? Nobody's interested in that shit anymore!"

The Reserve Officers Training Corps (R.O.T.C.) was finding it increasingly difficult to carry out its program on Penn State's main campus. Because of the growing concern among many of the students who were in R.O.T.C., the advantages of ultimately becoming an officer in the United States Army were highlighted at every juncture throughout college life during that spring of 1962.

Just as he had been doing for the past two weeks, Joe maintained a stone face while moving across the campus to attend his class in military science. Up to then, he was able to endure the few hecklers that lined up outside the building. Then Joe decided that he had an obligation both to himself and to his real father; there-fore, he was determined to go against the single advice given to the R.O.T.C. students by their instructors whenever the topic rose: Ig-nore the hecklers, regardless of what is said.

Instead of going inside with the others, Joe stopped at the front door and began to address the fifteen or so demonstrators with, "Believe me, I know how you people feel about our growing involve-ment in Southeast Asia, but why do you have to come down so hard on those of us who have chosen to pursue our education a little differently from the usual . . ."

For about three minutes, it appeared that Cadet Talanski was doing all right; at least there was some semblance of calm in the atmosphere. Then everything went sour when Joe attempted to an-swer one heckler's question as to why he was wearing "that shit-colored uniform."

"Well, asshole, I'm going to tell you something right now!" shouted Talanski as he dropped his books and assumed a wide-legged, clench-fisted stance. "My father wore a uniform just like this one, and he died fighting for his country. . . ."

"His country? You mean Poland? He probably didn't know where the hell the front was!"

Laughter erupted all over the area. Joe then got even angrier, because he interpreted the hecklers' comments as being sub-de-grading.

"I'll be damned if I'm gonna stand by and let creeps like all of you put *my* father down!"

Talanski surprised himself at the utterance of such bravado in the face of radical odds, because he couldn't recall when he had ever before shown emotional aggression related to anything even remotely connected to his real father. However, he felt good about it and was indeed ready to do battle with the hecklers either singu-larly or collectively.

Someone in the crowd yelled, "You're the creep, you gung-ho bastard!"

Another joined with, "Yeah! Let's teach this dumb sonofabitch a lesson he won't forget!"

Three guys rushed Joe from the side. Quickly turning he met one with a solid left hook to the solar plexus. Unfortunately, this did not prevent the other two from pinning him against the wall while trying to rip the uniform from his body. One adversary came in too close as he tried to knee our hero in the groin. Joe managed to get a headlock on him and put all of the strength of his 195-pound frame into tightening up on the neck. The unlucky heckler's face was changing colors in rapid succession. Hard punches and kicks that Joe was receiving didn't seem to bother him anymore now that he had a tangible object upon which his reactions might be transferred. In other words, he just held on to the long-haired, bearded head under his arm.

"Let him go, you bastard!" screamed a girl as she scratched and bit the arm that was holding her friend's head. "My God! He's strangling him to death!"

Through the maze of this riotous mob scene waded the campus police, clubs jabbing and flailing. When the melee was over, several people, including Joe, had to be taken to the dispensary.

Student unrest and protests were rapidly growing popular on many American college campuses. It seemed as though demonstrating and taking over administration buildings had become the prime focus of student entertainment. No campus was truly safe from the prying eye of television. In record time, the nearest video and radio station always dispatched a news team to where it was even *thought* there was going to be a juicy riot, for whatever reason.

In the case of the fiasco that occurred on Penn State's campus that warm spring afternoon, a cadre of news people had been contacted by, as usual, a group that was against what it perceived to be blatant federal encroachment into the mainstream of campus life. Since that prior December, little brushfires, so to speak, were flaring up here and there with relationship to rumors dealing with the school's administration being overly wooed by the prospects of getting larger multi-million-dollar grants from the federal government. At the same time, school officials were very much aware of the fact that there were strong alumni associations and other revenue sources that were not exactly enthusiastic about State's catering to the wishes of the R.O.T.C. Program.

Subsequent investigation into that afternoon's disturbance revealed that there was a premature eruption. The demonstrators were supposed to have been waiting for some Pentagon officials to arrive on campus for the purpose of making a cursory inspection

24

of the R.O.T.C. facilities. And the relatively small number of demonstrators that arrived early were just warming up until their ranks could be reinforced by an expected hundred and eighty more. The so-called organizers of the demonstration were late in arriving on the scene; therefore, the early arrivers decided to entertain themselves by heckling a few uniformed candidates. As fate would have it, what was supposed to have been nothing more than a preliminary bout turned out to be the main event.

A quasi-administrative committee composed of the Assistant Dean of Student Affairs, one associate professor from the history department, one instructor from the military science department, and two students, was formed. The purpose of this team was to make an in-depth investigation and report its findings to the Dean of Student Affairs. At the time, no one realized what kind of an impact the incident would have. However, when the American Civil Liberties Union became involved because of alleged use of excessive force, the upper eschelon of the school's administration decided that something concrete had to be done. Dr. Ernest McMillan, Dean of Student Affairs, called in his assistant, Dr. Solomon Rosen, and briefed him on the real importance of the matter.

"What I fail to understand, Sol, is how in the hell did this thing get out of hand and grow?"

"Based upon what our committee has found so far, Ernie, the demonstrators were peaceful and well within their rights of assembly when that cadet . . . er . . . ." Dr. Rosen quickly thumbed through his notes, "um . . . oh, yes, here it is. Talanski. Yes. Joseph Bernard Talanski. Well, it appears that Talanski passed several derogatory remarks, and the other students responded accordingly."

"Then would you say that this Talanski fellow was the prime initiator of the fracas?"

"Well . . . Ernie, I don't know if I would be ready to commit myself to that extent yet, because I still can't, for the life of me, figure out why a lone cadet would take on, as it were, a whole group, and, furthermore. . . ."

"Wait . . . just a minute, Sol. I know exactly what you're saying, and I agree. However . . . the fact of the matter remains that, this time, the powers that be are eager to squelch this thing via the quickest and most facilitative way possible. I'm telling you, it seems as though everybody, including the president, is anxious about the far-reaching repercussions of this thing. Just to give you some idea, the other night, at the Southeastern Alumni Association Meeting, Tom Marshall mentioned to the president how disappointed he was that State would allow such negative publicity to hit the campus. Now you *know* what that did to the old man!''

"Yeah, I can very well imagine. However, when you stop to think about it, Ernie, State hasn't been doing too badly at all if you compare the few little demos that we've been having here and there with the goddamn massive riots, shootings, and all of the other things that've been happening on campuses over in New York and Ohio. Hell, I would say we're in pretty good shape.''

Dr. McMillan was nodding in agreement with his colleague; nevertheless, they both recognized the fact that the current problem was not going to just go away. Something more definitive had to be done by central administration in order to satisfy the headhunters out there.

"I had my secretary contact the R.O.T.C. office yesterday,'' said the assistant dean. "I wanted to review Joseph Talanski's jacket file before meeting with the committee. Didn't find anything glowing. He's been in the program for two years; missed several muster calls for which he was reprimanded and placed on probation. I would say the kid's pretty lacklustre, non-descript.''

"Interesting—no pun intended,'' said the dean as he lit his pipe, "but this morning I personally perused the young man's regular file. Seems, although he wasn't a chronic discipline problem at George School, he had an unusual proclivity for, shall we say, losing the big one? He had been given a four-year swimming scholarship here but lost it even before arriving on campus that September—got tossed off George's team after being caught raiding the girls' dorm.''

"You know, Ernie,'' the assistant dean said as he leaned back in the stuffed chair and crossed his legs, "I wonder if our Mr. Talanski has the kind of clout that could cause us trouble were we to . . .''

"Say no more, Sol. I do believe our thoughts are running in complete agreement. Why don't you make a few strategic telephone calls, then let your committee do its work.''

When Dr. Rosen met with the other members of his committee, there was unanimity as far as everyone's desire not to create any more adverse publicity for the school. However, there was disagreement among them in terms of how the various interest segments should be satisfied without causing more trouble further down the line. What it amounted to was that the R.O.T.C. unit wanted to improve its image and popularity, but not at the expense of having to make any kind of public apology. The Students for a Democratic Society (S.D.S), in its desire to gain a firmer foothold on Penn State's campus, did not want to go all out on this situation since its main thrust had to be aborted because of the minor fracas that was fast becoming a major pain. And the school's administration wanted only to handle this situation in such a manner that no further embarrassment would accrue to the university.

"Captain Levers, I can very well understand how difficult it must be," said Dr. Kirsted of the history department, "for R.O.T.C. people to try to just hang on to good candidates, especially when there's such focusing out here on students' rights and do-your-own-thing emphasis."

"Even so," interjected Seymour Goldman, an honors senior majoring in political science, "I think the federal government has to realize that when it sets up a military training unit on a college campus, it should *join* the main stream of college life, not try to divert it and convert it."

Dr. Rosen, knowing how stinging Goldman's remark must have been, quickly tried to ease it with, "I don't think any of us on this campus, or for that matter any other campus, expect R.O.T.C. to alter its basic rules and regulations just to accommodate some of the super hothead students who might be in the program. . . ."

"That's right, sir," joined the captain. "We do have a pretty good screening process for prospective candidates, but, as we all know, there isn't a screening process for any organization in the world that's completely one hundred per cent foolproof *all* the time. Granted, a few bad apples are mistakenly placed in the basket with the good ones. But, as fast as we find them, they're removed from the program."

"Well, Captain Levers," said Debbie Smith, an honors sophomore majoring in psychology, "we obviously have identified at least one bad apple. What do you military people intend to do about it? And, if I may, Dr. Rosen, I would like to piggyback that question on to this one for you: What is the *school* going to do about it?"

These questions served as the basis of discourse for nearly two hours. At times, discussion became semi-heated; however, Dr. Rosen

27

always stepped in to soften the harsh statements rendered by others, and he did this very skillfully.

"So, might it be accurately said here that the committee is in agreement?" asked the assistant dean. Upon hearing the positives from the members, he smiled to himself as he thought how easy this was after all.

Dr. Rosen's secretary did the necessary transcribing and finished the report that afternoon, because the two students were eager to see whether or not their time was wasted and whether this committee was formed just to look good on paper. The committee felt that its eight recommendations were reasonable and feasible. Therefore, subsequent follow-through by the administration was crucial.

"Very good, Sol," said Dr. McMillan as he adjusted the telephone receiver. "I especially like recommendation number seven, because it would denote some degree of immediate relief. Beg pardon? Oh, yes . . . no problem . . . let's face it, his past record would definitely substantiate what we intend to do here. . . ."

Since only one week remained in the spring term, Joe was permitted to take final exams with the understanding as per the decision that came out of the meeting he had with the Student Discipline Committee and the assistant dean of the university. Also, Joe was informed that he was being dropped from the rolls.

During a lull in the squad's close-order marching practice, the drill sergeant addressed his groups rather harshly.

"Some of you guys, even after being together for a year, still move like you have two left feet! Exams are over, so you don't have any reason for not concentrating on getting ready for summer camp! In five minutes, I want you young troopers to fall in! And, this time, do it right!

After the sergeant had moved out of hearing range, one cadet uttered, "That freaking bird ought to fly off into the sunset, or something."

"Yeah, I agree," joined another cadet as he removed his helmet liner and leaned against a tree. "Especially since I'm just like you guys—can't keep a cadence step beyond ten yards. Too bad Talanski's not here anymore to help us through this shit."

"Hey, now that was one gung-ho cadet who knew how to drill forward and backward. Heard he was kicked out of school because of the crap that happened with those campus hippies."

"Yeah. Well, if you ask me, I think Talanski got one helluva raw deal."

"So you're probably right, but you know somebody's ass *had* to be hung out to dry in order to keep peace in the valley—a real scapegoat if I ever saw one."

"I still can't figure out how they could justifiably put the blame for the entire chain of events on Talanski's shoulders. Boy! Talk about your bum raps! That one was a classic!"

"Hey, let's face it, guys; there're some poor slobs who just can't win for losing. Oh, hell, time's up, fellas. Here comes the Sarge. Okay, let's fall in—and try to do it right!"

Three

Stomping Ground

1

Working at Schmidt's Brewery in Philadelphia was not exactly what Joe had in mind; however, it was a good-paying job. Besides, he was determined not to go home. The embarrassment of his having to face family after being kicked out of school was something that he just wasn't ready to do. So, against the wishes of his mother, Joe did not come home to Pittsburgh. Instead, he chose to take a job loading trucks.

Marie Callahan tried desperately to convince her son that he was making a bad decision. However, she found the task unrewarding over the telephone.

"Joey, please believe me," pleaded his mother as she held the receiver with both hands, "your life is not ruined just because you can't go back to Penn State. There're plenty of other schools that'll accept you right now if you apply."

"Mom, you don't understand. It's not just being kicked out of college that makes me feel so rotten. It's the whole chain of things that've been plaguing me since . . . since . . . I don't know . . . day one of my life! I can't seem to do *anything* right!"

"You're not the only person in the world with problems, Joey, and I wish you wouldn't do this to me! I need you home . . . right now . . . here with me! I'm losing you, Joey, and you don't seem to care one darn bit!"

Marie never could control her Irish anger whenever things did not go her way. And now, at a time when perhaps the right choice of words would prompt her son to come home, she failed to make the ideal combination.

"Mom, I gotta go now; the bus is loading. . . ."

Joe's mother became practically hysterical when he was ready to hang up. It seemed as though she just couldn't hold back her true feelings any longer.

"Joey, Joey, why Philadelphia? If you *have* to go somewhere other than home, why not to New York, or anywhere, but not Philadelphia!"

"Mom, don't worry . . . it's all right. Nothing's going to happen . . . hey, look, Mom, I'm a big boy now. Nothing's going to happen to me. I can take care of myself. . . ."

It had been almost eight years since Joe was spirited out of Philadelphia by his parents. And since then, they never so much as suggested that he even think about that city again, to say the least about returning. Marie still shuddered whenever she thought of how close to death her son was on the night that Madge Talanski was murdered. It took nearly six months of seeing a psychologist on a weekly basis for Joe to return to what his parents considered normalcy, because the traumatic episode had left him unusually quiet and pensive. As a matter of fact, Joe's parents and grandparents were of the unspoken opinion that he was still suffering from mental scars.

After three months of hard work loading those trucks, Joe felt good. None of the old solemn and pensive moods stayed with him more than a few minutes at a time, because some of his co-workers were always drumming up something to do after six o'clock, especially the single ones.

"Hey, Joe T, you wanna go partying with me?" asked Fred Blueswicz. "Listen, I got a friend who's a member of the Northeast Sons of Poland Club, and he can get us a couple of memberships for twenty bucks a piece. There's a big dance goin' on there tonight, and I'm sure a lot of single skirts'll be on the scene."

"Oh, no, fella! You're not going to pull that shit on me a second time! Hey, Blue, this is Joe T, remember? I'm the same guy who went with you to Cabrelli's last month and almost got my head torn off because of your mouth!"

The incident to which Joe was referring occurred at a little neighborhood Italian bar on the south side of town. When the bartender had asked to see some identification, Fred immediately went into why it wasn't necessary for them to show anything.

"What d'ya mean *I.D.,* mister?" Fred shouted as he halted his friend's hand from pulling out the wallet. "My pal and I are definitely twenty-one plus, and we're insulted that you're calling us down on it. I bet we've been in practically every bar in Philly, and this is the first time we're being challenged on age! However, I might go so far as to say I'm flattered, but I need a little something to wet the old whistle. So make that two doubles of Seagram's Seven and draw two good old silver noggin' brews."

Even though Fred was twenty-five and could have easily produced proper identification, it just wasn't in his character to let things run smoothly. He always seemed to get untold enjoyment out of causing disturbances whenever there was an audience. That day was no different.

The bartender was obviously becoming quite annoyed with these two strangers, especially when the shorter one made a ridiculous request.

"My friend and I are being insulted, and we want to see the manager right now," Blueswicz demanded as he banged his fist on the highly polished oak bar.

Joe couldn't believe what was going on. His co-worker was creating trouble in a rough neighborhood. A couple of the other patrons got up from their seats and closed in on the pair.

"Hey, Vinnie, dese guys buggin' you or what?" asked the beetle-browed one as he took a firm grip on an empty beer bottle.

Immediately, Joe pulled his friend away from the bar and toward the door as he said, "Damn it, Fred, look what you got us into now! Look, fellas, my electric-mouth pal sometimes overloads his circuits. But he doesn't mean any harm—just likes to break balls once in a while, you know? Now if you gentlemen will excuse us, we'll be leaving in peace."

"Bullshit!" yelled Fred as he unsuccessfully tried to shake loose from Joe's vise-like grip. "We're not going anywhere!"

Luckily, a cab had just turned the corner when Joe spied it. "Taxi!"

When the vehicle pulled up, Fred, much to his friend's surprise, was the first to jump in.

"Well, what the hell are you waiting for? Let's get outta this wop place!"

"Fred, you're a crazy bastard! Shut up before you get us both killed!"

The disastrous experience loomed uppermost in Joe's mind as he finally convinced Blueswicz that he was not interested in going with him to the Northeast Sons of Poland Club.

2

Traveling alone became standard operational procedure with Talanski, and by December, he had developed quite a facility for dating older women who didn't mind spending their money on a strappingly handsome guy.

"Shipley is really a nice school, Joe," commented the gorgeous blonde as she gracefully slid into the passenger's side of her fire-engine red 1963 Mercedes sports car. "I'm sure your sister likes it."

"Yeah, Susan's a super kid. I just wish I could spend more time with her and Mike. You know, Bonnie, I haven't seen her and my brother since last February. Even though we're not a close family, we . . . well . . . I guess I'm what you might call the black sheep of the group. Can't seem to find the right words to say to people, especially my mother."

Bonnie had heard Joe speak of his brother and sister before, but this was the first time that she could get him to talk extensively about his mother. As the sleek Mercedes seemed to flatten out rolling hills and straighten curves in the road, Bonnie ignored that the machine was zipping along between seventy-five and eighty miles per hour. Her attention was focused on this handsome hunk of a man whom she had met only a month ago.

Bonnie St. Clair was by no means a pushover. This playgirl of thirty-three certainly knew how to handle herself when it came to men. Not only was she from a rather wealthy real estate family in Quincy, Massachusetts, but she was also doing very well as a clinical psychologist on staff at the Jefferson Medical Center.

Although she had not yet married, she was a viable force when it came to dealing with men. Not only was Dr. St. Clair a very popular beauty in the upper social set of Philadelphia's Main Line stratum but she had practically half of Jefferson's male resident physicians jockeying for a date with her. However, since meeting Joe Talanski,

Bonnie dropped virtually all other outside interests and devoted more time than necessary to her new patient. Oh, yes, Joe was her patient.

He was introduced to Dr. St. Clair by the physician who miraculously brought him back from the edge of death as a result of what had happened in Germantown. That was the first time Joe had been in the neighborhood since Christmas 1954. There was a chill in the autumn air that made the night feel colder than it actually was. Joe didn't know what made him take a trolley back to the old neighborhood where he and his Aunt Madge had lived. Nevertheless, there he was, standing beneath the lamppost across the street, staring at the turn-of-the-century brownstone where he used to live. An intoxicating feeling seeped through Joe's body. He felt extremely lightheaded as grotesque memories of that terrible night drifted in front of his mind's eye. First, there was Aunt Madge's diminutive body being practically ripped apart by bullets. Blood, viscera, and pieces of bone splattered the wall. Second, came that gigantic mountain of flesh who stood menacingly between a frightened little boy and a long, steep staircase of escape. Third, came two bodiless hands that seemed to be drifting out of a murky purple mist. And, in slow motion, the ghostly white hands replaced those of the little boy. Fourth, the hands, with the little boy's body in tow, drifted toward the gigantic mountain of flesh that was poised at the top of the stairs. Fifth, the hands gave the mountain of flesh a hard push that sent it tumbling down a deep dark hole, screaming as it fell.

"Hey, man, you got a cigarette?" asked a strange husky voice that broke through Joe's consciousness. From the murkiness of the past to the presence of the moment came a confused and frightened boy who, in one night, experienced enough horror about murder to cause him to have many restless nights. But, up to now, he forced himself to push the realities of Christmas Eve 1954 deep into the most obscure corners of his mind. Until tonight, Joe had been successful in keeping himself away from the house. Something happened, something he couldn't explain. Instead of going out with the fellas on that Friday payday, as he usually did, Joe let his formerly suppressed curiosity rise to an uncontrollable height. Now, he was a little sorry—but it was too late.

Talanski, noticing how the four black youths sort of eased themselves into positions around him, became quite nervous. He knew

34

that he was going to have to fight or take to flight. Either way, he could not possibly come out a winner, especially since there were no other apparent options.

"Sure, pal," responded Joe as he quickly took out the pack and offered cigarettes to all four. "Say, do you guys live around here?"

The question did not exactly come out the way he meant it; however, the die was cast.

"What kinda gotdamn question is that, honky?" growled one of the four as his cigarette-holding hand froze in stop action a few inches from curled lips.

"Yeah," said another, "are you trying to say that the neighborhood is too good for us?"

Laughter erupted among the black youths. Perhaps they were laughing at the fact that this poor white boy had stumbled into Satan's Stomping Ground, an area so named by police because of the high number of homicides that had taken place since the complexion of the neighborhood had darkened considerably. Even some of the precinct's black cops were reluctant to walk those streets alone.

"I'm sorry if I've caused any offense," our nervous hero said as he began to grope in his jacket pocket for the penknife he usually carried—it wasn't there. "But I used to live in that brownstone right there, and since I hadn't seen it in eight years, I thought . . ."

"Aw, man, bullshit!" yelled the leader as he grabbed Joe by the collar and slammed him against a wall. "We've heard enough of your crap! What the hell you take us for, anyhow? You come up here on our turf like you some kinda gotdamn dude looking for . . ."

"Some fine black ass," one of the other attackers interjected while grabbing for Talanski's wallet. "Uh, huh, that's what this honky's lookin' for!"

"Or maybe the mothafucka's lookin' for some *real* stuff, ya know?" said another. "Could be another one of those narco squad dudes! I say we waste this turkey right now!"

The leader released the victim with a heavy shove into a narrow alley and growled, "Yeah, man, you probably right. He's part of a setup—I can see it all over his white face!"

Unfortunately for Joe, he had invaded the Stomping Ground when the entire neighborhood was paranoid. Also, he was not aware of the fact that it was rapidly undergoing ethnic changes. Very few whites still resided there, and most of those were elderly people who, for one reason or another, couldn't seem to break out of the environment.

Breaking out of his present situation was uppermost in Joe's mind, but how? It was quite apparent to him that his attackers definitely meant to make him another statistic. His mind was now bent on how to escape with his life. The narrow, garbage-covered alley held little promise. An eight-foot metal fence behind him offered no hope since turning his back on the gang would probably be a fatal mistake anyhow. And trying to fight his way out of the alley would be useless.

"Yeah, I'm gonna stick it to him all right," grimaced the leader as he clicked open a seven-inch-blade Italian stiletto.

The alley was just wide enough for the other three companions to fit in so they could witness this bit of entertainment.

"C'mon, Bubba baby, off that fucka for good!"

"Right on, man!"

But the leader was not in any special hurry to dispatch with the stranger. Without turning around, he snapped his fingers and said, "Hey, one of you dudes light up a joint for me, 'cause I wanna enjoy workin' on this faggot. I even might be generous enough to blow a little in his face before I lay him out for good."

"Here, Bubba. This is my last one. Was savin' it for later, man. But that's cool. Just lemme get a one . . . oh, yeah . . . maybe one more . . . aw shit. Damn! This is a good one, too!"

While the four gang members were gloating over what they just knew was going to be an easy mark, caution was relaxed as the marijuana cigarette passed from hand to hand.

Speaking of hands, Bubba, feeling that everything was under control, was in the process of taking another deep drag on the well-smoked joint while changing the knife from one hand to the other.

With almost lightning speed, Talanski sprang upon his much-larger assailant. The other three were momentarily stunned by the unexpected lunge as the two bodies tumbled against trash cans. This was for all of the marbles, and Joe knew that he could very well lose his life in this stinking alley if Lady Luck refused to smile in his direction.

Nobody ever physically challenged big Bubba Green and survived to brag about it. Six-feet-three inches, two hundred and thirty pounds of meanness reacted immediately. None of Bubba's boys came to his assistance—they knew better. Besides, he let it be known many fights ago that "There ain't no mothafucka between heaven 'n hell can beat my ass one on one! So you guys just back off!" Bubba was right—up to that point. Several adversaries were maimed beyond full recovery, and three died later as a result of injuries received. Therefore, this latest event with a crazy paddy boy was looked upon as just another easy mark. However, there was one big difference this time: Bubba Green was the *attackee* instead of the *attacker*.

With one arm around the gang leader's eighteen-inch neck and the other arm serving as leverage, Joe caused him to drop the stiletto. Both bodies scrambled furiously, punching and being punched. Although Bubba was stronger, he just couldn't seem to beat this latest victim. Perhaps it was because this latest victim felt so much combination of fear and rage that his glands were causing him to perform beyond the ordinary. Joe's face was swollen and numb, but his fists kept working like two electric trip-hammers. And, because of the small alley space, neither man could do much dodging.

Upon seeing a police cruiser, the look-out yelled to his comrades, "Here comes a red car, y'all!"

Bubba, finding himself in an unusual predicament and also realizing that he couldn't afford to get caught, shouted, "Get this sonofabitch off me!"

No sooner had the gang leader made the request when someone picked up the knife, grabbed a handful of Joe's hair, and plunged the full blade deep into his back. Talanski fell face down into a garbage heap as blood streamed from the wound. Everything turned black. Silence.

3

"It looks pretty bad, gentlemen, but we'll do all we can to save him," said the doctor to the two policemen who had found Joe lying in the alleyway.

"C'mon, Paul, we can't do anything else right now. Let the meds take over. We'll get a statement from John Doe here later, maybe."

"You mean if he lives."

While the two officers were walking toward the hospital's emergency room exit, something kept stirring in Paul Kruger's mind. He was pretty sure that he had seen this *John Doe* before—and under other gruesome circumstances.

"Maybe he's a supplier, Paul. Why else would a white guy be up in that neighborhood? Hell—he couldn't have been looking for a little action—even the prostitutes gave up on that place years ago; so why . . ."

"Prostitutes! Damn it, Mike, now I know where I saw that guy before! The face, Mike, the face! You know I never forget the face!"

"What the hell are you talking about?"

"The face on our Mr. John Doe! Unless I'm way the hell off base, that fella—he was a young kid then—used to live in that neighborhood. Crap! Too bad those perps took the guy's I.D. Mike, I'll bet you a fin that this is the same kid who Dick Mason and I found in the house with two stiffs. If I recall correctly, the dame was his aunt. Hey, don't look at me like I'm crazy! Just drive."

Instead of going home at the end of his midnight shift, Kruger spent an extra hour going through the file, clippings, etc., on the 1954 Talanski—Swensen homicides. By the time he finished, he thought heavily on how the late Lt. George Clayburn, contrary to investigation reports, quietly maintained that the kid was connected, in some manner, with those deaths. Now Kruger's curiosity completely overwhelmed him to such an extent that he couldn't wait—had to go back to the hospital, regardless of the two A.M. hour.

"Look, sweetie, I'm familiar with the rules and regulations," Kruger said to the nurse as he practically shoved her into the room. "All I want is to see this guy for myself—like right now."

All kinds of life-support apparatus were connected to the pale body. Even so, the officer squinted at it just to make sure that his eyes were not playing tricks. Kruger was convinced that the man lying in the bed was the frightened little Talanski kid. Now, more than before, the officer was determined to get answers to some questions that had been plaguing his mind for years.

Kruger spent the rest of the night catnapping in an uncomfortable chair in the lounge area. After getting this hot on the trail, he was not about to let some old hospital rules stand in his way. Even the usually-tough night supervisor of nurses couldn't convince the seasoned veteran cop that the patient would not be physically or mentally up to making a statement.

"I can understand what you're telling me, miss, but it's very important that I be the first person this guy talks to when he comes around. Look, I promise, I won't be hard on him. Just have to question him about his being stabbed—routine stuff."

A kind of purplish fog seemed to enshroud Joe's mind; everything was bordering on the opaque. The pain that darted from one side of his head to the other was unbearable, even moreso than the stab wound. Upon opening his eyes, Joe saw a figure leaning over him. Assuming that it must be one of the doctors, our hero said, "How bad is it?"

"Ah, so you're awake. How do you feel?"

"Not good, doc. I got a lot of pain, especially in the head."

"Do you feel strong enough to answer a few questions? First of all, I'm not a doctor, kid. I'm Sergeant Paul Kruger, Philadelphia Police Department. My partner and I found you up in Germantown last night, bleeding and unconscious."

"Damn, now I remember! Some black guys mugged me, and . . ."

"What's your name, kid?"

"Talanski . . . Joe Talanski."

Kruger, but for the fact that he knew that his hunches were usually right, would have jumped for joy. However, he maintained his cool investigative demeanor and continued. "You're lucky to be alive, Joe Talanski. What were you doing in that neighborhood, anyway?"

"I used to live there with . . ."

"Yeah, yeah, I know all about that, kid, but why did you *really* come back? Was it because you were looking to tie up some loose ends? Wanna tell me more about that Christmas Eve night back in '54?"

If Joe was in great physical pain before, he was in greater mental pain now. The barrage of questions shot at him by Sergeant Kruger unnerved our hero to the extent that he began shouting for the nurse. Joe's yelling brought not only one nurse but three nurses and two interns who happened to have been in the area.

The policeman's probing coupled with the heavy after-effect of the medication sent Joe into a psychotic rage, "The sonofabitch killed my aunt! And he was gonna kill me too! I had to do something!"

In the midst of all of the confusion that was taking place in the room—flailing arms, tubes being intertwined, intravenous apparatus falling, attendants trying to restrain the patient—Kruger relentlessly hung on to his questioning. "So what did you do about it, kid? How did Swenson happen to break his neck? Did you have something to do with it?"

"Yes! Goddamnit, yes! I pushed that sonofabitch down the steps! And I'd do it again—and again—and again—and again. . . ."

While the orderlies were holding Joe down for a needle, Kruger, now wild-eyed and acting like a pit bull that wasn't about to let go of his quarry, kept throwing questions at the helpless form in the bed. In spite of the head nurse's protests, the policeman just barreled ahead as though the true life-death situation depended upon his working this suspect into a frenzy. And, undoubtedly, Kruger was good at it. However, before he could really get into his gear, the powerful injection was already beginning to take effect.

"I'm afraid our Mr. John Doe can't undergo any more questioning now, Sergeant," the head nurse said, smiling. "He's going to be under heavy sedation for the next three to four hours."

Nevertheless, Kruger was not deterred from pursuing positive identification. When he returned to the hospital later that day, he had secured all of the data he needed concerning Joseph Bernard Talanski. The veteran cop's steps quickened as he rounded the corridor.

Nineteen years on the police force and only up to sergeant made Kruger a bitter cop. His contempt for those younger punks downtown was never hidden; always up front with whatever was on his mind had frequently caused Kruger to lose out whenever promotion recommendations came around. Being tactful was never one of his strong suits. How often did Kruger latch on to solid-gold leads and just try to ride roughshod over everyone else's? This latest thing was red hot, and he planned to use it to his advantage in proving how good he was in turning up new evidence, evidence based upon leads that his buddies down at the precinct didn't know existed.

I'm gonna ram this one right up their rear ends, thought Kruger as he walked briskly through the corridors.

When the officer arrived at the doorway, a nurse stopped him and said, "Sergeant Kruger, I know you must be here to see the John Doe you brought in."

"Yeah, that's right, sweetheart, and I'd appreciate it if you people would let me do my job this time and stop interfering in police business, understand?"

Kruger went to the right bed but found the wrong patient.

"Okay, miss, let's stop playing games. Where's the guy we . . . ."

"That's what I've been trying to tell you," she replied. "Apparently, the patient . . . ."

"His name's Talanski, Joseph Bernard Talanski."

"Thank you. I'll be sure to enter that on our records when . . . ."

"Please . . . er," Kruger read the nurse's I.D. badge, "Miss Lester, where is he?"

As the nurse led Kruger to a small single room off the back hallway, she informed him of the inexplicable drop in Talanski's condition.

"Dr. Mahan, one of our best surgeons, operated on him, and even he is puzzled by the lack of this patient's responsive recovery. It's as though he doesn't want to get better."

After escorting the police sergeant to the room, Miss Lester disappeared around the corner, leaving only a faint trail of light perfume.

Kruger looked at the prostrated figure lying in the bed and thought about how he found that same figure several years before. A brief feeling of pity passed through the veteran cop's heart as he surveyed the surroundings. However, policework must not be hampered by such feelings, so on with it.

"Is your name Joseph Talanski?"

"Yeah," came a whispered reply, "and I know who you are. You're one of the officers that came to my aunt's house the night she was murdered, right?"

Kruger's face registered mild surprise. He didn't expect the suspect to open the subject; nevertheless, the surprised look was only momentary.

"Okay, pal, since you mentioned it first, suppose you tell me what really happened that night. Never mind your aunt's cause of death. What I want to know is whether or not what you were yelling the other day was true."

41

Again, the police sergeant expected Talanski to do anything but cooperate. Cracking through hardened lies was commonplace with this veteran cop. He could peer deeply into a man's eyes, far down into his soul, and tell whether or not he was lying. Therefore, Kruger was prepared to deal with reluctance in any form. Surprisingly, though, the officer's straightforwardness must have triggered in the young man a latent response that had been just waiting all those years for the right moment to rise to the surface. Even during the time when Joe's parents had him undergo several trips to the psychiatrist it was never considered that the kid had killed the killer. And since the shrink never raised the question, Joe, apparently, pushed that singular deed to the rear of his mind. Maybe it was because he did not view himself as a killer that none of those horrible nightmares resulted in his losing a real grip on reality.

Kruger, during the nearly three hours that he spent in the patient's room, found himself more in the role of sympathetic priest than the hard-nosed cop. As Joe openly related incident after incident concerning his rather short life, the venerable old officer concluded that this guy had suffered enough and was in need of a genuine helping hand.

"Look, kid, I'm no Mr. Know-It-All, neither am I used to sticking my neck out. But, for some strange reason, I feel kinda close to you, and . . . well . . . I guess I just wanna help, okay?"

Even though Kruger was basically a hard-nosed, by-the-book cop, there were times when that armor plate of his did not fend off the arrows of emotion. And this was one of those times.

"The doctors tell me that you could be doing a helluva lot better toward getting out of here if you'd just try. They seem to think you want to cash in your chips early, kid."

Joe re-positioned his head on the pillow as he replied. "Sergeant, to tell you the truth, I really don't know how I'm supposed to feel at this point in my life. But I do know I've been screwing up everything I touch . . . nothing seems to go right. . . ."

"Hey, whoa, now just take it easy, kid. You're not the only person in the world who's had problems. Listen, I'm gonna give you something that just might turn out to be a great help to you," Kruger said as he rummaged through his small notepad for a scrap of clean paper. "I don't know how you feel about shrinks, kid, but I can personally tell you that this one is good—not just because she's my cousin's daughter, but because I've known her to sweep the cobwebs out of some of the guys' heads down at the precinct—and, believe me, that ain't easy!"

Joe took the piece of paper and read it: "Dr. Bonnie St. Clair, Staff Psychologist—Jefferson Medical Center—Evergreen 2-1899."

Four

Age Factor

"Maybe you should have called your sister to let her know you're coming—and bringing a friend," Bonnie said as the powerful Mercedes sports car gunned to a stop in front of the Shipley School's ivy-covered dormitory.

Joe laughed as he got out. "Hey, Bonnie, this is Susie I'm going to see, not the Queen of Sheba."

Because she and Joe had been waiting in the housemother's office for nearly an hour, Bonnie perceived something that she didn't think was favorable. Not being able to hold back any longer, she stubbed her cigarette and said, "I don't think Susan wants to see you. Why else would she . . ."

"What? What the hell are you talking about? Of course she wants to see me! I talked to her on the phone back in early October, and she said she wanted me to come out here to visit her! That's my little sister up there in the dorm, not just some broad who slipped me a phone number!"

Joe's voice had become so loud that several other visitors showed alarm. Nevertheless, our upset hero ranted on. Maybe it was because he tried to ignore the truth or was just plain angry. At any rate, Bonnie was the one who verbalized what had occurred to both of them; therefore, she had to receive the full force of Joe's rejected feelings.

During the silent period that followed, Bonnie did a lot of introspection. *Serves me right,* she said to herself, *I should've known better than to spend so much of my free time with this one patient. Now, damn it, I'm hooked . . . I love this gorgeous hunk of a man, and it's terrible! How can I possibly help him with his problems while I feel this way?*

Bonnie's little reverie was interrupted by the tall matronly woman who approached them. "I'm sorry, Mr. Talanski, but Susan wishes me to convey the message that she is very much indisposed at this time and that it is quite impossible for her to see you."

Joe felt as though his whole world was falling apart and he was losing control of everything. When Bonnie saw him tighten his lips and begin rocking back and forth in the chair, she knew that if she didn't do something positive at that very moment, all of the progress made in the past therapy sessions would be lost.

"Miss Holcroft, may I have a word with you?" asked Bonnie while the tall housemother stood straight with closed hands, body language definitely sending out the signal that it was time for the two visitors to leave. The hard, cold stare that the housemother was giving Joe did not help matters at all. In fact, he was just about ready to unload his verbal anger on her when Bonnie spoke to him. "Excuse me for a moment, Joe, I want to talk to Miss Holcraft in private. That is, if you don't mind."

"Go right ahead," he replied while reaching into his jacket pocket for cigarettes. "But I'm sure these people haven't even notified Susan that I'm here. Otherwise, she would've been . . ."

"It's all right, Joe. I'm positive we can clarify matters," Bonnie said as she gently ushered the dorm mother out of her friend's hearing range. "Suppose you just wait here for a few minutes while I speak to Miss Holcroft. I'm sure there must be some mistake."

When the two women entered an unoccupied office, Bonnie began with, "I want to apologize for this little imposition, but it was necessary under the circumstances. You see, Mr. Talanski had been happily planning this trip out here to see his sister for a long time, and . . ."

Miss Holcroft interrupted with, "I understand how he must feel, but what I don't quite understand, Miss . . . er . . ."

"St. Clair—Dr. St. Clair."

"Dr. St. Clair, the reason I was so long in returning from Susan's room was because the poor child outright refused to come down! Naturally, I became concerned since I couldn't persuade her to tell me anything beyond confirming that Mr. Talanski is her step-brother."

Although Bonnie was surprised to learn that Susan's feelings toward Joe were not compatible with his, she was reluctant to discuss anything further with Miss Holcroft; however, it was obvious that this matron did not mind revealing all she knew. Therefore, Bonnie urged her on. "Why do you suppose a child of just fourteen would not want to see her brother, whom she hasn't seen in almost a year?"

"Good question. Also, why would a young girl of fourteen find it necessary to telephone her mother in order to discuss her brother's visit?"

"What?"

"That's right. She called her, but, apparently, no one was home. And when I questioned Susan about her unusual behavior, she began to cry. Nevertheless, the poor child stood firm on her refusal to see . . . your friend."

Bonnie distinctly noticed the slight innuendo. "What are you driving at, Miss Holcroft? Are you suggesting . . ."

"I'm not suggesting anything! However, during my twenty-three years here at Shipley, I think I qualify quite well when it comes to discerning young girls' fears about . . . certain things."

"Certain things? Oh, my God, you *are* suggesting something! And that something is the most . . ."

"Now just a minute here, Dr. St. Clair, I don't intend to spend the rest of the afternoon debating on an obvious issue! Prior to today, Mr. Joseph Talanski had not set foot on this campus, but his sister has been here since September! Now I'm very close to all my girls. So why do you suppose Susan never mentioned a second brother to me? She frequently talks about the one who is a freshman at Penn. *Suggesting?* No, Dr. St. Clair, I'm not *suggesting* anything other than I do believe that this entire matter is somewhat bizarre and I also think there is nothing more for us to discuss!"

The day was pretty well ruined, and Bonnie knew it. She also knew that trying to explain things to Joe was not going to be an easy task, especially in light of the fact that he had been happily talking about the family during the recent therapy sessions. Although Dr. St. Clair was aware of Joe's embellishment of certain bits of information, she didn't back him into a corner for more details. It became obvious to her that Joe really wanted a closer relationship with his family, but various circumstances were preventing it. Through those sessions, Bonnie found herself devoting more personal time to this client than perhaps she should have. In the beginning, she was merely fascinated with his good looks. Now, she was in love and feeling totally incapable of dealing with Joe on a professional level. It seemed as though none of her words were really getting through to him. "Oh, maybe your sister is just not feeling

46

well and doesn't want to be bothered with anyone today. For Heaven's sake, Joe, you have to realize that Susan is a young lady now, and her body is going through the normal monthly cycles, which cause . . ."

"Bonnie, stop talking for a second, will you?" Joe said as he returned to the housemother's office. "It could be what you're suggesting, but why should we go away guessing when all of this mystery could be cleared up with one phone call?"

After he convinced the stern Miss Holcroft that he would leave upon making one short call to Susan, the housemother reluctantly assented to his using her telephone. Miss Holcroft dialed and asked the person who answered the hall telephone to knock on Susan's door.

"Remember, Mr. Talanski, I must insist that you limit your conversation to just a few minutes, because this whole matter seems odd to me."

Joe faintly smiled as he held the receiver to his ear with one hand and gently closed the door behind the two women with the other. He was sitting on the edge of Miss Holcroft's desk as he waited for his sister to come to the telephone. Bonnie and the housemother moved out of listening range; however, they could see Joe through the two large plate glass windows. The quick rise from the desk top and wide smile told the women that he had made contact.

"Susan, baby, how're you doing? Gee, it's great hearing your voice again! Come on downstairs so I can look at you! Haven't seen you and Michael since . . . What? What do you mean you can't see me? I'm right here, Susan. All you have to do is . . ."

Bonnie watched as Joe's facial expression changed from happiness to dejection. She didn't have to hear the conversation to know that all was not well. After he hung up, Joe walked hurriedly out of the office and, without stopping, took Bonnie by the arm as he moved toward the exit door.

"What happened? What did Susan say?"

"Not now . . . not in this place. Let's just get on the road. If you don't mind, Bonnie, I'd rather not talk about it," Joe responded as they approached the car. "And here, take your keys. I don't feel like driving."

For the most part, the ride back to Philadelphia was in silence. Only the purr of the motor could be heard. Bonnie surmised that whatever the nature of the conversation that Joe had with his sister, it was indeed a disturbing one. Nevertheless, she decided to wait for him to open up. A half-hour passed.

"Are you hungry?" came the surprising question from the passenger.

"I sure am. How about you?" Bonnie answered, smiling. "It's been a long time since breakfast—coffee and juice."

"Can't understand why you starve yourself. You look good all the time, sweetheart," Joe said, kissing the index finger of his left hand and touching Bonnie's right knee. Her response was instant.

"Hey, mister, you'd better cut that out before you go to prison for creating a dangerous electrical situation."

Even though his feelings were terribly hurt by the brief conversation that he had with his sister, Joe was trying to cover up that which was obvious to Dr. St. Clair. Nevertheless, she thought it would serve no beneficial purpose to quiz him concerning the conversation or even mention the afternoon's fiasco. Bonnie wisely decided to let Joe determine the conditions under which he might wish to talk about it. However, she always believed in giving chance a little help. By taking advantage of the brief happy mood that Joe displayed, Bonnie altered plans somewhat. "Why would you prefer eating at an old greasy-spoon joint when you could eat at a new greasy-spoon joint . . . like my place?"

For the first time that afternoon, Bonnie heard her patient laugh with gusto, and she intended to keep him that way until she could get to the root of his latest problem.

"Do you like Chinese food?" Bonnie asked, while they waited for the light to change.

"Umm . . . and how," Joe replied. "But I didn't know you could cook Chi . . ."

"Hey, now who said anything about cooking?" Bonnie interjected, as she negotiated an illegal U-turn midway up the block and pulled to a jerky stop in front of the Golden Dragon Restaurant. "I thought I'd give this place a try and see whether there's any truth to the rumor that my egg foo yung is not as good as Chan's."

Since the restaurant was not crowded, Bonnie suggested that they eat there instead of taking out. Oddly enough, both of them wanted to talk about some sensitive things; therefore, the secluded booth in the corner was perfect. Conversation was lightly humorous through the won ton and main course. "Umm . . . Chan's chop chop is good, but I know it doesn't compare with yours, babe."

"Now just how would you know that, Mr. Talanski, since you haven't tasted my cooking?"

"Oh, well . . . er . . . I realize that I haven't been extended the glorious honor of partaking of your delicious victuals, madame, but it would seem improbable that a sweet and gorgeous lady such as yourself would not be able to prepare the most exquisite of gourmet delectibles."

"Well, now, if that isn't one heck of a line to lay on a gal who's nine years your senior! It's a good thing I don't take it seriously, because . . . "

"Bonnie," Joe interrupted as he reached across the narrow table and held her hands, "you've been good to me, probably more than you should be, as far as doctor-patient relationships go, but I've grown to love you . . . and I'm afraid."

Granted, Dr. St. Clair would have preferred that the ensuing conversation take place in a more appropriate setting, but she knew that once a patient begins to open up, it would be counterproductive to stop the flow of words. However, her femininity forced her to ask the question, "Does my being nine years older than you have anything to do with our relationship?"

Joe was surprised that the age factor was highlighted at the moment, but he dealt with it in an honest manner.

"Bonnie, you know how I feel about you. I told you three weeks after I had started coming for therapy that I loved you. Age never entered our discussions then. I don't consider anything important other than the fact that you mean a helluva lot to me, sweetheart, but I'm not so naive as to believe that our relationship is going to last."

A sad frown covered Bonnie's face, and she squeezed her lover's hand while saying, "It will last if we want it to. Yet, right now, I'm wondering if there is another woman who . . . "

"Don't say it!"

Joe's booming order caused the waiters and other patrons to look in astonishment, or at least in anticipation of some excitement. A few minutes later, he called for the check, and they left.

"Even at the risk of having you think of me as being a pushy person," Bonnie said, as she pulled away from the curb, "I'm going to insist that we go to my apartment for a drink, okay?"

Laughingly, Joe replied, "Okay."

The young garage attendant at the plush Colonial Arms recognized the car immediately, and he hurriedly came out of the booth in his usual anticipation of gunning that beautiful machine into its parking space on the upper level. But it was different that night. Dr. St. Clair only waved to him as she proceeded to park her own car.

"Who was that with her?" asked the other attendant as his young co-worker disgustedly closed the booth's sliding door.

"How the hell would I know? Some guy, I guess."

"Nice answer, Pete. That's why your smart ass'll never make full-time here. Always wisin' off with somethin' stupid. I'm tryin' to help you get ahead on this job, kid. I've been workin' round these kinds of places for a long time now, and I know how to see and don't see. Know what I mean?"

The young fellow looked quizzically at the older man and replied, "No, I don't know what you mean."

"Well, first of all, with this place bein' the high-class joint that it is, you got a lot of jet-setters livin' here—singles, married ones, and them that play both angles. But it really don't make no difference which way they go, 'cause they make big money, and they do whatever the hell they wanna do, get me?"

"Yeah . . . kinda. . . ."

"*Kinda!* Damn, kid! How long you been workin' here now?"

"Almost a month. But what does that have to do with the price of tea in Japan?"

"There you go again, wisin' off! Look, Pete, the people who live here love their privacy, and they show their appreciation by tippin' us guys when they come and go, right?"

"Right. But what . . . "

"But what, my ass, kid! In simple language, they sometimes have people in the car that they would rather we don't see. These are mostly professional people livin' here, but they got hot rocks the same as me 'n you. They pick up shit out there 'n bring 'em home for a few hours—or maybe the night."

A sardonic smile spread across Pete's face as he said, "What you're telling me is that our beautiful Dr. St. Clair has picked up on some stud out there and doesn't want the world to know about it, right?"

"Now you're gettin' the picture. 'Specially since the guy ain't the one she's been seein' up to awhile ago. Yeah, she used to go out with one of them sharp doctors over at Jefferson Hospital, but I haven't seen him 'round for couple of months now. I forget his name, but I ain't forgot the big tips he used to give me when he came to visit with his lady friend. Now that I'm talkin' 'bout it, I remember him and doc had a big argument one night over there by the elevator.And less than an hour later, he came down—musta been madder than a wet rooster—slapped a five-note on me, jumped in his car, 'n burned rubber all the way outta here. Listen, there're many things these jetters do, but, I'll tell you this. You can collect a lotta tips when they find out you can keep their business private, know what I mean, kid?"

"Sure, Walt, I know—just like you've been keeping Dr. St. Clair's private, right?"

"Fuck you, kid. Go get us some coffee. It's gettin' cold down here tonight."

Meanwhile, high above the garage, in apartment 1406, Dr. St Clair and her guest were sitting on the luxuriously made, white, crushed-velvet sofa. The expensive, hi-fidelity phonograph had just finished playing a Sinatra ballad when Joe slowly stood up, stretched, and said, "As usual, Bonnie, you've been great. But I don't want to wear out my welcome . . . so . . . I think I'd better hit the road."

"Why're you rushing? You don't have to work tomorrow. And even the farmers come to town on Saturday night. What do you say I whip up a small pitcher of my world-famous martinis for an evening of relaxation?"

Joe was only mildly surprised at Bonnie's aggressiveness, because it was a little over two months before this beautiful woman had all but seduced him after his third visit to her office. At that time, Talanski, heavily impressed by her independence, brilliance, and money, also did his best to turn on as much charm as he could muster. However, neither he nor Bonnie had planned for love to creep into the picture. Doing simple, non-complicated things, such as going to the zoo, The Ben Franklin Institute, riding bicycles in Fairmount Park, and going to the movies, appealed greatly to Bonnie. As she commented so often, it was a lot of fun for her to relive those activities that were a part of her fun-filled days when she was in college and graduate school.

51

Bonnie never had to concern herself too much with the financial aspect of growing up, because the St. Clair family had been independently wealthy since the turn of the century. Bonnie's great-grandfather amassed a sizeable fortune in New England real estate. Until Bonnie's Aunt Priscilla decided to turn her attention toward college and a career in teaching, most of the other St. Clair women were satisfied with the niceties learned in the various New England finishing schools. And, like several of her relatives who had moved southward, Bonnie was just dying to get away from home so she might kick up her heels. Fortunately, her father, although a rather mild-mannered man who was never one for complaining about the rich but sedentary life, did not try to stifle his youngest of three daughters' zest for a different lifestyle.

However, Mr. St. Clair did make sure that there was always a tidy amount in Bonnie's checking account. He had a direct pipeline to all of her banking transactions via one of his former classmates at U.P.'s Wharton School, who was first vice-president of Franklin National Bank. Also, Bonnie's father made sure that there was someone to look after her safety-wise; therefore, he contacted his cousin, who was a member of the Philadelphia Police Department.

Yes, beautiful Bonnie St. Clair could devote her leisure time to building a tabloid of gentlemen pursuers. And since she seemed to possess more than her share of brilliance, passing examinations with high grades was standard operating procedure. Undoubtedly, Bonnie was not only a big hit with many of the young and old Philadelphia Main Line social strivers, but also well-to-do eligible men all up and down the eastern seaboard.

"Sounds good," Joe replied, "but I don't want to spoil your night . . ."

"Believe me, you won't be spoiling anything," Bonnie said excitedly, as she practically ran to the kitchen and started grabbing objects needed for drinks. "Just relax, take off your shoes, and enjoy the music."

While she was pouring the vermouth, Bonnie felt arms slip around her waist from the rear.

"You're really one beautiful woman," came a whisper into her ear.

"Woman? Bet if I were about ten years younger, you would've said *girl,"* Bonnie replied, turning around with pouting lips.

"Why're you so hung up on our age difference, babe? I love you. So what else matters?" he said, kissing her tenderly.

"Hmm . . . then move in with me, darling."

Joe was practically numbed by the suggestion. Although he had spent several intimate hours in Bonnie's apartment on a couple of previous occasions, he never once considered living with her, nor had she previously mentioned the thought.

"You mean here in your apartment? Oh, no, Bonnie. I'm already a piece of disease to my family. I don't need to spread further."

"Look, stop putting yourself down, Joe. The world's not coming to an end just because you had a few disappointing words with your kid sister."

"A few? Bonnie, it's just not that simple. You know what Susie told me this afternoon on the phone? She told me that everybody back home is disgusted with me for getting kicked out of college. . . ."

This was the moment that Dr. St. Clair had been awaiting. Her patient was finally opening up about the telephone conversation that he had with his sister. Therefore, she remained silent and listened.

"Like I told you, I thought Susie and I were tight. I mean, I really love that kid . . . and Mike, too. Sure, we're only half-related as far as the rest of the world is concerned. But they're *real* family to me . . . real brother and sister—none of that step-crap. Like I told you, even though the three of us haven't spent much time together, I love them."

Bonnie didn't want anything to interrupt Joe's flow of words so, without asking him, she poured a couple of martinis and sat down at the kitchen table, knowing that Joe would join her. He did, but not before gulping the contents of the small glass and refilling it. Bonnie was tempted to make a comment; however, she decided that her client should not be disturbed.

"Susie's words really hurt me this afternoon. Told me she didn't want to go against Dad's wishes. Can you beat that? My own father . . . building a wall between me and the other kids . . . well, maybe he doesn't really consider himself to be my father . . . just my mother's husband when it comes to me . . . hey, I thought you doctors were suppose to heal . . . never mind . . . don't bother responding to that . . . you haven't done anything to me. . . ."

Bonnie remained attentive to Joe's every word as he rambled on while putting away three martinis and two cans of beer. An hour later, Joe passed out while trying to balance self-pity and liquor consumption. His girlfriend viewed the seemingly lifeless hulk that was draped over her kitchen table as a wasted cause for that night. She thought about reviving him, but a better idea crossed her mind: put him to bed.

While Bonnie was fruitlessly attempting to raise the sleeping form to at least a sitting position, the telephone rang. She started not to answer it, but it continued relentlessly.

"Hello, Bonnie? Ralph!"

Perhaps it was a good thing that Bonnie had not completely revived the guest, because the voice on the other end of the line belonged to someone whom she was trying to forget when she met Joe. Dr. Ralph Lindstrom, a divorced thirty-eight-year-old cardiologist, up to the time he took a six-month leave of absence from Jefferson, was one of Dr. St. Clair's several pursuers.

"Ralph! When did you get back? Why didn't you call?"

The questions were fired at Lindstrom in such rapid succession and with a voice that sounded so full of enthusiasm that he smiled as he put down the lightweight carry-on bag and switched the telephone receiver to a more comfortable position. Bonnie was the first person with whom Lindstrom had made familiar contact since the end of his airline flight from Brussels. During their ten-minute telephone conversation, Bonnie decided, as she looked at the drunken figure, that she wanted more out of a relationship than she was getting. All of a sudden, the beautiful woman realized that she missed the more mature attention given to her before she began dating someone who was obviously not in her league.

"The breakthrough in successfully performing human heart transplants is coming fast, Bonnie. If you'll pardon the pun—it's only a heartbeat away, and I intend to be right in there with those few doctors who're presently building one helluva knowledge resource. I learned a lot over there, and now I need more time for laboratory experiments. . . ."

The excitement in Dr. Lindstrom's voice raised Bonnie's desire to see him again—soon. And while he was talking, she thought how ridiculous her actions with this youngster had been during the past several weeks.

My God! I must be crazy! thought Dr. St. Clair as she continued to divide her attention between the telephone conversation and the intoxicated form draped over her kitchen table.

"Hello! Are you still there?"

"Oh, I'm sorry, Ralph. Of course I'm still here. I think it's wonderful, and I want you to know I'm really happy for you."

"Happy enough to have dinner with me tomorrow night?"

"Well . . . I don't. . . ."

"Hey, Bonnie, I'm sorry. What a nut I am! Here it is, I've been away for nearly three months, and I'm acting as though all a gorgeous woman like you had to do was just sit around waiting for some jerk like me. I'm sorry, Bonnie . . . I really am. Perhaps I'll see you at the hospital on Monday and we can have coffee if you . . ."

The more Dr. Linstrom talked, the more Bonnie realized how much she missed being the center of attraction among her many male admirers, and she wanted to get back into the mainstream of her familiar social atmosphere.

"I would be delighted to have dinner with you tomorrow night, Ralph. . . ."

Right there in a telephone booth at Philadelphia's International Airport, a cardiologist almost had a cardiac arrest. He was happier than happy. Even the little old bag lady who was picking through a wastepaper can nearby was momentarily startled when the booth's door flew open and a grinning man rushed out, apologized for bumping into her, pressed a ten dollar bill into her hand, and then disappeared.

Bonnie glanced at the clock. Almost midnight. She then glanced at her sleeping friend who was snoring heavily because of the twisted position of his neck on the table. Without bothering to awaken Joe, Bonnie turned off the light and retired to her spacious bedroom. After she got out of the shower, our humming psychologist admired her beautiful body while dabbing expensive cologne behind each knee. The flimsy white nightgown gave Bonnie the appearance of a Greek goddess. That night she did something for the first time since moving into the huge apartment—locked her bedroom door.

Momentarily, Joe could not turn his head too well. The subtle throbbing increased when he stood up to turn on the kitchen light.

55

"Oh my gosh! That clock *can't* be right! Three-thirty? Damn, I must've passed out. Where's Bonnie?"

Joe splashed cold water on his face and then carefully tiptoed across the living room toward the door. He thought that it was best not to disturb Bonnie, since he wasn't too sure whether he had created a terrible situation. Joe, not being aware of the call that Bonnie had received, assumed that she just became upset when he did not express enthusiasm about moving in with her.

Maybe I shouldn't try to see Bonnie right now, Joe thought as he touched the doorknob. *Damn! I must've really made a jerk of myself, getting drunk and passing out. No. On second thought, I'm not going to leave without apologizing. Maybe she's still awake.*

Joe was no stranger to Bonnie's bedroom, so he expected to go right in. Upon finding the door not only closed, but locked, he retreated to the large couch in the living room and made himself comfortable for a few more hours of shut-eye.

The bright sunlight pouring through the huge picture window caused Bonnie to blink and turn over. She peeked at the clock—seven-thirty. Thoughts of last night's telephone conversation with an old flame brought about a smile. Ralph Lindstrom, whether he knew it or not, came back on the scene in perfect timing. Bonnie was eager to rekindle their relationship. Suddenly, her early-morning reverie was interrupted when a light odor of coffee seeped in.

"Oh, my God," said the blonde beauty while slowly getting out of bed. She knew that there was a bit of unsavory business that must be taken care of immediately. However, she wasn't quite sure as to how she should handle it.

"Top 'o the mornin' to ya, m'love," came Joe's lively greeting as he diverted his attention from the sizzling bacon to the barefoot doll standing in the doorway. "Hey, how 'bout a kiss—or is it against house rules to cavort with the hired help?"

Reluctantly, Bonnie eased up to the cook and gave him a light peck on the cheek. It was apparently not enough, because the cook laid aside the spatula and took the lady of the house in his arms.

"No," was her response while pulling away, "not now, Joe. It's much too early in the morning for that sort of thing."

"Or too late after last night," was his light-hearted reply. "Wouldn't you know it—Talanski fell asleep on the job again. Here, let me pour that for you. So . . . I've been thinking about what you said last night, Bonnie, and . . . well . . . I like the idea of moving in . . . damn, that doesn't sound right . . . sharing your apartment sounds better.''

Bonnie tried not to let her lately developed true feelings come through in a hurting way to Joe, but she knew that things had to be made clear before he left. So, picking her words as carefully as she could, Dr. St. Clair began with, ''Joe, I want to apologize for backing you into a corner last night concerning that topic. I've been taking undue liberties, making unreasonable demands on your time. . . .''

By then, Joe began noticing the fidgety way Bonnie was running one hand through her golden tresses and tapping the table with the other. He couldn't help noticing these unusual actions, because they were not what he had ever before noticed about Bonnie, who always seemed to be in control of every situation. However, Joe didn't want to interrupt her at that juncture, because, although he had a feeling that Bonnie was not building up to something pleasant, he felt compelled to let her get it all out.

She continued with, ''I think our relationship needs to be redefined in terms of . . .''

''Whoa, wait. . . .'' Joe interjected, ''I never thought it was necessary to *redefine* anything, Bonnie, I mean, after all, you and I came together because we fell in love. Now what's so complicated about that? You're the one who seems to have this hang-up on age. . . .''

''*Age?* Now who the hell is talking about age? I haven't mentioned it this morning! So why should you?''

''Aw, come on, Bonnie, you know that's been a major stumbling block ever since we started . . . well . . .''

''Shacking up? That's the term you're looking for, right?''

''Jesus Christ almighty, Bonnie, what's gotten into you? Here I am, trying to repair whatever damage I caused last night, and . . .''

''Look, just forget it, okay? The whole damned mess is my fault! I admit it! I practically forced your weak mind into . . .''

''*Weak* mind? Now it all comes out! Just because you got inside my head, Dr. St. Clair, doesn't mean that I'm ready to succumb to the idea that I'm just a piece of meat!''

''And just because you got inside my body, Mr. Talanski, doesn't mean that *I* am ready to succumb to the idea that I'm just a piece of meat!''

"Oh, now that's what I call viciousness! Maybe I'd better leave," Joe said as he got up from the table.

Bonnie was somewhat ashamed of herself for verbally fighting Joe. She, above anyone else, was most aware of the devastating psychological changes he had been going through, yet she could not separate her womanly feelings from her professional feelings. As a result of her becoming intimately involved, the doctor-patient relationship suffered a major setback, and Bonnie felt that it was totally her fault. Perhaps the thought of being pursued once again by gentlemen of means was stimulated. At any rate, she did not consider her present love life to be solidly in place, and this bothered her greatly.

Usually, Joe covered the walking distance between the subway entrance and the rooming house in less than five minutes; however, that early Sunday morning, it took him twice as long. With hands shoved deeply into the pockets of his mackinaw jacket, he walked slowly along the narrow cobblestone street, his mind engrossed in the latest perplexing situation. No sooner had he closed the foyer door when his landlady poked her head from around the corner of the staircase where she had been cleaning.

"Oh, Mr. Talanski, I'm glad you're in. You got a long distance telephone call last night from a lady who said she was your mother. You're to call Operator Six."

"My mother? Er, all right, Mrs. Krantz, thanks," Joe responded, as he headed for the public phone on the wall outside of the landlady's apartment.

After the seventh ring, the operator was going to hang up; however, Joe asked her to let it go for another half-minute. It was early Sunday morning, and he assumed that his parents were still in bed. The assumption was right.

Bob picked up the receiver reluctantly, because he thought the hospital might be calling him on another emergency.

"Dr. Callahan here. Er . . . yes, operator. It's Joey."

A mixture of relief and disgust registered on Bob's face as he handed the receiver to Marie. She eagerly took it and started right in with, "Joey, why did you upset Susan like that? No, there's nothing wrong with you visiting her, but you might have at least given her the courtesy of calling first. . . ."

58

While his mother was rapidly telling him about the embarrassment that he had caused the family to date, Joe was trying very hard to hold down an angry tone. One argument that morning was enough.

In an unusually calm voice, he said, "Mom, you know, it certainly is funny. I left the 'Burgh, because I was causing too much embarrassment. Came all the way to Philly to kinda pull things together . . . and what did you and Dad do? Why, what else? Send Mike and Susie right into this area! Now that's what I call real planning. Then, of course, stupid me, believing that we're all family, and that it's normal for a guy to visit his brother and sister, dared to go to their schools unannounced.

"Well, I'm sorry, Mom . . . sorry as hell. Sorry for causing embarrassment to the family; sorry for being a constant reminder to you of a time you'd like to forget; and sorry that I was even born. . . ."

Instead of her attempting to calm her son, Marie let him rant on about many troubled thoughts. She did not offer any suggestions for solving the problems other than, "I don't know what else you could reasonably expect us to do, Joey. Your father and I have tried to give you everything you basically needed for growing up. You've been messing up! Look what you've done to your college education so far! Right now you should be looking forward to graduating in June instead of wasting away life chasing trashy tramps around that trashy city! And furthermore, I . . . " Click.

Perhaps the last thing Joe needed to hear at that time was how terrible he was doing in general. But his mother went on relentlessly in her determination to let him know the degree of her displeasure with all of his actions and inactions since being kicked out of college. This, coupled with the fight that he had with Bonnie, was too much for Joe; therefore, he just hung up the receiver.

Five

Separation of Inseparables

1

In spite of the several invitations to Christmas dinner, Joe turned them down. He was in no mood to take part in any of the holiday festivities that were going on around town. His somber mood was noticed by a few close friends down at the brewery, but it took wild Freddy Blueswicz, as usual, to bring things into laser-sharp focus.

The locker room was just about empty when Blueswicz seized the opportunity.

"So, Joey, baby, what's happening with that beautiful blonde dame, what'shername?"

Although he wasn't quite ready for this kind of inquiry, he took it in stride. The question really pierced him to the marrow, but he tried not to show his true feelings.

"Her name is Bonnie, Bozo! We just don't see each other anymore, but she's still a great woman!"

"I can believe it, now that she's dropped your ass. Phew! How could any broad put up with your shit!" Blueswicz said as he playfully tossed a wet shower towel at his friend.

Near closing time, the bartender notified the last two customers. Undoubtedly, Joe and Fred were pretty well tanked up during the several hours that they spent boozing at Belchek's Tavern. Topics of conversation ran the gamut, but, ironically, accord was reached on most aspects, even down to patriotism.

"... And because I was trying to defend the in ... (hic) ... tegrity of the government of these U ... U ... (hic) ... nited fucking States, I got kicked out of the fucking R.O.T.C. and ... (hic) out of the fucking school," complained Joe. "I'll tell you, man, it was a rotten goddamned deal!"

Fred leaned forward, almost falling off the bar stool, as he tried to make his point. "You know why you got a ... (hic) ... rotten deal, partner? I'll tell you why you got a rotten deal. Because them people in charge ain't . . . (hic) . . . nothing but a bunch of Communist bastards! That's right! Commie bastards! You and me, we bust our fuckin' balls tryin' to do what's right, and the fuckin' Commies that run them schools could care less about upholdin' anything but their goddamned pants!''

"All right, fellas, I'm ready to lock up now," the bartender said as he dipped several glasses into the rinsewater.

"Okay, okay . . . Say, Louie," replied Fred, who was definitely three sheets into the wind, "what d'ya think about these bunch of hippie wierdos tryin' to take over the goddamned school?''

The topic piqued the bartender's interest, apparently because after wiping his hands he cast forth with, "It's not just the hippies. How about all these people right here in Philly on welfare, especially the blacks? I work every day of my life, and I still can't make the kind of money they make just sitting around! Just before Thanksgiving, a couple of 'em held me up right here in my own place! Not only did they take every damn cent in the register, they even fleeced my customers! Scared the shit out of one guy so bad that we had to call the first-aid squad! I'm telling you, if I could've gotten my hands on my trusty old Army .45 I would've blown 'em right through the goddamned window!''

Fred immediately chimed in with, "Well, for Chrissakes, a whole fuckin' tribe jumped my partner here last fall! Stabbed the shit out of him, right, Joey, babe?''

"Yeah, they almost punched my ticket. But, Lou, you mentioned Army. Were you ever in?''

"Was I in? Damn right I was in—served three and a half years with the Third Division, Rock of the Marne. I was in the same outfit with Audie Murphy! Fought from North Africa to. . . .''

"My father was in the Army," Joe interrupted, "He was killed in action." The statement followed so quickly that Talanski surprised himself. It was the first time that he had mentioned his real father to anyone in a long time. However, the topic was highlighted, and the bartender had nothing but words of praise for those who served.

"You know something, Joe," said Fred, "there ain't nothin' out here in these damn streets except a lot of junkies tryin' to live off the system. Just like down at the brewery, everybody's out to beat you out of a job. I've been in Philly all my life, man. I know that if you're Italian, you don't have much of a chance in gettin' some of them so-called white collar positions. And if you're Polish, forget everything, man! They don't even want you to clean their fuckin' toilets!"

"You're right, kid," joined the bartender. "Us Poles practically built this country, and . . ."

"Hey, slow down, fellas," Joe interrupted, "I doubt if we're going to solve any of these sociological problems tonight, so I'm splitting this scene. Goodnight, Louie. You coming, Fred?"

The cold air went right to the bone while a strong wind brought the chill factor down to a rather intolerable level. The two friends hustled down the subway steps, momentarily enjoying the sudden rush of warm air coming at them from below.

The syncopated clacking of the train's wheels and the intermittent blinking of the lights caused Fred to close his eyes and nod while Joe stared intensely at an armed forces recruitment poster. He became oblivious to everything around him other than the poster figures that seemed to be sending out a beckoning message.

Next day, Joe had a hard time trying to concentrate on his work. A couple of truck drivers had to remind him of special orders that were supposed to have been filled. By lunch hour, he had made a decision. All that was left to do was to see if Fred would go with him.

The two friends paid for their hoagies at the counter and sat in a vacant booth. Normally, the little restaurant would be packed with people from the brewery, but it was practically empty. The hoagies disappeared within ten minutes, leaving the guys plenty of time to casually smoke a couple of cigarettes.

"So," began Joe as he turned sideways and rested both feet on the seat, "are we going to do it together, or am I going to do it without you?"

Fred squinted while deeply inhaling and said, "I may be sorry as hell for this later on, man, but . . . well . . . I'm gonna do it, okay?"

"Way to go, Freddy!" yelled Joe. "If we hurry right after work today we can catch that office before closing time!"

"Wait a minute, man," Fred remarked as he gently restrained his jubilant friend. "I still have some doubts in my mind. Don't get me wrong now! I'm ready to serve just like any red-blooded American, but why not wait till we're drafted, ya know?"

"Look around you, Fred. Is it really worth staying here busting our butts when we could be seeing the rest of the world? And there's a lot of world out there beyond the Philly city limits! Besides, the recruiting sergeant guaranteed us that we could stay together for the entire enlistment. Now what else could you possibly want when old Joe T. here is gonna walk you through it?"

Fred, faking a punch to his talkative friend's stomach as they left the restaurant, said, "I guess you're right, man. Besides, somebody has to look after your ass since you can't seem to do it right yourself . . . especially when it comes to broads. Maybe me and the Army can at least try, eh?"

Joe laughingly replied, "Freaking right! Look out, Uncle Sam! Here come two of your best damn Polack nephews this side of the Schuylkill River!"

2

After Talanski and his friend Blueswicz completed basic training, they were sent to the Special Forces School at Fort Bragg, North Carolina. Both fellows were so physically and mentally gung-ho that it wasn't long before they were wearing their green berets. The training was extremely demanding and psychologically challenging, but the two guys from Philly threw everything they had into it. Frequently, Joe and Fred depended upon each other for encouragement when the going got rough.

Less than three days after graduation, the entire regiment was placed on alert. Everyone was surprised that the move happened so suddenly, because there wasn't even enough time allotted for spending a leave at home. Consequently, many of the troops just hung around the base or whiled away a few hours in some of the local bars.

"No, put your money back in your pocket," Joe said as he ordered two more bottles of beer. "Ha, ha, it's funny the way we're sitting here sopping up this sauce. You'd think we would've had enough of it back at the brewery!"

Someone poured a lot of coins into the orange and red jukebox. One sad song after another came on, spreading a somber mood over the whole dilapidated bar. Even Fred was overcome. He leaned across the table and playfully tapped his friend on the jaw while saying, "Joe, I still don't know why I let you talk me into joinin' up. I must've been almost as (hic) drunk as I am now. No siree, buddy boy, this stuff ain't hittin' on shit!"

Talanski just smiled at his friend, took a long swallow on the luke-warm bottle of beer, wiped his mouth with his sleeve, and falteringly replied, "Bull crap, Freddie, baby. You . . . (hic) . . . you eat this shit up. No way could (hic) any G.I. be tabbed 'Soldier of the Cycle' without putting his heart into every phase of the training. And when you stepped up there this morning, I was (hic) damned sight proud of you, good buddy."

Talanski and Blueswicz were inseparable. Their commanding officer was very proud—so proud that after he was apprised of a top-secret mission, he automatically included the T-B Team. It really didn't matter to those guys, because, by autumn of 1963, they had become pretty bored with the same old routine of going through so many combat training programs. As Joe often commented, they were "*too* damn good!" Maybe that was why the two friends were assigned as part of the Special Forces training cadre.

Captain Ralph Lowry wasted no time in contacting fifty of his best troops. It didn't matter to him that none of these men had ever seen action. When the Korean War was raging, most of them were still in elementary school. No experience, but a lot of guts. Lowry himself, just thirty years old, saw only three weeks of action before the cease-fire in Korea. Since then, he was a frustrated warrior who liked nothing better than the prospect of getting into some *real* action. Promotions came very fast for this rather gung-ho individual. After completing Officers Candidate School at Fort Benning, Georgia, in 1955, Lowry signed up for tactical ranger training. He became an expert in the marital arts and strategic missions.

The eager captain and his fifty men were flown out of Fort Bragg at three o'clock on the morning of October 15th. Lowry, the only officer on board, politely refused acceptance of preferential treatment, because he wanted to be back there with his men.

Except for one refueling stop in Hawaii, the big jet flew straight to Vietnam. Although Capt. Lowry did not know the full details of the mission prior to take off from Fort Bragg, he wasn't too concerned. The mere fact that he was selected was enough to elevate his hopes of doing something heroic.

It was shortly after midnight when the jet's wheels touched the tarmac at Saigon Airport. A small delegation of American and South Vietnamese officers hurriedly greeted Lowry's group. Within minutes, the captain and his men were driven to the site of an old French chateau located not far from the Presidential Palace.

"We hope that you will find these quarters to your satisfaction," said the Vietnamese general as he closed the door to his office, which was the huge drawing room. Dust had collected on the relatively few books that were still on the shelves. Lowry smiled when his eyes fell upon an old copy of Moliere's works. For a moment, he expected some exotic oriental ladies of the evening to step from behind one of those beautifully hand-painted dressing screens. No such luck. At the long teakwood conference table sat two other American officers, five Vietnamese officers, and two Vietnamese civilians.

Colonel Govan Thompson opened the meeting with, "Captain Lowry, either you're the smartest green beret officer in the world or the dumbest sonofabitch in the universe!"

Lowry was pleasantly surprised as laughter permeated even the musty old drapes that were still hanging in remembrance of better times under French rule. Not being one to lie down under the cutting edge of humor, Lowry countered with, "Well, sir, I guess I'm *almost* the dumbest sonofabitch in the universe, because I still can't figure out why all of you high-ranking gentlemen would call lowly Lowry halfway around the world; meet with him at this ungodly hour; and then tell him half of what he already knows!"

More laughter. Then Col. Thompson went right to the heart of the matter. "You've probably wondered why there were no written orders cut on you and your men."

"Yes, sir, you're right. I've been wondering about that ever since we left Bragg."

One of the civilians spoke. "Captain, our present government has become totally insensitive to the needs of the people. We are suffering greatly because of the President's unwillingness to heed the suffering groans of the masses. He is being poorly advised by his brother and others who are drunk with power. . . ."

The morning sun had already begun to stream through the tattered drapes when the briefing ended. Empty cognac bottles and ashtrays filled with cigarette and cigar butts were quickly taken away by grinning shortstepping houseboys who were very happy that the long meeting had finally ended.

On the way out of the room, Colonel Thompson put his arm around Lowry's shoulder and said, "Remember, Ralph, this is an invisible mission—the media's not in on the action. So if you men do it, don't expect any high accolades, because, as you know, the United States is not supposed to be involved in the overthrow."

"Don't worry, sir, we'll pull this thing off and be home before supper cools."

The "thing" to which Capt. Lowry referred was the secret coup that was scheduled to take place on the first of November. President Diem had already lost the moral support of his closest ministers, and practically every high-ranking military officer was either ready to turn his guns on the present government or, at least, refuse to turn them in defense of it. The entire world was watching the situation in South Vietnam, and feelings were mixed as to what should be done—and by whom.

The military computer, operating in strictest confidence with the Central Intelligence Agency, came up with several names of low-ranking, gung-ho officers who were highly trained in specialized tactics. Ralph Lowry was selected. And he, in turn, hand-picked fifty of the best berets on the post. Among the chosen few were Talanski and Blueswicz.

3

At three-thirty in the morning on November 1, Sergeant Lonnie Robertson was awakened personally by Capt. Lowry. A strong flashlight beam, when focused up close on shut eyelids, has a way of causing even the soundest of sleepers to rise.

"This is it, Lonnie. The coup is coming off ahead of schedule."

"What happened, sir? I thought we were still weeks from flying to the interior," the sergeant said as he got out of bed and reached for his trousers.

Lowry and Robertson worked very well together. They were from the same hometown, and, for the past two years, Sgt. Robertson had served as Lowry's field first. Although the feisty old by-the-book Sergeant had planned to retire a year ago, he let himself be talked into re-enlisting so that he could, as he often said, "train a few more young troopers with guts enough to finish special forces school." Besides, Sgt. Robertson and Capt. Lowry often spent after-duty hours drinking and talking about their desire to utilize their skills in combat. Also, since both men were devout bachelors, they did a lot of womanizing together.

While Robertson was hurriedly getting into his gear, Lowry informed him of their latest orders.

"Begging the captain's pardon, sir, but why in the flying hell are orders being changed at the last minute?"

"I don't know, Lonnie, other than perhaps the brass wanted to make sure that any prior leakage of information would not hurt international relations. Right now, I want you to get six other men and meet me behind the motor pool in twenty minutes."

As the armored personnel carrier sped toward Saigon, the sound of small arms fire and exploding mortar rounds could be heard in the distance. The assault on the Presidential Palace had begun.

"This is it, man," Talanski said to Blueswicz as the vehicle stopped less than a half-mile away from the action, "Now we'll see how effective we've been as technical advisors for the past few weeks."

By noon of the following day, the entire world was watching the bloody coup on television. Newspeople were arriving and recklessly setting up their equipment so as not to miss one head being blown off. All safety precautions were abandoned for the juicy prospects of getting even closer to the gory action. Unfortunately, some of the cameramen lost their lives in trying to capture the full flavor of this coup.

It didn't take long for the insurgents to begin laying plans for celebrating after the word came that the assassination of President Diem and his brother, Ngo Dinh Nhu, had received tacit American approval. On November 4, the United States recognized the new government in Saigon. Two days later, Capt. Lowry received orders to move his men out of the area immediately.

"What do you make of it, Captain?" queried Sgt. Robertson. "I mean, we did the job. So why the heck is headquarters sending us into Tay Ninh Province? How much advising can we do without getting shot at?"

"Beats me, Lonnie. But I'll tell you something. Word has it that the VC are building up for a mid-winter offensive. So . . . I guess our unit has to go there to teach, oh, I'm sorry . . . to *advise* the South Vietnamese Rangers how to defend their perimeter. The thing I don't really like is this *show 'n tell* shit. We're only a heartbeat away from war; Uncle Sam's not going to take too much more of that duck-and-run crap. We'll be fighting for real by this time next year."

Neither one of the soldiers noticed anything different about the many people that were selling vegetables and other goods. Scrawny little children climbed all over the jeep, trying to outsell one another for the Yankee dollar.

"Those melons look good, Sergeant. Let's get a couple to take back to camp. Hey, get down from there, kid, before you break your neck!"

Lowry was shouting at a ten-year-old boy who was trying to climb onto the truck's tailgate. Both Americans had their attention diverted, so they did not notice the man on the bicycle. Besides, just about everyone rode bicycles as the chief means of transportation. However this particular man weaved his way through the heavy maze of humanity until he was even with the front of the American jeep. Unfortunately, Sergeant Robertson, who was driving, stopped the vehicle momentarily. This gave the cyclist just enough time to take a hand grenade from beneath his garment, pull the pin, lob it into the jeep, and fast-pedal down a nearby side street. The explosion killed not only the two Americans but also nine other people, including the kid who was trying to hitch a ride.

Word about the tragedy travelled like wildfire among the green beret unit. So incensed were those young warriors from Fort Bragg that the brass at the American Headquarters quickly decided that the unit should be moved immediately.

"I don't care who we fight at this point!" Fred growled while he and the rest of the troops were loading their gear into three giant CH-46 Sea Knight helicopters. "If I'm gonna get my tail blown off, I would at least like to know who the hell I'm supposed to be fightin'! All of these goddamn people look alike! I mean, how can you tell the so-called enemy from the man on the street?"

Joe was more subdued about the whole matter and everything surrounding it. "Hey, Fred, why get all sweaty? We knew what we were getting ourselves into when we signed up for this so-called secret mission. Hell, advisors are no more than . . ."

"Sittin' ducks," Fred interjected. "Yeah—freakin' sittin' ducks! You advise one guy how to use certain pieces of weaponry, and the s.o.b. turns around and uses it on you! I mean, I don't quite understand our involvement. Why don't we just declare war on North Vietnam? Shit, it's common knowledge that they're the people behind these freakin' black-pajama-wearin', bicycle-ridin', grenade-throwin' bastards!"

Joe could sense that his friend's concern ran much deeper than what was being verbalized, and, right after Lt. Allen told the unit of departure details, Joe put his arm around Fred's shoulder and said, "Hey, buddy, don't worry about it. Nothing's gonna happen to us as long as we stick together. Remember, I was the one who talked you into joining this man's Army, so you know I'm not going to let anything happen to Mama B's boy! Besides, as long as we're together, who the hell can hurt us, right?"

"Damn right!"

At that moment, a barrel-chested, bow-legged sergeant first class hopped down from the helicopter's doorway where many of the troops had queued up for boarding. After he counted off the number of men while walking down the line, he stopped and placed his arm between Talanski and Blueswicz.

"All right, now listen up, men!" yelled the non-com. "From here on back, line up at the chopper over there! This one's full!"

Immediately, Joe said, "Sarge, excuse me, but my partner and I have never been separated since . . ."

"Goddamn it, soldier, do you think we got time to cater to every request we get? Flying this chopper is my business—and I do it damn well! So when I say something, I know what I'm talking about! Now if you insist on having your bunkmate with you so you can hold hands, well. . . ."

Laughter erupted across the tarmac as Blueswicz and the other troops moved their gear over to the helicopter that had just been refueled. Within the next ten minutes, all three of the big Sea Knights were loaded with green beret personnel and ready for takeoff.

Joe was lucky enough to get one of the bucket seats near a window. He watched Fred disappear through the aircraft's huge doorway. Most of the other men were busily chatting, but Joe was preoccupied with the thought of not sitting next to his friend. For some strange reason, Joe's mind began to churn up all kinds of anxieties.

"Hey . . . hey . . . Talanski, are you awake?" asked one of the G.I.s.

"Huh? Oh . . . yeah," Joe responded as he turned his attention to the speaker. "I was just watching them loading up the other two choppers."

"Where's your partner in crime? I didn't see him come on board."

"Who, Fred Blueswicz? He's on that one over there. Seems as though they had enough on this baby."

"I'm surprised you two guys ain't together. Shit! This is one of the few . . . no . . . hell . . . the first time that I'm seeing one without the other! Damn! Do you think you can stand it! I understand this flight takes all of a big whopping hour!"

"Ha, ha, go soak your head in liquid lead, prick," Joe quipped.

The three Sea Knight helicopters roared and whipped up a lot of wind as they rose. The powerful engines drowned out all conversation. Joe kept his eyes on Fred's craft, which was about three hundred and fifty yards off to the left. Suddenly he saw a bright orange ball, followed by thick black smoke, and then bits fall earthward! The shock waves of the mid-air explosion reached Joe's craft seconds afterward. Panic broke out in the other two choppers.

"Good God!" someone shouted. "Did you see that? We're all gonna die up here! Those people planted bombs on us!"

Crew members tried as best they could to calm the troops, but inflammatory words combined with fearful thoughts caused the pilots of the remaining crafts to mutually agree that they should land immediately and check for time bombs.

Through all of this, Joe never spoke. He just stared straight ahead as the tears flowed profusely across both hands. Losing his best friend under those circumstances was too much for him. He had silently freaked out, but no one realized to what extent until the helicopter had landed on the edge of a rice paddy. As soon as the door was opened, Joe leaped down and ran, clutching his M-16 rifle, toward some peasants who were working nearby.

"You sneaky sons of bitches, I'm gonna waste all of your asses!"

70

Had it not been for the alertness of a few fellow berets who tackled him before a round was fired, Joe probably would have emptied his banana clip.

Six

Good Blood, Bad Blood

1

On the morning of February 4, 1964, Corporal Talanski was assigned to provide a small group of South Vietnamese Rangers with some instruction covering the rudiments of how to get effective firepower from the .57 recoilless rifle. As Joe had related to one of the other American soldiers who accompanied him on the assignment, he didn't mind giving up his day off, but he *did* mind having to travel for almost two hours by jeep into one of the dense forest regions of Tay Ninh Province.

They were only thirty minutes away from the outpost when all hell broke loose. Artillery rounds whistling in dropped close enough to prompt Joe and the other green beret to pull the jeep off the main road.

"Holy shit! We'd better turn this thing back toward camp!"

"You're right, Joe. I don't know what's going on up ahead, but something tells me that we should get the hell outta here before. . . ."

Private Lindhurst never completed that sentence, or any future sentences, because he was killed instantly when a shell burst sent shrapnel flying in all directions.

"Jeff! Jeff!" yelled Talanski as he struggled to his feet after being knocked down by the impact.

Joe saw what was left of his buddy. "Oh, my God," he groaned upon viewing the almost-shredded corpse. Regardless, Joe knew that he had to get out of the targeted area immediately. Grabbing both M-16's, he started running back toward the base.

Within the next five minutes, the road became cluttered with humanity and livestock. Some of the people had all of their worldly possessions piled into carts. Joe tried unsuccessfully to negotiate for a bicycle; no one was about to give up the best means of transportation in the area.

It was shortly after two o'clock in the afternoon when he finally reached camp. The atmosphere had certainly changed radically since that morning. American military advisors were scurrying around while loading up every piece of movable equipment.

"What the hell's going on?" he asked a soldier.

"Ah, Talanski, it's a good thing you're back, fella! Headquarters has ordered a pullout—the damn Viet Cong launched a big offensive about forty miles from here, and they're swarming all over Tay Ninh! Better grab your gear and throw it on one of those deuce-'n-a-halfs—no choppers are coming to lift us out this time!"

"What's the difference?" Joe said as he quickly stuffed things into his duffle bag. "You stay down here, you get blown up; you go up there, you get blown down. So what? Hey, and another thing, we're not even officially in this friggin' war yet! Which reminds me, I got to drop these dog tags with the lieutenant."

"Dog tags? You'd better put 'em around your neck!"

"They're not mine—belonged to that kid Jeff Lindhurst—he bought it this morning."

Talanski's unit filled seven trucks and vacated the area. As soon as the American advisors pulled out, all kinds of people came creeping into the abandoned campsite from the thick surrounding jungle. Most of them were Viet Cong sympathizers who had been anticipating this big day for a long time. By sundown, the VC had reached the formerly-held South Vietnamese post and were well-received.

The word coming from headquarters was that Lt. Boyleston's beret unit would have to wait until daybreak before any South Vietnamese Rangers could be flown in to give cover. Therefore, the Americans found it necessary to pitch camp overnight, an idea that they did not relish at all.

"Phew!" We're sitting ducks out here, Lieutenant," commented Sgt. Pellham. "And this isn't even our war!"

"I know what you mean, Sergeant, but orders are orders—we wait right here on these coordinates so that the choppers don't have to look all over for us. In the meantime, I want you to post all-night guards around the perimeter and keep a fire going."

"Begging the lieutenant's pardon, sir, but don't you think it would be safer to stay in total darkness? All power lines around here are down, so the VC can't exactly zero in on our location."

"I know what you mean, but do you see those people out there cramming the road trying to move south? Well, they know we're here—and I'm sure there're a lot of VC sympathizers among them. So, Sergeant, we have to be very suspicious of those innocent-looking, scared farmers and their families. I don't want the same thing to happen to some of us that happened to Captain Lowry and Robertson. No telling how many of those little sneaky bastards out there have hand grenades hidden under some fruit or whatever! And it wouldn't take a whole lot of effort for somebody to come in close enough and lob a few. At least we'd stand a better chance if we can at least see what's happening out there."

Heavy artillery resounded in the distance throughout most of the night, and only a few of the Americans even considered shutting their eyes for one second. Then, about five o'clock in the morning, all shelling stopped. Through the faint glimmer of daylight, Talanski and his guard-walking partner, Phil Abernathy, noticed the big reduction of the amount of human traffic down on the road.

"What d'ya think, Joe?"

"I think we'd better get ready for some action. It's too damn quiet out there. Something's happening around us . . . I can feel it in my bones, man."

"What are we supposed to do if the VC start firing on us? It's not like we're at war yet, and . . . "

"Bullshit, Phil! The only difference between our situation and these few South Vietnamese Rangers who're traveling with us is that they *know* they're at war, but Uncle Sam is still pussy-footing around this thing like it doesn't exist! What happened to Fred and those other guys was real, pal!"

The dawning of a new day brought with it anxiety that circulated rapidly among the troops. Final preparations were made in anticipation of helicopter arrivals. The heavy equipment was to remain with the Rangers, and all American advisors were to be lifted out.

Suddenly, the morning calm was punctured by a voice coming over a loudspeaker; first, in Vietnamese, then in English. "Lay down your arms, Americans. This is not your concern. Why do you insist upon bringing death to the people of Southeast Asia? We can settle our own disputes without your unsolicited help. Yes, *unsolicited,* because we want to unite our country. This is only an argument among

74

our people . . . much the same as the argument among your people during the Civil War. Let us resolve our own differences. We do not need you as advisors. Also, Americans, the helicopters that you are expecting were destroyed. There is no way for you to get out of Tay Ninh unless we grant it. How many of you are there? Forty? Fifty at the most? What chance could you possibly have against a VC human wave of over a thousand? Now, here is, as you say . . . the clincher. Even if you should foolishly decide to fight and die, your government will not call you heroes. Your government will not even acknowledge your presence here in Vietnam, because, remember, you green berets were part of a secret mission to help overthrow the Diem regime. Do you really think that the Pentagon would allow such embarrassment just to save a few gung-ho troops who, on paper, are not even here? You will have three minutes to lay down your arms."

The South Vietnamese Rangers, to the man, did not hesitate. They rapidly placed themselves into battle position around the perimeter. Captain Hoa and his men were so programmed to their cause that they never considered surrendering. And the American officer in charge of the berets was so impressed that he gave the order for his men to deploy for battle.

"Oh, shit! This is it, man!" shouted Talanski as he slammed the bolt of his M-16 and dropped to the prone position behind a tree trunk. The stone-faced Ranger beside him placed six grenades between them.

Those were the fastest three minutes on record. Again, the voice sounded. "The allotted time has expired, green berets. What is your decision?" Silence. "I ask you for your decision. Are you not capable of making a decision?"

Upon hearing the last question, Lt. Boyleston's anger completely suppressed any reserved feelings that he may have had about the consequences. In fact, from behind the broad tree trunk, the American officer quickly stepped out, .45 in hand, and yelled, "Fuck you!"

The firefight that ensued was very intense. VC guerillas made several attempts to overrun the position, but they were turned back each time. After a half-hour, casualties mounted on both sides. However, the VC suffered almost three times as many hits. Sporadic shots were fired instead of heavy barrages.

The early-morning dew began to evaporate rapidly as the sun rose higher in the sky. The heat of the day was coming on, and agonizing groans of dying and wounded men could be heard begging for water, the medic, and death. Fighting had become isolated shots fired at anyone on either side who tried to rescue the fallen.

"Talanski!"

"Yeah, Sarge, over here!"

"You and your buddy cover me. I'm gonna try to ring up headquarters again."

The thirty yards between the dead radio operator and Sergeant Reynolds did not appear to be impossible to cover in a quick sprint. The stone-faced Ranger, although he did not understand English, knew what had to be done. As soon as Reynolds motioned fire cover, the Ranger laid down a steady burst. No sooner had the sergeant reached the tent when several mortar rounds whistled in. Reynolds was killed by the first one. The second shell blew Lt. Boyleston and his firing partner right out of their position. Nothing was left that could be labeled whole or intact bodies—torn flesh and bone bits flew in every direction.

Immediately following the barrage, yelling, frenzied voices of over two hundred VC sounded at the bottom of the hill. The Americans and Rangers were so caught up in the concussion and shock of battle that numbers meant nothing. A real din was created when the enemy began banging on what sounded like pans and other objects. However, in spite of the noise, there was no charging up the hill. Strangely enough, not even one VC could be seen moving beyond the treeline. This lasted for about two minutes, after which that familiar voice blared once again over the loudspeaker. "Now, foolish Yankees, count your dead! Does it make sense? They died for nothing! There will be no hero's recognition or honor coming out of what has happened here this morning! Only war produces heroes! You are not heroes! You are only fools! You do not even have a reason to fight us! You are nothing more than intruders in a family quarrel! So where is the glory that you seek? Why would you die for nothing?

"This is your last chance, Americans, to hold on to your lives, because my dedicated comrades have grown impatient with your delay! Consequently, if you do not surrender within the next fifteen minutes, the wrath of Viet Cong will be unleashed against you in all its fury! Unfortunately, our misguided countrymen who are with you will be killed! And, for this, we hold you totally responsible! Their families will lose them because of your foolish resistance!

"I am warning you, advisors! Take some meaningful advice, and lay down your arms! If you refuse, we will overrun your position; take you as prisoners, and subject you to the worst torture imaginable! Incidentally, castration is the first step, followed by bits of ground glass pushed deeply into your anal passage!"

The green berets were on the verge of giving up when one of them took it upon himself to yell back down the hill. Talanski had been designated as the new non-commissioned officer in charge, and he did, in fact, let his feelings be known.

"All right, you sons of bitches down there, you have to bring ass to get ass! If you want any part of this hill, come on up now! What're you waiting for—your goddamn nerve to support that big mouth? This is Corporal Joe T talking to you! And in ten minutes, if you don't come up here, we're coming down there! So, either way, bastards, get ready!"

All of Joe's men were surprised. They certainly did not expect him to rattle off such a response. But they loved it. And the thing that really added encouragement to everyone was the gesture made by the stone-faced Ranger when his buddy gave an accurate translation of Talanski's words. The stone-face actually grinned and gave the thumbs-up sign.

As the time ticked away, heartbeats became increasingly faster and perspiration flowed in rivulets. Three minutes to go.

"You're crazy, Talanski," said Jim Stryker, "but I guess we're all crazy since we're ready to go down fighting."

"Not necessarily, Jim. Look, those VC down there are not about to put on another charge up this hill. They suffered a helluva lot more casualties than they anticipated, plus I think they've run out of mortar ammo. No, Jim, what I think they're *really* waiting for are replacements. The way I see it, right now, we have the psychological, as well as the firepower, edge. And if we don't . . . well, who the hell's gonna be around to complain?"

All of the troops piled into the four trucks that had survived the bombardment. Floored clutches and revving engines were under the control of young, sweaty, Americans who gripped those steering wheels like Saturday night hot-rodders on a dragstrip.

Suddenly, six American helicopter gunships swooped into the area. There was no ground fire. The squadron commander, Lt. Raymond Kalziewski of Trenton, New Jersey, was both surprised and relieved that no confrontation occurred, even after the choppers circled several times above the heads of the VC.

Since the radio had been destroyed, Talanski had no way of communicating with the gunships except by having his men frantically wave their arms. Lt. Kalziewski, after ordering the other five choppers to continue circling and cover, landed his in a small clearing near the trucks. The officer quickly sought to make contact with the person in command.

"Where's the officer in charge here, soldier?" asked Kalziewski.

The man looked puzzled and then he responded. "He was killed, sir. Joe . . . excuse me . . . Corporal Talanski's in charge, sir. There he is over there near the lead truck."

Lt. Kalziewski sprinted around the craters to where Joe was giving last-second instructions to the drivers. When one of them saw the officer approach, he shouted, "Attention!"

"Never mind, men. At ease. Talanski, are you in charge of this crew?"

"Yes, sir."

"Well, I don't know how you men did it, but the VC down there must have decided to pull out. From the air, we could see just a trickle of movement after they spotted our choppers."

"The way I figured it, sir, we ran up their casualty list pretty high, and that was probably the reason why they tried to psyche us down from here."

While the lieutenant and corporal were conversing, word came over the chopper's radio that a large contingent of Viet Cong regulars was reported moving rapidly toward that sector.

"I knew it! Those slick bas . . . excuse me, sir, but I think we'd better get the hell out of here before. . . ."

"You're right, Corporal! Get those trucks rolling fast! We'll fly cover until you men are back at the control point!"

Even though the United States was not at war with the People's Republic of North Vietnam, no diplomat or elder statesman could have double-talked any of the Special Forces troops that were crammed into those trucks and were trying to get out of another confrontation. Lady Luck was riding with Talanski and his men.

The bumpy, winding road yielded no hazards other than livestock and unconcerned farmers. Slowing down always caused the Americans to be on their guard against grenade throwers. However, the trip, in that respect, was uneventful. And when the troops finally arrived at the control point, most of them looked forward to having a little rest and recreation. However, headquarters had other plans for the small band of green berets.

So while the trucks were still en route to Phu Cuong, a small town less than thirty miles away from the capital, American high brass down in Saigon decided to ship what was left of the unit back to the United States.

"I agree with you, sir," said Major Hutton to Colonel Van Buren. "We would be hard put to explain why we let a handful of G.I.s almost catapult us into World War Three."

The colonel was still fuming over the matter when he said "I just cannot, for the life of me, understand the rationale behind sending those men into Tay Ninh Province in the first place! Although, word around headquarters has it that they were originally brought over here on some secret mission."

"Secret mission?"

"Yeah. They had some role in advising the regime that pulled off last fall's military coup here in Saigon. And another thing, why in the flying hell didn't someone realize that the presence of Americans in Tay Ninh would still not stop the Viet Cong from pulling off their planned offensive?"

"You're right, Colonel. Our boys should never have been sent up there. It's bad enough that some of the Cambodians are giving obvious support since Tay Ninh is so close to the border. Well, how do you want us to handle this, sir?"

"Just as though it never happened, Major . . . that's the way we'll do it. Send word to have the unit hold up in Phu Cuong overnight. Give the boys a little time to unwind . . . kick up their heels a bit. In the meantime, I want you to make all of the necessary arrangements on cutting orders for the entire group to be flown out of here for the States tomorrow morning."

2

Most of the men were so elated over the idea of going home that they didn't bother to go into town. Perhaps their unscheduled baptism of fire erased some of the previous notions that they may have had about war being glorious. And even though the Ranger base did not exactly have all of the comforts equal to American installations, the G.I.s were satisfied. However, Corporal Talanski, was too restless to wait out the next eight hours.

Joe tried unsuccessfully to get a few of the other guys to go into town with him, so he decided to go anyhow. There were many things swirling around in his head, and he wanted a change of scenery. Losing Fred weighed heavily on Joe's mind; nevertheless, he was trying to rid himself of all sad thoughts, at least for that night.

Talanski was a little hesitant about going inside the bar, because he saw only orientals. Then someone shouted, "I say there, Yank, come on in! It's all right, you know."

The voice belonged to the big red-faced Australian soldier who was sitting in a rather dark corner with a Vietnamese girl. As soon as Joe saw the friendly face to whom the voice belonged, he felt much better and ready to share an evening of entertaining conversation.

"Reginald Beasley's the name, Yank, and this is . . . er . . . oh, what the hell . . . she doesn't speak English, American, or Australian, but she certainly is pretty, eh?"

"No doubt about it, Reginald, she's definitely that! By the way, my name's Joe Talanski."

The two allies laughed and joked about everything while consuming several cans of beer.

"Damn, Reggie (hic), this swamp water's almost as (hic) bad as the stuff I used to brew back home."

"Joey, m'boy, the trouble with you is you're still (hic) too bloody sober! Anyway, I think it's bloody well time for you (hic) and me to wet our whistles on something better, mate." Beasley immediately called the owner to the table and said something to him in Vietnamese. The bent-shouldered man's features broke into a broad grin which revealed a mouth full of gold-capped teeth. He then led them out the back and through a winding narrow street to a house that appeared to be better kept than any of the others.

"Now we're going to have some real fun, mate," Beasley said as they entered the small parlor. "A friend of mine told me about this place. Nothing but quality opium and clean girlies are served up here."

Ordinarily, Joe would have reneged on smoking opium, but when the scantily dressed, pretty, almond-eyed beauty took him by the hand and led him to a bedroom upstairs, he just couldn't resist. Reggie and the second girl disappeared into another room on the first floor.

Except for his socks and combat boots, Joe had completely disrobed. The creaky old bed groaned rhythmically under the continuous gyrations of its occupants. Well into the night, every corner of the house was covered with odors of incense and opium.

3

"Comrades, this is the hour to make contribution toward freeing our land of intruders," spoke the same bent-shouldered man who had led the foreigners to the brothel. Only this time, he was not the grinning little man who had been so accommodating. There was dedication of purpose wrapped around every sentence.

"What happened at Tay Ninh represents the true beginning of our people's fight to rid the country of these beasts. We were victorious against the French, and we shall also be victorious against these latest intruders."

Undoubtedly, the loosely knit group of twenty-seven young men were VC sympathizers who eagerly wanted to do their part. Guns, ammunition, anything that could be gotten from the intruders would help the cause. And, as fate deemed it, Joe was in the wrong place at the wrong time.

When two VC sympathizers burst into the room, a shrilling scream was the only sound that Talanski's prostitute could emit before she was snatched by the hair and had her throat cut.

"The gun, Li, the gun! Grab the gun," yelled the prostitute's killer. "I'll take care of this American dog!"

Although Joe's head was still swirling from a combination of liquor and opium, he still had enough vision to see through the cloudiness of his brain.

"Shoot! Shoot, Li!"

But while Li was trying to manipulate the M-16's bolt, Talanski leaped across the bed and slammed him against the wall with a near-body check that ice hockey players use so often. Li's comrade immediately attacked from the rear. Luckily, Joe received only a glancing stab in the shoulder.

Whether Talanski's high-pumping adrenal gland or just plain anger kept him going is hard to say. But there's one thing for sure: he wheeled around, grabbing the attacker by the arm and throat. Joe flipped him to the floor without letting go of either. Fingernails dug firmly into the VC's neck until he dropped the dagger; whereupon, Joe seized the weapon and drove it into the attacker's belly. He jerked the dagger up and down until pieces of the bowel fell out of the lifeless body. The one called Li had leaped from the window, Talanski's rifle in hand.

Beasley ran up the stairs to check on his friend. He found him, grotesquely bleeding and naked, rocking back and forth. Joe was holding the dead girl as he pleaded, "Don't (cough) . . . leave me . . . (cough) again . . . Aunt Madge. Please don't leave (cough) . . . don't leave me again."

About ten minutes later, two United States military policemen joined the local police who had previously arrived at the scene. The VC's body had been removed, but the prostitute's was still there on the blood-soaked bed and cradled in the arms of an equally blood-soaked babbling G.I.

Unfortunately, none of the townspeople, including the police, could speak English. And, when Beasley had earlier sized up the situation in terms of his probably being court-martialed for being in that off-limits establishment, he decided to disappear in advance of the arrival of authorities. Perhaps his decision was also prompted by the erratic actions of the American bloke who had apparently gone balmy. At any rate, just like in Philadelphia several years earlier, Joe was in no frame of mind to explain anything.

"Watch out, Frank," cautioned the M.P. to his partner, "he's holding a dagger."

Although Joe had not made any menacing gestures toward the onlookers, he eyed them with apprehension as he continued to talk to the corpse. "Don't do it . . . (cough) . . . Aunt Madge, please . . . please don't (cough) leave me again."

The M.P. who had moved close to the bed without taking his eyes off the G.I. motioned to the other who was still in the doorway.

"Bullshit, Frank! I say we don't chance getting stabbed by this basket case!" And with that, the cautious one aimed his .45 at Joe, saying, "All right, soldier, drop it before I blow your fucking brains out! Like now, fella, like now!"

"Hold it, Chuck! I think we can do this another way. Just cover me. Okay, buddy, you can leave your Aunt Madge with us. We'll see that she's taken care of. Now come on with me . . . er . . . what's your name?"

"Joey," came the soft reply.

"Okay, Joey, you can let us handle things. No problems now, Joey, because . . ."

Whack! While his partner was trying a calmer approach to the situation, the other M.P. rushed forward and struck Joe effectively on the head with his pistol, rendering him unconscious.

"Damn it, Chuck, that wasn't necessary!"

"Oh, no? Well, if you think I'm gonna put my butt on the line for some doped-up jerk who's killed a gook whore and calls her his aunt, you're crazy!"

4

Joe's military fate was in a holding pattern, and headquarters seemed to be undecided as to direction. For nearly three months, he had been confined to the company area at an American base on the outskirts of Saigon. No one from home had written to him, nor had he bothered to write. His disposition, according to the base commander, was sullen and given to extended periods of silence. Even the head physician had become impatient with Joe's refusal to talk logically and cooperatively. It was because of this attitude that Major William Hiltbrunner, a psychiatrist, became involved in this unusual case.

Prior to seeing his new patient, the major reviewed Talanski's 201 file and had a briefing with Colonel Van Buren.

"How do you like your coffee, Major?"

"Just black, thanks."

"So—now that you've reviewed Corporal Talanski's file, what do you think?

The major squinted through the spiraling haze of blue smoke coming from their cigars and replied, "Well, according to what I've been able to glean, this Talanski, up to now, has been a pretty good soldier, no prior military problems. But I have the distinct feeling that you didn't call me in on this case just to hear that, sir."

"Okay, Major, it's only right that I level with you one hundred percent," replied Van Buren as he got up and made sure that the office door was closed. "This Talanski has really placed us in one helluva situation after getting us out of another helluva situation."

Major Hiltbrunner looked puzzled, but he had enough experience in dealing with mind-boggling cases to know that he was about to be let in on something that the colonel, apparently, hadn't discussed with too many people. So the doctor settled himself in the cushion-backed chair, took a slow sip of coffee, remained quiet, and patiently waited for the colonel to open up.

"I know what the soldier's file contains. And I also know what it does *not* contain. Talanski was part of a small cadre of elite green berets specially brought over here to take part in a highly classified activity."

The doctor slightly raised his eyebrows, but he didn't speak.

Colonel Van Buren continued. "No entries were made, or will be made, because our government is still not officially at war with North Vietnam; even though we're getting our tails shot at and blown up every day by perpetrators. All you need to know about the secret mission I alluded to is that Talanski's outfit took part in the coup which overthrew Diem. A lot happened to that fifty-man unit. The commanding officer was killed; fifteen of 'em were blown up in a helicopter; and twenty-one were killed in a firefight when they were attacked during the big Viet Cong offensive in Tay Ninh. Hey, and you know what's so damn sad about this? We're not even at war with these sons of bitches!

"How the hell am I supposed to nail a kid who, under different circumstances, would be accorded a battle commendation for saving what was left of his unit plus a Ranger attachment? The high brass down at headquarters in town don't want to touch this thing with a ten-foot pole, and to. . . ."

"Pardon me for cutting you off, Colonel, but I think I see enough of the picture to be of some help to you."

Van Buren raised his cup in toast and replied, "If you can, it certainly would be appreciated, because right now Talanski's presence serves as an embarrassment to us. And the burden of this whole matter is sitting squarely on my shoulders, Major."

"I understand, sir . . . well, now, how about letting me see and talk to Corporal Talanski?"

Fifteen minutes later, the subject in question entered the Orderly Room and addressed the master sergeant that was on duty. "Corporal Talanski reporting as ordered, Sergeant."

Major Hiltbrunner very closely scanned the figure who was standing at attention in front of Colonel Van Buren. After the formal introduction, the major requested a few minutes alone with Corporal Talanski. Most willingly, the colonel agreed and added, "Take as much time as you need, Major."

5

Based on the psychiatrist's report, Colonel Van Buren expedited all of the necessary arrangements for Joe to be shipped back to the United States within forty-eight hours. Instead of returning him to Fort Bragg, the Army assigned Joe as a patient in the psychiatric ward at Fort Campbell, Kentucky. At first, he resisted the idea totally, but, after reconciling himself to the fact that it was futile to resist, Joe narrowly missed being confined to a padded cell, although his restless nights frequently gave rise to nightmares that caused him to cry out for help.

"I don't think it would be wise for us to release this one yet," said Major Louis Dellacorte to the other six army physicians as they sat around the oval conference table. He passed the records folder to another colleague.

"Hmm, Joseph Talanski again, I see," Capt. Kent Langley commented, taking the folder. "How long are we supposed to keep him? It's been . . . umm, let me just check the date here . . . ah, yes, since May of last year. Talanski's not suffering from physical injuries, so why are we keeping him?"

At that moment, Lt. Col. Walton Fulcher looked over his bifocals at the young officer, smiled, and asked, "How long have you been in the Army, Kent?"

"Almost two years, sir."

"Hardly time for you to learn all of the seemingly odd things that we do, but you've definitely been in this man's Army long enough to know that there's not always a rational explanation offered for each cockamamie decision. However, since you're rather new to the staff, I'll let you in on a bit of information concerning the Talanski case.

"When he was flown in here ten months ago, orders were that we should hold him for at least one year. The poor bastard had just about lost all touch with the present—continuously talked in terms of things that had happened when he was a youngster, especially the loss of some aunt. Also, Talanski did some heroics that saved a few of his buddies over in Nam—but unfortunately we weren't at war with Hanoi then so the upper brass tried to hush-hush the matter. On top of that, he murdered a Vietnamese prostitute who . . ."

"Begging the Colonel's pardon, sir," interrupted one of the veteran junior officers, "but we have made substantial progress in at least bringing Corporal Talanski back to reality. So maybe we can think seriously about giving him a medical discharge in a couple of months."

"Exactly," said the colonel. "That's precisely what we're going to do to cover our butts. No one wants any embarrassment, or worse yet, a demotion because of a bad decision at this juncture. For whatever reason, although no one upstairs has seen fit to discuss it with me, I get the feeling that the Army would greatly welcome such a move on our part, especially now that we have more troops in Vietnam."

"Right, sir, but judging from the present state of our military build-up over there," added Major Craig James, "I would say that Talanski's combat experience might be a big plus factor if . . ."

"Whoa! Hold on there, Major," Van Buren interrupted. "I'm fully aware that on the eighth of this month the first American Marine battalion arrived at Da Nang and also on the nineteenth the first full Army battalion arrived also. But our boy Talanski is in no kind of mental shape to be sent back. No, gentlemen, I think the best thing for us to do at this time is to just hold him for maybe another three or four months and then give him a medical discharge."

"That's a good decision, Colonel," said Major Dellacorte as he quickly flipped the page to the next case.

Four months later, on July 28, 1965, Joe was honorably discharged from military service. Also on that date, President Johnson announced his decision to send greater numbers of American fighting men to Vietnam.

Seven

Pleasing Others

1

The Callahan household was unusually filled with activity on that hot August morning in 1965. Mrs. Callahan had risen early to prepare a delicious breakfast for Michael and Susan. Dr. Callahan, upon catching the pungent odor of bacon and eggs intermingled with fresh coffee, couldn't force himself to stay in bed; even though the night before he had not gotten home from the hospital until well after midnight.

Both parents were very proud of their children. Michael was home for the summer and working as an assistant in the hospital's pharmacy.

Susan, armed with her 142 I.Q., had no problem getting into Tufts University after completing only three years at Shipley School. However, being the kind of free spirit that she was, Susan had not decided what she wanted her life's endeavor to be, although she was always quick to say that she wanted to join the Peace Corps for a couple of years after college.

Yes, the Callahans were generally pleased with the progress of two of their children. But the third one was a problem to them, and now the entire family was buzzing with projected thoughts about how to deal with the problem.

Susan was the first to raise the topic. "What time is Joey's train due in, Mommy? The reason I ask is because I thought I would get in some more driving practice by . . ."

"Hey, Susie," interrupted her brother, "give us a break, will ya? Let's face it. You may have memorized everything in the manual, but your dexterity leaves a heck of a lot to be desired."

"Oh, I don't know now, Mike. Your sister's not half as bad as some of the kids I see driving around on permits," Dr. Callahan countered.

"Excuse me," said Mrs. Callahan finally, "but I think someone did originally want to know what time Joey's train arrives. Three-twenty this afternoon, if it's running on schedule."

"Gee," Susan said with a smile, "can you believe it's been almost three years since any of us has seen Joey? He used to be a lot of fun back in the old days. Do you think he's changed? Gee, I certainly hope he's not smoking marijuana, or . . . "

Mrs. Callahan winced as the painful thought stabbed her mind. She then shouted, "Susan, for heaven's sake! That's your brother you're talking about!"

"Well, gee whiz, Mommy, he did spend a lot of time in the hospital! And besides, my friend Regina told me that one of her cousins, who's in the marines, was . . ."

"All right, all right, Susan," Dr. Callahan interrupted, "I don't think we want to hear about it. But, yes, Joey had a few problems in the service; however, he's okay now. The main thing is that your brother's coming home today, and we want to make him feel one hundred percent welcome, right, gang?"

Mrs. Callahan, eyes brimming and trying to stop the tears from spilling, could not help but reach across the table and affectionately squeeze her husband's hand. She then got up to refill the coffee cups.

Michael's black '63 Volkswagen Beetle typified everything that he valued. He was not one of those outrageous, impetuous, pot-smoking, hippies that enrolled at college for seemingly the prime purpose of causing discord among the student body and nausea among the administrators. No, Michael was a solid book-plugging conservative student who held his father as the ideal pattern to follow. Never once, since he got into a shoving match with another boy back in junior high school, did Michael ever give his parents any reason to feel anything but pride in their rational-thinking, level-headed, handsome son.

Michael, although very much aware of the heart-rending feelings that his mother had down through the years in trying to reconcile relationships between his half-brother and the rest of the family, never acted like a spoiled brat. He did not try to corner all affections due to a son.

During their younger years, since Michael and Joey lived primarily in different cities, the brothers had not gotten to know each other on a solid base. However, now that both of them were grown men, Michael was actually looking forward to establishing a real brotherly relationship. And, as he heavily considered his thoughts, he was oblivious to what Susan was saying.

"Hey, hey, Michael, gee willikers! Are you still on this planet?"

"Huh, oh, I'm sorry, Susie. Guess I wasn't listening too closely. Well, so you and Judy are going to play doubles this morning, huh?"

"Oh, Michael, I talked about that nearly ten minutes ago when we left the house. You *do* remember where the courts are, don't you? If not, let me drive since. . . ."

"Forget it, kiddo. The last time I let you practice on ole Black Beauty here, you darn near burned out her clutch! Seriously though, Susan, I was thinking about Joey and how nice it's going to be to see him again."

"Yeah. The last time I saw him was when he came to visit me at Shipley, and that seems like centuries ago. You know, I still feel pretty bad about it . . . not coming downstairs to talk to him 'n all. But what did I know? I was only a kid then. Besides, I saw Joey and some washed-out blonde drive up in a sports car. Humph, from the way she was pawing all over him, he sure wasn't concentrating on seeing me."

"You never mentioned this before. Why?"

"Well, I didn't think it was important. I still remember how stupid I was in telling Joey a big lie when he called me on the dorm phone. I told him Mommy didn't want me to talk with him because it might upset my schoolwork to hear about his goings-on down there in Philly."

"Tsk, tsk . . . Susie, you really shouldn't have done that. Maybe that was the reason why Joey stopped coming over to Penn to see me. Oh well, all of it's history now. He's coming home this afternoon, and that's all that matters, right, babe?"

"Right," smiled Susan. "But I wonder why he had to spend a year in the hospital if he wasn't hurt physically."

"Who told you about that?"

"Michael, I may be young, but I'm not stupid. Even little sisters have *some* intelligence you know. Besides, I heard Mommy and Daddy discussing it last winter. I *do* know how to listen when I'm not supposed to be listening. Besides, what's the big deal? So Joey had a few brain strains while he was in the Army. Some people go through their whole lives without one to strain."

"Okay, Susie, (ha, ha, ha) you made your point. I guess you're pretty perceptive after all."

"Never mind the *perceptive*, Bozo. What about *pretty?*"

At that moment, they arrived at the tennis courts, and Susan's girlfriend yelled to her, "Hurry up, Susan, before we lose our court time!"

2

Joe was only mildly surprised when he did not see his mother on the platform. However, he was extremely surprised to see his step-father. Dr. Callahan had made last minute changes in his appointment schedule so that he could be free for the rest of the afternoon.

It had been a long time, but very little had changed in terms of superficiality. Both men treated each other with congeniality, but no genuine warmth emanated from the brief handshake. It was as though they were embarrassed by their own actions or inactions. Bob always knew that this offspring, whether present or absent, remained a troubling object in his marriage. How frequently did he wonder whether he should have left Marie alone after the first dance at that company Christmas party of long ago. And, also, how frequently did he want to kick himself for even entertaining that thought after Marie consistently demonstrated her devotion to him, Michael, and Susan. Yet, Bob felt that his wife would have been much happier through the years if he had adopted Joey, thus making a more solidified family.

Even though both men strained to carry on conversation during the half-hour ride from the train station, there were still wide expanses of silence while each tried to think of another light topic.

"So how's Grandpa these days?"

"Feisty as ever, Joey, especially since he retired last spring after working thirty-three years at Westinghouse. His new love is boxing."

"Boxing? What's he doing, going to all of the little club fights in the 'Burgh?" laughed Joey as they turned the corner of their street.

"I wish it were that simple. Right now, your grandfather is seri-ously considering investing a few bucks in a fighter over at O'Hara's gym in East Liberty. You have to see this situation for yourself. Maybe after dinner, you and I could pop in. I'm sure he'll be there. That's the only place where he consistently goes on Thursday nights."

When Marie heard the car pull into the driveway, she quickly terminated her phone call with, "Oh, I think that's them, Ma! Gotta go now! What? Of course . . . but why don't you and Papa come over for dinner? Oh, it would be such a lovely homecoming for Joey, Ma. Great! See you at six! Gotta really go now! Bye!"

Marie was like a child on Christmas morning. And her delight was magnified even more when she saw Bob's arm around Joe's shoulder as they walked across the lawn to the huge, curved front porch. Marie could not restrain from bursting through the door and greeting her son.

"Joey, Joey, Joey, oh, how I've missed you," she said kissing and hugging him. "Welcome home, sweetheart."

He responded emotionally also as tears came to his eyes. "Oh, Mama, it's so good to see you again! It's been such a long time!"

Trying to eat delicious pot roast and field all of the questions that everyone threw at him did not cause Joe any discomfiture. As a matter of fact, he was enjoying every minute of being the center of attention. Joe had previously thought it would be terrible, being in the presence of the whole family. How wrong he was! And when Dr. Callahan insisted that Joe sit at the head of the large, mahogany, dining room table, he was *really* set.

"So, Joey," said Susan sipping iced tea, "how many beautiful girls did you meet in the service?"

Michael almost choked on his mashed potatoes. "Susan, for crying out loud, what kind of a question is that?"

"Hey, it's all right, Mike—nothing wrong with her question. Now, umm, let me see . . . er, nope . . . I'm afraid I can't. You know, Susan, I had to take a little time to think hard about that . . . and guess what."

"What?"

"I can think of several young ladies who were definitely beauti-ful, but, unfortunately, Susan, none of them were as beautiful as you."

That remark added to the general warmth and happiness of everyone.

3

Mr. Flaherty and Joe spent a lot of time together during the next couple of weeks. It was as though they were trying to re-discover each other. Some days, just the two of them would spend a couple of hours drinking boilermakers at Patty's Bar.

One afternoon while Joe and his grandfather were having a few, sudden cheers rang out from many of the patrons when two obviously special persons entered.

"There's Jimmy Doolin and his manager!" said Mr. Flaherty excitedly.

"Who's Jimmy Doolin?"

"Shades of St. Patrick!" responded the grandfather, smiling as he stood up and took Joe by the arm. "Don't let anyone in this joint hear you ask that kind of question, Joey m'boy! Jimmy Doolin's gonna be the next heavyweight champ of the world in two or three years! He's dynamite, kid! Saw him fight 'cross town last month. Put away this colored guy in the first round! C'mon, I'll introduce you to him."

While driving home, Talanski's ears were bombarded with nothing but boxing. Although he was not that interested in the sport, he was happy to be in the company of his grandfather. Joe kept a fixed smile while the old gentleman just rambled on about the "manly art," as he heralded it.

Then, for some reason that was still in left field, Joe re-adjusted his position behind the wheel and calmly said, "I think I'd like to try my hand at boxing, Gramps."

"Ha, ha, ha! Well, I'll be darned! Must be that strong Flaherty strain coming through your hide!"

"No kidding, Gramps, I'm serious. I really would like to give it my best shot. Hey, I know a few things about boxing!"

"Joey, you're talking about the ultimate sport—Spartan bravery. Being out there all alone to win or lose! No team to back you up. Just ability to hit, take a punch, and endure, m'boy, endure!"

Joe could feel the excitement in his grandfather's voice. Maybe the thought of gaining everyone's respect was coming through; maybe the thought of doing something violently legal was coming through; or maybe the thought of making everyone in Pittsburgh cheer the name *Talanski* was coming through. At any rate, Joe didn't have to think twice about the decision to ply his to-be-refined wares in the squared circle. For the past three weeks, he had seen enough exhibition training sessions and listened to his grandfather proclaim the attributes of several Irish boxers enough to last him a lifetime. However, Joe even surprised himself with the ease in which he assured his grandfather that the decision was solid.

"I'm really not trying to pluck your shamrock, Gramps, but I'm going to box—or my name's not *Talanski!*"

4

"Anybody home?"

"Yeah, Joey, come on up," answered his father. "I'm trying to get these last few things in order here."

Joey, as had become his practice in helping to strengthen his leg muscles, bounded up the stairs three at a time.

"How're you doing, Dad? All packed?"

Dr. Callahan was preparing to leave the next day for Chicago where he had been invited to read his latest published paper.

"Yeah, I guess so. Maybe I shouldn't say that, because your mother is pretty thorough when she packs my bags. Knows exactly what I need whether it's for one day or one week. Hand me those two folders over there, Joey. Thanks. If I leave these, I might as well not go. They contain most of my rough notes.

"So, big guy, how're you doing? Tough workout this morning?"

"You *know* it! Hey, but I'm hanging in there with the best of them down at the gym."

"Yes, your grandfather has told me how good you're getting. Well, there's one thing for sure, we'll be at your first fight next Thursday.

Joe broke into a broad smile as he shoved both hands into his rear pockets and leaned against the door jamb.

"Oh, and another thing, I just want to say how happy you've made all of us, Joey. I know there have been many rocky periods for you, and I know I've been responsible for some of them. You may find this hard to believe, but I consider one of my biggest regrets is not having legally adopted you when. . . ."

"Hey, Dad, that's not important. I still consider you my father, since I was only a baby when my real father was killed in the service. Besides, I'm happy that my name's Talanski, because I am determined to make it mean a helluva lot one day. And, to me, that's the challenge that means everything."

After an early dinner, Mrs. Callahan drove her husband to the airport. Joey went along, because he was going to be dropped off at the gym. When our aspiring gladiator arrived at the Lucky Clover Gymnasium, which was just a little more than a renovated upstairs flat, he headed straight for the small dilapidated locker room.

Joey, in his usual happy mood, was lacing up his shoes when the owner, Harry O'Hara, and another man came over to him.

"This is the kid I was telling you about, Champ," said the owner as he motioned for Joey to stand up. "Talanski, I want you to meet the second greatest heavyweight of 'em all who . . ."

Joey's eyes were already bulged, and his heart had skipped several beats! He couldn't believe it! "Oh my gosh! Danny Murphy!" Joey interrupted. "This is certainly my pleasure, Champ! I'd recognize you in a crowd of millions! My grandfather talks about you all the time!"

Irish Danny Murphy, between 1951 and '56, was heralded as the 'Burgh's next Billy Conn. After taking on and beating all opponents in Amateur Athletic Union competition, he turned professional one month following his winning the A.A.U. regional heavyweight division title on his twenty-second birthday. Murphy breezed through the first nine bouts, with none lasting more than three rounds, and they were via the knockout route. As the competitors got better, Murphy had to settle for sporadic K.O.s; nevertheless, he amassed an impressive record of 16–0 before losing a split decision at St. Nicholas Arena in New York. Irish Dan also lost his future as a prize fighter that same night. Back in the dressing room, while still fuming and cursing about the decision, he pushed a stiff left jab through the full-length mirror. The doctors saved the hand, but the ligaments were irreparably damaged.

"Harry here tells me ya jumpin' up to the pro ranks without doin' no amateur stuff. Is that right, kid?"

"Ah, yeah, well, I figure since I'm already twenty-five and have no formative experience in the A.A.U., why waste the few good years in front of me trying to get it? My legs are strong; my wind is strong; my chin is strong; and my left jab is strong. So, I guess what I'm saying is maybe if I can keep all those things together for a few years, I might make a few dollars while having some fun."

Murphy, smiling briefly, said to O'Hara, "You're right, Harry, he *is* a thinking one. I just got little piece of advice for ya, kid. Tell 'em to take the full-length mirror outta your dressing room."

5

The mid-March blizzard didn't stop any of the contestants and real fight fans from coming out, although the huge Duquesne Gardens was hardly needed for the sparse crowd.

Thirty-six seconds into the first round, Talanski feinted a left hook and zipped over his opponent's guard with a classic right cross that resulted in a clean knockout. The Callahans and Flahertys went crazy with joy!

A week later, Mr. O'Hara arranged for Joey to fight in Scranton. It was almost a carbon copy of his first fight. Our boy cold-cocked Hurricane Hansen in two minutes, eleven seconds of the opening round.

By November, Joey had fought six times, winning all via the knockout route and within three rounds. He was fast becoming known among local promoters, and his grandfather was already out there beating the publicity bushes.

"There is a Mr. Timothy Flaherty here to see you, Mr. Clancy," said the shapely young blonde speaking into the office intercom.

"Thank you, Grace. Ask him to come right in."

When the door was closed, the white-haired, cigar-smoking, portly gentleman sitting behind the desk shed the stern, strictly business countenance for a big broad smile and open arms.

"Timmy m'boy, how the hell are you? I haven't seen much of your potato face since I left the plant ten years ago!"

"Ah, Johnny, Johnny, it's good to see you again! You know, when I called this morning, I didn't really expect 'em to let me talk to you, what with all your big business appointments. Begorra, man, you must've kissed more than the blarney stone to get all this!"

"Ha, ha, ha, ha. Timmy, you haven't changed a bit . . ."

The two old friends spent a few minutes reminiscing about days gone by; however, they both knew why this meeting was necessary.

"Tim, your grandson's doing all right for himself out there. Saw his last fight. No doubt about it, the kid looks good, and as I told you on the phone, I'd like to aim him in the right direction—for a fee, of course."

"Johnny m'boy, I'm happy to see you doin' so damn well, but, you know, believe it or not, there's still a helluva lot of us back in the old neighborhood who're *not* doin' so damn well! Talk about the luck o' the Irish!"

"Whoa, hold on now, Tim. Don't get your dander up before you hear everything. Look, I know you got raw talent there, but it's not going to do Joey any good unless he can really display it on the right circuit where he can be seen and bring in some meaningful bucks. For openers, I can get him on the Mancuso-Lipman card down in Philly next February."

Clancy, being quite proficient in compromising and persuading people to see things his way without making them feel pressured, talked to Flaherty for nearly an hour about the bountiful advantages Joey could reap by seizing the opportunity immediately.

Tim Flaherty felt good when he left his old friend. In fact, he felt like doing some celebrating on his own. And at what better place to do that than the Oakland Cafe? From the minute Flaherty entered and saw several other retired acquaintances, he started belting one boilermaker after another.

"So, Tim," said Billy O'Hagen who was practically infamous for saying the wrong thing at the wrong time, "tell me one goddamn truth right now since we're on the subject. Why the hell don't you get your grandson to fight under a good shamrock-green Irish name?"

The blood rushed non-stop to Mr. Flaherty's ears. And although he had always hated the name *Talanski*, something triggered a response in him that even he didn't expect, especially since he never liked the circumstances that caused the name to come into his precious family. Perhaps it was the idea of having some outsider raise the topic that moved the seventy-five-year-old bantam rooster. At any rate, he reacted with dispatch by replying, "My grandson's name's got nothin' to do with his ability to kick the shit outta all comers! Besides, what's wrong with *Talanski* anyhow? He likes it—we like it! And I'll lick any mick in 'Sliberty that speaks out against it!"

Even Billy O'Hagen knew better than to press the issue any further.

All the way home, Mr. Flaherty whistled one Irish ditty after another. No doubt about it, he felt good and wanted the world to know.

"Timmy, is that you?" came his wife's voice from the kitchen.

"Now who else would you be expectin', m'love? I know you're gettin' prettier as the years go by 'n every son of Erin this side of the Atlantic wishes you was his, but that's too damn bad, because you belong to Rosie and John Flaherty's handsome son, Tim!"

Now whenever her husband had that much to say without being prompted, Mrs. Flaherty knew that he had been drinking again. But, unlike some men after returning home from several hours of imbibing, Mr. Flaherty usually displayed a happy and philosophic mood. Whatever was on his mind found its way into semi-picturesque terms.

"Supper's almost ready," Mrs. Flaherty said as she came downstairs with an armload of clothes for the washing machine. "Having delicious stew and hot soda bread, so I hope you can belly up to that."

"Umm, now, light o' my life," he replied as he gave her a kiss on the cheek, "you know you're the best scullery wench west of County Cork, and I count myself damn lucky to have you as m'own."

Mr. Flaherty followed his wife into the kitchen where the washing machine was also located. After taking two cups from the counter, he went to the stove for the coffee pot and said, "Sit down for a minute, m'love, I wanna talk about somethin' that means a lot to a real man."

"Timmy, you've been drinking again," chided Mrs. Flaherty as she took the pot from him and poured the coffee.

"By the staff of St. Patrick, woman, of course I've been drinkin'! How else can a sane man stay sane in this insane world?"

Having been married to Timothy Flaherty for fifty-three years, his wife knew that this was time for her to remain silent and let him do all the talking.

"It ain't no secret that I didn't approve of Marie marryin' a Polack. But, you 'n me, we know the kind of disgrace that would've come to this family if she hadn't—what with her bein' in a motherly way 'n all."

Now this topic was certainly not new to the ears of Mrs. Flaherty; nevertheless, she knew how much anguish her husband suffered, and she always listened consolingly.

"You can step on a man's face 'n maybe you'll find trouble. But, dammit, step on a man's name 'n that's a *sure* way 'o findin' trouble—even if the name's *Talanski!*"

Surprise registered on Mrs. Flaherty's face; however, she only nodded her head encouragingly as her husband continued.

"I guess I never really got to know Carl as a son-in-law. Guess that was my fault. Marie loved him, 'n he worked hard to make her happy during the short time that they had together. Ella, by God, you don't know how often I tried to bring myself to see some kind o' good in him! But I guess both my pride 'n prejudice just wouldn't let me do it—even for Marie's sake."

"Don't be so hard on yourself, Timmy," responded his teary-eyed mate as she reached across the table and gently squeezed his hand. "I was just as much at fault as you were. If I had been a more understanding mother and a more persistent wife, you would've attended the wedding and gotten to know Carl as a person—and not just a South Side Polack."

"He musta been a real brave fightin' man, Ella. I mean, to volunteer to go on practically a suicide mission 'n lay down your life for your buddies ain't easy for just *anybody* to do! Joey's *got* to have a lot 'o his father in him, because he's a brave man also. The kid's been through fire 'n brimstone, probably more than we'll ever know. Even stayin' back there with his aunt's murder, he saw 'n swallowed a lot. . . ."

"You're right, Timmy. And God only knows what that child's been going through between the time he was expelled from college and the day he got off the train last year. But he's been a good boy, and he really loves you, Timmy. It's certainly no secret that he seems

99

to seek out his gramp's approval before any other—you're why he's taken up boxing!''

Mr. Flaherty never did get around to relating to his wife what happened earlier that afternoon.

Eight

Discovery and Re-Discovery

Joe trained exceptionally hard for the Philly fight, and everything was beginning to fall into place. However, one week before the bout, the question of his name surfaced again, this time by one of his stablemates.

"Hey, Joey, I got nothin' against *Talanski,* but I do have somethin' against you ruinin' big opportunities just because of a fuckin' name! Hell, man, Joe Louis changed his! Who knows, maybe it brought him luck, I don't know. But there's one thing I *do* know, and that's wearin' green trunks and a Polack name's gonna confuse the hell outta the crowd! And sometimes, especially when you're in there with a tough South Philly dago like Carmine Reventi, you need all the help you can get!"

Granted, Larry "The Destroyer" Kennedy was not one of the most articulate persons in the world, but he could lay out his true feelings very clearly. Joey and he had become friendly not only because of their association as stablemates but through their living in the same neighborhood.

To Talanski, it seemed as though a lot of people in the fight game were interested in his taking on a Celtic surname, and this was beginning to wear him down. However, it occurred to Joey that his grandfather hadn't pressed the issue. Perhaps this is what made him decide to approach the old gentleman after the workout.

It had been several weeks since Mr. Flaherty had decided not to burden his grandson with the name situation, and he was quite pleased that no one else had mentioned it. For all practical purposes, Mr. Flaherty had pushed the subject to the rear of his mind.

Snow had just begun to fall when Joey popped happily into the passenger side and said, "Hi, Gramps! I thought you were coming early enough to catch the sparring session. Think I've really perfected that combo well enough to stick and move, you know?

Should've seen Charlie trying to counter me, Gramps. I mean I was really putting it all together this afternoon!''

"That's good, Joey. I knew you'd get it," said Mr. Flaherty as he reached over with his right hand and slapped the boxer's knee. "Now, all we have to do is polish up a few dull spots 'n you're ready for Reventi, right?"

"Yeah . . . but, between now and then, Gramps, I'm going to play down *Talanski* and take on the name *Kelly*. What do you think about that? Ha, ha, ha. Is that Irish enough for you?"

Joey had given serious thought to assuming a new ring name, but it was only after his stablemate and a few other guys around the gym pointed out various advantages that he finally decided to do it. Besides, Talanski felt that his grandfather, especially, would be pleased with the change.

The vintage car shuddered when Mr. Flaherty stomped on the brake.

"Holy shit . . . , I mean, wow, Gramps. What was that for? You all right? Want me to drive?"

The old man, momentarily, did not reply or release his vise-like grip on the steering wheel. With eyes riveted straight ahead and clenched teeth, Mr. Flaherty hissed, "Don't *ever* even *think* about changin' your name for the ring or any other reason, do you hear?"

Then he somewhat relaxed, got control of himself, and continued with, "I'm not droppin' you off at home now. We gotta talk, Joey, and I can't really say what I want around Marie and the others. We need some privacy—just you 'n me."

Of course, Joe was taken completely by surprise by all of this, and he was totally confused—so much so that he could do little more than just look puzzled at his grandfather and say, "Well . . . er . . . okay, Gramps. Where do you want to go?"

"Oh, I don't know . . . hey, how 'bout us goin' over to the North Side? I know this nice little pub where they serve some o' the best corned beef sandwiches in the 'Burgh, 'n, besides, none o' my crowd would be there now, because it's too close to suppertime."

The huge red-faced bartender must've weighed at least three hundred pounds. Even the apron, which was practically up to his armpits, hardly stretched around the enormous stomach.

When the combination walnut stained-glass door swung open, letting in a wintry blast that disturbed the green and white cloths that neatly covered several tables, the bartender and the one other patron turned their eyes toward the two newly arrived figures who immediately headed for the corner booth in the rear.

"What'll it be, gents?"

"A boilermaker for me 'n a glass o' orange juice for the kid here," came Mr. Flaherty's reply as he took a fresh cigar out of his flannel-shirt pocket.

It would've been sheer fiction for anybody to think that one boilermaker was going to be enough for the old man, especially when he had to brace himself to say what was on his mind. After talking about boxing in general and gulping down his third whiskey, Gramps was ready.

"What I really want to talk to you about, Joey, is this business of changing your name from . . ."

"Yeah, I knew you'd like the idea, Gramps . . . a solid green Irish name that . . ."

"Whoa! Wait a minute, 'n slow down! What makes you think you can do any better by changin' your damn name?"

Joey was taken somewhat aback by his grandfather's reaction. But before he had a chance to reply, the venerable old gentleman continued in a calmer tone.

"Joey m'boy, it's no secret that your father 'n me . . . well, we never really got along. No . . . no, that's not the whole truth. I have to be honest all the way if I'm gonna tell you what's on my mind."

Talanski, seeing the inner struggle surface plainly in his grandfather's face, tried to help him along by saying, "Gramps, you must know by now that I'm fully aware of why you didn't attend my mother and father's wedding. I couldn't have been more than ten when I found out. Don't ask me how or who told me, because I don't even remember. Anyhow, the fact that you chose not to attend never had what you might call a negative impact on my feelings for you, Gramps."

To cover up the emotion that was about to spill out of his eyes, the old man yelled to the bartender for another round of drinks. "'N make that a double vitamin C for the kid! Gettin' back to the name thing, Joey, I just want you to know that I don't think you should change it . . . not for the ring . . . not for some crazy notion . . . not for nobody!

"Your father, Carl, laid down his life for this country. He was a hero. Well, I don't have to tell you. You've seen the medal and citation certificate often enough, right?"

"Right, Gramps, but what . . ."

"No buts about it! The name that Uncle Sam cherishes and put here for all to honor, Joey, is Talanski! Hear that? *Talanski!* And it's a damn good name, one not to be traded in for any other!"

"But, Gramps, I thought . . ."

"Yeah, yeah, I know, and you were right, I'm sorry to say. All these years, Joey, I've been a . . . a . . . a plain, hard-headed, stubborn old jackass. I let m' foolish pride stand between me 'n your father. He was a good husband to your mother, 'n he thought the world of you, Joey. On top of that, he was pretty smart—was in line for a big promotion over at the steel mill.

"I guess what I'm tryin' to say, son, is that your father, Carl Talanski, was a man—a real man among men. And, dammit, I wish to Christ he was right here in this pub right now, 'cause I'd tell him so! Change your name? No, Joey, don't ever think about doin' that again. If anything, honor it all the days of your life."

Undoubtedly, Timothy Flaherty felt relieved and good after having talked to his grandson that day. It was as though a heavy weight was lifted from the old man's heart.

Philadelphia fight fans are among the most supportive in the country when it comes to cheering local talent on to victory. And the huge crowd at the Arena that night had come to see South Philly's favorite son, middleweight Manny Mancuso, pulverize Gene Lipman, a black, stick-and-move jabber from Chicago. Those two were the main event to round out the five-bout card.

The fans were really a mixed bag. Even the uppercrust from the Main line had representation, and among them were Dr. and Mrs. Ralph Lindstrom. Although Ralph had always been a fight fan, he was not too successful in convincing his wife to become one also.

Neil Crenshaw, a longtime fight promotor and restauranteur, often gave Dr. Lindstrom a couple of ringside tickets to show his unending appreciation for the cardiologist's ability to keep a worn-out heart from exploding in trying to pump blood through three hundred and forty pounds of pampered fat. Dr.Lindstrom employed every conceivable method in trying to get Crenshaw to lose tonage, but nothing seemed to work. The rich businessman's penchant for delicious food was too strong; therefore, he just stopped all notions relating to dietary matters.

After the handsome physician and his beautiful wife got out of their new Porsche, the eager parking valet hopped in and gunned the precisioned machine up the ramp. Surprisingly, though, the couple did not become unglued at the seams. They were a devout sports car couple but refused to let over-zealous parking lot attendants ruin their many evenings out by causing concern as to how the cars were parked. However, Dr. Lindstrom could not pass up the occasion to make a timely comment to his wife.

"I'd like to place that guy's testicles between the gear cogs and shift into first without using the clutch."

Although it was a bone-chilling night, the crowd filed into the Arena quite jovially. No one seemed to mind the fact that the parking area adjacent to the building was closed, making it necessary for the fans to walk almost three blocks.

Once inside the already smoke-filled Arena, Dr. Lindstrom, with his gorgeous wife clutching tightly to her Russian sable coat and husband's hand, sailed expertly through the sea of fans until he arrived at the ringside section.

"Hiya, Doc!" came the familiar raspy voice, "I'm glad you could make it!"

"Neil, how're you doing?"

"Fine! How else, with Philly's best pill-pusher looking after me?"

Laughingly turning to his wife, Dr. Lindstrom said, "Sweetheart, I want you to meet Neil Crenshaw, the ogre who's been forcing all of these great fight tickets on me since last spring."

"Pleased to meet you, Mrs. Lindstrom. You have a terrific husband here. If it weren't for him, I probably wouldn't be able to still enjoy the finer things of life."

"It certainly is a pleasure to meet you, Mr. Crenshaw. Ralph has spoken of you often, especially when there's a big fight coming to town."

"Ha, ha. That's nice, but please call me Neil, okay?"

"Okay, Neil, but only if you call me Bonnie."

105

While the two men were busily assessing the various merits and predicting outcomes, Bonnie nonchalantly surveyed the interesting people around her. She was only partly listening to Ralph and Neil when she heard one of them mention the name Talanski. She casually interrupted the two fisticuff aficionados with the question, "Who's Talanski?"

Unfortunately, or maybe fortunately, neither of the men ceased his discourse long enough to offer a verbal reply. However, Ralph did quickly give Bonnie his program and signaled the section attendant for another.

Long-buried thoughts were exhumed as Bonnie's eyes raced randomly over the sheet of paper. Could this Joe Talanski be the same Joe Talanski who was once her lover? Impossible!

The second bout could not begin soon enough for Bonnie. Minutes later, the noisy crowd stood up to cheer Carmine Reventi as he bounced assuredly down the aisle behind his handlers. If all he needed to win the fight was a strong rooting section, then the proverbial deal was in the white house. Reventi was a plucky lad of only twenty-one, but he had ring savvy that just came naturally to him. Since he was thirteen, Carmine had come up through the South Philly Police Athletic League boxing program, putting away opponents through sheer power.

"Wait'll you see this kid go to it, Doc," said Crenshaw as he also stood up clapping. "He's a machine, a real stone merchant! Can bang you on the arms and give you a headache! Saw him fight back in November. The other guy never knew what hit him—Reventi dissected the poor slob."

"*Dissected?*" Ralph laughed, joining his friend in applauding the fighter who bounced toward the squared circle amid a mixture of Italian and English yells. "Maybe this guy's got a scalpel in each glove!"

"Yeah, he must, because in the eight pro bouts he's had so far, the kid's won 'em all by the knockout route. But, then again, his manager's not rushing him up against any *real* talent—you know, bum of the month, cannon fodder, confidence builders? For instance, who's this bum from Pittsburgh? I'll tell you. He's just another stepping stone for Reventi!"

Bonnie listened intently to Crenshaw's words while at the same time craning her neck to see Talanski. Although only a few minutes had elapsed between the favorite son's grand entrance and the intrusion of the opponent, it seemed like an eternity to her. As a matter of fact, the hoopla for Reventi was so great that his opponent's arrival to the ring was practically spontaneous.

My God, thought Bonnie as she viewed the once-familiar muscular frame, *it's him! It's Joe! What on earth is he ever doing here—in that ring—in Philadelphia?*

She even noticed the scar tissue from the old stabbing wound. Suddenly, our gorgeous lady felt extremely light-headed. It was as though she was viewing the entire scene from out in space. Bonnie remembered the helpless, mind-jumbled, over-sized, handsome boy whom her cousin had pleaded with her to help. Now look at him. She could see that he was a boy no longer. He was a man.

"Remember, kid," cautioned Reventi's handler, "good, hard jabs . . . so we can find out what this guy knows."

Round One. Reventi moved quickly to the center of the ring and began with a head fake followed by a sharp left jab. Talanski was then barraged with a series of pin-pointed jabs, a couple of left hooks, and a stinging right cross that had him bobbing and weaving on the ropes when the bell sounded.

Shouts of encouragement from the South Philly contingent could probably be heard all over town. Young, greasy-haired, olive-complexioned fellows, who were there to cheer their rising hero on to another knockout, completely ignored the mild requests of attendants to refrain from using profanity and be seated.

"Fuck you, man," someone yelled. "That's our Carmine in there!"

Round Two. Talanski backed his opponent into a neutral corner and immediately went to work. Short, power-packed body blows caused Reventi's knees to buckle twice. However, he managed to wheel Talanski around and get in a few clean shots of his own.

At the end of Round Three, Crenshaw waved for the hot dog vendor while asking his friends, "Hey, how 'bout a little refreshment here, Bonnie? Notice I didn't ask Doc. He always puts a damper on my *favorite* recreation."

"Never mind," Ralph laughingly said. "When we decide to staple your intestines, maybe we ought to do your lips also."

The physician had no sooner sat back in the seat when his beeper sounded. Reluctantly, Ralph had to take care of an emergency situation that only he could do at such a late hour.

Bonnie was not bent out of shape because of the interrupted evening. This occurred frequently, and she, as usual, began putting her coat on too.

"You don't have to leave, angel," Ralph said after he had returned from the telephone booth. "It took me long enough to get you out to the fights, so I'll be damned if I'm going to let your debut be spoiled."

"Oh, that's all right, Ralph. I've seen enough to . . ."

"No, sweetheart, I want you to enjoy the fights. Then I won't have to go through any red tape in getting you out here in the future—right, Neil?"

"Aw, c'mon, Doc, you don't really expect me to get into this. But I'll say this much. Tonight's card is one of the best I've seen this year."

"Okay, okay," laughed Bonnie. "I'll stay. Besides, I'm enjoying it!"

"Good. Neil, would you see Bonnie home?"

"Hey, no problem, Doc."

"And don't bother to wait up for me, honey, because the operation will probably last all night."

Although Joey lost the fight on a split decision, he and his corner didn't feel too upset, because the referee had given him all but the first round. The place probably would have exploded if Reventi had not been named the winner.

Talanski, unlike his opponent, had no difficulty getting out of the ring and back to the dressing room, because there was only a handful of fans waiting to greet him. Besides, it really didn't matter that much to our hero. His mind was on calling home to find out the latest report concerning his grandfather, who had been hospitalized a few days earlier with a heart attack.

Just before Joey and his attendants disappeared behind the stands, a beautiful blonde woman called to him from only a few feet away. Bonnie knew that it would be somewhat awkward to explain to Neil why it was so necessary for her to see this fighter from Pittsburgh. Therefore, she didn't bother to mention it. Instead of going to the ladies' room, Bonnie stood near the corridor leading to the dressing area.

During the few moments that Joey saw Bonnie before he was whisked away, he managed to force a smile across his swollen face, and she managed to shove a folded note into his hand.

Nine

Shades of Understanding

1

As soon as Bob had finished in the operating room, he wasted no time in getting down to the third floor. All elevators were either too far above or too far below the sixth, so he used a nearby stairwell. The brilliant physician didn't bother to change out of his greens, because the call from Miss Aikins, the head nurse, was urgent. Bob saw her behind the counter when he rounded the corner.

"Thanks for notifying me, Ginny. Came as fast as I could."

"Oh, it was no problem, Dr. Callahan," replied the nurse while joining him en route to room 309. "I knew you'd want to know if your father-in-law took a turn for the worse."

Marie, her mother, and Michael were standing at the bedside looking helplessly at the pallid form of Mr. Flaherty. Contrary to her husband's insistence, Mrs. Flaherty began to cry softly. It was then that the tough old bantam rooster opened his eyes and spoke in a raspy voice. "Ah, Ella, Ella, m'love, thar you be garn tarnin' on the waterworks."

"Well, it's about time you woke up, Gramps," said Michael in a forced jovial tone. "Look who's here," he continued while putting his arm around his father's shoulder. "Big pill-pusher and little pill-pusher."

After quickly kissing Marie on the cheek, Bob took the old man's hand and smilingly asked, "How're you feeling tonight?"

"Not too good," came the faint reply, "but I'm not complainin'. Where's Joey? Ain't he here yet? Marie, where's Joey? I gotta see m'grandson, Joey."

"He's fighting down in Philly, Papa," Marie responded as she quickly wiped her eyes before bending over the bed and kissing her father on the forehead. "But he promised he'd fly straight back to see you, okay?"

Michael motioned for his father to join him at the nurses' stand.

"Gramps doesn't look so good tonight, Dad. Do you think the medication should be increased?"

"Under the present circumstances, no, Mike. Perhaps the best thing that we can do for him is to just be around. The fluid build-up in his vena cava is progressing too fast. And you know what that means."

"I know, Dad. All we can do is try to make him comfortable."

It was nearly midnight when Marie finally persuaded her over-tired mother to let Michael drive her home. However, Mrs. Flaherty made her grandson promise to bring her back to the hospital by noon. She wanted to be there to make sure that Mr. Flaherty ate something. The half-hour drive gave Mike's grandmother a chance to let him know that she was not terribly upset with her husband's condition, because, as she put it, ". . . he's a good man who always worked at making a good home for his family. . . ."

Earlier, Bob had told Marie that her father would probably pass shortly. Being a physician's wife plus having a son in medical school sort of conditioned her to facing the realities of adverse medical situations. However, she still hung on to hope.

1:15 A.M. The dim nightlight cast a somber atmosphere through-out the private room. Mr. Flaherty's low groaning caused his dozing daughter to get up from the cushioned chair and rush to the bed.

"What's wrong, Papa? More pain? Here . . . let me buzz for the nurse . . ."

A weak hand waved off the fast motions and signaled for Marie to come sit on the bed. Her father's voice was barely audible, so she leaned forward while holding his hand.

"Joey . . . (cough) . . . is Joey here?"

"No, Papa, he's probably on his way back from Philadelphia now."

"I . . . (cough) . . . I don't care any . . . (cough) . . . anything about dyin', Marie. But . . . I do care about . . . (cough) . . . I do care about how bad I was . . . (cough) . . . I was to you, Carl, and little Joey all . . . (cough) . . . all them years. . . ."

"Oh, Papa, don't try to talk now. . . ."

The old man's milk-glossed blue eyes widened as he mustered just enough strength to raise his voice slightly above a whisper. "Marie, I'm sorry for not bein' (cough) not bein' a good father. . . ."

"Oh, Papa," she said as she gently kissed and pressed the gnarled hand. "You're a good father and grandfather."

"That's just it. I didn't do right by Carl, and (cough) he gave his life for you, me, and this whole (cough) this whole damn country. He deserved better treatment than what he got from me. I was a stubborn jackass then and (cough) and I'm still a stubborn old fool now. Here I am, tryin' to hold on to this terrible piece o' life I been livin' 'n I know (cough) better than the doctors that I ain't got long for this world, Marie."

"Shh, stop trying to talk so much, Papa. You're straining all of . . ."

"Never mind. I'm ready to meet Saint Peter, Saint Patrick, 'n the rest right now, but I certainly would like to (cough) to see Joey before I go. I ain't been exactly a good Gramps to him, Marie. The lad deserved more attention from me than what he got. Oh, God, I love that boy, 'n I wish I could tell him so tonight."

Tears welled up in the old man's eyes and trickled down the side of his wrinkled face.

"That's all right, Papa. Joey'll be here in the morning. He's probably left Philadelphia. . . ."

"Philly. That damn town's bad luck for Joey. I never shoulda had him fight down there (cough). Never shoulda talked the kid into bein' a bawxer anyhow. He did it for me 'n me stupid (cough) stupid pride. Jus' wanted to please his old gramps, don't ya know. I love him, Marie, I love him, 'n I want you to please tell him (cough) tell him yourself, because . . .

"Not enough time left on me clock, darlin'. I'll be (cough) be gone before sunrise," the old man said as he turned his face to the wall.

Marie, feeling that her father needed to sleep, released his hand and settled quietly in the heavily-cushioned chair. Several minutes later, as she nodded between consciousness and subconsciousness, Marie thought she heard her father utter Joey's name. However, it didn't matter, because, as the gray mantle of morning began to make its encroachment on the black canopy of night, Tim Flaherty departed this life.

111

2

The dressing room monitor was mildly polite but very fast in his movements toward keeping the flow of combatants, winners and losers, moving through the drab facilities. He moved from one dressing room to the other, quickly opening doors, saying a few words of good luck to the waiting fighters, congratulations to winners, and encouragement to losers.

"Hurry up, Billy," shouted Ed Bennett, the punchy retired middleweight who had accompanied the two boxers from Pittsburgh. "We gotta get a move on if we expect to make the owl flight."

As soon as Ed had spoken, the dressing room monitor poked his head through the door, passed a warm greeting, and reminded the fighters' attendants that the room had to be vacated within the next ten minutes. Joey didn't have to be rushed, because the sweat-covered note moved him exceptionally fast. It was only after he had stuffed the last piece of gear into the neat bag that his grandfather had given him for Christmas that Joe informed the other two of his date.

"How do you like this guy, Ed?" yelled Billy, laughing, from the shower stall. "One night in Philly and already he's a goddamn ladykiller! Eh, what the hell! That burly black guy puts my lights out in the second round, but I still don't get a come-on from some gorgeous blonde. So tell me, how d'ya rate, Joey?"

"Ha, ha! Maybe someday I'll share the secret with you, but right now, gotta go!"

"Still think you're makin' a mistake, kid," Ed interjected. "If your grandfather's sick as you say and in the hospital, you really should be on the plane with us."

Although Joey knew that the old guy was right, he passed it off lightly with, "Gramps is tough as nails, Ed. Besides, he's probably going to nail my ass to the barn door when he finds out that I let that greaseball take the fight."

"Hey, got nothin' to be shamed of, kid," Ed said as he patted Joe on the shoulder. "You did good out there. Hell, if it wasn't for the damn rough guinea crowd, I'm sure you woulda gotten the nod. Don't worry, Reventi don't wanna meet you again, but he's got to. When the sonofabitch comes to the 'Burgh, you'll kick his ass in style, right, babe?"

Talanski was only half-listening. He was busily trying to get out of there. However, Joey did respond with, "Yeah, when we square off again, I'm gonna take that bastard out in the first round. Okay, guys, see you at the gym on Tuesday."

As the cab whizzed north on Broad Street, Joey's mind flashed memories of times when he and Fred Blueswicz used to comb the town looking for fun after working all day at the brewery. Fred. What fun they used to have flicking in and out of places where they weren't supposed to be. Joey continued smiling as he thought about how full of life Fred had been and how much confidence Fred had in him when they decided to join the army together. Joey was like all the family Fred had, and, aside from the badgering and constant pursuit of broads, those two fellows were self-decided brothers whose love for each other ran deep. Joey was enjoying those pleasant memories until a traffic light turned yellow.

It was an electrical shock wave blasting through his head. The ex-G.I.'s eyes saw the yellow fireball engulf the helicopter that was carrying his friend. Joe could almost feel the searing glare as he gripped the back of the front seat while at the same time yelling, "Fred! Oh, my god, Fred!"

The cab driver, being quite accustomed to all kinds of nuts, registered only mild surprise—didn't even turn around.

"You all right, buddy?"

"Whew! Yeah, I'm okay. Sorry about that, pal. I could've caused an accident."

Frequently looking at his fare through the rearview mirror, the cabbie finally asked the question, "Were you in Vietnam, chief?"

"Yeah, for a few months before we got into it."

"Hey, you were lucky. Now, that place is a real hell hole. I see what's happening on T.V. just about every night—got a nephew over there. Hey, but, like I said, you were lucky, chief, if you got outta there before Johnson declared war on those bastards. At least you didn't have to be shot at, right?"

"Yeah, right."

The driver, after hacking in Philly for eleven years, knew when fares wanted conversation or silence. So, he shut up.

Joey's thoughts turned to Bonnie, the gorgeous reason for his heading to the Golden Dragon Chinese Restaurant instead of to the airport. To say the least, he was surprised to see her at the fights.

Not that Joe harbored any animosity toward the beautiful psychologist, but he had thought that this was one chapter in his rocky life that was finished. However, when Bonnie suddenly appeared again and slipped a note to him, Joe could think only of those fun-filled times that they had prior to the last time he saw her back in November of '62. And for Bonnie to have set up this meeting so secretly stirred his curiosity even more. The time for getting answers to a lot of questions was at hand, because the cab had come to a final stop in front of the huge neon dragon.

Upon entering the once-familiar restaurant, Joe was immediately greeted by a waiter who whisked him off to the curtained booth where Bonnie was seated. Instead of sitting on the opposite side of the table, Joe sat close enough to feel the gorgeous form pressed against his right arm, hip, and leg. No words were spoken until after the smiling waiter had closed the curtain.

"Hi, Joey," came the greetings as two perfectly-sculptured hands folded gently around the swollen fingers and bruised knuckles of his huge right punching weapon. "You're still looking good, I see."

He smiled, leaned, and kissed those lips that used to send him into a whirlpool of passion. The force was still there. And in that brief moment, tongues flicked alternately.

"Seeing you made me forget how bad I felt for losing tonight, because you're as delicious as ever, Bonnie."

Surprisingly to both of them, conversation was not at all strained or contrived. Within forty-five minutes, marriage, military time, broadened psychological service, Pittsburgh homecoming, and the fight game were covered while the couple did very little justice to Chan's egg foo yung.

Shortly after leaving the restaurant, Bonnie and Joe found themselves intertwined and drenched in each other's sweat at a secluded motel just north of Pennsauken on the Jersey side of the Delaware River. It seemed as though they purposely avoided getting into all of the reasons why things did not work out during their previous relationship. High passion completely overwhelmed them until a few minutes before daybreak when the sleepless couple began to settle down to earth.

After lighting Bonnie's cigarette, Joe and she relaxed their nude bodies among the damp, mussed sheets.

"Yes, it's true that Ralph and I have a wonderful marriage, that is, if money is the common denominator."

Joe detected the slight cynicism in Bonnie's tone, so he let her continue without interruption. It seems that in spite of all the material things available to her fingertips, she did not have the object of her constant dreams, a baby. Dr. Lindstrom was ever so attentive to his beautiful wife, but having children was not one of his priorities. Both of them had agreed to wait until all career plans had fallen into place.

"Well, I don't see anything wrong with what you and your husband decided. I mean, after all, just think about how great your children's future's going to be because of this careful planning. Some people would give anything to have just a small fraction of what you and your husband have, especially when . . ."

"His name is Ralph."

"What?"

"I said his name is Ralph, damn it! Why is it so hard for you to say his name?"

Joe raised himself and looked puzzledly at Bonnie. "What's wrong? It's not hard for me to say *Ralph!* Wow! I see you can still get pissed off over nothing. . . ."

"Nothing! You might consider it to be nothing, but it's very important to me that you understand. Ralph is solid gold; I mean, he's an excellent doctor, excellent husband, and . . ."

"Hey, wait a minute, Bonnie," Joe interrupted in the calmest tone that he could effect under the circumstance. "Why are we arguing when both of us know that tonight is only a brief re-encounter of a relationship we used to have? I don't intend to hurt or complicate your life, and I'm sure that you feel the same about mine. Look, sweetheart, we once laughed and loved heavily. But that was a long time ago. Now, we're both in completely different worlds, and this night should. . . ."

Bonnie couldn't help but smile and jokingly say, "I see you've become quite the psychologist yourself, Joseph. Really, I don't believe anyone else could have put things more cleverly into proper perspective than you've just done. But don't think for one minute, love, that I'm some frustrated wife who's out here looking for kicks."

"Bonnie, I don't know what all this has to do with our lying here tonight simply re-capturing some of those plain, old, personal, and private moments that we used to enjoy together. Hell," Joe continued as he laughingly reached across the gorgeous body next to his for the pack of cigarettes on the small table, "I'd have to be the last person in the world to qualify for sitting in judgmental seats—the way my life's been screwed up since day one. So why don't we just take what tonight has to offer us and enjoy, okay?"

"Okay," Bonnie responded while simultaneously taking Joe's cigarette and stubbing it. "I think it's time to stop talking."

The top sheet fell to the floor as reunited lovers passionately embraced in re-discovery.

3

Nine days had passed since Mr. Flaherty's funeral, and everyone was beginning to make the necessary mental adjustments. That is, everyone except Joe. He just couldn't seem to get himself together. Nothing was the same. His friends down at the gym unsuccessfully tried to get him back into training, but something was missing. The desire for boxing seemed to have disappeared when his grandfather died.

Aside from thinking about securing some kind of gainful employment otherwise, Joe had made up his mind to leave the 'Burgh. He spent a lot of sleepless nights brooding about the old man whom he had finally come to know.

On this particular night, Marie also had difficulty in sustaining a sound sleep. She heard footsteps going down the stairs and into the kitchen. Not wanting to disturb her husband, Marie slipped quietly out of bed and put on her robe. Ten after one and snow was beginning to come down rather heavily.

When his mother entered the kitchen, Joe was in the midst of preparing hot chocolate.

"What're you doing up at this hour, Mom? Have trouble sleeping?"

"Well . . . sort of . . . but I guess that comes with age."

"Ha, ha. Mom, you still don't look a day over thirty. Naw . . . come on . . . I'm not kidding. You look good."

"Flattery will get you everything. Here, move out of the way; let me finish making the hot chocolate. How 'bout a nice ham 'n cheese sandwich to go with it?"

116

"Not at this hour, but I certainly would like for you to stay down here awhile, Mom. Got a few things on my mind."

For three hours, Joe and his mother talked about everything from college days to the present. For the very first time, mother and son felt absolutely comfortable in discussing such a wide range of topics without becoming upset and angry with each other. Surprisingly, Mrs. Callahan was a very attentive listener. As a matter of fact, her general demeanor encouraged Joe to elaborate greatly on various military and post-military events that he had not discussed with anyone prior to then.

"And believe it or not, Mom, our little unit was called on the carpet for defending ourselves!"

Mrs. Callahan felt good about chatting with her Joey. While he was talking, she hung on to every word and gave welcome commentary on several points, especially when Joe related that he thought it was time for him to leave the 'Burgh.

"While I don't really want you to leave, I think I understand why you feel you have to go. Papa used to always tell me that you would find your way, because you have a strong heart."

Joe felt a little embarrassed to hear his mother speak praisingly of him. But he realized that she also was trying to make adjustments in her life. Never before had Joe known his mother to be so calm and understanding. Ever since high school, their conversations were more of the encounter type—his mother consistently shouting him down. Tonight was different.

"You know, Mom, since Gramps died, I've been doing a lot of thinking about boxing. At this point in time, I don't really know if I want to stay in it or not. Gramps would probably turn over in his grave at hearing me say this, but . . ."

"I don't think so, Joey. You know, believe it or not, your grandfather had a lot of faith in you, and I'm not just talking about since you came home from the Army. Even while you were living in Philadelphia, he was always the one who used to try to convince me that you'd be all right."

The more Mrs. Callahan talked to her son that night, the more she surprised herself in finding out how easy it was for just the two of them to carry on a sustained conversation without any angry outbursts. Joe and his mother were actually listening to each other with interest.

117

Three days later, Talanski boarded the 9:22 P.M. train for Miami. He had absolutely no idea as to what he'd do there. The only reason why Florida was selected was because, while rummaging through the mish-mash of things, at the bottom of his old Army duffle bag, Joe came across a jungle survival manual that contained the address of a close comrade who served with him at Fort Bragg and also on that ill-fated secret mission in Vietnam. Although Joe had no knowledge of what had happened to Paco Sanchez after they were debriefed, he decided to chance looking him up.

Paco Sanchez was older than his two friends and had already been in the Army eight years. However, because of his periodic absences without leave and strong inclination to goof off in general, he was always in trouble. Joe smiled to himself as he thought about the time when he, Fred, and Paco had to fight their way out of a bar when some local toughs made several racial slurs about Hispanics. What ignited the fuel was Paco's reply: "You fucking hillbilly bastards can kiss my Cuban ass!" And Blueswicz had consumed just enough bourbon to prompt his adding, "Yeah, 'n while you're doing that, you can double back 'n kiss my Mexican ass! And while you're at it, you can kiss our other friend's Puerto Rican ass, okay?"

Joe wasn't sure whether Sanchez had fully recovered from the wounds he suffered in Tay Ninh Province. The last time he had seen him was at a field hospital north of Saigon.

It wasn't until Joe had been in town for nearly a week that he finally made contact with his Army buddy. The inquisitive stares that he received from people as he walked along the streets of Little Havana gave him an uneasy feeling—a flashback to when he was jumped in Philly.

Joe was so deep in thought that he hardly noticed the police car parked outside of the dilapidated apartment house. The officers became quite curious when they saw him stop and look at a small piece of paper.

"Let's check him," said the driver as he opened the door. "We just might be on to something here."

Joe was approached from the side and rear by the two Metro-Dade policemen.

"Just a minute, pal. We want to talk to you," said the one who stepped in front.

"Good, officer, because I'm a little lost here trying to find this address," responded Joe, giving him the piece of paper.

As soon as the officer saw the name that was written on the crumpled sheet, he passed it to his partner and said, "There're a few questions we'd like to ask you."

Joe became quite perturbed, but he was wise enough not to show any kind of reluctance. He figured that being a stranger in the area gave him no room for arguing.

While checking Joe's I.D., the other officer, who had been silent up to that point, asked, "What brings you to Miami, Mr. Talanski?"

By the general drift of the cop's many questions, Joe assumed that he was suspected of having some kind of narcotics connection with persons in the neighborhood. However, the officers were not too informative as to particulars. It was a wasted afternoon as far as Joe's efforts to locate his friend were concerned. He even tore the slip of paper into shreds as the taxicab picked its way through rush hour traffic and carried him back to his rented room.

Ten

Reunion

1

Cleaning out fish pools was not exactly the most prestigious job in Florida, but, as our Joey Talanski had told several people with whom he had struck up friendly and beer-drinking relationships, "It pays the rent." As a matter of fact, Joe developed quite an attachment to his job at Ocean World, Miami's marine research laboratories.

Biologist Dr. Harry Compton reminded Joe of his grandfather. He was a feisty old gentleman who was particular about the care and feeding of the fish, especially the big ones. However, the senior biologist eventually noticed that the new man did an excellent job in performing his duties on the tanks. During lunch hour, Joe frequently ate right there while watching the sharks.

One afternoon, Dr. Compton, upon arriving in the area to take some algae samples, noticed Joe sitting on the apron of the pool that contained three huge mako sharks.

"You'd better watch yourself there, Mr. Talanski," warned the biologist. "They're not fussy about what or on whom they chomp."

"Oh, hi, Doc! Why don't you join me over here?"

The biologist decided to spend a few minutes talking to the new worker, because, for some unexplained reason, he liked him. Perhaps it was Talanski's apparent interest in sharks. At any rate, Dr. Compton sat down beside the young man.

"Joe, I've been noticing that you always linger around the pool. Do you know anything about sharks?"

"Not really, Doc, only what I've seen in the movies. They just keep swimming all the time, don't they?"

"Well, most species do. You would think that after so many millions of years sharks, like other animals, would've gone through drastic change cycles. But not these creatures; they're basically the same."

During the many lunch hours to follow, Dr. Compton developed a fondness for the young man who expressed a sincere desire to learn more about sharks. Perhaps it was because Talanski showed a genuine interest in them that the seventy-three-year-old marine biologist took to him. Or maybe it was because Joe was one of the few persons at Ocean World Labs who spent any time chatting with the old gentleman.

Although Harry Compton's colleagues, all younger than he, respected the scholarship of his many research projects, they thought his retirement was long overdue. Several of the hotshot Ph.D.s were eyeing Dr. Compton's position, and he knew that they laughed about him behind his back.

One day, while the old gentleman and his friend were eating their lunch, Dr. Compton continued the conversation that he had begun earlier. "Now if I could only prove my theory, Joe, I'd be the happiest man in the universe."

"Well, it doesn't sound too far-fetched to me, Doc. I mean, after all, sharks are probably no less intelligent than some land animals. Maybe we just haven't been studying them in the right manner."

"Ha, ha, and just what is the right manner, Joe? I've done just about everything conceivable, and I still can't get the desired results. I even fashioned a darn good and sophisticated response-reward mechanism about eight years ago with a hammerhead, a blue, and three makos."

"Oh, yeah? What happened?"

"Well, aside from one of the attendants who was helping me damn near losing his life when he accidentally slipped into the pool, nothing."

"Even so," came Joe's reply as he stood up and walked over to the edge, "I think they're fascinating. Just because we don't understand them doesn't mean that they are without understanding. . . ."

"Profound! Absolutely profound, my boy!" said the old man as he also approached the edge of the pool. "Now if we could just program those guys in there, we'd be all right, huh?"

The intended humor was lost on Joe, because he appeared to be wrapped in deeper thoughts. Dr. Compton, placing his arm around Joe's shoulder as the two of them stood there, continued, "I've applied to the National Geographic Society for a substantial funding of my next shark project. Think you'd be interested in working with me?"

Without so much as a smile, Talanski looked into the wrinkled face and replied, "For some strange reason, Dr. Compton, nothing would give me greater pleasure."

2

Joe had given up trying to contact his former comrade-in-arms, Paco Sanchez. He wasn't listed in the telephone book, and that original address drew nothing but a blank. Besides, Talanski's involvement in the many after-work hours spent helping Dr. Compton set up various shark experiments dominated his interest.

It was well past eleven o'clock on a rainy night in October when Joe mounted the stairs to his third-floor efficiency apartment. As usual, the stairwell and hallway were shadowy dim. Just as he was about to unlock his door, a dark form suddenly appeared. Talanski wasn't alarmed, because the building housed all kinds of weirdos. However when the dark form moved closer, he became suspicious, causing his muscles to become tense and ready to unleash.

"Hey, Jose. Joe Talanski," whispered the form. "It's me, Paco. Paco Sanchez. Let's not talk here in the hall, man (cough)."

"Well, I'll be damned!" Joe exclaimed upon recognizing his old Army buddy. "You were the whole reason why I came to Miami months ago, and I'm just now hooking up with you! Damn, it's good seeing you again, Paco!"

The two former green berets clasped hands and hugged.

"Shh, not so loud, *amigo*. Let's go inside before the goons who were following (cough) me pick up my trail again."

No doubt about it, one-time robust and handsome Paco Sanchez had gone through some terrible changes. Joe could hardly believe his eyes. The once-dashing Cuban was practically skin and bones.

"My god, Paco, what the hell happened to you? You stop eating or something?"

"No, Jose," came the immediate answer as the two sat down over a pint of cheap rye at the kitchen table. "But you might say I'm on a (cough) low-Pepsi/high-Coke diet."

"You sound bad, Paco, and where the hell did you get that cough?"

"Same place I got a lot of other stuff that's giving me problems, man."

By then, Joe sensed the need for his becoming less talkative and more of a listener, because Paco was nervously moving in his seat.

After the friends briefly recounted some of the good times that they had together in the service, they became sad upon mentioning the special mission to Vietnam prior to the outbreak of declared hostilities.

"Believe it or not, Jose, I always think about those good and bad months that you, me, and Fred went through over there in Nam. Shit, we were fighting a goddamn war while Washington was trying to decide whether to come in, right, bro?"

"Yeah, that's for sure," said Joe, "but at least some of us were lucky."

Talanski's eyes suddenly became watery as he poured more whiskey into both glasses and continued talking.

"A toast, *amigo!* Here's to Fred Blueswicz, one of the best pals a guy could ever have. God bless."

"Vaya con dios."

Both glasses were drained of their contents.

"Incidentally, *amigo,*" Paco continued, "I sort of lost track of you after you got us off that hill in Tay Ninh Province. Where did they send you, man?"

The question burned like a white-hot poker jammed into Joe's ear. Not since during his stint as a psychiatric patient in the hospital at Fort Campbell did he have to give an oral recount of the carnage that took place at the whorehouse in Phu Cuong. And he was not about to regurgitate that now. The army shrinks, plus therapy, were successful in helping him to be able to deal with himself. No way was he going to let any exhumation of the nightmares and other thoughts drive him back into mental chaos. Therefore, Joe answered his friend's question with the lie, "Hell, man, they gave me a soft job teaching weaponry to recruits at Fort Dix. Did that 'til I was discharged in July '65."

The two comrades continued talking about light and humorous things for nearly an hour when all updating was completed. Then it was Sanchez who finally got down to the real reason why he had suddenly appeared on his friend's doorstep."

"I need your help, Joe."

"What kind of trouble are you in? And, Paco, hey, don't hold out on any information that I might need to know. Just keep in mind you're talking to me, Joe Talanski—with you all the way."

"I knew I could count on you," said Sanchez as he reached across the table and squeezed his friend's hand. "Remember when we used to get drunk and I would always cry while boring you guys about how miserable it was for all of us poor people down in the *barrio?*"

"You weren't boring us."

"The hell I wasn't, bro! Ha, ha, no way could anybody listen to the same stories one binge after another and not get bored. Hey, but that's all right now, because I got my hands on some stuff that could lift half of Miami out of poverty for the next million years, man."

"What are you talking about, Paco? Did some of that agent orange get into your booze?"

"Joe, baby, now I know I used to do a lot of kidding around, but this time I'm as serious as a goddamn coronary, man!"

"Okay, good buddy, you have my undivided attention."

After lighting another cigarette, Talanski's friend continued, "I got a tiger by the tail, Joe. Lemme explain. When I came home from the Army a couple of years ago, I hooked up with the Trailblazer."

"Trailblazer?" chuckled Joe.

"Yeah. You probably haven't heard of this dude. He took over his uncle's business, so to speak. Anyhow, the Trailblazer runs coke and grass from here express to the Big Apple and the Windy City. Nothing but best motors and tires on the cars, man. Guys 'n gals are placed in designated motels along the routes. It's like the goddamn Pony Express, man, high-speed driving all the way. We get stuff from seaplanes that land three miles outside the inner harbor reef and bring it in by motorboat. Well, to make a long story short, I've been raking in some good bread—sometimes over ten grand a month when I'm hot for the road."

"So you're into the narcotics club, Paco, which doesn't surprise me."

"Hey, man, everybody's into something, even the cops. Remember back when you first came to Miami and you were in my old neighorhood looking for me? Well, how the hell do you think I found out about it? The two cops that talked to you that day also work for the Trailblazer. They're just a few of many who are hired to serve as watchdogs on runners like me."

Joe was mildly surprised but not overwhelmed, because the drug market was extensive throughout the area. "So what does all of this high-powered money-making have to do with me, Paco?"

Upon hearing this question, the Cuban quickly moved his chair closer to the table and leaned forward as though he did not intend for even the ghosts of past tenants to hear what he was about to say. "Six months ago, one of the seaplanes ran into some rough weather and couldn't land. The water was too choppy. At the same time, the damn thing must've developed engine trouble. The other guys and me were in the boat waiting for it to land so we could get the bales.

"When the motor started sputtering, the pilot must've decided that he didn't want to chance coming in so he turned on both spotlights as he circled. This gave us three guys in the boat a chance to see where the drop was going to be made. I'm telling you, Joe, that was no night for any second guessing about those high waves. I thought we'd be swamped for sure. As soon as the plane dropped the four bales, it gunned for altitude and headed south."

During his friend's long explanation, Talanski was becoming impatient. "So what happened, Paco?"

"Wait, man, this gets hairy now," the Cuban responded as he poured himself another drink. "While Ramon was trying to snag one of the bales with a gaffing hook, a goddamn wave hit us broadside and swept him overboard. Right away, I grabbed the life ring to throw to him. Instead of the other guy helping me to pull in the poor bastard, he jumped in to try to save Ramon. It was black as pitch out there, bro, and I wasn't about to leave the boat! Anyway, both of 'em disappeared, man. Not even a damn scream could be heard over the howling wind.

"Somehow, I managed to pull in three of the bales. One was split. I checked it, expecting to find the usual combination containers, some marijuana and some coke. All of those waterproofed packs held six kilos apiece of pure cocaine, man! I mean the real stuff!"

"So what was so alarming about that? If you chose to make some fast money in the drug world, my friend, then nothing should surprise you, not even when everything goes wrong."

"Hey, Joe, tonight's the first time I'm seeing you in three years. Let's not turn this meeting into a frigging lecture, okay? I know what the odds are against me getting retirement benefits in this job. And that's exactly why I'm coming to you. I need your help, because you're the only person I feel I can trust at this point."

"Whoa, hold on, Paco! Look, I'm not getting myself involved in this narcotics crap! My life, so far, has been one helluva mess. Everything I've tried to do always seems to come out wrong. You were there with me on that hill in Nam, right?"

Talanski's own words were causing him to become upset. Now that he had begun talking about himself, he could not stop.

"Well, the way I was treated by top brass after we were rescued, you'd think I was responsible for almost starting World War Three! Then there was the bloodbath I got into at that whorehouse! I mean who the fuck could have worse luck than Joe Talanski? And now you come in here talking about some dope stuff? No thanks, pal, I don't need any part of it."

Upon hearing this Sanchez realized that he would have to tell his friend everything surrounding the deal if he expected any kind of help to be forthcoming.

"Joe, all my life I've been in and out of trouble. Sometimes I started it, just to break the boredom. There was nothing between heaven and earth I feared, man. But that was when I had only myself to think about. Now, I got Dulcina, my girlfriend, and her three kids. *Amigo,* I really love this woman, and I'd marry her right now. Only, she's still married to Juan Pelones in Cuba. And we don't know if he's still living. You see, he was mixed up in a plot to knock off Castro's Minister of Agriculture, but when word leaked out, Pelones and others were rounded up and sent to prison. Luckily enough, he was able to secure secret passage to Miami for Dulcina and the children. All of this happened before I met her two years ago."

Joe was silently taking all of this in while at the same time trying to figure out what part did his former green beret comrade want him to play in the matter. Finally, not being able to hold off talking

126

any longer, he asked Paco, "How can I help you in this matter? Before you answer that, let me tell you that I don't have any money."

"Money? Shit, that's the least of my worries," Sanchez replied as he got up and pulled back a portion of the drawn window shade so that he could see if anybody was standing across the street. "What I'm *really* worried about is whether I'll be able to swing a big deal before I'm taken out."

"What do you mean *taken out*, Paco?"

"Well, man, I guess I should tell you this, because, right now, there ain't nobody else I can trust. Like I said, the other two guys drowned. Wasn't nothing I could do for them, man, so I headed back to port.

"Just before rounding the jetty to come into the cove, I saw all these goddamn red lights flashing on the shoreline. Right away, I knew something had gone wrong, so I whipped the motorboat around and headed down the coast to a secret place I've known for years. Later on, I found out that the Trailblazer and others were busted by the Miami vice squad. Somebody had tipped them off, man."

Joe was confused, so he said, "Thought you told me that this Trailblazer dude had the cops in his pocket."

"He does, man, but not the whole friggin' department! However, I did manage to get word to a guy, and he told me to hold all information until someone contacted me. Up to that point, I hadn't explained what happened. Two weeks later, Trailblazer's second-in-command called me. Naturally, I'm thinking three bales, which I had stashed away so well that even the best dogs in any town's K-9 unit would have a helluva time trying to sniff 'em out.

"Madame Fortune must be finally in my corner, Joe, because, while I was riding in the car with the two dudes that came to get me, I learned a couple of things: the plane crashed that night, no survivors; everyone assumed that the bales were destroyed also."

"Excuse me for interrupting you, Paco, but I notice you're not giving me names that . . ."

"Joe, believe me, you don't want to know any names. This crap's heavy, man, and I wish I didn't know any either. As I was saying, that whole night's operation was written off—four bales of pure cocaine, man. We're talking big bucks, *amigo*—like close to three and a half million, street value!"

Talanski almost choked on the drink. His head began to spin like a top. Three and a half million dollars was a sum too astronomical for his mind to internalize. However, he managed to say, "Paco, if you're planning to rip off your group, you'd better damn well know what the hell you're doing every step of the way!"

"It's already done, man."

"What?"

"I said I did it—sold the three bales to a contact over in New Orleans for cash. Made out fairly well on the deal, *amigo*, considering that I had to make sure no connections could foul me up. Anyway, I got eight hundred thousand, and, if I start spending it, I'm freezer meat, Joey!"

"What do you mean? Thought you said everybody assumed that the bales were lost?"

"Well, not exactly, because those two crooked cops have been shadowing my every friggin' move for months now. I'm sure you remember the time when you were questioned by the police in my old neighborhood. Yeah, well those creeps are always sniffin' around, and they certainly ain't doing it for Metro-Dade, you know?"

"So what you're telling me, Paco, is that you've got this money stashed somewhere other than in several banks, right?"

"Yeah, that's true, but it's not because I don't trust banks, *amigo*. It's just that I got this gut-level feeling I'm being set up for a hit and I'm afraid it might come before I can funnel some cash to people who're very important to me.

"You know, it's funny, Joe. When I was in the army, I didn't give a damn about anything; nothing moved me to worry beyond the next meal. But that was before I found a good woman, Joe. What I really want to do is take Dulcina and the kids to Argentina. I figure I can start a new life down there and live comfortably.

"I don't know what it is, *amigo*, but this is one woman I really love! You have to meet her. How can I put it? Remember how broad-crazy I was in the Army? Well, I'll tell you something, Joe, and this is the honest-to-God truth. For over a year now, I haven't touched or dated any other woman besides Dulcina Pelones. She's my whole world, Joe—I mean the whole ball of wax."

It was almost two A.M. when Talanski's comrade-in-arms finally wound down. Paco left out no superlatives in describing how great

128

Joe was and how the two of them together could team up and get around the various obstacles that stood between them and over three-quarters of a million dollars in cash. Yes, Paco was sincerely willing to give Joe a hundred and fifty thousand.

"All I want you to do is shadow the bastards who're shadowing me, because I have a feeling, Joe, that they're getting ready to do something that's not going to be in my best interest. In other words, *amigo*, I'm asking you to please help me to stay alive."

Undoubtedly, Talanski was moved by the apparent dependency that his friend showed. Quick memory flashes of times gone by passed through Joe's mind, three buddies sharing fun and hardship. He reached across the table for Paco's hand as he said, "I couldn't do a helluva lot for Fred when that chopper exploded, but I'm going to do my best to keep you safe, Paco. And if it's in the cards that we both cash in our chips together, then so be it."

In a way, Joe could hardly believe that such a statement had come out of his mouth. Granted, he still felt pain in his heart every time a memory of Fred Blueswicz flashed across his mind. But to go all out with reckless abandon? Perhaps Joe was just plain tired of losing the people whom he loved and cared about. At any rate, he did intend to put forth maximum effort in keeping Paco Sanchez among the living.

Eleven

Naked Trust

1

The two well-dressed Latinos who were standing near the doorway of Club Tropicana looked rather awesome, even though they were smiling and exchanging pleasantries with patrons who were pulling up in flashy, late-model cars. The hot afternoon sun had already disappeared below the tiled rooftops of Little Havana's apartment houses, and a cool evening breeze was beginning to blow gently across the faces of the many people that were sitting on their stoops while watching the birth of another multi-colored neon night on the strip.

When one of the two men saw a particularly beautiful woman step out of a cab, he said something to his partner, and both of them quickly escorted her through the club's side entrance. Disco music with a smooth Latin rhythm surrounded the woman and her escorts as they made their way through the dancing crowd that seemed to change colors to the pulsating *salsa* beat of sound-coordinated disco lights. The trio ascended a short stairway at the end of a hall that led to a more remote part of the club. Modern art done in bright pastels lined the walls on both sides of the heavily carpeted floor.

"Please wait here, señora," said one of the men as he showed her to a small room. "I'll let Mr. Corazon know you're here."

Luis Corazon, owner of the disco club and wearing a very expensive white raw silk suit, was sitting behind the heavy Mediterranean desk smoking a freshly lit Cuban cigar. Although he was only thirty-one, Corazon was rich. His business ventures started paying off for him when he was only twenty-five, and a constant stream of millions of dollars flowed through his hands. However, Luis always focused attention on business first and pleasure last. This is why he was so eager to meet and talk with the beautiful woman who was waiting outside the office door.

"She's here, Mr. Corazon."

"Good, show her in," the suave owner said as he motioned for the three men, with whom he was previously conversing, to leave his office via another door. No one seemed to mind the abrupt ending and exiting. Perhaps it was because the three plainclothes policemen did not want anyone to connect them with Luis Corazon, one of Miami's biggest drug dealers.

As the lawmen approached their car, which was parked in a narrow alleyway, one of them commented, "You know that young punk is getting too big for his britches; I don't think I can stomach much more of his fucking arrogance."

"Hey, Jeff, don't rock the boat, will ya?" replied Officer Bill Noonan. "As long as he's willing to pay, what the hell are you complaining about? Besides, where else can you pick up a grand a week for just looking the other way? Come on, fella, let's face it, you never had it so good."

"I have to agree with Jeff, Bill," said the third officer. "The Trailblazer's getting too. . . ."

"Wow!" Noonan interrupted. "Don't let that little prick hear you call him *Trailblazer*. He's come up in the world, and he wants to be considered a regular businessman, ha, ha, ha. Can you picture that? Now, he wants everybody to address him as *Mr.* Corazon."

Bill Noonan, Steve Lindscott, and Jeff Saunders represented the Trailblazer's direct pipeline into city hall. And, for the past seven months, he had been expanding his informational network among some of the inner harbor police. The money output was very high, but Corazon considered the investment a worthwhile one, especially since his operations were pretty much free of police interference.

However, Luis Corazon's dislike for losing anything drove him to keep his secret informers working overtime to find out more about the air shipment that was supposed to have been lost during the storm. Certain sources, after checking and shadowing, suggested that Trailblazer talk to a Mrs. Dulcina Pelones.

When Corazon's eyes took in the statuesque form of the woman who was ushered into his office, he immediately stood up and came from behind his desk to greet her.

"Ah, Señora Pelones, it is a pleasure for me to see that the telephone voice truly belongs to such a lovely lady. Please permit me to kiss your hand."

This gesture did very little to assuage the woman's inner fear, because, although she had not known of the man standing in front of her prior to the day before, Dulcina Pelones had been visited by the same two well-dressed men who met her at the club's entrance. It seemed that Trailblazer was told that Paco Sanchez's ladyfriend was a political refugee who might know something about the *cache*. Instead of confronting the situation head on, as he would've done in his grubbing days, Corazon chose to do a little research into the beautiful lady's background so as to build a firm foundation on which he might approach her on the basis of mutual trust—that is, if he could hold down his usually uncontrollable bad temper.

After the waiter had brought in two tall, frothy, piña coladas, Corazon opened the real conversation with, "Señora Pelones, I believe that you and I can be of valuable service to each other. It is no secret that your friend, Paco Sanchez, works for me. However, what does *appear* to be a secret is the whereabouts of my personal property which he was supposed to deliver to me."

Over a rather brief period of time, Paco's love for Dulcina had grown tremendously. There was something special about this woman that the former romancing green beret had not seen in others. Undoubtedly, he wanted to marry her, in spite of the fact that, although they were lovers, Dulcina had told him repeatedly that she still loved her imprisoned husband. Nevertheless, Paco was relentless in his pursuit of consummating their relationship in matrimony. Perhaps this is why he had revealed to Dulcina his grandiose plans of buying Señor Pelones's freedom through certain Cuban officials who were very close to Fidel Castro. Paco had also revealed to Dulcina the story concerning his drug deal. So, when the Trailblazer made his opening statement, Dulcina knew perfectly well the surrounding circumstances, yet she tried to avoid implication.

"I'm not sure that I understand what you're talking about, Señor Corazon. What does Paco's business life have to do with me?"

"Life," replied the Trailblazer. "Now there's the whole thing in a nutshell. It's funny you should mention the word *life*, because that's what I'm talking about here.

"Look, I'm not gonna play games with you, lady! The fact of the matter is you and that goddamn Sanchez have ripped me off, and I don't like it! Now either you get him to deliver my property to me or all of you—I'm talking kids, too—are gonna be fish food, *comprende?*"

The sudden change in atmosphere was not surprising to the frightened woman. She was all alone at this time, because she chose not to tell Paco of the visitors or her arranged visit to Club Tropicana. Perhaps that was a big mistake, because now she felt weak and helpless, especially since her kids' lives were also being threatened.

"Please, Mr. Corazon, don't hurt my children," pleaded the woman as she began to cry. "They should not have to suffer because of my mistakes."

Luis, realizing that he had struck paydirt, wanted to make sure that he would get Mrs. Pelones's full cooperation. Therefore, he added, "Lady, we're not just talking kids here; we're including your husband, too. You see, I happen to have direct contact with certain officials in Cuba who would make sure that he meets with a fatal accident when . . ."

"Oh, please, please, Mr. Corazon. I'll do anything you want!"

"Good," a smiling Luis replied as he offered the sobbing woman a pure silk handkerchief that he took from his pocket, "because full cooperation is what I must have from you starting right now. And, Mrs. Pelones, under no circumstances do I want you to breathe a word of this to your boyfriend. Just find out from him two things: where the rest of my property's at and the amount of bread he has stashed. Okay?"

"But I do not have any idea, Mr. Corazon, where . . ."

Luis clinched his teeth as he reached out and covered the frightened woman's mouth. "Shh . . . don't even say it. Just do whatever you have to do to find out the information I asked you for. Got that? I expect to see you again within forty-eight hours. Don't bother to call or come here. We'll be in touch."

By the time Dulcina left the disco club, she was a petrified woman who was thoroughly convinced that this man would definitely destroy the entire family. Unfortunately for Paco, he was the least of her worries.

2

As the pale moonlight bathed the two nude bodies that lay perspiring on the already-soaked sheets, silence dominated the small motel room while the couple relaxed after making love. A few minutes later, the man remarked, "I hate myself for lowering you to this rotten level I'm on, Dulcina. You deserve much more respect than this."

"But you *do* show me respect, Paco. How could I possibly ask for more of anything from you?"

"That's just it, my darling," he replied. "You are too contented with me. But, at the same time, you refuse to be my wife."

"Paco, we've gone over all this before. You know I can't marry you, or anyone else, while my husband is still suffering in prison."

"I know, Dulcina. It's just that I love you so much. I'd lay down my very life for you! And I'm at the point now where I don't give a damn who knows it! I love you, *cara mia!* What do you want from me? Just name it and it's yours. What, money? I'll give you everyth . . ."

Smack!! Before she even had time to think about her instant reaction, Dulcina slapped Paco across the face. The movement totally surprised him, because she hadn't done that before. And what surprised our lamenting suitor even more was the follow-up kiss that Dulcina gave him.

Sanchez couldn't help but make the comment, "I wish you'd decide if you want to kill me or kiss me."

"Oh, Paco, don't joke around like that, please!"

"I'm not joking, baby, because you're the most important person in the world to me. Whatever makes you happy, Dulcina, is what I want to do for you. And I don't care if my love for you is making me act stupid these days. I really don't care. As long as you just let me stay around you, I'm satisfied."

Dulcina began to cry while her lover continued speaking words of persistence and affirmation. Then she just couldn't hold back any longer; she had to tell Paco about her visit with Luis Corazon.

While his sweetheart talked, Sanchez was listening and thinking intently. He knew that if there ever was a time when he needed to call upon his survival skills it was then. But things were a lot more complicated. The safety of his girlfriend and her children loomed foremost in Paco's mind. He knew that the Trailblazer wouldn't think twice about carrying out his threats. There were enough assault and homicide cases in the *barrio* to give valid reasons for fear.

As soon as Paco saw Dulcina safely into her apartment, he left in a rush. Time was a big factor, especially since less than twenty-four hours remained. The ex-G.I. drove in a circuitous route, since he did not want to take the chance of being followed by Corazon's men or certain members of the Metro-Dade Police Department. When he was satisfied, Sanchez went to the apartment of the one person in whom he had the most trust.

3

Knock, knock, knock!

"Okay, okay, I'm coming," came the voice from within. The sleepy occupant finally arrived a the door.

"Quick, close the door, *amigo!*"Sanchez exclaimed as he quickly brushed by the somewhat confused man.

"Holy shit, Paco! This is getting to be a goddamn habit! I mean, twice now you've come to see me, and both times it's like cloak 'n dagger! What the hell's happening?"

"Sorry to have to barge in on you, Joe, but I need your help right now! The Trailblazer is on to me, man!"

"Okay," Talanski replied as he sat down at the small kitchen table, "so he's on to you—so what? All you have to do is leave the area."

After nervously lighting a cigarette, Sanchez said, "It's not that easy now, man. He's thrown my girl and her kids into the crap also. No, *amigo*, I can't run under these circumstances. Look, I don't care about myself at this point. But I'm not going to let anything happen to my lady!"

Joe could see that his Army buddy was beginning to unravel; therefore, after calming him down, the two comrades began analyzing the problem.

"Okay, you say you have money, but all of the cocaine is gone, right?"

"Yeah, I got only a few kilos of marijuana left, but I don't know if that'll help. Trailblazer is basically a ruthless rat. He'd probably

135

have us blown away anyhow if for no other reason than to let this serve as a warning to any of his other drivers who might have ideas about ripping him off."

"From what you tell me, Paco, you have to make a run for it tonight."

"But . . . "

"But, hell, man! You do have a choice! Either get Dulcina and the kids out of Miami tonight, or stay around for a mass wasting of all of you! It's now or never, Paco."

"You're right, but what about Dulcina's husband?"

"Look, whether or not the Trailblazer has that kind of influence you don't really know. But any way you turn the coin, you're the loser if you stay here. Incidentally, you *do* have enough money to get out of the country, don't you?"

"Oh sure, *amigo*, Money is the least of my worries. What I have in the bank, I'll let stay. I'm not taking any chances on being spotted by Corazon's men. They've been watching my pad ever since he got wind that the bales might've been saved.

"Anyway, my sister has access to the money I have in a couple of savings accounts. She and the rest of my relatives can fight over that—maybe close to sixty thousand, man."

"Phew," Talanski uttered while shaking his head. "And I went to college for a few years—didn't pay off. Gave my country the best that I had to offer—wasn't good enough. Tried to box—never made any real money. Ha, ha, I'll tell you, Paco, Madame Good Fortune has definitely not smiled on this kid since the day he was born! And you talk about sixty grand being nothing? Well, to me, old buddy, it's, ha ha, something to only dream about, you know?"

"Hey, don't be too hard on yourself, *amigo*," Sanchez said as he got up to use the telephone, "there's one damn thing I know: if it hadn't been for your quick thinking and guts, I would've come out of Nam in a fucking body bag. So don't try to sell yourself short to me, man, because I *know* what kind of heart you have.

"I'm gonna call Dulcina and tell her to get the kids ready. We're getting out of town before sunrise."

"Now you're talking sense," Joe replied, slapping his friend on the shoulder. "I'll be dressed in five minutes; we don't have any time to waste."

"We? No, pal, I can't let you get involved in this thing. You have to stay here after I split, because that bastard would off you in a minute!"

"Go on, make your call, and stop worrying about me, will ya? Tim Flaherty's grandson may not be worth a damn, but he's a survivor, okay?"

Sanchez smilingly took a moment, and then he said, "Okay, you stubborn *gringo.*"

After calling Dulcina, Paco lit another cigarette, sat down again at the kitchen table, and began thinking about some of the things that Joe had said. He was deep in thought when Talanski reappeared and nudged him.

"All right, let's move out, soldier! We don't have that much darkness left."

"Damn, Joe, you're still a beret at heart, right?"

"Wrong. Make sure that butt's out. Don't want this roach kingdom to go up in smoke; although, ha ha, that would probably be a positive step toward urban renewal."

"Excuse me, man," Paco said, just as they were leaving the apartment, "but I have to go to the john—must be nervous tension."

"Hurry up. Every second counts."

While in the bathroom, Sanchez took several envelopes that he had and hurriedly stuffed them into an old brown paper bag. He then shoved the bag under the tub. Although Paco did not use the toilet, he flushed it and came out.

"Okay, I'm ready now, *amigo.*"

The two former comrades-in-arms cautiously made their way through the Miami streets, making sure to avoid driving on main thoroughfares. Fifteen minutes after leaving Joe's apartment, the friends arrived at the wharf where Paco was to rendezvous with Dulcina and the kids. Since his adopted family had not yet appeared, Sanchez filled in the time by again reviewing the plans with his buddy.

"When we get set up in a place in Rio, I'll contact you. Probably won't be for about a month, man, because those tramp steamers sail like they ain't never in a hurry."

"No problem, Paco. As long as I know that you're safe, then I'm satisfied."

Through various sources and the paying out of over forty thousand dollars in cold cash, Sanchez, within just a few hours after finding out about the Trailblazer's meeting with Dulcina, had made arrangements for them to get out of the country. Specifically, the group was supposed to travel by motorboat to certain map coordinates fourteen miles southeast of Miami. There, a ship was to be waiting to pick up Sanchez and family.

Knock, knock, knock!

"Are you sure you can trust this guy?" asked Joe as they waited for someone to answer the door of the shabby little fish and bait shop.

"Well, Ramon's not exactly the Pope but we've done a few things together that tell me he's okay," Sanchez replied, just as a dim light flicked on.

When the door opened and the shopkeeper saw Paco's friend, he said in Spanish, *"Quien es el gringo, hombre? Usted sabe que . . . "*

"He's my blood friend, man. And, don't worry, he can be trusted," Sanchez said while quickly stepping inside. "Joe, I want you to meet Ramon Garanza. Oh, and, Ramon, keep it in English."

The three men, after going over last-minute details, were about to drink some more beer when they heard a car drive up just outside the door.

"That must be Dulcina," Paco exclaimed, jumping from the table and rushing to the door. When he opened it, he immediately noticed the frozen look on her face, but what he didn't notice was the gun that was trained on her back from the taxicab.

The Trailblazer, not trusting the nervous woman who had left his office, decided to have her apartment secretly watched around the clock. And when a taxi brought Dulcina home at two A.M., the watcher called his boss. Of course, the Trailblazer decided to close in. He sent three of his men to collect Dulcina, the children, and Sanchez. However our crafty friend was not on the scene, because he was at Talanski's apartment.

"You'll have to help me with my little one," said Dulcina. "He fell asleep on the way here, and I can't lift him out of the cab."

"No problem, sweetheart. I'll get him. Hey, Joe, give me a hand with the kids 'n luggage, will ya? Damn cab drivers get paid to sit on their asses."

138

Sanchez and Talanski had no sooner approached the cab when the driver pulled a .357 magnum on them and snarled, "All right, you two yo-yos, get face down on the ground! Hurry up!"

"Oh, shit!" exclaimed Paco upon recognizing the cabbie as one of his relief drivers on several cocaine runs. "Frank, don't tell me you're gonna do me in!"

"Sorry, man, but it's nothing personal," Frank Claymont responded. "I'm just followin' instructions. I ain't got nothin' against you, Paco, but, if you move, I'll blow your fuckin' head off, *comprende?*"

Ramon, after taking a few minutes to size up the situation, made his decision and yelled to the gunman from inside the bait shack. "Hey, chief, you want me to help you? Can I call somebody?"

"No, that's all right. The other guys should be getting here in about another five minutes or so. Say, on second thought, why don't you come on out here, and maybe you can help me watch these people."

"Great," came Ramon's reply as he approached the group. "Mr. Corazon should be pretty happy about this. I took a big chance in stalling these guys until you got here."

Paco could hardly believe his ears, and it didn't take long for his anger to push him into action. He sprang up from the ground and lunged for the surprised gunman. Everything happened quickly, but Joe's reaction was right on time. He also lunged for the gunman who managed to get off only one shot, which struck Sanchez in the stomach. Before Claymont could get off another blast, Talanski knocked him cold with a hard right to the chin. In the meantime, Ramon was truly caught between a rock and a hard place, so he took off running down the wharf. However, he only got thirty yards away when a fatal thud hit him between the shoulder blades. Sanchez, although near death himself, had mustered enough anger and strength to pick up the fallen revolver and take the ultimate revenge against such betrayal.

"Come on (cough, cough), *amigo,*" gasped Paco while struggling to stand up, "help me get (cough) Dulcina and the kids down to (cough) dockside."

"You're bleeding pretty bad, Paco," Joe replied. "I gotta get you to a hospital right now!"

The wounded man insisted that he was strong enough to travel and that there was no time to do anything else but get out of Miami.

Through all of this, Dulcina remained very calm. She did not show any outward signs of cracking under the strain. This bothered Talanski, but everything had happened too fast for him to figure things out. However, when Dulcina all but refused to go, plus suggested that they call an ambulance to come to the wharf, Joe became highly suspicious.

"I don't think it's a good idea to move you, my darling," Dulcina said as she bent over her lover. "I'm going to go inside and call the emergency squad. Here, hold his head up, Joe. I'll be right back."

Talanski didn't bother to reply, because the pieces of this puzzle were beginning to fit into place, and he did not like the picture that was certainly taking form. Besides, Paco had passed out because of heavy blood loss. Joe knew he had to move fast if he was going to save his former comrade-in-arms.

As soon as Dulcina heard the crank up, she ran out of the bait shack, yelling to Joe, "Wait! Where're you going with my children? Stop!"

"Come on, Dulcina, if you want to go," he shouted as he began pulling off. "I have to get Paco to some hospital right now! No time to wait around for an ambulance! Get in the back, and keep that shirt balled up and pressed hard against his stomach! Maybe it'll slow down the bleeding!"

Not more than five minutes after the taxi had disappeared around the corner into the morning mist, a big black Lincoln screeched to a halt in front of the bait shack.

"Holy shit!" exclaimed one of the three passengers, "Trailblazer's gonna have our heads! We shoulda gotten here sooner! Now how do we explain this?"

"We don't," replied the man in the back seat. "I tried to tell that fool not to get hung up on trying to nail Sanchez here in Miami. He's got a good operation going here, so why let pride cause unnecessary problems? All Trailblazer had to do was to send Sanchez on a run to Cleveland, or some other place far enough away from here, and have his outside contacts do three things: put the squeeze on Sanchez for information; get the coke or the bread; and then off the sonofabitch."

"Yeah, you're right, Al," said the driver, "because we don't need to draw attention to this, which brings to mind that Pelones broad. I tell you, getting mixed up in Cuban exile crap could blow the whole cover off our operation."

"Well, what do you think we should do about these guys?" asked one of the hoods that helped put the unconscious cab driver into the car.

The leader of the group responded. "We'll take Claymont and the stiff to Trailblazer, 'cause no way is he gonna believe what went down here. Hey, see what you guys can do about reviving Claymont, he's got a lot of explaining to do."

"Hurry up, nurse," shouted the small-framed Filipino doctor who was one of the few physicians on duty. "Get him ready for the O.R.! He has lost a lot of blood. I don't know if we can save him."

The corridor of the emergency area at St. Mary's Hospital was crowded with gurneys that contained groaning and semi-conscious victims of Miami's Saturday night. The nurses and doctors, mostly interns, really had their hands full. However, Joe refused to be polite and wait for the intake clerk to complete her paperwork.

"Look, lady, I don't give a damn about procedure! I'm going up with him! Are you coming, Dulcina?"

"Uh, oh, yes, Joe. I'm going, too."

After telling her children to stay in the lobby, Dulcina hurried as fast as she could behind the fleeting figure who did not bother to wait for the elevator.

While his semi-conscious buddy was being prepared for the operating room, Joe seized the opportunity to talk to Dulcina in the small waiting area. No one else was there, so he did not have to worry about being overheard. After getting a couple of coffees from the vending machine for himself and the woman, Joe sat down on the vinyl couch beside her and, in a low tone, asked, "Why did you do it?"

Dulcina, looking straight into the eyes of her lover's friend could tell that he was aware of what she had apparently done. Therefore, trying to fabricate a story would've served no believable purpose. Besides, Dulcina was sorry for what she had let happen on the wharf.

141

"I am not going to convince you, Joe, that I couldn't have prevented Paco from being shot. Yes, I could've prevented it—but only by sacrificing my children's lives—never mind my own. That man they call Trailblazer has a cold heart, and I'm sure he will try to do something terrible to me and my children. So, yes, I gave him information to save my family, but I didn't want to! Can't you see, Joe? I had no choice!"

Although Dulcina did not expect Talanski to agree with her, she felt relieved for having told him the truth. He continued to listen rather coldly to the distraught woman's explanations, but her plight did not seem important to him. Only the plight of his friend dominated Joe's thoughts.

A few minutes later, a doctor appeared in the doorway of the small waiting room.

"Are you Mr. Talanski?" asked the Filipino intern.

Joe's heart skipped a beat as he replied, "Yes. Have you started operating on Paco yet?"

"Ah, no, and I'm not sure that we can. The bullet caused extensive damage around Mr. Sanchez's vital areas, and . . . ."

"You mean he's dead?"

"No. We managed to stop the bleeding, but the crisis still exists. Right now, he's asking for you."

Dulcina also moved toward the room, but the physician suggested that only one at a time go in.

Seeing his friend in such terrible condition caused Joe to gulp heavily in trying to hold back impending tears. Tubes and various pieces of life-support mechanisms practically hid the bandaged patient.

As Joe quietly approached the bed, Paco's eyes slowly opened, and a faint smile quivered across his face while he struggled to say, "Joe, I'm (cough) afraid I really did it (cough) this time."

"Don't try to say too much right now, Paco. We can talk after you . . ."

"No, *amigo,* this hole (cough) in my gut's taking me out . . . I (cough) can feel it. Got to talk fast, 'cause they filled me (cough) with a lot of pain killers, man, and I . . . (cough) feel the sleep coming over me. But I have to . . . (cough) tell you . . . something before I go under."

Paco's voice was getting weaker, so Joe leaned over while holding his hand. "You old war horse, you'll be out of this place in no time. Just take it easy."

A tear trickled down the ailing man's cheek. His eyes widened momentarily as he seemed to be mustering his last bit of strength to make a final statement.

"I want . . . (cough) . . . I want you to promise me something, Joe."

"Sure, Paco, anything. Just say it."

"Look in the . . . (cough) . . . look in the lining of my jacket over there first (cough) and then I'll tell you what I want you (cough) to do."

Talanski was puzzled, but he quickly did his dying friend's bidding. The expensive green raw silk sports coat was completely lined with satin.

"Rip out the . . . (cough) rip out the inside. Hurry."

Upon doing this, Joe's heart practically stopped beating, because the coat started raining money.

"What the hell do you have here, Paco?"

"Never mind, man, just . . . (cough) make sure you get every . . . (cough) . . . every single bill."

The money, mostly in large denominations, totalled one hundred sixty thousand dollars. Sanchez had, in no time, originally planned to wait for a few days until he could transact a drug move that was supposed to net him another hundred or so thousand, but the plan went sour when word got back to the Trailblazer that one of his roadrunners was dealing in high finance.

Joe never considered himself to be a pillar of honesty, and he had some serious thoughts about keeping the money. After all, who was Paco Sanchez? This dying wretch, to whom nothing was valuable unless it could be measured in dollars and cents, had no more right to the money than anyone else. The thought occurred to Joe, and he was quickly leaning toward that direction. With this kind of money, he could set himself up in some kind of business in another state. A slight smile came over Talanski's face while he was standing at the window watching the morning sun spread a beauteous golden mantle over the eastern sky. A new day was dawning, and his thoughts of taking the money for himself were also dawning.

"Amigo," said Paco in a strained voice, "I'm . . . depen . . . depending on you to (cough) to take care of Dulcina for me."

"Take care of Dulcina?"

"You gotta understand, Joe, that I've been (cough) a scoundrel all my life. Big disappointment to just . . . (cough) just about everybody who ever cared anything for me. I left a trail of broken hearts halfway around the world."

Talanski didn't interrupt his friend's rambling, because he knew that the end was near. Not too many guys had gotten to be real close pals of Joe. His aloofness kept most casual acquaintances from further developing into bonded ties. Maybe it was because Talanski felt that every time he attached himself to someone real special, something tragic always happened. Joe could still see the bright orange explosion ball that snuffed out the life of his best friend over in Vietnam.

Paco continued, *"Amigo,* you have to understand that I love Dulcina with all . . . (cough) . . . with all my heart and soul. Yeah, yeah, I know she's still married to (cough) somebody else, but I don't care . . . especially now, man. I know I'm not gonna leave this . . . (cough) . . . hospital alive. . . ."

Tears began to flow from Paco's eyes, and his already-wispy voice became choked with emotion.

"I tell you, *amigo,* I don't know of three . . . (cough) . . . don't know three good things I did in my life. Been hitting schemes for years. Nobody in the *barrio* got a good word for Paco Sanchez . . . (cough) . . . and I can't blame 'em. But I love Dulcina, Joe, and you just got . . . (cough) . . . got to help me to save her and the kids. She's the only woman I've ever loved. Now ain't that a damn shame, *amigo?* I've had broads all over . . . (cough) . . . everywhere, but this is the only one who's ever meant anything to me, Joe. You know what I'm trying to say?"

Talanski, now filled with mixed feelings about keeping the money, just nodded his head affirmatively as he gently squeezed Paco's hand saying, "Yeah, good buddy, I understand and don't worry; everything's going to be all right."

"No, I bought it this time. My ticket's punched, Joe. I know . . . (cough) I can trust you to give the money to Dulcina."

"If . . ."

144

"No ifs, *amigo*. Damn it. I haven't lived like a . . . (cough) like a good man, but maybe I can . . . (cough) I can die like one. What d'ya think?"

"Paco, you're the greatest. And don't worry about Dulcina and the children. I'll see to it that they get the money and are also out of the Trailblazer's reach."

"You're a good man, Joe. I knew I . . . (cough) . . . I could count on you to bring us through—just like you did over in Nam."

If Talanski had any prior notion of telling his dying friend about the woman he loved, he abandoned the thought right there at the bedside. The gift of naked trust was offered to Talanski, and he could not refuse it.

Coughing spasms gripped Paco's torso like a vise. Joe called for help, and, within seconds, a team of doctors and nurses burst into the room. However, just before an injection was given, Sanchez whispered into his comrade's ear, "Look under tub in your bathroom. Keep it—I want you to have it. *Adios, amigo.*"

The sun-withered, little, elderly lady stepped cautiously out of the elevator. She was aided along by a skinny and poorly dressed lad of twelve. Although Joe did not know them, he felt compelled to speak.

"Excuse me, ma'am, but are you related to Paco Sanchez?" our hero asked.

When her eyes of eighty-one years met his, Joe knew the answer. Señora Flores was Paco's grandmother and the kid was his nephew, Tito.

"My grandmother she don't speak English," the boy quickly responded. "We come to see Uncle Paco. Is he hurt bad?"

Dulcina conferred with Mrs. Flores in Spanish, just as a nurse came to lead the boy and his grandmother to Paco's room. Although the little old lady had not previously met Dulcina, she knew of her from the many times that Paco had promised to bring the young woman to the house.

4

"What'll it be, pal?" asked the bartender.

"Double bourbon on the rocks," Joe responded.

His entering was not unnoticed. Lola, one of several prostitutes that frequented the Orchid Lounge, eased smoothly over the stool beside him.

"Hi," she said in a sultry voice. "My name's Lola. Mind if I sit here?"

If there ever was a time when Talanski needed someone to talk to, it was then. Not that he was looking for a holy confessor, but he did feel the overwhelming urge to unload on somebody.

"Uh, no, not at all," Joe responded his eyes quickly absorbed the beautiful blonde. "Are you alone?"

"Now, that's supposed to be part of my line," she smiled, "but I guess it's all right for a handsome fellow like you to use it."

Talanski lit the woman's cigarette while at the same time telling the bartender to give her whatever she was drinking. This posed no problem, because the owner of the club had long ago instructed his bartenders in how to treat and look out for the "ladies of the evening" who used the Orchid Lounge as a base of operations. In other words, the tall cocktail glass contained plain iced tea that had the appearance of scotch on the rocks.

After about ten minutes of small talk, Lola and Joe left the bar through a side exit that led them into a palm-tree-dotted courtyard, which was lined with gorgeous tropical plants and flowers all the way to the entrance of the motel's office.

"Just wait out here for a second, sugar, I'll be back with the key," Lola purred as she switched her fine frame.

Within those few moments that he was standing there looking at his reflection in the fountain, Joe thought about the whirlwind of events that had taken place in his life during the past six days, and he said, "Joe Talanski, you're the biggest fool in Florida."

Lola emerged, bouncing, from the office and led her latest "John" across the patio and up the wrought-iron steps to a room on the far end of the balcony. Within a matter of only a few minutes, the experienced prostitute had her customer undressed and in the undulating waterbed. However, things were moving too fast for Joe. He also wanted conversation and plenty of time for developing it.

"As you know, sugar, time is money in my profession, so if . . ."

"Five hundred for spending the rest of the night with me, Lola."

The offer was too tempting for her to refuse, especially when she thought about how much it would help toward paying her tuition at the University of Miami where she was a junior majoring in marine biology. Yes, Lola was doing financially well working out of the Orchid Lounge, and she managed to keep her job-related activities off the Coral Gables campus.

That double shot of bourbon made Joe want to talk instead of getting on with the business of the evening.

"The three of us were like brothers, and those guys really depended on me to keep them straight under all circumstances. I don't know why, but they trusted me. Now look at 'em, Lola; Fred got blown up in a freaking chopper over in Vietnam while I watched, and Paco was blown away right here in town while I watched. Seems as though that's been what I do best, watch the scenes while people close to me die. Hey, do you want to hear something funny? I used my head once—used it to butt a bastard down a flight of stairs. He had just blown my aunt away. Ha, ha, ha."

"Are you sure you're all right, sugar?" asked the nude figure who was lying next to him.

"Who, me? Sure, I'm okay," Joe replied while reaching for the whiskey bottle. "Don't you know nothing ever happens to me? Just the people I love get screwed up. Frankly, I don't think death gives a damn about this kid. The son of a bitch totally ignores me! Ha, ha, ha."

Lola was quite accustomed to listening to all kinds of tales coming from her "johns," but there was something indescribably different about this guy that fascinated her—and they had not yet sexually engaged. Two A.M. and Talanski was still talking; however, Lola found this one's trail of tales so fascinating that she eagerly followed it without becoming weary or bored. Three-fifteen. Joe was drunk, and he began to nod off while trying to maintain a clear line of thought.

"You've had too much to drink, sugar," Lola said as she gently ran her hand through his hair.

"I don't (hic) doubt that," he replied while slowly reaching for the bottle.

"No, no more. You're already four sheets into the wind," said Lola as she moved it out of reach.

Joe limply dropped back on the pillow and stated, "You're probably right. I (hic) I don't need any more of that. After all, I gotta (hic) stay awake. Know why?"

"No, sugar, and you don't have to explain it to me."

"I'll tell you why. Because (hic) because the last time I was (hic) was in bed with a prosti (hic) prostitute, the whole goddamn room was covered (hic) covered with blood."

"Covered with blood?" Lola excitedly ejected as she sat up with renewed interest.

Talanski wiped a tear from the corner of his eye and replied, "I didn't even know (hic) the kid's name. Couldn't have been no more (hic) no more than seventeen. The bastards broke through the door and started shooting. They killed her, poor kid. But don't you worry. I won't (hic) let anybody hurt you, Lola."

"Sure, sure. Now you just lie down here with me," she replied.

Within a few minutes after he laid his head on the pillow, Joe was sound asleep. Usually, Lola left her customers when they were unconscious, but, for some strange reason, she had no desire to do it this time. There was something strangely fascinating about the handsome body lying next to hers that made her feel like a starry-eyed, aroused teenager rather than the indifferent strictly-business pro that she was.

Several hours later, Lola was awakened by the fresh morning breeze that filled the room. Not feeling the warm body touching hers made her awaken fully and sit up with a start. It was gone. Five one hundred dollar bills were lying on the little night table.

Lola's experience included having been with men who, for a variety of reasons, did not consummate the sexual act. However, this was the first one that titillated her curiosity so greatly. She felt a strong urge to see him again. The throbbing desire was unabating as Lola hurriedly dressed. Why hurry? This guy, like all of the others, was probably not interested in carrying on a relationship that would go beyond the sack.

The freshness of the morning air mixed with the sweet fragrances of the courtyard's flowers made Lola feel terrific. She bounced lightly along the beautiful floral path to the office.

"Morning, Ed. And how is my favorite clerk?"

"Oh, good morning, Lola. Cal told me, when I relieved him at midnight, that you were up in 214. Interesting night, huh?"

"Well, I suppose I could honestly call it an interesting night. By the way, Ed, did you see the guy when he came out?"

"Yeah. He stopped in to ask about catching a cab to St. Christopher's."

"Oh? And what is that?" Lola asked as she peeled off two ten dollar bills to pay for the room.

"It's a little Catholic church over on the south side. Not exactly a well-to-do neighborhood either, mostly Latins. I was curious as hell why a white guy would be going over there, so I asked him. He said he was going to the funeral mass of a friend."

Upon hearing this, Lola did something that surprised even herself. She aimed her green Thunderbird convertible toward South Miami, with her destination being St. Christopher's.

5

"The Lord giveth, and the Lord taketh away," said the priest in Spanish as he made the sign of the cross over the closed casket. "Blessed be the name of the Lord."

A warm humid breeze caused the small cemetery's palm trees to sway gently, and most of the thirty-two mourners breathed deeply so as to get the full benefit from the fresh air. The tiny church, even in mid-morning, was very hot. And, when the brief service ended, everyone, even Father Gonzalez, was eager to get out to the adjoining cemetery.

When the simple gray casket was rolled past Talanski and into the fall sunlight, he inaudibly said, "*Adios,* Paco, you've really put me in one big helluva mess. I don't need this kind of trust to be laid on me."

The whirlwind of events that had taken place in Joe's life since his arrival in Florida made him wonder whether he would be able to endure the mental anguish that tore at his brain.

"Why did you have to depend on me to take care of these people?" Talanski thought as he looked at the saddened faces of the few mourners. "I don't need this kind of pressure, Paco. I got enough problems otherwise."

"Do you wish to drop your rose into the grave, my son?" the priest asked when he noticed that Talanski seemed to be deep in thought.

The two gravediggers, who were sitting beneath a tree while waiting for the service to end, were very interested in this particular funeral.

"I knew Paco was going to wind up like this one day. That *hombre* was always traveling in fast company. I'm surprised he lasted this long," the older man commented.

The younger man, shaking his head and getting up while leaning on his shovel, responded with, "For the money he was haulin' in, I guess he had to be dealing in narcotics. Understand he ripped off some drug dealer for a couple of hundred grand."

"Lotta good that's gonna do him now. Say, who's the lone *gringo* over there?"

"Damn, Pop, don't you know anything? He's probably a narco agent with the Miami Police Department. What other reason would a white dude come to this funeral if it's not for checking out the people?"

"I don't know, Julio, but all you youngsters better leave that dope alone, or you'll check out like Paco over there."

At the conclusion of the graveside service, Joe was approached by his late friend's grandmother and nephew.

"Mr. Talanski," Tito said quietly, "my grandmother she wants me to tell you again she is very grateful for the money you gave us from Uncle Paco."

After making quick glances around them, Joe replied, "That's all right, kid. Just remember what I told you the other day. Your Uncle Paco was pretty lucky in some of his stock market investments, and he wanted you and your grandmother to move out of the *barrio* and live comfortably. You do understand, don't you, Tito?"

"Sure, I understand, Mr. Talanski," said the youth. "I might be only twelve, but I understand more about Uncle Paco's business than what you think I know. Us kids in the neighborhood learn about everything fast. Don't worry. I know how to keep my mouth shut. I didn't even tell my cousins about the money, and I'm not going to either. Because the story might leak out and those men who shot my uncle would do the same to us."

Joe smiled. "You're a bright kid, Tito. And I have the feeling that you're going to see to it that you and your grandmother get some real worthwhile benefits from the money. Just remember—thirty thousand dollars can go a long way if you let it."

The grandmother, although not being able to speak English, could tell by the soft tone of Joe's voice that he was still deeply concerned about her and Tito's welfare. And, in Spanish, she smilingly spoke slowly so that Tito might translate each word correctly.

"You are a good man to give us this money, Mr. Talanski. I know that our Paco was getting into trouble, because he was making money too fast, and what he was doing was against the law. I don't know much about you, Mr. Talanski, but I do know you are honest and you have a heart of gold. Because if you wanted to keep the money for yourself, we could do nothing about it. Heaven will bless you. Go with God."

When Tito had finished translating his grandmother's words, Joe embraced both of them and left the cemetery.

6

At first, Talanski paid no attention to the green car that pulled alongside the curb where he was standing. But when a beautiful blonde honked the horn, Joe's reverie was interrupted.

"Hey, mister, do you need a lift?" asked the smiling lady behind the sunglasses.

Talanski immediately recognized her as being the gorgeous prostitute with whom he had spent the night.

"I know you didn't expect to see me again so soon, but . . ."

"Look, I paid you—left the money on the dresser. Didn't you get it?"

Now Lola was no prude by any stretch of the imagination, but to hear this new customer refer to their previous night's session in such a cold businesslike manner made her wince. And she couldn't explain it—no more than she could explain why she had trailed this guy afterward.

"Yes, I got the money; however . . ."

"I know I had too much to drink, but I also know we agreed on five hundred dollars, right?"

"Right. But I didn't come all the way down here to talk about money," she replied in a huffy tone. "Now are you going to get in the car, or are you afraid of me?"

Joe smiled as he slid in beside the gorgeous figure. "Umm, I hope this is not going to cost me a . . . "

"Hey, will you just shut the hell up about money? Maybe I shouldn't have come down here."

"Well, why did you?"

"You were such an interesting guy last night that . . . oh, I don't know . . . I just wanted to see you again. But, look, I'm making a perfect fool of myself—sorry. Perhaps you should just get out of the car. And I'm very sorry for causing you any kind of embarrassment."

Talanski continued to look puzzled. Why else would this prostitute go beyond herself to see him again if money wasn't the reason? Because he certainly didn't captivate her with his sexual prowess. Then it occurred to him that he may have caused her some kind of insult by not following through.

"You're not the one who should be sorry for my stupidity last night. I certainly was a jerk, and I hope you'll accept my apology. If you don't want to ever see my face again, Lola, I would understand, plus this . . . "

Impulsively, the woman quickly leaned over and kissed the babbling mouth of her passenger. Then she calmly said, "Suppose we stop this idle chit-chat and get you over to Ocean World. Aren't you working today?"

Joe looked only mildly surprised, because he assumed that he must have talked about his job along with a million other things, only a few of which he could recall.

As the green Thunderbird convertible zipped through traffic, Talanski admiringly noticed the ease with which Lola handled the car. Joe also noticed a couple of books and some note pads on the back seat. Picking up the book entitled *Plankton Forms*, he asked, "Do you read stuff like this?"

"Naturally, silly," replied the laughing driver. "How else would I expect to pass the course?"

"Pass . . . what . . . are you in school?"

By the time they arrived at the employees' entrance of Ocean World, Joe and Lola's conversation had covered bits and pieces of Penn State University and the University of Miami.

"Sure wish you had time to come in and meet Dr. Compton, Lola. He's really a down-to-earth guy."

"Maybe some other time when both of us are not so busy. Right now, I have to get home and go over some notes for a math exam. Why are you staring at me like that?"

"Oh, no special reason other than I'm just noticing how the color of your eyes perfectly match the color of the car—sea green."

"Now, if I were a teenager, Joe, I'd take you seriously," laughed Lola as she reached across her passenger and opened the door for him to get out. "But thank you anyway, even though, deep down inside, you probably wanted to say that my eyes match the color of money, right?"

"Damn, how could I be so stupid to forget you're a working girl with no time to waste on the likes of me unless I can come up with the bucks."

Joe then discerned the uneasiness that Lola reflected as she put the car in gear and smiled weakly.

"That's right, sugar," the prostitute replied. "If you don't have the green, don't cloud my scene."

The sports car's tires screeched when the driver negotiated a fast U-turn and sped out of the parking lot. She took one hand off the steering wheel and wiped away things that had begun to cloud her vision—tears.

Book II

One

Emergence of a Thinking Machine

1

Tremendously loud claps of thunder boomed, and streaks of lightning frequently stabbed the high waves as the hurricane gathered intensity in its rapid movement along the Northeastern coast. Cape Hatteras was barely touched, but, from Norfolk up through the mouth of Chesapeake Bay, the swells were almost twenty-five feet high. "Bertha" was only the second hurricane of the season, and already she was making her mark. However, the turbulence between the heavens and the ocean could almost be matched with the turbulence that was created below the surface. Murky currents were so heavy that even the strong swimmers were having difficulty in maintaining equilibrium. And, although the twenty-eight-foot great white shark was doing her best to stabilize her movements, she was still being tossed about like a piece of tumbling seaweed.

The pregnant leviathan tried to catch as many blue fish as she could under those conditions, but luck was not with her at all. The great white mother-to-be missed every single one. She had been in pursuit of this school of blues for almost three days, but her near-delivery condition hampered her from succeeding.

Several hours later, after the storm had veered out to sea off the coast of Atlantic City, the weakened and half-starved great white swam slowly in descending concentric circles as she sought anything that was edible. However, the increasing pain caused her to cease looking for food and concentrate on something more important—giving birth. At a depth of eighty feet, the great white began straining her bowels. The trail of blood attracted four mako sharks that happen to have been in the area. Under normal conditions, the makos would not have considered attacking the great white. But these were not normal conditions. The second pup was about three-quarters of the way out of its mother's womb when the largest (twelve

157

feet and over a thousand pounds) of the makos struck. In a churning mass of mangled meat, the pup was ripped and swallowed ravenously. The excruciating pain practically numbed the great white, but she mustered every ounce of her massive body to do battle. Fighting defensively was out of the ordinary. She had never experienced being attacked in the past. Now, she was actually fighting for her life. Even with her belly slashed open and intestines showing, the great white spun around to face a frontal attack. One mako that had come too close to the frenzied mother was practically decapitated. Immediately, the other three makos attacked and ate most of their fallen comrade's body. While they were busy doing this, the dying great white tried to get as far away from the scene as possible. Something seemed to signal her that there was a more important task than fighting.

After leveling off her descent at three hundred feet, the mother began straining again. Unlike the other pups, this female was much larger. As soon as the hundred and twenty-five pounder was dropped free, she began making the swimming motions that would have to be used for the rest of her life. There was no time for motherly attention, because the remaining three mako sharks had caught up and were circling for the kill. It was as though the great white knew that her most important mission in life had been accomplished, namely, giving birth to the future queen of the deep. Moments before the three makos hit her simultaneously, the mother's eyes briefly scanned the area for her pup. Perhaps she sensed that it had escaped and was safely out of harm's way; therefore, the need for continuing her own life no longer existed. Within a matter of seconds, huge chunks of flesh were torn from the great white's body, and what was left of the carcass sank to the ocean's floor to be eaten by crustacean scavengers.

2

During the next ten years, the great white developed rapidly. By spring of 1973, she had grown to a length of thirty-two feet and possessed unusual intelligence. Not only had she perfected skills in hunting food but also in entertaining herself. One of the great white's favorite stunts was leaping out of the water up to six feet above the surface. In order to do this, she would dive straight down to a depth of almost one hundred feet, level off, accelerate horizontally at a rate of nearly thirty miles per hour for about fifty yards, then aim her massive body upward. Breaking the surface felt good to her, and she did it frequently. Through consistent practice, the great white learned to arch her back so that she could re-enter the water head first. Soon, she discovered that she could catch seals faster this way, because they would mistake her for a harmless porpoise. By the time the seals realized danger, the great white would have snatched one on each leap. She was wise enough not to crunch into the body until she was far below the surface on the dive. Telltale blood streams would signal danger after the first leap. As it usually happened, she was able to catch nearly a dozen before they realized their peril.

In 1976, our heroine's curiosity about the world around her almost cost her to lose her life hunting among the caves of the Australian Great Barrier Reef. After gobbling down the few morsels of a dead giant squid that the huge sperm whale had overlooked, she decided to investigate beneath the jagged precipice. With a couple of stiff flickings of her tail, the great white moved cautiously into a black cave. She had penetrated nearly forty yards into darkness when she smelled the first squid. The grotesque monster, upon seeing this intruder, prepared to attack. Four tentacles encoiled the great white's body while the sharp parrot-like beak kept snapping away on her flank. Never before had she felt such pain. With lightning speed the great white spun around and headed back toward the entrance. Three more tentacles were fastened tightly to her head. The shark's gills were covered by the squid's powerful suction discs. Now, the great white could not breathe. The weight of the giant squid impeded her movements; however, the great white managed to gather enough strength to shoot for the surface. She came close enough to the jagged overhang to ram the squid's arrow-shaped head against the rocks. Black sepia fluid spewed forth as the shark did this repeatedly. But each time she weakened, because her tentacle-covered gills could not function in processing oxygen. On the third ramming, the huge pink body of the squid finally fell off. Being able to breathe again restored the great white's aggressiveness and insatiable hunger. She pursued the near-death cephalopod and sank her teeth into its relatively soft head. Five minutes later, the entire giant squid had disappeared down the shark's gullet.

3

The waters off the coast of New Zealand felt warm and soothing to the great white. She spent a lot of time just nosing around some of the objects that raised her curiosity, and these seemed endless. Unlike the image that sharks were supposed to display, the now thirty-four-foot heroine was not perpetually in search of food. Frequently, she passed up tasty tidbits, because of the pleasure she derived from observing other marine animals. Once, the great white swam back and forth in front of a huge six-hundred-pound green turtle. Repeatedly, she gently butted the frightened animal, causing it to tumble. When the great white grew tired of this activity, she just turned and swam away.

Killer whales are methodical hunters that fear nothing in the sea. A pod of eleven had pursued and cornered a young sulphur bottom whale about fifty miles east of Tierra del Fuego. Although the hopeless leviathan was almost sixty feet in length, it was no match for the black and white hunters. Three of them made a bold frontal attack and ripped out the sulphur bottom's tongue. Then the entire pod lazily circled it and waited patiently for the victim to die. Unlike sharks, killer whales prefer dining casually rather than in a frenzy.

The great white, after observing the attack from afar, decided to join in on the feast. This was her first close encounter with killer whales, and it proved to be an important segment of the great white's learning experiences. Barreling through the pod at nearly top speed, our heroine snatched about four hundred pounds of flesh from the dying sulphur bottom's underside. She made a wide turn while gulping down the tasty morsel. Before the great white could reach the carcass again, the entire pod of eleven killer whales angerly shot out to meet her. All adversaries were surprised. The great white was unaccustomed to fending off such fast and aggressive attackers. At the same time, the killer whales were unaccustomed to having their challenge to fight accepted.

The largest (fifteen feet) whale aimed straight for the great white's mouth in an attempt to tear out her tongue. Luckily, she veered left, and the killer latched on to one of her lateral fins, almost ripping it off. Meanwhile, the other ten orcas closed in for the kill. Then the great white did something that perplexed the whales. Instead of threshing wildly about or diving deeper, she sped straight upward, breaking surface and topping a perfect arc at nearly eight feet in the air. With mouth as wide open as the gates of hell and lips pulled back to show all of her jagged, razor-sharp teeth, our heroine re-entered the water head first. The tons of toothed pressure that she applied to the orca that was at the end of the arc completely severed his caudal areas. While continuing her dive to a hundred and thirty feet, the great white swallowed the tail section and swam quickly away. Six members of the pod pursued her briefly and then returned to join the others that had already begun feasting on what was left of their dead comrade.

4

An intense tropical storm blew hard across the waters of India's Bay of Bengal. Strong currents dislodged huge rocks from submarine mountains, and life of every form was disturbed. Even the creatures that were known to be strong swimmers had difficulty in trying to navigate themselves through the murky deep. Shifting sand drained over precipices. Noises caused by falling rocks and boulders reverberated for miles. Seaweed and other various kinds of plants were violently dislodged from their comfortable niches and tumbled about in much profusion. Fishes of all kinds darted aimlessly about trying to get out of the turmoil that was happening all around them.

A school of twenty-seven tiger sharks was so disturbed by everything that, in its haste to find calmer waters, they totally ignored well over a hundred seals and sea lions. The tiger sharks did not like the idea of being tossed around by the super-currents that became even more violent as they swooshed over the underwater hilltops. Apparently, the seals and sea lions felt that they were relatively safe as long as they remained in the throes of the choppy current. However, danger was still present.

Far below the surface, where the storm had very little influence, lurked the lone great white. She was aware of the turbulence that was taking place five hundred feet above her. This is why she chose to let her hunger wait until the waters were calmer. For several hours, our heroine swam slowly around. With just a slight jerky motion of her tail, the gigantic body glided smoothly. Hours passed by, and the great white felt hunger pangs gnaw on the walls of her stomach. Nibbling on crabs while trying to wait out the storm was not enough. She now wanted blood meat—and plenty of it.

The black pupilless eyes and twitching blunt nose led the great white into the same general area where seven blue sharks were feeding on two marine tortoises. Under normal circumstances, the great white would have passed over this meal, but hunger drove her. Building up a tremendous rate of speed, she opened her cavernous mouth and headed straight into the midst of the blue sharks. After clamping tightly on a twenty-footer that still had a tortoise flipper dangling from his mouth, our heroine never stopped or looked back as she leveled off at thirty feet from the surface. Undoubtedly, the blue shark was already dead when the great white loosened her hold and proceeded to gulp down huge chunks of delicious meat. Within fifteen minutes, she had completely devoured almost half a ton and was once again descending to lower depths so as to escape the turbulence caused by the storm.

On the way down, the great white noticed a gigantic form emerging through the murkiness. Although she had just finished a meal, she wanted more. The form was that of a sperm whale. Tampering with one of these leviathans under any conditions is not very smart, especially a hungry one that was unsuccessful in its attempts to pull a delicious giant squid from a cave. The orifice was too small for the fifty-eight-foot whale to push his head through. When he attempted to open his mouth after forcing the issue, he couldn't. And all he got for his effort were several painful bites administered by the giant squid's parrot-like beak. After many fruitless attempts from many angles, the sperm whale finally gave up and started his ascent to the surface. Not having any natural enemies proved to be the whale's undoing, because, although he saw the great white, he paid no attention to her. The only thing that the leviathan wanted to do now was surface for air. Maximum time under water had almost expired.

Our great white made one wide turn and then gunned her muscle engine as hard as she could. With mouth fully open and all teeth bared, the eating machine aimed straight for the sperm whale's head. Crash!! Crash!! Crunch!! She rammed into the unsuspecting objective with such force that he tumbled over several times. Blood spewed from the whale and from the massive hunk of flesh that was trailing between the shark's jaws. The great white's body shuddered repeatedly as she tried to swallow every tidbit. By this time, the whale had gone into shock, because its blowhole area was totally destroyed. The mammal's mechanism for separating water from air was ripped apart. Sperm whales are known for being aggressors under normal conditions, but this one's present condition was certainly not normal. It was perhaps the first time in its now-diminishing life that any creature, other than its own kind, ever dared to initiate an attack.

An opened mouth and rows of blood-stained jagged teeth again were aimed at the fleeing whale, which finally reached the surface. However, its sense of equilibrium was damaged so much that the mountainous waves, caused by the raging storm, rolled the whale onto its back. This time the great white hit with such force that the upper portion of the whale's body was lifted nearly three feet out of the water. Death could not come quickly enough. As the dead mammal sank slowly, eight tiger sharks appeared, yet they were reluctant to attack the sperm whale's lifeless body. While the tigers were apparently trying to muster enough courage to go in, the great white eating machine was enjoying the last of the tasty chunk of blubber that she had torn loose. Now our heroine was ready for another pass, and she did not take too kindly to the idea that these eight intruders were eyeing her quarry. The great white then began making wide circles around the tigers as they made circles around the sinking dead whale. Three of the sharks grew bold enough to attack. One became so rapacious that it completely engulfed itself in the gigantic blood-draining hole made by the great white's two passes. As the relatively small nine-footer emerged from the gigantic wound, it did not look soon enough to its left. The huge jaws of our heroine closed like a pair of pinking shears on the tiger shark's body with such pressure that it was totally severed. The sight was indeed a gruesome one. Flesh from the sperm whale's body hung partially out of the mouth of the great white's mouth. While making a wide circle, she forced it down her gullet. The remaining seven tigers zoomed in on both the whale's carcass and what was left of their unfortunate comrade.

The great white's appetite was satisfied for the time being; however, she felt the urge to keep up her attack on these seven intruders. After going about two hundred yards away from the site where the tigers had begun their eating frenzy, the great white flicked her powerful tail fin and turned around. Seaweed clung to her enormous body as she negotiated attacking position. The murky water was filled with all kinds of detached plants, thus impairing the great white's vision, but her acute olfactory nerves gave her all the accuracy she needed as to location. This time, she tried something different. While speeding toward the objective, her mouth was only partially open. She intended to ram at top speed.

By the time the feeding tiger sharks saw her, the great white was upon them. Thump! Practically every large piece of cartilage in one tiger's body was fractured or completely shattered. Blood immediately streamed from its mouth, nose, gills, and anal passage. Death came upon contact. The force was so great that the great white's forward momentum carried her nearly eighty feet, even after impact. She enjoyed this latest tactic immensely. No sooner had our heroine made her usual wide turn when three sand sharks joined the tigers in the feast which now included the body of the ramming victim. The great white was enjoying every minute of this game. At maximum speed, she raced toward the three sand sharks. However, instead of barreling through them, she tried even another new tactic. The great white, upon coming within a mere six feet of the feeding sharks, veered sharply to the left, thereby causing her body to become one huge whip. The sound of cracking cartilage could be heard throughout the expansive area. Although she was not hungry, our heroine made a picturesque turn and seized the sinking body of one of the dead sand sharks. The tigers seemed to know that it was far too dangerous for making any rash moves toward grabbing the other bodies, so they just continued swimming in wide circles until the great white had finished dining. Through streams of blood and pieces of viscera, our heroine kept her black pupilless eyes on the audience as she moved her pectoral fins in order to make a slanting motion. Once cleared of the carnage area, the great white made a few stiff tail flicks and glided effortlessly away.

The calm waters of the Mozambique Channel felt good on her body, especially after she had spent several weeks hunting seals off the coast of Tanzania. These small creatures, being swift and shifty, were accustomed to out-maneuvering most of the various species of sharks in that area. So, when the great white came upon the scene, it was still business as usual for the hundreds of seals that hunted schools of fish around the small rocky islands near Zanzibar.

Sliding off the craggy ledges into the water to intercept the passing of a large school went nearly five hundred seals. Their barking and flapping flippers indicated the great fun they were having in chasing and catching thousands of fish. It had become a game with the fat well-fed seals. A typical day for them consisted of lulling away the morning hours basking in the equatorial sun. Waves dashed against the rocks where the more aggressive, larger seals stretched out. These smart mammals would remain just barely beyond the full dousing so as to be covered with a light misting spray that cooled their bodies. And, as the sun rose higher in the sky, one could see the seals move closer to the water line in intervals of ten minutes. The sleek shimmering coats of these docile animals struck quite a reflection.

As was the usual behavior, those seals that were occupying the higher ledges kept their eyes riveted to the channel. These centurions served as lookouts, so, when a large school of fish was spotted, they barked in a particular manner. This signaled the others to hit the water. Within one minute, the rocks were completely deserted by every seal that was physically able. Only those pregnant females that were just hours away from giving birth remained.

Large schools of fish also attract sharks. Nevertheless, these Zanzibarian seals were used to dealing with the risk in a unique manner by following certain procedures that usually worked very well for them. They waited until the school was within approximately a half-mile of the shoreline. By swimming between the school and the open channel passage, the resourceful seals drove thousands of fish closer to the rocks. And, since most of the sharks stayed clear of the turbulence caused by the pounding waves, the seals had no trouble in dividing their attention—half devoted to the skillful business of catching fish and the other half devoted to keeping a wary eye out for sharks.

However, some of the seals, instead of concentrating on securing food, decided to make sport of several bold sharks that had ventured within three hundred yards of the jagged rocks. When nine seals swam near the sharks, anticipated excitement mounted among the rest of the barking group. Reaction was fast. The sharks began pursuing the seals with reckless abandon. At top speed, the little mammals darted straight for the rocks with fifteen mako sharks in hot pursuit. Given about another hundred yards, the pursuers would have caught up with them. But the rocks were only a few feet away when the seals made their perfect leaps at the highest rise of the waves. It was precisioned timing that allowed the seals to land well up on jutting ledges. Five of the makos were apparently so engrossed in catching these tasty, warm-blooded morsels that they completely ignored the perils of being caught in pounding waves at high tide. Right behind the seals leaped eight of the relentless sharks. However, they were not as skillful as the seals in avoiding little clusters of rocks that became visible only when the waves receded and left waterless traps. Although the sharks' huge streamlined bodies were superbly agile, they were a hindrance out of water. Even with the waves breaking over them, the struggling hunters could not get themselves into a proper position to fall back into the water.

For several hours, the merciless sun beat down upon the contorted and trapped creatures. Their gills had all but ceased functioning, yet death came slowly. With emotionless eyes and baked skin, one shark looked harmless enough to the young seal pup whose curiosity just overwhelmed it. After waddling around the shark that was lying on its back, the seal pup slowly eased up to the head region. With the final ounce of strength left in its body, the mako shark lurched forward and clamped its jaws around the careless victim. The sight was indeed grotesque, because the huge shark died while holding the dying blood-covered seal locked tightly in its death grip.

The afternoon sun was unbearable, but the gregariously disciplined seals did not venture into the water for even a cooling-off dip. Instead, they lay or waddled around in their chosen little areas. And, as usual, the more important group leaders enjoyed being in their personal areas close to the spray while high above the rest were the channel watchers.

Mixed odors wafted through the clear blue-green waters to where the great white was searching for food. She hadn't eaten anything of sizeable bulk in three days. Up from a depth of one hundred and fifty feet, the graceful form rose to the surface. The great white's high dorsal fin sliced silently toward the distant rock islands. Her nose indicated an abundance of fish not too far away.

Amid the usual exciting barking and flippers flapping, hundreds of seals splashed into the water and headed out to intercept a large school of fish. Being accustomed to performing this activity at least once a day afforded these intelligent animals the opportunity to perfect their fishing techniques down to a science. Random activity in trying to force the school to go in the desired direction was not necessary, because those particular seals that served as major herders were experts in doing their jobs. And those that served as shark watchers were also experts. However, something went wrong that day.

The great white's olfactory pits were filled with the delicious odors that got stronger as she streaked forward to within five hundred yards of where the seals were having an easy time catching fish. Instead of barreling in on a full head of steam, the great white dove to a depth of about three hundred feet before leveling off and heading toward the feasting area. When she was directly below the desired location, she aimed her huge body straight up. This time, the great white didn't fully extend her jaws until she was only fifty feet from one of two shark watchers that was on patrol. Although the unlucky seal tried to head for the surface, it was quickly caught and swallowed. When the great white's enormous head broke through the foam, sheer panic struck among the seals. They fled in every direction, twenty-nine of them foolishly south into the open Indian Ocean.The great white governed her speed so as to hang back just far enough to pick off the victims one by one. Within an hour, she had eaten all twenty-nine.

For the next several days the great white stayed in the vicinity. By placing herself only a few yards away from the rocks, she was able to catch several seals as they slid into the water to chase fish schools. Then one day, the seals went out but did not return. Instead, they followed the coastline northward and set up new residence on rock islands forty miles away.

6

At the mouth of the Congo River, the great white hesitated as though she was trying to decide whether to venture forth into these muddy waters. Then several strange creatures appeared momentarily through the brownish hue. The great white's hunger once again complemented her high sense of curiosity in order to make a decision. Several light flicks of the powerful but graceful caudal region sent the streamlined form gliding smoothly through the murkiness to investigate the strange creatures more closely. Unfortunately, when she arrived in the area, the crocodiles had gotten out of the water to join others that were sunning themselves on the bank.

For the next couple of days, the great white scoured the riverbed and found many forms of delicious crustacea. However, her hunger was now calling for something more substantial. This is why she surfaced when about ten shadows passed over her.

The ten crocodiles also had designs of their own, because the object looked like a fish. As the great white slowly swam around these creatures, one of them had the audacity to sink his teeth into her tail fin. Surprised and angered by this act, she wheeled around but not with enough force to dislodge the nineteen-foot reptile. Attracted by the thrashing water, which usually indicated that some large delicious animal was trapped and about to be devoured, more crocodiles quickly slid into the river and headed straight to the action site. Although the great white was being attacked, she did not abandon all thoughts of calculated strategies that had worked well for her in the past. Luckily, she had not gone too far up river, else what she was planning would not succeed.

By lowering her massive head, the great white dove straight down. Fifty feet. The determined crocodile was still hanging on. Seventy feet. The reptile was beginning to weaken, because it was not used to moving that fast under water and its body was being crushed by the rapid descent. One-hundred-ten feet. The bull crocodile, in desperation, unlocked his jaws and frantically tried to find air. The great white continued her dive to within just a few feet of the bottom. Meanwhile, the crocodile's lungs had burst, and the completely disoriented reptile bit his own tongue. Blood streamed from the wound as the dying animal was caught in a state of suspension at eighty-five feet below surface.

Blood. Food. After leveling off, the great white aimed herself toward the top and bulleted straight for the crocodile. With her jaws fully open and lips pulled back over those double rows of serrated teeth, she snatched the hopeless reptile and immediately began feeding. Her body gave a vigorous shudder when the crocodile's head disappeared down her gullet.

There was a lot of activity happening topside. It seemed that several hippopotamuses were attacked as they were wading and feeding in shallow water. When the crocodiles appeared, some of the hippos foolishly fled into deep water and tried to outswim their attackers to the other shore. Their efforts were futile. Every one of those ponderous horses was slashed to death. They didn't stand a chance against those crocs. So much blood was spilled into the water that the brownish hue changed to scarlet red.

By the time the great white had picked up the scent, the hippos had been dismembered and eaten. Now, nearly forty well-stuffed crocodiles were lazily swimming toward the bank where they were probably going to sun themselves and sleep for the rest of the day. Looking at this seemingly solid mass of twitching tails and moving feet signaled the great white eating machine that there was more food above.

Crash! When the shark's massive body broke through the crocodile jam and continued upward almost ten feet into the air, bedlam erupted among them, especially after eighteen of the reptiles suffered broken bones, cracked vertebrae, ruptured spleens, and other injuries as a result of this gigantic stranger's ramming plus falling on them. The great white seized a croc as she re-entered the bloody water and dove to a depth of almost one hundred feet where she gulped it and readied herself for another pass at the group.

One of the few reptiles that had not received any injuries joined in the frenzy. This fourteen-footer tore off what was left of a dead comrade's tail section and was heading for bankside with it. Suddenly there rose the gigantic head of the great white fifty yards away. Something must have told the crocodile that this was going to have to be his strongest fight, because he quickly released his booty and submerged to meet the challenge. At top speed, these two creatures from different worlds headed toward each other, mouths open as the distance closed to less than twelve feet. The last thing that the crocodile viewed in his life was a cavernous maw. After the great white bit completely through half of her opponent's body, she swallowed it with a lot of effort. The rest of the reptile's body spewed blood as it slowly sank to the bottom where crustaceous scavengers waited.

Several days later, the great white left the Congo River for the refreshing brine of the Atlantic Ocean. Uninhibited and full of curiosity, she headed in a northwesterly direction.

Two

Love Is Strange

1

Dr. Wesley Prescott, the president of Ocean World, picked up the receiver on the first buzz.

"Yes."

"Dr. Prescott, Dr. Compton is here for his two o'clock appointment," said the secretary.

"Fine, Rhoda. Ask him to wait a few minutes." The president then whirled around in his huge leather chair and said to the five people seated near his desk, "Now that the arrangements for next month's quarterly meeting have been made, I think we had better get on with the business of dealing with Compton's work."

"Or lack thereof," came Dr. Jason Kromyer's pointed interjection that caused laughter among the group.

"Now, now, Jason," came the president's snickering reaction, "how about showing a little respect for our senior-most citizen. After all, old Harry used to be very good in his work before all of you young fellows came in with your new techniques, which brings us to the center of the current problem.

"Then we all are in agreement that Dr. Kromyer here is the best person to take over Compton's position as head of the upcoming Caribbean Project, right?"

The Caribbean Project to which Dr. Prescott was referring had top priority in the current research plans of Ocean World. However, to explore marine life around several sunken volcanoes was going to require more money than was originally budgeted. Therefore, the Ways and Means Committee had decided to try to get the needed three-hundred-thousand-dollar shortage via goodwill offerings at the annual dinner meeting of Ocean World's Board of Directors, which was scheduled to be held at the Flamingo Palace, a plush hotel in Miami Beach.

Undoubtedly, the meetings were always meant to be more social occasions than business. Four multi-millionaires were included in the membership, which was primarily composed of people who donated large sums of money outright or could at least clear the way for Ocean World to receive large grants.

While sitting in the president's outer office, Dr. Compton reflected on how cold and impersonal the staff at Ocean World had become since he started there over forty years ago. Even a young man with a Ph.D. in marine biology had a rough time trying to make economic ends meet during those Depression years. But old man James Cassidy, founder of Ocean World, made sure that all of his employees, especially the professional staff, did not have to grub for a living. It was like one big happy family. Then things started changing right after Cassidy died in 1946. So as to keep the research going financially, the new owners opened a small aquarium for public admission, and the big emphasis was placed on bringing in all kinds of exotic sea life for display purposes. Compton soon found himself sailing and flying all over the world in search of "sea freaks," as was his term. While Harry was on a three-month jaunt off the coast of Madagascar, his wife died. Since the marriage had been childless, he was left quite alone.

Throwing himself totally into his work, Compton earned the reputation of being the Frank Buck of the seas. There was no place that he wouldn't go to follow some inside information on the location of various marine creatures. And for nearly fifteen years, Compton enjoyed the popularity among his colleagues. He not only became known to the National Geographic Society but also Jacques Cousteau himself. Unfortunately, while Harry was doing some work near Borneo, he caught a rare fever that did some damage to his heart. It didn't take long for the debilitating illness to slice Compton's effectiveness by fifty percent. More out of respect than anything else did the management of Ocean World permit him to remain head of the Special Projects Division, commonly referred to as SPD. However, the time had come for trimming staff, and Compton was among several veteran members to be considered.

The secretary's words snapped him out of his reverie. "Dr. Prescott will see you now, sir."

"Huh? Oh, thank you," came Harry's response as he picked up his worn leather briefcase and entered the president's office.

After several light, friendly remarks were exchanged as coffee was poured, Dr. Prescott reconvened the meeting.

"Ladies and gentlemen, suppose we set aside our regular agenda for the moment while we listen to Dr. Compton. He requested to meet with us this afternoon about something that he stated was of great importance to Ocean World."

One member leaned over and whispered to another, "About the only thing of importance that old Harry boy could tell us would be that he's retiring."

"Thank you, my colleagues, for permitting me to come before you today," Dr. Compton opened, as he pulled from his briefcase a rather thick folder. "I know some of you are wondering just how much longer I'm planning to retard the wheels of progress here at Ocean World...."

This drew a remark from Dr. Alice Randall, the first woman biologist hired by the laboratories ten years prior. "I totally disagree with you, Dr. Compton, because the wheels of this company would've stopped turning long ago had it not been for people like yourself, especially when you refused to listen to all those subtle sexist babblings about how terrible it would be to take a woman on the Great Barrier Reef Project five years ago...."

"Harumph, ahem ... ah, yes, Alice," interrupted Dr. Prescott as he lightly tapped on his desk. "I'm sure that all of us here can appreciate the excellent work ... and foresight ... of Dr. Compton, but suppose we move on."

The same whispering member uttered while smiling, "Damn right; he took along a piece of ass he could jump on whenever he could get it up."

Compton continued. "First of all, for those of you who are wondering how much longer this old coot plans to hang around the labs, well, I will be retiring in six months, the thirty-first of December."

"We'll all miss you, Dr. Compton," said the whispering member.

"I'm sure you will—as much as the Ancient Mariner missed the albatross that fell from around his neck. However, I didn't come here to waste your time with small talk.

"Colleagues, I am well aware of the fact that we need some kind of gate-crashing attraction that will bring in some more money.

173

I'm also well aware of the fact that you don't think I can do the job anymore. Maybe you're right, and then again maybe you're wrong. But there's one thing for certain, esteemed colleagues; I do believe that the record of my past accomplishments has earned me the right to remain head of the Caribbean Project."

Dr. Prescott almost choked on his coffee as he sputtered, "Harry (cough) I don't know how you found out so soon, since the Committee took it under discussion just this afternoon, and . . ."

"Pardon me, Wes, for interrupting, but I think it's important for you people to hear what I propose to do! Now, I have here in this folder a compilation of information, from reliable sources, about a sea find that would boggle the minds of everyone who . . ."

"Harry," said the president, "there isn't a person in this room, nay, the state of Florida, who would challenge your expertise in marine exploration. But, let's face it, the Caribbean Project is going to require the leadership of a younger person, one who can physically be involved. . . ."

As various other members rambled on about the necessity for change, Compton could see that any further statements coming from him would be bordering on begging. So he retreated from the field of verbal battle.

2

On the fifth ring, Joe managed to reach the telephone which was buried beneath a pile of debris. "Hello. Ah, Lola, how are you? What? Oh, no problem. I figured I must've said a few things that ticked you off. I seem to have a bad habit of doing things like that. Sure, I want to see you, but I don't want to ruin your Saturday night. Business is probably good on the weekends when . . . no, Lola, I'm not trying to be sarcastic . . . hello, hello. . . ."

The woman felt deeply wounded but she couldn't quite understand why. Calling one of her johns should not have proposed a problem. After all, she had done that many times in the past as a matter of stirring up revenue. But this Joe Talanski was causing Lola to have feelings that were definitely not conducive to a successful prostitute. Becoming involved with a john on a genuinely emotional level was a no-no, and, Lola felt that this relationship with Joe had already gone too far.

All day, the troubled lady of the evening had second and third thoughts about calling her customer again. She finally decided to do what she really wanted to.

"Hi . . . I'm impressed. Never thought you would've identified my voice, especially when you talk to so many different women who call. Ha, ha. I'm still impressed. Look, I'm sorry I hung up on you this morning. No, no, there was really no good reason for me to do it."

As the two bantered back and forth with idle chit-chat, Joe detected so much pleasantry in Lola's voice that he decided to be even more presumptuous.

"Say, would you do me a big favor, Lola?"

"Sure, as long as it's within reason."

"Now you know I don't deal in rhyme or reason, doll, but, anyhow, I was wondering if you could come over here tonight, and . . ."

"You mean come to your apartment tonight?" asked the surprised woman, almost dropping the telephone.

Then Joe thought how stupid it was of him to suggest such a thing for a Saturday night, what with Lola's busy and lucrative schedule.

"Hey, it was just a dumb thought of mine, Lola. I must be crazy to think that . . ."

"Joseph Talanski, will you shut up for a second, please! Boy! Talk about women with motormouths! Yes, I would love to come over this evening."

Within a couple of hours, Joe had straightened up the little efficiency and gone to the supermarket. At seven-thirty, he responded to a gentle rapping at the door. When Talanski's eyes absorbed the beautiful blonde adorned in a sleek black satin dress, he gasped for breath.

"Oh, my gosh! Are you sure you have the right place, lady?"

As she entered, Lola remarked, "Well, when I was graciously extended the invitation to come to a classy joint like this, how else might I have dressed?"

Later, as Joe cleared the table, he insisted that Lola not help but just sit there at the small kitchen table and talk to him while he quickly cleaned up the area.

175

Sipping wine, she said, "You know, you never appeared to be the domesticated type."

"Oh? Then what type did you think I was, ma'am?"

"You know what I mean. Even the spaghetti was surprisingly delicious."

Joe turned to an FM radio station that played pop music mixed in with traditional love songs.

"Can you also dance, *monsieur?*"

As they held each other softly while gently swaying to "Love Is a Many Splendored Thing," a new feeling seemed to take hold. It wasn't meant to be verbalized, so neither Joe or Lola spoke during the song—and even when it ended by trailing right into another, "Night and Day."

The unfelt electrical currents that seemed to course through the couple's bodies as they danced caused unusual sensations, sensations that could not be translated into sexual desires.

In the quietness of his mind, Joe tried desperately to reconcile these strange feelings that surrounded him.

Why am I beginning to have such tender thoughts about Lola? I must be crazy! After all, the bitch is nothing but a whore, and I've dealt with whores before. I think I'm falling in love with you, Lola, and I can't explain why. We've already been to bed, so what's the big deal? Oh, Lola, you're so soft. Damn! You're a damn sex merchant, bitch; and guys just don't fall in love with prostitutes. What are you doing to me? This can't go anywhere. We're in two different worlds. How many men have you held like this? How many of them have you screwed? I enjoy having you around.

"I enjoy having you around, Lola," whispered Joe into her ear.

"What?" she asked as she gently leaned back and looked into his eyes. "I bet you say that to all the girls."

As Sinatra crooned, Lola's feelings mounted.

Who is this guy that has me acting like a teenager in love? I think I am falling in love with you, Joe. Lola, have you lost your mind? Falling for a john is definitely a no-no. Umm, he makes me feel so good when I'm just in his presence with nothing going on. Watch out, Lola! Remember the last time you fell seriously for a guy? I'm a professional, and this schoolgirl infatuation certainly has no place in my life. I don't want to be hurt anymore.

When the song ended, Lola softly said, "I'd better go now."

And without thinking, Joe blurted out, "No! You must stay here! I love you, Lola."

Silence. He then felt completely embarrassed. However, before he had a chance to apologize, Lola put her arms around his neck and kissed him with a feeling that had all but been forgotten. She felt like a giddy teenager falling in love for the first time in her life.

"And I love you, too, Joe," she responded.

There they were, two worldly adults who thought that they suffered under no delusions as to what the real world was all about. Yet, they were allowing genuine feelings of love to drape over their formerly protective shields against naivety. Joe and Lola were well aware of the vulnerability to which each was permitting exposure. But they didn't care. Nothing existed outside of that apartment on that hot summer's night. It was as though they were finding true love for the first time in their lives.

The heat prompted Joe to suggest that they try to cool off. "Wanna share a shower with me?" he asked.

Although Lola was taken somewhat by surprise by the question, she answered in the affirmative. As the refreshing water streamed over them, they remained silent as if each pondering thoughts that were not to be shared. After pat drying, the naked forms stretched out on the bed. Lights were turned off, allowing only the pale moonbeams to illuminate the room. There seemed to be no great hurry for sexual engagement. The lovers were very content in just holding each other.

Then Lola broke the silence with, "I have to tell you something."

"Umm, just keep on telling me how much you love me, Lola. I have to hear it at least every . . ."

"Darling, I do love you," she interrupted, "but what I have to tell you goes against a strict rule that I made for myself two years ago when I became a prosti . . ."

"No!" Talanski firmly said as he placed his hand over Lola's mouth. "Please don't say that word tonight. We may be trying to lose ourselves in unrealistic feelings, but who the hell else cares outside of us?"

The more Joe talked, the more Lola realized how much she loved him and had to have him for her very own. Of course, she knew that trying to hold on to his heart was a task not to be taken lightly.

After kissing him, she continued. "I want you to know that my real name is Kristina Flaubert."

When she noticed that Joe's body did not give any indication of retreat from hers and also that he chose to remain silent while holding her closely, she proceeded.

"I was born and grew up in Fond du Lac, Wisconsin. My mother's background is Danish and my father's French. I'm the youngest of four children. My two brothers, they're both married, jointly own a mid-size dairy farm just outside of Brandon, a small town southwest of Fond du Lac. My sister, Nanette, is also married, and she and her husband are schoolteachers in Milwaukee. Am I boring you?"

"Of course not, darling, I want to know everything about you," was Joe's response as he kissed her on her forehead.

"Well, you asked for it. After I had won first prize in a local beauty contest, I knew I wanted to get as far away from cow manure as I could. Ha, ha. Even had thoughts about going to college outside of the state. This went over like the proverbial lead balloon, because no rational-thinking person would ever consider going to any other school except the University of Wisconsin or the University of Milwaukee. But my folks always considered me to be different, so they weren't too surprised when I told them, at seventeen, that I was not planning to study biology in college and pursue medical studies so that I could eventually become a doctor like Uncle Charles and his daughter, Claudia. So, it didn't come as any big surprise to anyone when I turned down a full academic scholarship to UW. But what really shocked the hell out of them was when I decided to come to the University of Miami. No one, I mean no one, could deal with that. A 'milk maid' from Wisconsin—creamy white skin and all—going to Florida? Ha, ha, my dad almost had a stroke! As he said, right up to the day I boarded the plane, he just couldn't understand why an intelligent girl like me would want to go to Florida among all those rednecks, Cuban foreigners, colored people, and Jews. Wow, I mean my father was pissed! Would you believe that it took my cousin, Claudia, to calm him down? Like I said, she's a doctor, a gynecologist, with one heck of a lucrative practice right there in Fond du Lac. Joe, you should see her. She's really pretty, but, at thirty-six, Claudia's not married yet. No, she's not a lesbian—at least,

I don't think so. Anyway, when Claudia found out I was planning to major in marine biology, she was right in my corner.

"Now, you're probably wondering why I became a prostitute, right?"

Without saying a word, Joe gently squeezed her and kissed her hair.

"Well, it's not a long story," Kristina (aka Lola) began as she leaned over to get the cigarettes on the night table. "Near the end of freshman year, my dad informed me that he was tired of paying money to, let's see, how did he put it—oh, yeah, a school that condoned drugs and beach bumming. Ha, ha, ha. Oh, man, you really have to know my father! He was determined to get me to transfer, and I was just as determined to stay down here. So, after final exams, I moved in with a girlfriend who had a gorgeous apartment near the beach. Now, I had assumed that Shelly's folks were paying her way also, that is, until she introduced me to the owner of the Orchid Lounge. That was two years ago. Shelly later met and married some well-to-do Cuban guy. I understand they live in Union City, New Jersey. At any rate, I took over the lease, and I've been able to take care of all financial needs plus I have enough money in the bank to cover next year's tuition. Right now, Joe, money is the least of my worries.

"You . . . you're the greatest worry I have," she responded, kissing him on the chest. "I'm losing control of my emotions, Joe, and I don't know whether that's good or bad. All I know is that, for the first time since high school, I'm in love, but this guy is like a piece of floating plankton. He just seems to be aimlessly drifting on the sea of life."

Joe smiled and said, "Why don't you stop seeing that . . ."

The sentence was never completed, because she placed her lips over his and sucked heavily on his tongue.

"Move in with me, Joe . . . please."

The request not only surprised but disturbed him also. He remembered another time when another woman he loved had made the same request.

Joe partially sat up and replied, "I don't think it would be the right thing for me to do, Kris. I'm not going to take advantage of your being nice to me. . . ."

"Nice to you! Damn it, mister, I'm not just being nice to you! I love you! Can't you understand? Oh, I love you so much, Joe, and I want you to love me!"

"I do love you, Kristina, but I know I shouldn't because . . ."

"Because I'm a whore?"

Without answering immediately, Talanski got up from the bed, put on his robe, lit a cigarette, stood at the window, and then replied, "I have had all kinds of shrinks look inside my head. Don't ask me what they found, because I really don't know. But there's one thing that I do know, and that is that I love you, for whatever reason. Playing the game by society's rules, I'm not supposed to love you and you're not supposed to love me. What a hell of a combination—a born loser and a . . . a . . . "

"Prostitute. Yes, a prostitute," Kris added as she buried her face in the pillow and began to cry. "I'm not blaming anyone, not even my father, but now I'm sorry as hell, because I love you."

"Oh, Kris, Kris . . ."

"No, no, don't try to rationalize our relationship, Joe, because it just doesn't make sense. I know men have the kind of pride that will not let them love women who give their bodies to other men. And it's a rule everybody plays by."

Talanski cradled Kristina in his arms and held her quietly. They didn't say anything for almost fifteen minutes. Then she softly said, "If you truly love me, Joe, tell me to stop seeing other men, please."

"From now on, I want to be the only man in your life, Kris. Stop seeing all others, and give yourself to me totally."

On the fifth ring, Talanski picked up the receiver.

"Hello . . . Dr. Compton, how are you? . . . No problem, really. That's all right. Sunday mornings are casual, and I try to keep them that way. Sure, I could come over this afternoon around three. Oh, by the way, sir, would it be okay for me to bring someone with me? I really would like for you to meet her; she's studying marine biology in college, and . . . yeah, doc, she's also very special to me . . . good, we'll be there."

When Joe hung up, a pair of soft moist lips kissed him on the back and asked, "What was that all about, darling?"

"Huh? Oh, so Sleeping Beauty has finally awaken, I see."

"Umm, I could stay right here in this bed with you for the rest of my life."

"Hey, that's the best offer I've had today. Come here . . ."

"Easy, tiger man," Kris purred as she slipped her beautifully contoured bare body out of Joe's arms. "Let me show you another side of me, one that you haven't seen yet."

"Wow, you mean there's more?"

"Of course, silly. I want to fix you the best breakfast you've ever had, okay?"

"Okay."

"Now, who was that on the phone?"

"Oh, just one of my old flames calling to see if . . ."

Joe never finished the sentence, because Kris placed her hand across his mouth and said, "Don't. Please don't ever joke like that. My feelings for you are as naked as my body and they hurt a lot."

3

The old house in which Harry Compton lived was of Victorian design, built by Harry's father in 1895. Mr. Compton, a carpenter and forty-six years of age, married rather late in life. However, his young bride of twenty-two, a private music teacher from Boston, bore him seven children over the next ten years, all born at home. Harry, the youngest, never knew his mother because she died during childbirth. Esther, the oldest of the four girls and three boys, learned to cook and keep house. Poor Esther learned so well that she turned down several offers of marriage rather than leave home. She died an old maid of forty-nine, six months after Mr. Compton passed.

Since the rest of Harry's brothers and sisters had families of their own and were not interested in the old house during the Depression years, the deed was turned over to him for the consideration of one dollar.

While working full-time at Ocean World and pursuing a master of science degree in marine biology at the University of Florida, Harry met and married Peggy Morris, the pretty but sickly daughter of one of his professors. Although they were childless, Harry and Peggy enjoyed many happy years together in the old house. And when she became too ill, Harry hired a housekeeper (Mrs. Penn) to take care of things while he was out of the country. After Peg died, Mrs. Penn stayed on to cook Harry's meals and clean.

"Oh, you must be Mr. Talanski and friend," said the smiling, chubby, little woman who answered the door. "Dr. Compton is expecting you."

Mrs. Penn led them across the foyer's highly glossed parquet floor and through the polished sliding doors into the den. And what a den it was! Full bookshelves from the floor to the high, ten-foot ceiling lined the walls; rolled-up maps and sea charts practically covered a solid teakwood desk; small marine fossils were used as paperweights; a large leather-covered globe rested on a mahogany stand; and the most dominating feature of the den was a huge four-by-eight lighted aquarium that contained a variety of sea life.

"Oh, Joe, so happy you could make it! Well, now, this pretty lassie must be the one! How are you, my dear? Joe often talks about you! So now I'm finally meeting you. Ha, ha. Hey, Joe, you're right. She *is* beautiful!"

From the very start, Kris liked Dr. Compton, and she was hoping that Joe's suggestion might come to realization, specifically, her securing a part-time job at the lab at Ocean World. Both visitors were fascinated with the memorabilia, photographs, and various other marine items that the old gentleman showed them over coffee and some of the housekeeper's delicious black forest cake. Kris was especially captivated by all of this, and the good doctor was very impressed with her knowledge of his favorite topic—sharks.

"Dr. Compton, I know there have been numerous studies done on sharks," she said as she watched the small sand shark in the aquarium, "but what about the many discrepancies that still exist about the great white?"

"Funny you should mention the great white, Kris," the host replied, "because it's the topic that has been dominating my thoughts for the past three months. Ah, yes, *carchardon cacharias,* the great white shark, the most mysterious creature in the ocean. Discrepancies, my dear? Yes, there are hundreds among us, plus I have several theories, based upon my explorations and experiments that continue to confuse even me. In other words, the great white shark is mind-boggling, which brings me to the reason why I asked you to come here this afternoon."

Dr. Compton then proceeded to tell Joe and Kris about the Caribbean Project and how he was being systematically squeezed out.

"None of those people at Ocean World could even carry your microscope, Doc," Joe remarked. "I know I just clean tanks, but during the ten months I've been there, I've noticed how many of the other biologists try to pick your brain."

"Well, maybe Prescott, Kromyer and some of my other colleagues are right, Joe, in trying to get me to surrender without a fight. I'm getting too old to head up the Special Projects Division. Lord knows I can't take long stretches on the water the way I used to. Anyhow, I got a few medical problems that are a pain in the butt. Nevertheless, I just have to go out there one more time, because a reliable source has given me some information that could possibly lead to the greatest feat of my entire career."

"And what is that, Dr. Compton?" Kris asked excitedly.

The venerable old gentleman, without answering immediately, got up, put on his spectacles, went to his desk, and moved several charts until he came to a particular one.

"Come here. I want to show you something," the host said. "During the past six years, there've been several sightings of enormous great whites in this area between Chub Cay and Morgan's Bluff on Andros Island in the Bahamas. Think of it, folks. If one could be brought back, it would be the super attraction at Ocean World! And I'm planning to set sail within two weeks. How would you like to be on board, Joe?"

"Wow, Doc, I sure would, but I couldn't get the time off for . . ."

"Don't worry about it. I can easily make tentative arrangements for you to accompany me—and be paid your regular salary, of course."

Upon hearing all of this, Kristina felt an arrow of sadness pierce her heart. She wanted nothing to prevent her seeing Joe every day, and the mere thought of not having him close to her all the time raised feelings of selfishness and jealousy that she had previously not known. Nevertheless, Kris knew that Joe would agree to go; therefore, without thinking things through, she blurted out, "I'd like to go also, Dr.Compton! Classes are over for the summer, and I've taken all but one final exam, which will be on Tuesday. You don't have to pay me, because . . ."

"Kristina," Joe interjected, "slow down! Can't you see you'd be putting Dr. Compton in a precarious position? Besides, it probably is too risky, and I wouldn't want anything to happen to you."

The bolt of anger that streaked across Kris's mind prompted her to say, "Joseph Talanksi, I've been a solid B-plus student in marine biology for six semesters, and I dare say that I would probably be of more assistance than you!"

"No need to become upset, my dear," responded Dr. Compton, "because, in all fairness, I could certainly use another person on board who is knowledgeable in the field. Well . . . the trip does not exactly have the blessings of the current powers that be at Ocean World, because they would rather have me retire immediately. Joe, I'm sure you heard little unflattering remarks about me around the place recently."

"Well, to tell you the truth, Doc, sure, I've heard a few people say things, "Joe said. "But I don't consider their comments worth a nickel. Hell, those jerks are just jealous of your past record and popularity through the years."

"I've scraped together all of the financial resources I have," the old biologist said, "and a few influential friends around the town are willing to invest enough money to cover expenses. But do you kids want to hear something funny? Except for Alice Randall, none of my colleagues offered any kind of technical assistance to me. Well, that's right; I don't need those people now, because, with you two, Joe and Kris, I have all I need."

Talanski placed his arm around Kris's shoulder as he said, "You needn't worry, Doc. Kris and I are with you all the way."

The smiling student never felt better.

Three

Almost Made It

1

It was nine-thirty in the evening when the tall, handsome, middle-aged gentleman strode into the Orchid Lounge. And although he was dressed in a dark blue, three-piece business suit, his objective was strictly recreational. George, the bartender, recognized the gentleman immediately.

"Mr. Logan," he said, "how're you doing? It's nice to see you again. In town for a while?"

"Hi, George," the gentleman replied as he took a stool at the bar. "Good seeing you again also. Make it a Jack Daniels on the rocks."

Logan, Frank Logan, was the pseudonym that Scott Ballinger, investment banker from Palm Beach, had chosen for himself six months ago when a business associate introduced him to the happenings at the Orchid Lounge. And each time Ballinger's business travels had brought him to Miami subsequently, he never failed to check out the atmosphere at what had become his favorite watering hole. Needless to say, the management and workers were well aware of the necessity for them to protect the anonymity of high spenders who were there for some action with ladies of the evening.

This was Ballinger's fifteenth visit to the Orchid Lounge, and he had been looking forward to spending some pleasant moments with his favorite girl, Lola. She was the one who made him feel young again; therefore, he always made it financially well worth her while. After their second night together, Ballinger became so happily relaxed with Lola that he told her his real name and all about his wife and four kids. Naturally, he did not omit telling Lola about his meteoric rise up the corporate ladder. However, on that particular night, Lola was not at the Orchid Lounge, and the bartender

185

informed Ballinger that she hadn't been around in several weeks. Now, giving out girls' telephone numbers and addresses was a no-no, and Ballinger was very much aware of that standing rule. Yet, the persistence of the patron, especially when side money entered the discussion, began to whittle away at that standing rule.

"I understand fully why your boss doesn't want the ladies' telephone numbers given out," Ballinger said as he casually fingered a twenty-dollar bill, "but Lola and I have a special relationship going on between us, George, and it certainly would be worth this if you could help me out."

A handsome potential customer seldom escaped notice, and as soon as Mimi, an auburn-haired beauty, tuned in to what was happening, she slid off her seat and glided fluidly up to the tight space next to Ballinger at the crowded bar.

"Oh, Mimi, I'd like you to meet someone," the bartender said. "Mr. Logan, this is Mimi, one of the Orchid's loveliest."

When he looked at her, Ballinger decided to try to make the most out of the night, so he smiled while offering the curvaceous figure his seat.

"Nice meeting you, Mimi. May I buy you a drink?"

After they had talked for about five minutes, Logan gently placed a fifty on her knee and left. A half-hour later, Mimi exited from a cab in the circular driveway of one of Miami's plush hotels and glided smoothly across the ornate lobby to the elevator. Even the night bellman took special note of the gorgeous figure.

Ballinger quickly responded to the light tap on his door. "Hi, sweetheart, I'm glad you could make it. Come on in."

After their first round of lovemaking, during which Mimi gave one of her best performances, the Palm Beach banker began asking questions about Lola, whom Mimi knew very well.

"Tell you what," Ballinger said to the naked form beside him, "if you can make contact with Lola right now, then you've made another fifty on top of the two hundred, okay?"

Jealousy, be it ever so mild, has a way of creeping into the strangest scenes. Mimi tried very hard to stifle her anger, but she wasn't quite successful.

"Oh, shit! Just how good *is* Lola? What can she do, or has done, that's so damn special?" Then, just as quickly as she became angry, Mimi felt embarrassed and small after those few words had spilled out of her mouth. If she could have snapped her fingers and disappeared, she would have. But all Mimi got for her little explosion was an indifferent stare from the customer.

"I'm sorry," she barely uttered while getting up and reaching for a towel to wrap her nakedness. "I had no right to say that, and I'm truly sorry, Frank. I don't know what got into me, for heaven's sake. Anyhow, sure, I'll call Lola for you."

The telephone rang many times, but Kristina didn't answer. She was spending the night, just as she had done for the past week, in Joe's apartment.

"Well, I guess the least I can do to try to convince you that I'm not entirely a shrew," Mimi said, smiling, as she reached for pen and paper, "would be to give you not only Lola's number but also her address."

This act met with such gratefulness that Ballinger gave the girl a twenty as he took away the towel and pulled her down into the bed.

2

Kris opened her eyes and found her lover resting on his elbow staring affectionately into her face. "Good morning," she smiled.

"Good morning, love," Joe replied, lightly kissing her on the lips and each nipple. "I was just lying here admiring your beauty. Did you know that the sunlight streaming over your body is making those blonde hairs give you a golden hue?"

"A what?" Kris responded, laughing as she hugged him.

"Really," Joe said, pulling the sheet back to permit her sculptured form to be bathed in full sunlight. "Your body's taken on a golden mantle, and you know how precious gold is."

"Oh, stop kidding me, Talanski," Kris said as she hit him on the head with a pillow and simultaneously looked at the clock. "You don't want to be late for work, so let me rustle up a nice breakfast, all right?"

"No, thanks, baby. You know I don't have much of an appetite in the morning. Say, are you coming out to see Dr. Compton this afternoon?"

"Of course," Kris responded. "I have to help him stock the boat's lab equipment. Wouldn't miss that for the world! Oh, darling,

I'm just so excited about this! Can't wait until we hoist anchor nine and a half days from now!''

While Kristina was talking, Joe watched her admiringly. Then he decided to reveal what had been on his mind.

"Marry me, Kris.''

"What?''

"I want you to be my wife, the mother of my children.''

"Don't play around like that, Joe, please. I like jokes, but . . . but . . . well, I don't think this is funny,'' she said in a quivering voice.

Joe held Kris's shoulders, looked her squarely in the eyes, and said, "This is not a joke, Kristina. I want to marry you and spend the rest of my life with you. This is not a whim, and I want you to know that I'm dead serious about. . . .''

"Shh, my darling,'' she tearfully whispered in his ear. "Don't make any reference to death. Oh, I do love you so much, Joey, that it frightens me.''

"*Joey*. You've called me by that name before, Kris. I didn't say anything—just enjoyed hearing it. Several people who've had great impact on my life called me *Joey*, and I remember them with love.''

"God, Joey, you've changed my whole life! Oh, yes, yes, I'll marry you and follow you to the ends of the earth! I love you, love you, love you!''

For the next five minutes, the two nude lovers lay silently embraced. Then Kris broke the mood with, "What about my street life, Joey? I can't expect you to be able to forget what I was when you met me.''

"If Lola is dead, never to rise again, then what more can I ask? All we have to do is hold on to each other and move ahead with our lives. When you and I finish Dr. Compton's enterprise, then we're going to make some concrete plans, okay?''

Kris became sensitive to their nudity, and she said, "Heavens! Here we are, talking about good things and buck naked! Really!''

"There's nothing for us to be ashamed of,'' Joe said as he pulled back the sheet. "We could very well consider nudity to be symbolic of our love—nothing to hide from each other.''

A half-hour later, Talanski found himself rushing to leave for work. Kris leaned against the door jamb of the bathroom wistfully watching him shave.

"I could spend the rest of my life watching you."

"Ha, ha. What?"

"I'm not kidding," she said, moving in and hugging him around the waist from the rear. "I get such a pleasure watching you do anything."

"You're weird, lady."

"So are you, mister. Maybe that's why I'm happy."

Joe wiped the excess lather off his face, turned around, and replied, "Know something? We'd both be happier now if I had held on to the money that Paco stashed behind this damn tub. Just think, Kris, I had eighty-six thousand dollars cash and gave it away, not to even mention all the money I gave to Paco's girl and her kids. Why would . . . ."

"Please, Joey, don't—I thought we agreed that you did the right thing. You have to be a special kind of good person to be that honest, even when you're doing it for a real close friend. People like you don't come along everyday, darling, and I love you for it. Besides, you fulfilled the wishes of a dying friend when you could've easily kept every penny and be a rich man today and for many. . . ."

"That's exactly what I mean, Kris! You and I could really live on. . . ."

"Oh, stop it, damn it, stop it!" she shouted. "Do you think our paths would've crossed under a different set of circumstances? Let's forget about the recent past, Joey, and think about just the two of us building our future together."

"I love you so much, Kris."

Needless to say, Talanski was twenty minutes late for work, and his tired, but happy, lover didn't leave the apartment until three hours later.

3

"All of the necessary papers will be drawn up by our office," Ballinger said as he shook the client's hand. "And a special bank messenger will bring them to you on Tuesday for signature."

The portly, white-haired gentleman to whom Ballinger spoke was none other than Armstead Livingstone, president of southern Florida's most successful land development company. Ballinger had just beaten out several other investment bankers who had been trying to get the business. In short, it was indeed a victory, a tug of words that had lasted over three months.

"Well, Scott, I can truly say we're satisfied with the way you've drawn the financial picture for us," Mr. Livingstone said as the meeting was breaking up. "How about joining the group for lunch?"

Even though Ballinger was happy about this latest bit of success, which was typical of his rapid rise in the corporate world, he wanted to shed his three-piece image for the rest of the day and do something more physical. The big guy had brought his tennis gear on this business trip and was eager to get out on the courts at the hotel.

"Gee, I certainly would like that very much, Mr. Livingstone," Ballinger replied, "but I really have to get back to Palm Beach by four this afternoon. There're a few things I want to do at the office before tomorrow."

"Ah, yes, I admire you young bucks," Livingstone said as he lit a cigar. "You're smart and always forging ahead. Say, how would you like to come work for me, Scott?"

"Ha, ha, well, I'm flattered, Mr. Livingstone, but . . . "

"Never mind answering now, but just keep my offer in mind," the executive leader advised. "Because Florida is starting to get a lot of blue-collar retirees from up north who're looking for affordable housing down here, especially up in the Seminole County area."

While driving the rented car back to his hotel, Ballinger reflected on Mr. Livingstone's offer. With four kids to educate, a mortgage on a lavish home in Riviera Beach, a lovely wife who had expensive taste; plus various other factors that required more than his one hundred twenty-five thousand per year, yes he intended to give the offer more thought later.

As soon as he entered his room, Ballinger called the bank and briefed his boss on the clinched deal.

"Excellent, excellent, Scotty! I knew we had made the right choice in sending you down there! What? Oh, don't worry about the papers. We'll take care of the mechanics from here. Listen, why don't you stay in Miami tonight and drive back tomorrow afternoon? Hell, you deserve it. Oh, and, Scotty, when you come back, we have to talk about moving you into Merton's slot. Ha, ha . . . of course I'm serious! You've shown us all we need to see."

By the time he had hung up, Ballinger was floating on Cloud Nine, but the upwardly mobile executive had one more call to make.

"Scott, that's wonderful!" exclaimed his wife. "I knew darn well you could do it! Yes . . . uh huh . . . yeah . . . what?? Oh, my god, Scott, I can't believe it! That's fantastic! I'm so proud of you!"

Ballinger also informed his wife that he would be driving home the next day. But what he did not tell her was that he planned to engage in a few celebration activities that night.

After blowing out all the competition down on the tennis courts, Ballinger returned to his room, physically tired but mentally rejuvenated. This was definitely a night for going to the Orchid Lounge. Then he thought about someone else. The telephone rang twice.

"Hi, Lola? Frank Logan from . . . well, now, that really makes me feel important. Right, this is Scotty, but, since I wasn't quite sure that you'd remember me, I thought I'd give the old stage name. Hey, do I detect a little disappointment in your voice?"

Even though she had tried to cover the conversation with light chit-chat, Kris knew that the past was catching up to her, and beads of perspiration rose on her forehead while rivulets streamed from her armpits.

"Before this conversation goes any further," Kris said in a matter-of-fact tone, "I want you to know that I am no longer . . . no longer in the business, and I do not . . . what? No, Scott, I haven't found a new religion. It's just that I'm not interested in engaging in those activities any more."

Unfortunately, Kris's words had little or no effect on Ballinger, because he felt that this was his day to win anything. His ego was at an all-time high, and he was not to be denied. Even though it was obvious to Ballinger that the girl was trying to end previous connections, he was relentless in his pursuit of conquering once again.

"How I got your telephone number is not that important, Lola, but what *is* important is that I *must* see you tonight . . . well, just tell your new boyfriend whatever, but you and I have to see each other again—just for old time's sake, okay?"

Kris felt a combination of anger and fear. She envisioned herself being pulled back into the quicksand by former customers, a consideration to which she had given very little thought. Now, for the first time, she was frightened, so much so that she hung up the receiver without saying another word.

"Hello, hello! Why, that bitch!" exclaimed Ballinger. "Nobody hangs up on me, especially some little whore!"

<h1 style="text-align:center">4</h1>

Kris felt good about the short meeting that she had that afternoon with Dr. Compton. Plans were falling into place perfectly, and she was simply ecstatic that they would soon be lifting anchor.

After stopping to pick up a couple of ingredients for the French apple pie that she was going to bake for Joe, Kris decided that she would surprise him and prepare a nice dinner for just the two of them at her own apartment. Originally, they had planned for her to pick up Joe at six P.M., and then they were going to go out to eat. And, except for the terrible telephone call that she had gotten earlier, Kris was still a very happy woman.

The doorbell rang. "Just a minute, Mr. Santos!" came the cheerful voice from within. Earlier that day, Kris had spoken to the building's superintendent, Jaime Santos, about a leaky faucet. When she opened the door, her heart almost ceased to beat, because there stood one of the many men whom Kris had never wanted to lay eyes on again.

"And just who the hell is Mr. Santos?" asked the tall handsome man holding a bouquet of roses. "Ha, ha, ha. Wow, Lola, you're looking delicious as usual; therefore, this Mr. Santos is out of luck tonight. May I come in, or do we have to talk out here?"

"How the hell did you get my address?" came the angry question. "Come in, but you can't stay! I told you over the phone . . . "

"Over the phone, under the phone—I can't really trust a little chatty object that doesn't let me see the beautiful face plus hangs up on me. But all is forgiven, my dear, and these are for you."

The gentleman followed Kris into the kitchen where she filled a vase with water for the blood-red roses.

"As I told you earlier, Scott, I am out of that stage in my life, and I'd like to put it all behind me. I'm engaged to be married next month to a man who means all the world to me, and . . ."

"All the world's a stage, but I don't consider this little performance worthy of an Oscar, Lola."

Rage took over her demeanor. "Wait a minute, mister! Just who the hell do you think you are? Don't you dare even try making small of me or my *fiancé!* I think it's time for you to leave, Scott! We don't owe each other anything!"

"On the contrary, Lola," replied Ballinger, "I think you do owe me the courtesy of at least a more in-depth explanation of your decision. After all, we met on a low level, but, you must admit, Lola, our subsequent meetings were on a much higher plane. I came to trust you with some of my inner thoughts that I've never shared with anyone else, including my wife. Long ago, Lola, I stopped looking at you as a businesswoman; I considered you to be both my intellectual and conversational equal. Believe it or not, you're the only woman, other than my wife, I've treated like this. Look, I don't blame you for deciding to turn your life in another direction. Matter of fact, I still don't understand why you ever got into that line of work. You certainly have a lot more on the ball than just a body and pretty face. We used to do many cultural things together, things that didn't require jumping into bed. Lola, I guess what I'm trying to get over to you is that I think you owe me at least a smoother exit than this, don't you agree?"

Undoubtedly, Kris was impressed with the way Scott described his feelings; however, she had absolutely no intentions of playing Russian roulette with her future life. Perhaps fear of not being able to give Joe an acceptable reason for her even talking to an old acquaintance of this nature prompted Kris to become agreeable to Ballinger's suggestion.

"Lola, if we could just spend an hour over light drinks and conversation at that little club we used to go to on the outskirts of Ft. Lauderdale, I would consider it an honor, and we could part as friends. Please say yes, Lola."

Forty-five minutes later, Kris and Ballinger pulled into the circular driveway of the Flamingo Club. During the entire trip, Ballinger spoke glowingly of his family and that he intended to spend more time at home. Several times, Ballinger expressed his appreciation to Kris for her having been so understandingly discreet and how, after their second meeting, he looked upon her as a smooth friend and not a prostitute. Nevertheless, Kris was getting negative vibrations about the decision to go with her former customer. But it was too late to turn back.

After the *maitre d'* seated the couple at a rather secluded table on the veranda, Kris became very uneasy with the whole atmosphere, and she told Ballinger that she wanted to be taken home immediately. Of course, the super executive was not pleased to hear this; however, he agreed, but only after she showed enough patience for him to finish his bourbon and she her ginger ale.

"I know I shouldn't be so inquisitive about your private life, Lola," Ballinger said as he took a sip of Jack Daniels on the rocks, "but I was wondering if this Mr. Nice Guy of yours is really deserving of you. Not only do you have beauty but brains to match. I still find it hard to believe that you're just a high-school dropout."

"Well, it's true, Scott. I guess all of us are not interested in school, at least I wasn't. There's plenty to learn out here if we keep our eyes and ears open."

"And what about the heart?" queried Ballinger as he leaned forward and placed his hand on Kris's knee. "Do you think we can learn anything from the heart, too?"

She eased the hand away and stood up. "Scott, never mind. You stay, but I'm leaving right now. Cabs are outside."

"Phew, my, we can get angry in a hurry, can't we?" Ballinger said as he also stood and drained his glass of its contents. "But I guess that's a woman's prerogative. No problem, sweetheart, I'll take you home. I'm very sorry if I offended you. It's just that I used to be able to . . ."

"How many times do I have to tell you, Scott, that I've changed, and I am very much in love with one man?"

Kris felt herself becoming emotional and distraught. Tears began to form rapidly. As soon as she went into the ladies' room, Ballinger turned to the bar. He quickly ordered and gulped down a double bourbon. Kris decided to make an important telephone call before rejoining her escort. Nervously, she dropped coins into the slots.

"Hi, Joey? Had you tried to call me? Hmm, I miss you too, sugar. Well, I had to pick up a couple of lab manuals here on campus . . . no, I didn't drive, because I had trouble starting the car after I left you and Dr. Compton this afternoon. So, when I finally

194

got it going, I just drove straight to my apartment instead of going down to the campus as I had planned . . . well, I didn't want to be an added burden on you. Oh, Joe, you're such a darling. I love you so much . . . no, because I was going to make something very special and delicious for your dinner at my place tonight. Let's see, it's almost eight o'clock now; I should be home in about an hour and a half, because, Sandy, she's the girl I'm riding with, has to see a prof concerning some course deficiency . . . sure, you have plenty of time to catch a short nap . . . no, don't bother to call. Just come on over when you . . . oh, and I love you, Joey."

When Kris hung up, she felt refreshed and ready to get back to Miami as fast as possible. No need to tell Joe about the real mess that had occurred, and was still in progress, because she intended to eradicate it.

One more drink at the bar did not seem like such a big thing, since his date was still on the telephone.

"Let me have another of the same," Ballinger said to the bartender. "Looks like we're going to be here longer than expected."

However, a couple of minutes after the drink was served, Kris reappeared on the scene.

"Sorry I took so long, but I had to make a very important call. Are you ready to leave?"

"Ready to leave!" exclaimed the fast-becoming-drunk Ballinger as he almost fell off the stool. "I thought you (hic) had decided to stay awhile longer since you practically ran out of (hic) the dining room and then spent a year talking on the goddamn phone!"

"I said I'm sorry, Scott," Kris responded in a soft tone. "That call was important."

"Oh, I'm sure it was," Ballinger said as he finished his beverage and they left. "Who'd you have to call, your boyfriend?"

Kris just shook her head in the affirmative while trying to remain calm in the annoying atmosphere.

A light rain had begun to fall, and Ballinger's driving was not exactly good for the weather or for the high truck traffic on Route One South. Kris's uneasy concern prompted her to say, "Scott, I think I should drive, okay?"

"Why?" he asked as he moved the speedometer up to seventy-five. "Do you also (hic) have a problem with my driving ability like you apparently (hic) have with my screwing ability?"

195

Kris was now very frightened, and she pleaded with the angry driver to slow down. "My god, Scott, you're going to get us killed out here!"

"Who the fuck cares, you little bitch of a whore, that mangy bastard you call your boyfriend?"

Maybe it was because of sheer rage that Kris reached over and slapped Ballinger as hard as she could. At any rate, the untimely action caused him to lose control of the speeding vehicle, and it swerved too far to the left. The slickness of the road caused their car to hydroplane right on through the divider and into the north-bound lane.

There was no way that the fully-loaded tanker truck could have avoided the head-on collision.

"Kris!" yelled Talanski as he popped wide-eyed out of a deep sleep and sat straight up in bed. He had no idea why he called her name. Something made him break into a cold sweat and feel weak in the knees. No answer on the phone. Within five minutes, Joe was in a cab and headed for Kris's apartment. Not finding her there at ten-thirty made him very tense.

"Damn, that's not like Kris to stay out like this," Joe thought as he opened a bottle of beer and turned on the T.V.

He felt frustrated, because there was no one whom he might call for some kind of information. Their world consisted of only two people, themselves. Joe stared blankly at the picture on the tube, but his mind was not tuned to it. After getting another beer from the fridge, our restless hero turned off the set and turned on the radio. He then lay on his back across the bed while listening to the station that played love songs. Frankie Lane sang "We'll Be To-gether Again," and, for some inexplicable reason, Joe's eyes became misty.

6

Gasoline fire lit up the rainy sky and highway patrolmen had their hands full trying to re-route traffic away from the burning vehicles. Trucks and rescue-squad people were on the scene; although there was very little that anybody could do.

"Get those hoses in place!" a fireman yelled. "The rain's not doing it fast enough! And clear those damn people out of the area; that tank's gonna blow any second now!"

The county coroner's van pulled up. "Where're the bodies?" the driver asked. "We were told there're two for the morgue."

"Yeah," the trooper responded as he led the way. "It was a miracle that the truck driver came away with just a few broken bones, but the other people didn't make it."

When Mr. Santos opened his door, he immediately recognized the two officers as Mitchel Rayburn and Edward Carson. The apartment house was on their beat.

"Hello, Mr. Santos," said Carson, "We're sorry to have to disturb you like this, but we wonder if you could help us out."

"Sure, gentlemen. What can I do for you?"

"Can we talk inside?" Rayburn said.

"Of course. Damn, I forgot my manners."

Once inside, the building superintendent wanted to know if any of his tenants were in trouble. The officers then proceeded to tell him the nature of their call.

A few minutes later, Mr. Santos and the policemen were at the door of 5B. Out of habit, the super knocked, not really expecting anyone to answer.

"Great!" Joe said to himself as he sprang from the bed and ran to the door. "She's finally home."

Mr. Santos was about to insert his master key when the door opened.

"Kris, baby, I . . . oh . . . ah, Mr. Santos . . ."

"Sorry, son, there's been an accident," the superintendent said as he and the officers entered. "Fellas, this is Joe Talanski, Miss Flaubert's friend."

"We're sorry to have to tell you this, Mr. Talanski," Officer Rayburn began, "but there's been an accident up on Route One, and we think one of the two victims was Miss Kristina Flaubert, according to info found in her purse, and . . . Mr. Talanski, are you all right?"

No, he was not all right. Joe felt as though he had been struck repeatedly in the back of the head with a lead pipe. His knees buckled, but the two officers caught him before he fell.

197

"I'm okay," Joe uttered, sitting weakly on the arm of the sofa. "Just have to pull myself together."

"Like I said," Rayburn continued, "we only *think* that it was Miss Flaubert. Can we possibly get in touch with some next of kin tonight? Both bodies are at the county morgue pending positive identification."

Speaking rather calmly, Joe said, "I'll give you Kris's home telephone number in Wisconsin. Do you think they'd let me see her now?"

"Sure," Officer Carson replied. "We'll drive you over there."

Three hours later, Talanski was slouched down in the stuffed chair. The small, dark living room was slightly illuminated by the full moon that finally appeared through the thinning rain clouds. Joe had a pint of cheap rye whiskey in one hand and a loaded .38 in the other. The radio was turned to their favorite station, and he was listening to an instrumental version of "When Your Lover Has Gone."

As fate would have it, the potent liquor raced through Talanski's bloodstream like molten lava down the side of a volcano and rendered him unconscious. The empty bottle and loaded gun fell simultaneously from his hands. When he awakened, sunlight was bathing the entire room, and his telephone was ringing off the hook. With great effort, Joe was finally able to reach it.

"Hello. Doc, I'm glad you called . . . I don't think so. As a matter of fact, I'm not too sure whether I want to walk out of this room . . . Doc, the world hates me, and I just can't cope anymore. I know you don't, and at this stage in my miserable fucking life, I don't care about trying to understand it either. . . . Yep, I've been drinking, and I don't give a shit. Oh, by the way, Doc, Kris is dead. . . ."

Needless to say, within a half-hour, Dr. Harry Compton had left the laboratory and was in his young friend's apartment trying to stabilize him while, at the same time, trying to comprehend the entire picture.

Four

But the Memory Lingers On

1

The boat that was used for the sea hunt had all kinds of state-of-the-art equipment. Electronic devices were in abundance, and the twenty-four-man crew was composed of people who could perform multiple functions. Several of the young biologists pitched in as deckhands as well as sonar operators. All of them were experienced divers and could handle the manual plus motorized winches.

No doubt about it, Ocean World, apparently, spared no expense for this venture. And when, three days prior to cast off, the organization approved all questionable budget requests, Dr. Compton was cautiously elated. He wondered why the Board, all of a sudden, would grant things that had initially been turned down. Answers to the mystery were clarified when Dr. Prescott summoned Compton to his office forty-eight hours before the boat was scheduled to lift anchor.

"Ah, Harry, come in," said the president as he met the veteran biologist with a hearty handshake at the office door. "I'm glad you could get away for a few minutes to meet with us on such short notice. This really won't take too much of your time, because I know you still have some last-second details to take care of before sailing."

It wasn't until Dr. Compton's eyes discovered Dr. Jason Kromyer sitting on the far side of the huge office that suspicion struck him like a thunderbolt. Immediately, Compton mentally braced himself for some kind of bad news, and it wasn't far behind the light social exchanges.

"Hurumph . . . ah, well now, suppose we get down to brass tacks here," said Dr. Prescott as he took his seat behind the large oak desk of officialdom. "Harry, as you well know, the Board has approved all of your equipment and personnel requests for this project . . ."

Oh shit, thought Compton, *here it comes.*

"Even the vessel," continued the president, "is bigger and far more appropriate than the one called for in your original proposal, right?"

"Wes," Compton began as he poured himself a cup of coffee, "why is it I'm getting the feeling that you're about to drop a bomb? Don't tell me that the board has decided not to let me lead this exploration."

"Ha, ha, no, Harry. All of us know full well that you're the best person to head up the project. With all of your past experience, we'd be foolish to do otherwise. But, however, we do realize that you're not as young as you used to be, and you can't physically do many of the things that require a higher energy level, Harry. So, we'd like for Dr. Kromyer to go along as your assistant."

Compton was not in the least bit surprised. He had an idea that the preparations were going along too smoothly. He also knew that young Dr. Kromyer, even before he had been chosen to succeed Compton, was gunning for the top job. To challenge the board's decision at that point would have been futile, and the old biologist knew that. Therefore, he outwardly went along with the idea so as not to jeopardize any part of the program.

"Sure," Compton said. "I think having Dr. Kromyer as my assistant on this voyage would be wonderful. I'm looking forward to working with you, Jason."

After a few minutes more of light conversation, Dr. Compton left his two colleagues in the offices. No sooner had the outer door closed when Dr. Prescott said, "You know, Jason, it's kind of sad when an old warrior waits too long before he decides to hang up his sword."

"Yes, that's true," replied Kromyer. "Especially when he's become too goddamn weak to even hold up his shield."

"Easy, young fellow," the president chided. "If you're around long enough, maybe somebody might make similar comments about you."

"Sir, I really didn't mean any disrespect, but . . . "

"Ha, ha, ha, don't worry about it, Jason. I think perhaps I'm getting a little sensitive these days, because I'm about ten years from retirement. And when I look around and see all of you youngsters armed with the latest knowledge in marine biology, I guess I get a little edgy about my own position here at Ocean World."

"With your expertise in so many areas, Dr. Prescott, I doubt that you need to be concerned about being replaced. I, for one, sir, certainly admire the way you handle sensitive matters. It's obvious that you properly place a great deal of importance on doing what is best for the organization."

Although he tried not to show an overabundance of appreciation for his young colleague's flattering remarks, Dr. Prescott could not help from smiling as he said, "Ah, thank you so much, Jason. I try very hard to give Ocean World high quality service."

When Dr. Kromyer was sure that no one was in the immediate vicinity as the elevator door is closed, he audibly said, "Old incompetent fuck."

2

Mrs. Penn greeted Joe in her usual warm manner. "Good evening, Mr. Talanski, it's so nice to see you again. Dr. Compton is waiting for you and so is the delicious supper I prepared this afternoon."

"Umm, Mrs. Penn, no doubt about it. I think you're the best darn cook in the Sunshine State!" Joe said as he planted a kiss on her chubby cheek. "Where's Doc?"

"He's waiting for you in the den. Oh, and, Mr. Talanski, I want you to know how sorry I am to hear about your fiancée."

"Thank you, Mrs. Penn. That's very sweet of you."

Joe found Dr. Compton pouring over some notes and charts in preparation for the voyage. Each evening, he always pulled out papers from previous sea hunts that were successful. It was almost as though he was trying to muster the courageousness and devil-may-care attitude that brought him so much fame in past years.

The two men dined on Mrs. Penn's tasty roast beef followed by her famous apple cobbler. After the meal, they relaxed over Napoleon brandy and a couple of Cuban cigars. Up to that point all conversation dealt with the voyage.

Dr. Compton related to his young friend what had transpired that morning in the president's office.

"What I fail to understand, Doc, is why the organization would give you so much more than you asked for if they are so anxious for you to retire."

The old gentleman smiled and replied, "Joe, my boy, until I walked into Prescott's office yesterday, I was overjoyed. Up to about ten years ago, I had unlimited access to everything. No corners were cut on my sea hunts, because Ocean World knew I always brought back a lot of money-making creatures. But, after my ticker started acting up, I had to slow down. Couldn't get to where the real action was anymore, namely, diving."

"I don't think you have anything to worry about, Doc. Everybody knows your track record."

"And that's the crux of the whole matter, Joe. I'm sure that when Jason Kromyer found out that we're going to try to bring back a live great white, he persuaded Prescott to let him go also. After all, what could be more prestigious for the soon-to-be named director of the Caribbean Project?

"To tell the truth, Joe, I'm tired. I've had my place in the sun, and I guess it really is about time I step aside and let a more vigorous and energetic person take over. However, we're going to give this voyage our best shot, my boy, because I have a gut-level feeling that it's going to be the most exciting one yet."

"Of course, Doc, and I'm right there with you," Talanski replied while reaching for the brandy bottle. "Just point me in any direction, and I'm off and running—or diving."

Dr. Compton noticed how unusually calm his young friend was, which prompted the question, "Are you all right, Joe? Anything I can help you with before we shove off tomorrow?"

"No, Doc, I'm fine. I guess I'm ready to do anything or go anywhere. Doesn't make a big difference to me."

"You know something, Joe? I should be ashamed of myself. Here I am, flapping off at the mouth about my concerns and not even giving you a chance to say much. And I know there must be a lot tumbling through your mind, because many things have happened in your life since you came to Miami."

After a few seconds of silence, Talanski said, "I loved her more than life itself, Doc. Why . . . why . . . why did Kris have to be taken from me so soon? Pour me another brandy, please . . . thanks. That kid's world was just beginning to develop into something beautiful,

Doc, and I was lucky enough to be part of it, even for that short period of time."

The venerable ocean explorer did not bother to interrupt or make superfluous commentary, because he felt that Joe should have this chance to let it all out, regardless.

"You probably would never guess how we met or under what conditions, and that's not important. The important thing, Doc. . . ." At this point Joe's voice became a little shaky and his eyes a little misty, "is that we loved each other more than anybody else could imagine. Kris and I would've been happy together for the rest of our lives—I know it!"

Pause. Then Joe continued.

"Bullshit! Just who the hell (hic) do I think I am anyway? Her dad was right the day he came to her apartment and (hic) found me there. Mr. Flaubert thought I was just a no-good bum (hic) who his daughter knew. Ha, ha, ha, and you know what, Doc? I am. Basically I'm just a bad penny that's bad luck (hic) for anybody who picks me up. Did you know that, during my few years on this friggin' earth, I've been (hic) nothing but trouble for everybody, huh? Did you know that? Poor Kris's downfall was loving me, Doc. I should've left her alone, not tried to change her. She would (hic) be living today if she hadn't met me. Oh, God, how I loved that girl!

"During the short time Kris and I were together, I got to know more about her, I mean deep down inside her, Doc, than (hic) a lot of couples who've been together for years. And as for the guy who also died in the crash, I feel positive that Kris wasn't fooling around on me, Doc. I guess it's (hic) kind of hard for anyone else to believe that, but I do, and I mean I have no doubt in my (hic) mind that Kris was anything but true to me. I'll never find another woman like her. Come on, Doc, let's drink to my lady."

Although it was quite obvious to Dr. Compton that Joe had certainly had enough brandy, he thought it would be almost sacrilege not to appease his friend in this act of recognition; therefore, he replenished their glasses as he said, "It's tragic that Kris is not here in this room tonight, sitting over there and the three of us toasting tomorrow's departure."

"You're so right, Doc, so right. But here's to you, Kristina Flaubert, my darling! Until I (hic) join you, rest in peace, baby."

When Joe sat the empty glass on the coffee table, he leaned back on the comfortable couch, closed his eyes, and fell fast asleep. Dr. Compton removed his shoes and stretched him out.

The house was silent, except for the biologist's occasional coughing as he bent over his notebooks. Then there was a gentle knock at the opened door of the den. Dr. Compton looked above the shade of the single lamp to see his housekeeper standing there.

"Mrs. Penn, I thought you had retired several hours ago."

"I did, sir, but you know how light a sleeper I am. I see Mr. Talanski is still here. Shouldn't he be in bed rather than trying to get comfort from that couch?"

"Oh, he'll be all right. What time is it anyhow?"

"It's almost two o'clock, and you're not going to be in the best of shape when your boat leaves at six."

"Ha, ha ha. Oh, I'll be just fine, Mrs. Penn, but I don't know about my crewman there."

"You really like Mr. Talanski, don't you, sir?"

"Uh huh, yes. I like him. For some strange reason, I liked the lad the very first time I saw him cleaning tanks. There was something magnetic about Joe that seemed to draw me to him.

"You know, Mrs. Penn," the old gentleman continued as he leaned back in his oaken swivel chair and looked at the sleeping form on the coach, "if my wife and I had had children, maybe we would have had a grandson like Joe. Yep, that would've been pretty nice."

"Oh, Dr. Compton, from what you've told me of Mrs. Compton and the pictures I've seen, I'm sure she was a real fine lady."

"The best, Mrs. Penn, the best. God hasn't made a finer woman. Yep, I'd probably have a grandson to whom I could pass on all of my old bad habits, right? Ha, ha. You go on back to bed. I still have some things here I want to review before morning."

"Good night, sir."

"Good night, Mrs. Penn."

Five

Cavern of Serrated Death

1

The *Sea Gull* was a small freighter that Ocean World had purchased in 1961. Since then, the ship was completely overhauled and converted into a rather sophisticated floating marine laboratory. It was manned by a crew whose educational levels ranged anywhere from twelfth grade to post-doctoral studies. One of the things that the lab wanted to do when it made such an investment was to make sure that every one of the crew members was familiar with *Sea Gull's* capabilities and limitations. This is why Talanski and several others were obliged to spend three full days on board the docked ship. Their extensive orientation covered all aspects of the vessel's functions.

Joe was particularly interested in the various pieces of equipment that were going to be used in the crew's attempt to do something that none of the other aquariums had done, namely, bring back a live, adult, great white shark.

Dr. Compton did not exactly have an easy time in convincing the board that the achievement of such an endeavor was within the grasp of Ocean World if he were given permission to head up such an expedition.

On the afternoon of the second day, the *Sea Gull* was plying the waters south-southwest of Andros Island. According to the private information that Dr. Compton shared with no one other than Joe, several great whites had been spotted in the area.

While some of the crew members were busily capturing a couple of huge sea turtles, Talanski and Dr. Mark Davenport were receiving final check off before being lowered in the shark cage. The sunny sky was totally devoid of clouds, and the beautiful blue water was clear; perfect for exploring.

Dr. Compton spent a few minutes briefing the two divers as their oxygen tanks were being secured. "Now remember, even though these waters appear peaceful, dangerous situations can occur unexpectedly. Don't venture more than fifty yards away from the cage, and make sure that your tetherlines are fastened to your belts and the cage. Remember, every thirty seconds look around you, I mean the full three hundred and sixty degrees. Because, if a shark should decide to strike, especially a great white, you will not have time to do anything but die. Okay, you'll be down for thirty minutes maximum. If you see anything that you think might require topside investigation, just signal us. Don't take chances. Any questions?"

"I'm wondering, Dr. Compton," Davenport said as he and Talanski were entering the cage, "whether it was such a good idea for us to be wearing these black wet suits. This color, plus flippers, might cause us to be mistaken for seals, a favorite food of sharks."

A few minutes later, the steel eight-by-ten cage carrying its two occupants was lifted over the side and lowered gently into the water. The *Sea Gull* had dropped anchor to about one hundred thirty-five feet. A coral-studded embankment with its vast array of colors and hues was absolutely stunning. The refracted sunlight was able to penetrate the depths just enough to give Joe a beautiful picture of the aquamarine world. He was so engrossed in his surroundings that caution was all but abandoned. Our impetuous hero unhooked the tether cord so that he might get a better view of the area.

Dr. Davenport looked up to see hundreds of blue fish streaking around the surface. Immediately, he focused his attention on the source, and he saw several seals in hot pursuit. No sooner had he resumed the algae inspection when his sixth sense caused him to turn around. At first, Davenport thought the shadowy outline that faintly appeared in the distance was that of a medium-sized sperm whale. However, as the outline grew more definitive, the young biologist recognized it to be a *carcharodon cacharias*—A HUGE GREAT WHITE SHARK! Being less than twenty yards away from the cage, Davenport quickly swam to it and closed the door. He then tugged on Joe's tetherline. It was not attached, and the gigantic shark was close enough for the diver to see its full body.

Oh, my God, thought Dr. Davenport as he tried to remain motionless inside the cage. *Joe's out there, and he has no idea what kind of danger he's in! Then again, maybe the shark attacked him beyond my visibility range.*

Seconds seemed like hours to the caged diver. Davenport thought about signaling to be raised, but he decided not to since his partner's situation was still unknown.

Come on, Talanski, he said to himself, *just give me some kind of sign!*

The shark, although its mouth was partially open, appeared to be more curious than vicious as it nosed around the top of the cage. Then, with just a flick of its tail, the huge fish turned and darted off into the distance until it was out of sight.

The biologist glanced at his watch. Seven minutes remained on their diving time. He felt a combination of fear and frustration, because he had never before encountered a great white, plus he realized that there was absolutely nothing he could do alone.

Joe was totally unaware of the circumstances which had developed back at the cage, but he was definitely totally aware of his present circumstances, namely, the appearance of three mako sharks. Talanski knew that his only chance was to remain calm and swim slowly back to the cage. Things seemed to have been working out well for him until one of the makos nudged his leg. This action indicated to our hapless hero that it was only a matter of seconds before the sharks would attack.

The great white that had given Dr. Davenport such a scare was newly arrived in the area from the Congo River basin of West Africa. This thirty-four-foot awesome female weighed almost eight thousand pounds. However, her stiff body motions and slow deliberate turns could be governed with just a light flick of her tail fin.

The cage was an object that the great white had not seen before, and her curiosity prompted her to make a close inspection. Perhaps it was lucky for Dr. Davenport that he did not panic or make any type of aggressive move, because this engine of destruction would certainly have gone into action.

Talanski had resolved himself to meet death in the jaws of the mako sharks that had surrounded him. He was too far from the cage to make a successful attempt at reaching it. Suddenly, the three sharks darted away in the same direction. Our careless hero was totally surprised but quite happy. However, his happiness was short-lived, because out of the thin veil of murkiness loomed the most horrifying sight that he had ever seen. Approaching Joe slowly, head on, was the great white shark that only moments before had nosed around the cage. None of the information that Talanski had read about sharks nor his experience of working around the aquarium tanks came to serve him. The great white's head grew larger and larger as she curiously approached this object that had stopped swimming and was practically motionless. The giant fish seemed to be in no hurry to gulp down this small morsel in front of her, and the inside of Joe's wet suit was drenched with perspiration and urine.

As the shark swam under Talanski, her dorsal fin brushed against his leg. Then she made a short turn and swam over him. This time, her dingy white belly came in contact with Joe's left hand. He knew that his moment of dying was only seconds away, but yet there seemed to be a prolonging of the inevitable. On the shark's third time around, it eyed Talanski closely in the frontal position. Huge double-rowed jagged teeth lined the cavernous mouth which the great white opened to about four feet. Her upper lip was curled back over the teeth and her tongue was depressed. She then partially closed her mouth and slowly veered off to the side. Joe was beyond the point of being panic-stricken. His mind was a blank on every subject. His heartthrobs were so intensified that he felt as though every single blood vessel in his body was going to burst. He looked into the deep black pupilless eyes of the fish as it re-circled and came within twelve inches. Then Talanski did something that perhaps no human being had ever done. He reached out his hand and gently stroked the nose of the great white shark. After Joe had inexplicably rubbed the fish for about seven seconds, she slowly turned her gigantic head and swam around the almost-senseless diver in a couple of wide circles. Then, with a tremendous burst of spontaneous speed, the great white shark accelerated, and disappeared into the depths.

Dr. Davenport was just about to give the signal for the cage to be raised when he saw his missing partner swimming frantically toward him. As soon as the two men were back on the deck of the *Sea Gull*, Mark practically snatched off Joe's goggles.

"Where in the hell were you, Talanski? And why did you unhook your line?"

Joe's face was ashen white and expressionless. Other crew members gathered around the retrieved divers. Dr. Davenport was extremely angry. Another crew member asked, "What happened, Mark? Did anything go wrong down there?"

"Did anything go wrong down there! No,"* replied the biologist as he was being helped in taking off his oxygen tanks, "except for the fact that Talanski went against all the safety rules, which could have caused both of us to be in some shark's stomach, I guess you might say that nothing went wrong!"

Dr. Kromyer and his assistant came topside just as Davenport was sounding off.

"What's wrong, Mark?" Kromyer asked. "Are you fellas all right?"

"Damn, ha, ha, ha. What're we playing around here, twenty questions or something?" the nervous biologist said. "Jason, I almost got my tail chewed by a shark because of that sonofabitch sitting over there looking as though he was the one who came face to face with the devil! He unhooked his line to go looking for God knows what while I was left uncovered! I didn't realize he was gone until something told me to look over my shoulder just in time to escape from the biggest *carcharodon cacharias* that I've ever seen! Mark, I'm telling you, it was well over thirty feet! The only thing that saved me was the cage, and, really, I don't know if even that would've held together had the shark attacked!"

Meanwhile, Talanski still had not said one word. When his tanks were removed, he stood up shakily.

"Hey, take this man below and have the medic check him out!" Kromyer shouted to a couple of deckhands.

"Jason, I'm telling you," Davenport continued as they headed toward the lab, "the shark was huge! If only we could harness that one, Ocean World would be the most popular marine entertainment center in the nation! None of the trained porpoises and orcas could even hold a candle to this baby! Jason, I'm talking b-i-g!"

"Umm, I can see you're pretty excited about that great white," Dr. Kromyer responded. "As you know, in spite of all the information gathered by marine biologists over the years, that species is still somewhat of an enigma. It seems that each time someone thinks he has pinpointed substantive data on *carcharodon cacharias,* several other pieces of information will give contrary views."

'Yeah, yeah, I know it all too well, Jason, but the least we can do is try to keep the shark in the vicinity. How about throwing bait over the side at various intervals during the night? Maybe that would hold its attention until tomorrow when we could send down a team with more equipment. I'm sure the old man would go along with the idea since a capture like this would really catapult him into the limelight again."

Until Davenport made the last statement, Kromyer was beginning to share his enthusiasm. But to have Compton get that kind of publicity might slow down his retirement, and the upwardly-mobile young biologist wanted absolutely nothing to stand in the way of his own projected rapid rise at Ocean World and beyond. Therefore, he knew it was imperative that he sort of turn the present action toward himself. Kromyer needed time to think.

"Uh, right, Mark. I agree with you one hundred percent, but maybe we should wait until later before approaching Dr. Compton. Right after you fellows went down this afternoon, he developed dizziness and went to his cabin to take a nap. I think this hot news will still be smoking an hour or so from now."

As Talanski was being helped down the stairs by two crewmen, they met Dr. Compton, who had just received word of the divers' return. He noticed the far-away blank stare on his young friend's face and asked, "Are you feeling sick, Joe?"

"I doubt he's going to answer, Dr. Compton," said one of the helpers. "He hasn't said one word since he and Mark came up. Dr. Rinquist checked him out and found nothing physically wrong. He suggested that we take him to his cabin, and let him lie down for awhile."

The crew chief, after talking further with his colleagues as they made sure that Talanski was all right in the cabin, opened the porthole for fresh air.

"Close it, Doc."

"Well, well, look who's back among the living," a crew member said. "I knew you'd be okay."

Talanski pulled Compton's arm and whispered, "I have to talk to you alone—right now."

"Gentlemen . . ."

"That's all right, sir. We understand. Anybody can get shaken from diving. See you later in the galley, Talanski."

As soon as the door closed, our nervous hero sat up on the side of his bunk bed and calmly said, "I saw Death himself, Doc. Down there . . . deep . . . I looked him right in the face . . ."

"Take your time, son. Just take your time, and tell me about everything that happened."

"I've been close to dying so many times, Doc, and you know something? Not until today . . . down there . . . I realized how painful the process could be.

"I was face to face with a great white shark, the biggest one in the world, Doc! I'm telling you it was close to me . . . so damn close that I touched it on the nose with my hand!"

"You what?"

"Yeah, yeah, I reached out, don't ask me why, reached right out and touched it! I swear! As God as my witness, Doc, I actually touched, not just touched but gently rubbed the nose!"

Dr. Compton remained calm during their conversation, thinking that his young friend might be experiencing post-diving jitters.

"I see . . . I see. Well, how did the cage hold up, Joe? Any damage done to the . . . "

"Cage? Doc, that's the scary part of all this! I wasn't in the cage . . . nowhere near it, as a matter of fact! It seemed like forever. I expected to be slashed apart. Now here's what really caused my heart to almost stop beating, Doc. As I rubbed the shark's nose, a peaceful feeling came over me momentarily. I felt safe. I actually felt safe!"

"I understand, son, and now I want you to try to get some sleep. We'll talk about this after you've had a couple hours of rest, okay?"

"All right, Doc, I do feel drained. Those pills they gave me are making me a little woozy. But we have to talk about this again."

2

After supper, Compton, on Kromyer's special request, held a work meeting with five of the bioligists who were considered to be experts in shark study.

"From what Mark tells us," said Compton, "this particular great white is the largest we've heard of in a long time."

"That's true, sir," Dr. Davenport replied. "I've been cage-diving for only a couple years now, and I don't claim to know everything about sharks, but I do know how to make a quick visual assessment of these unpredictable babies. And, believe me, this one was well over thirty feet."

"I remember having read about a thirty-nine-and-a-halfer caught off the Hawaiian Islands in the late 1930s," Dr. Clifford Baxter added, "but, personally, I haven't seen any over, say, twenty or so feet. And, of course, I'm talking about measured carcasses. Yet, I don't know of any expedition that's brought back a live one."

"I understand exactly what you're saying, Cliff," Dr. Compton added, "because, in all of the years I've been going on marine expeditions, not once did we ever give serious consideration to trying to capture a great white. Maybe it was just plain fear that man has had in every close encounter. As a result, all kinds of theories have been set forth about this mysterious fish that's found in every single ocean and sea of the world."

"Well, I agree with the theory that *carcharodon cacharias* is a thinking shark," said Dr. Matsu Kuromoto, a shark expert on loan from the University of Tokyo, "It not only is capable of basic reasoning but it is the only species that will retaliate immediately if molested or injured. Ten years ago, while I was on an oceanography exploration about three hundred miles east off Aoga-shima Island, I lost a good friend. He was attacked by a great white shark and carried away. Takada never had a chance."

"I'm not at all surprised, Mat," Dr. Wayne Steuben added. "We know that the great white does this, whereas other sharks will take a leg or an arm first. At least the victim might get an opportunity to call or signal for help. But the great white . . . well . . . it just takes the victim and gulps him down in a hurry."

"Okay, gentlemen," said Dr. Compton. "I suppose we could go on all night relating known incidents involving *charcharodon carcharias,* but we know that it's not going to help us very much in trying to capture one if we don't put our scientific knowledge into practical usage here. After all, the main goal of this entire exploration is to bring back a live great white. So what do you say we make some concrete plans for getting the one that two of our divers reported having seen this afternoon?"

It was nearly midnight when the meeting adjourned, and most of the men were ready for a good night's sleep. However, Dr. Compton was far too excited about the prospect of catching the shark to think about sleep. He knew that success in this venture would be the greatest of all his previous ones. And the hand-picked crew was also excited, especially after the various pieces of sophisticated equipment were found to be in excellent operating condition.

The beautiful pale moonlight shining over the rippling tropical waters was complemented nicely by soft cool breezes. Dr. Compton, while slowly strolling the deck and smoking his pipe, stopped to chat with Larry Foxx, whose midnight-to-four A.M. watch duty was augmented by his having to pitch three buckets of fish heads over the side once every half hour.

"Having fun, Larry?" quipped the old biologist.

"Oh, hi, Dr. Compton. I can't exactly say I'm having fun, but, judging by the thrashing around I hear down there every time I pitch the buckets, I'd say some pretty big makos and blue tips are having a feast. Sir, do you really think there's a great white in the area?"

"Definitely, Larry," responded Compton as he tapped his pipe while leaning on the rail. "No matter whether the water is cold or warm, the great white is there, my boy. Maybe one of the reasons is because it has no real enemies and it's extremely aggressive. If you injure one and don't kill it, you'll have the devil to pay. Many are the men who've looked into the colorless black eyes of the great white, but I don't know of any who've lived to tell about it. Undoubtedly, Larry, this species will attack *anything,* and I mean anything, little boats, big boats, you name it. *Carcharodon carcharias* is, without question, the mightiest engine of destruction at large in the open sea."

"According to what I've read," Foxx commented as he emptied a bucket over the side, "the great white is capable of limited reasoning and travels alone, never found in schools. How big do you think this one is, Dr. Compton?"

"Oh, I don't know . . . somewhere between eight and forty feet. Davenport and Talanski both swear that the one they saw was over thirty, but I guess it's kind of hard to pay attention to particulars when you're staring into the face of one of those babies.

"Well, I'd better turn in now. Tomorrow is already shaping up to be a very interesting day. Here, Larry, give me one of those buckets."

The old biologist pitched the smelly contents into the water.

"Presto! Now that will definitely bring us some good luck, sir!"

"Ha, ha, ha. I hope so, son, I hope so. Goodnight, and stay alert."

"Oh, I will. Goodnight, sir."

3

It was primarily because of her unusually high sense of curiosity that the great white allowed the strange object not only to touch her nose but also rub it. And, somewhere in the small brain that governed this leviathan, a soothing message was received. She liked the contact to the extent that the thought began to occupy a segment of her inner force. Nevertheless, the great white's overpowering motivation was food, and she found plenty of it swimming around the huge dark shadow overhead.

All night, schools of blue fish and tuna had been feasting on the garbage that was thrown from the boat. In kind, these hopeless creatures were falling victim to the mako, hammerhead, and tiger sharks that had been attracted to the scene also. Meanwhile, the great white, being the only one of her species in the area, did not have to rush. Ever so often, she darted through the thrashing objects near the dark shadow and came away with a mouth filled with a combination of garbage eaters and eaters of the garbage eaters.

On one pass-through, the great white did not move fast enough, and, as a result, she was nipped by a fourteen-foot tiger shark. Now that was a big mistake on the much-smaller fish's part, because the bite did more by way of infuriation than infliction of pain. Immediately, the great white turned her thick body and zeroed in on the tiger, which had the audacity to maneuver for a second attack. With her lips curled back over rows of jagged teeth, the great white gunned her engine toward the tiger, and clamped her cavernous maw on the fourteen-footer so hard that it was completely decapitated. Holding tightly to the delicious prize and with tremendous upward thrust, the great white burst through the surface of the churning waters for a good six feet into the morning air.

"Holy shit!" shouted a crewman who just happened to be scanning the area. "Did you see that?"

"What?" asked another. "You mean all the fish grabbing bait?"

"No, no . . . I . . . I just saw . . . shit . . . I don't know *what* I saw, Sean! But it was right over there, I'm telling you, no more than forty or so yards out!"

"Well, maybe it was a giant sea manta. They like to leap when . . . "

Feeling slightly frustrated and annoyed, Bill interrupted with, "Hey, Sean, I also know a little about marine biology, okay? And that was no damn manta! It looked more like a . . . a . . . oh, I don't know . . . a submarine minus a conning tower!"

"Great pal! Ha, ha, ha! That's one way to end a stupid conversation. Come on, let's go below and check out today's diving gear and the shark cage."

"Damn, Sean, wouldn't it be amazing if we could capture a great white today? Sure would like to be part of the exploration that brings one of those babies back alive!"

"Yeah, I know what you mean, but the likelihood is not that likely, Bill, when you consider what the odds are. Nobody has ever brought back an adult of substantial size. Speaking of size, maybe the thing you saw out there was one. Ha, ha, ha."

"Up your ass, Sean."

4

At 11:30 A.M., the steel shark cage was lifted over the side and lowered into the water. A lot of excitement surrounded this particular dive, because there was still strong belief that the great white shark was still in the area. Every piece of equipment used for the dive was checked and double-checked for performance. However, there was still some skepticism as to the effectiveness of tranquilizers.

"I certainly hope it works," said one of the four wetsuit-wearing divers as they prepared for submersion. "I mean, how the hell do we know whether the tranquilizer drug is strong enough?"

Dr. Kuromoto, leader of the dive, replied, "The combined dosages that we have in these darts are enough to knock out any animal."

"And if they don't work, guys, we can always use these special grenades, right, Matt?" asked Mark Davenport.

"Urr . . . well, let's hope we don't have to resort to that," Kromyer said. "Remember, our main objective is to bring the fish back alive! Of course, it could easily be destroyed, but that would be defeating our purpose.

"Hey, you're mighty quiet there, Talanski. What do you think about it?"

Joe was in a rather pensive mood, even though he had to beg Dr. Compton for permission to go down with the group. "All of you gentlemen know more about sharks than I can ever hope to know. But I will tell you this: being close enough to touch one and live to tell about it is . . ."

"Okay, okay, Joe, we understand what you mean," Dr. Kromyer interrupted as he turned his attention to the cage-to-boat radio source. "Don't forget, you're to stay within easy access to the cage. It's a beautiful day, and the water is pretty clear."

Gentle swells lapped the bottom of the cage which was held in position for a final radio check. When Kromyer was confident that all systems were go, he gave the thumbs-up signal to the crane operator, and the coral waters closed over the cage.

At a depth of seventy-two feet, marine life activity was very interesting to the four divers. Dr. Kuromoto unlatched the door to the cage and motioned the other divers to follow him. A giant sea turtle that was foraging for crabs along the bottom seemed unperturbed by the presence of these four foreign objects.

Although she was nearly three-quarters of a mile away, the great white shark sensed the presence of something different. With a light flick of her tail fin, she turned her huge body upward on a fifteen-degree angle from a depth of 240 feet and swam briskly in the direction of our divers.

Matsu Kuromoto was the first one to notice the sudden excitement taken on by the many groups of tropical fish that had been swimming in the area. Then he saw the reason, for out of the distance, and headed toward him, was the great white. Years of studying shark behavior didn't seem to offer Dr. Kuromoto any fingertip hints that he could call to mind. The enormously thick body and cold black eyes of the great white, which was now slowly circling him, were mesmerizing to the experienced shark hunter. Then, on the fourth complete circle, the creature curled its lips over those jagged teeth and headed straight for the unfortunate biologist.

Within a couple of seconds, there was not a trace of him. The shark had swallowed the comparatively small morsel whole. Except for the slight stream of blood that trailed out of the great white's mouth, there was nothing left of the Japanese diver.

Kromyer, Davenport, and Talanski were unaware of what had happened to Dr. Kuromoto. However, moments later, the three remaining divers were faced with life-threatening peril when four mako sharks suddenly appeared. The largest one, fifteen feet in length, began making aggressive moves toward the men. Kromyer did not waste any time in deciding what to do. He immediately shot the shark with his tranquilizer gun. Seconds later, the fish's movements slowed to a stop, and it began to sink. Under the sea, food is food, and the stunned shark's traveling partners made absolutely no distinction. They attacked the limp form and began a feeding frenzy. The thrashing and tearing of flesh attracted other species to the scene.

Meanwhile, our three divers were able to make it safely back to the cage. They wondered why Kuromoto was not there. On an underwater writing board, Kromyer wrote the name followed by a question mark. He then placed the special radio apparatus over his head in order to talk to the boat.

"Can you read me up there?"

"Yes, we read you loud and clear," responded the crane operator.

"This is Kromyer. We just had a close call with a few sharks down here but nothing serious. Dr. Kuromoto is not here in the cage with us. He should've been back by now. We're going searching for him. . . ."

"Hello, hello, Jason? This is Compton! What the hell's going on down there? Don't take careless chances, regardless!"

"No need to worry, Harry. I'm sure Matsu is somewhere in the area, probably poking around on the other side of this coral reef."

"By the way, Jason, how's Joe doing?"

"Oh, I guess your *protegé* is holding up all right; although, I still don't think it was such a good idea to have him along on this dive."

Just then, the whole cage shook, throwing its three occupants violently against the bars. Since Talanski and Davenport were not on radio hookup, they couldn't say anything, but all three of the men simultaneously saw the source about twenty feet above them:

the same great white shark that had devoured Dr. Kuromoto was nosing around the cable.

"Holy, shit!" exclaimed Kromyer as he held on to the side. "I see it, but I don't believe it! Harry, Harry, we've got a *carcharodon cacharias* down here! And it's a big one, the biggest I've ever seen!"

"Okay, okay, Jason, just calm down," said the veteran explorer. "That cage is made of heavy-gauge steel! Besides, sharks don't particularly like the feel of metal against their teeth. Let me speak to Joe."

Kromyer motioned for Talanski to hook up. He did, but never once taking his eyes off the creature that was now nosing around the cage.

"Doc, I swear, this is the same great white that Mark and I saw yesterday! Yeah, yeah, I'm positive! What should we do about Matsu out there, Doc? . . . There're a lot of 'em in the area, including hammerheads and blue tips! But I'd recognize this particular great one out of a million! I see . . . yes . . . but . . . well, we can't just leave him down here not knowing if he's dead or alive! I understand that, Doc, but . . . but I have to do what I have to do."

"Joe, now don't try . . . Joe . . . Joe! Damn it, kid, answer me! Mark? Yeah, Mark . . . just don't let Joe do something foolish!"

While Talanski fully realized that going out there to look for the missing member of their team was suicidal, he couldn't help himself. The impulse was much too strong for him to resist. So he took a flashlight, a spear gun, two hand grenades, and left the cage.

"Christ Almighty, he's gone! Talanski left! We couldn't stop him, Dr. Compton!"

"I understand, Mark, I understand," the old biologist replied in a forced calm tone. "Don't you and Jason take any chances. Stay in the cage. If the other two men are not back in exactly four minutes, the cage is being hoisted without 'em, do you read me?"

A rather large hammerhead swam within ten yards of the lone diver, who was completely out of the cage vicinity and on the other side of the coral mound. Joe readied his spear gun, but the shark turned and quickly disappeared. Then our impetuous diver saw something else slowly approaching him head-on.

The great white, in all of her enormous hulk, moved toward the thing that piqued her curiosity. It looked like the object she had swallowed just minutes before. However, even though her mouth was partially open, she did not feel the desire to eat this thing. Closer and closer the big fish slowly came, both jet-black eyes focused sharply.

Talanski, instead of shooting his gun, or making escape movements, remained almost motionless. The great white slowed down to almost a halt and gently bumped him in the stomach. Joe's mind was totally devoid of all rational things, except, of course, he realized that he was gazing his last gaze in this life. Yet, the numbing fear that gripped him the day before was not present.

With this strange-feeling object still on her nose, the great white suddenly shot upward on an eighty-degree angle. Although she broke the surface in great billowing foam, there was no leaping this time. Joe's heart nearly exploded as he was pushed into the full sunlight. Luckily, his two oxygen tanks and mouthpiece were not dislodged. Nearly a hundred yards away and on the opposite side of the boat, several crew members saw the diver's plight when an all-too-familiar pectoral fin sliced through the water toward the boat then back toward the diver who had begun stroking for the vessel.

"Diver off port stern!" yelled one of the men. "Shark closing in!"

Within seconds, rifle fire split the air as other crewmen tried to keep the shark away from the diver. Excitement was also happening on the other side of the ship—the cage and only two of the original four occupants had just been lowered onto the deck. And when the shark cry went out, the response was spontaneous. Even Dr. Compton, armed with a 30-30 rifle, rushed as fast as he could to the boat's rear and joined in the firing.

Exhausted by his present ordeal, Talanski was feebly stroking. The men began yelling to him.

"Keep coming! Don't stop now! You're almost here!"

"Where're the fucking sharks? Can anybody see fins?"

"There, there, right over there!"

More rifle fire.

When the stinging objects struck her back, the great white submerged quickly and passed beneath the vessel to the other side. Meanwhile, Talanski was within forty or so yards of life lines. He had already shed himself of the heavy oxygen tanks and goggles.

"That's right, kid," shouted Dr. Compton, "keep swimming! Just a little more and we'll have you!"

Then, about twenty yards away from the diver and in full view of everybody, the great white shark burst through the surface with a mighty leap of almost fifteen feet into the air. She did an almost perfect dolphin dive back into the water.

"There it is, there it is!"

"That guy's a goner! We can't get to him! He's gone down!"

The wake of the leviathan's re-entry created such a turbulence that Joe was momentarily submerged.

"That shark's got him. It's no need to . . ."

"Look! Look!" Compton yelled. "Hurry up! Get him outta there before the shark returns!"

Talanski bobbed to the top like a cork, and alongside him appeared the emerging form of the great white.

"Holy Mary, Mother of God!" shouted another crewman. "Will you look at that!!"

The shark had raised her huge head out of the water long enough for the spectators to see what many of them had never seen before, not even in the movies. Joe's hand was touching the sea monster's nose. Then it rolled on its side, showing the full thirty-four-foot length. During the fifteen seconds that all of this took place, no one moved or attempted to pull Joe out of the water. Undoubtedly, every person who was observing the scene was completely overwhelmed with amazement. The huge fish would slowly disappear and reappear.

"Hey," yelled Joe when it submerged for sixth time, "are you people gonna get me aboard, or do I have to go home inside this baby?"

"Better not make any sudden moves, Joe," said Dr. Compton in almost a whispering tone. "Sharks react to them and noise. Just slowly reach for this line we're lowering to you. When you get it, hold on tight, because we're going to pull real fast."

Joe wrapped the rope around his chest and gave a nod.

"Okay," shouted Compton to the crew, "pull, pull, pull, men, pull it faster!"

During this time, all eyes were looking for the shark to reappear, but it didn't.

Once safely on board, Joe assured everyone that he was all right; however, the loss of Dr. Kuromoto concerned him greatly.

For the rest of the day, the main topic aboard ship was how lucky Talanski was to escape death. Of course, there was a lot of talk about how they could possibly get the great white shark to Ocean World.

5

Amidst the scientific and technical jargon that was passing around the room, there were frequent shrugs of shoulders and admittings of not enough information known about this particular species of shark on which concrete judgments might be built. All of the biologists and technicians were still baffled by what they had actually seen in the water, plus by what Talanski told them about his encounter with the great white on both days.

"Yes, but, Joe," said Dr. Kromyer, "how do you account for the fact we lost Dr. Kuromoto if this shark is not vicious?"

"I can't. And do you want to know something else? I'm not sure that what happened to me, or maybe I should say didn't happen to me, can be explained. All I know is that I did, in fact, come face to face with a great white shark which, by natural reasoning should have gobbled me down without ceremony. Instead, the sonofabitch turned away, and that was after it came so damn close to me that I reached out and touched it on the nose, and I lived beyond the moment. Now how in the hell am I supposed to explain something like that, huh? Can any of you tell me, with scientific accuracy, what's going on?"

It was obvious to Dr. Rinquist, the ship's medic, that Talanski was beginning to show signs of a nervous breakdown, and, instead of having him continue answering all kinds of questions that were being tossed at him, the physician interceded with, "Gentlemen, Talanski has experienced something that no one else in this room has, and it's hard enough for him to try to verbalize the experience. So what do you say we just let him talk uninterrupted until he's ready to handle the more technical questions, okay? Go on, Joe."

After taking a deep drag on a freshly lit cigarette, Talanski began. "Like I told you not too long ago, Doc, death seems to be something that happens to other people around me—but not to me. Remember my telling you that, Doc?"

221

Compton smiled, leaned back in his chair, and motioned for Joe to continue.

"Well, I'll tell you folks one thing," the lucky diver said, "I've seen a few gruesome sights during my twenty-nine years on this earth, but nothing—I mean, nothing, gentlemen—has ever come close to being as frightning, or as pleasurable, than my two separate body-rubbing encounters with that fish. I was beyond being scared. By all rights, I guess I should've had a massive coronary, at least, ha, ha. But, I guess old Death did it again—gave me the cold shoulder."

Talanski proceeded to talk about the strange and mystifying effect that the shark had on him. However, his words were given very little credence by the scientific minds gathered in the room.

Dr. Reginald Blake just couldn't take any more of these ramblings, so he said, "Joe, when I, along with most of the others here, saw that bit of odd shark behavior, I can't say that I'm ready to accept what you're telling us as . . . er . . . as inexplicable.

"Jason, Mark, you guys were down there, too. Isn't there some kind of rational explanation you can give us?"

Before either of the two could respond, Talanski said, while standing up and moving toward the door, "Look, fuck you people, okay? I had a couple of experiences that no one else in this room has had, so that makes me a liar or crazy, right? Well, I've told a lot of lies in my time, and I'm probably crazy, at least that's what a few shrinks have said about me. So . . . I guess there's nothing else for me to say, except I'm tired as hell. Goodnight, fellas."

When the door closed, the room erupted into all kinds of buzzing.

"Okay, okay, gentlemen," said Dr. Kromyer, "whether we believe him or not is not too important at this time. What *is* important is for us to devise some kind of strategy for getting this particular *carcharodon carcharias* to Ocean World, and I'm not too damn sure if that's going to be an easy task. What do you think, Dr. Compton?"

The seasoned explorer tapped the ashes out of his pipe and replied, "That fish was the biggest one I've ever seen, plus its behavior was unlike any in my frame of reference. So I'm just as stymied as anyone else. But . . . and I know this might sound totally illogical . . . but I do believe that the only way we're going to capture this shark . . . now here's the clincher . . . the only way is through Joe Talanski."

After the meeting broke up, Kromyer and two close friends went to the galley for sandwiches and drinks. Since the area was rather private, Kromyer seized the opportunity to talk about something that had been on his mind, especially since the next day's venture was going to be an all-out effort to catch the great white shark.

"It's no secret," Kromyer said as he poured a round of scotch for himself, "I would certainly like to take over the whole operation of the exploration division when old Harry retires, but I really hadn't thought there was much of a chance for that. Now, I *know* there's even a better chance if we bring back this goddamn fish, because we're going to get some spectacular film footage tomorrow, guys."

Davenport added, "I think we can get close enough to the shark to take all the pictures we want, Jason, but unless they're done while something out of the ordinary is taking place, then we're not going to make much of an impression back at Ocean World."

"So what do we need to do in order to make the most of this once-in-a lifetime opportunity?" asked Bill Zeigler, an expert underwater photographer.

Kromyer quickly responded with, "After we've numbed the shark with enough injections, Bill, you're going to make sure that you get a lot of close-ups of Mark and me actually handling the fish while placing the three hoisting belts around it."

"Are you forgetting about the fourth man with us?" Davenport queried. "Talanski's going to want to be included in on everything we do down there, and we all saw some odd things happen today."

"I don't see that his presence is going to detract from our plans," Kromyer said. "In fact, I intend to stay close to him at all times just in case there might be something to the idea that he and the shark have some kind of (ha, ha, ha) understanding, as it were."

6

Although the great white's natural instinct prompted her to search the deep for food, which meant going several miles away from the long shadowy form that seemed to stay in one location, she always returned. As soon as the shark heard different sounds, she quickly rose from the cold three hundred foot depth just in time to see the lowering cage and its four occupants. The giant fish came close enough to brush against it.

"Okay," said Kromyer to Dr. Compton, "there it is again! We have the shark within range, Harry! Can you read me?"

"I read you, Jason," replied Compton. "Remember, don't try to do anything other than what we planned. Stay in the cage until you're absolutely sure that the shark is heavily sedated. Then you guys gotta move fast as hell in positioning the hoisting belts."

"Affirmative," came Kromyer's response as he hand-signaled directions to the other divers. "If this baby continues swimming as closely as it's doing now, we should have our task completed within the next twenty minutes. Okay, breaking contact for now, Harry. Time to go to work."

On one of her passes around the cage, the great white eyed one of those occupants with unusual interest. She then nosed head-on up to within inches of the bars. Her huge, wide mouth was partially open, but there was something about the slow frontal approach that was more of curiosity than aggression.

Bill had already begun taking footage of the shark when Mark motioned that they should start the tranquilization process. While the spear guns were being checked and positioned by Davenport and Kromyer, Talanski quickly unlatched the door and exited the cage. It was too late for anyone to do anything other than let topside know what had happened.

"He did it again!" yelled Kromyer. "That sonofabitch Talanski's out of the cage again, Harry! I told you he should never have been allowed to make this dive! He's crazy! Now when that shark finishes tasting his blood, it'll go looking for more! Great! Thanks to you, Harry, we'll probably lose both man and fish! Do you have any damn suggestions up there? Over."

Kromyer's words came clearly through the public address system; therefore, everybody working in the rigging area heard him.

"What the hell's wrong with that Talanski? He's really pushing his luck!" exclaimed one deckhand.

"Jason, I know how you feel," replied Dr. Compton, "and I can't say that I blame you, but, whatever you do, don't try to follow Joe. Do you read me? Do *not* follow Joe under *any* circumstances! I believe there's definitely some reason why that particular shark did not attack him yesterday or the day before. What it is, I don't know yet. In the meantime, you three fellows stick with the capture plan, okay? Over."

"Roger on the capture plan, Harry," Kromyer said. "You may as well lower the belts now, though. No point in waiting any longer. We want to be ready to swing into action when . . . holy shit, I don't believe what I see!"

Kromyer never finished his conversation with Compton, because something else completely captivated his attention. Consequently, he took off the special radio helmet and joined Davenport and Zeigler in marveling at the strange sight.

Talanski had come into view approximately twenty feet away from the cage, and he was not swimming frantically. As a matter of fact, he paused several times and looked over his shoulder. Then, out of the misty distance, came the object of Talanski's attention.

The gigantic great white shark moved slowly behind the diver. Man and fish proceeded to put on an underwater show that the known world had never before witnessed. In full view of his comrades, Talanski approached the shark and held on to one of its pectoral fins as the thirty-four-foot leviathan gracefully turned and disappeared into the mist. Needless to say, the three caged divers were completely awed. However, before they could react, Talanski reappeared alone and re-entered the cage. The awkwardness of their not being able to talk to one another added to the silent excitement. The other divers had a thousand and one questions that they wanted Talanski to answer, but discussion would have to wait until later. However, the situation did not prevent Davenport from putting on a radio helmet.

"Dr. Compton, Dr. Compton, do you read me? This is Mark. Over."

"I read you, Mark. Over."

"Sir, I don't know whether we're dreaming down here or what! But we just witnessed a first! Talanski was out there with the shark, touched it—no—held on to it, and the two swam away! Talanski came back alone! He's here in the cage, and he's not hurt or anything! Over."

"Okay, okay, just take it easy. Try to hold your composure, Mark. How're Jason and Bill? Over."

"No problem. All of us are safe. It's the weird chain of events that . . . ay, what the hell—no need trying to piece this puzzle together right now. We'll talk about it topside. Besides, this is the first time that one of our . . . oh, oh . . . we have company. Three—no, five big makos just joined us. Looks like we're going to have to wait until these babies clear out of the area before we can do anything else. Talk to you later. Over and out."

After what seemed like an eternity, the sharks finally decided to swim away. However, the temptation to shoot one was too great for Zeigler. He aimed the spear gun carefully and fired, striking a soft belly. Blood trailed from the wound, prompting the other sharks to attack their weakening comrade. Slashing and tearing chunks of flesh from the dying victim occurred immediately. Crimson became the dominant color, and it even drifted into the cage. Then, seemingly out of nowhere, reappeared the same giant white.

Very little meat was left on the dead fish, but the newcomer wanted it anyway. With lips peeled back over jagged razor-sharp teeth, the great white headed straight for the frenzied group and engulfed the entire carcass in her mouth. Needless to say, the other makos uncontestingly left the scene. Our three divers, even though some blood had slightly decreased vision, viewed the action and caught it all on film.

Zeigler was still taking footage when Talanski once again unlatched the cage door and swam out into dangerous open. This time his fellow divers did not attempt to stop him. Instead, they followed closely, spear guns ready. The great white had descended and was out of sight when her acute smelling apparatus signaled activity above. The shark immediately turned upward and reappeared within the divers' sight.

Upon realizing how vulnerable they were, fear took a firm hold on the four divers. Even Joe wondered whether he had made the last mistake of his life by assuming that this mighty engine of the deep would continue to go against its nature of devouring anything and everything representing food.

The divers were certain that the shark was about to attack them when three dark objects entered the water. The wide, dangling belts were lowered close enough to the scene to cause the great white to turn her attention toward them. And, during that brief moment, two of the divers quickly swam back to the safety of the cage. Once again, for some strange reason, Talanski chose to stay out there. However, this time, he was not the only one; Kromyer decided to remain and try to discover why Joe had not been attacked. Zeigler was busy filming while Davenport talked to Compton.

"Yeah, Bill and I can see what's happening out there, Harry, but it's still strange. Oh, wow, the shark is back, and . . . damn, it's moving above us! Let's see now . . . well, it's, ah, yes, a female. Harry, a big female. She's definitely over thirty feet long!"

"All right, all right," Compton replied, "try to tranquilize it! Aim for the area just behind the gills. About five darts should do it, Mark. We're gonna have to work quickly, because this species has to keep swimming in order to breathe and prevent sinking."

"Okay on those directions," Davenport replied, "but I think we're going to need more help down here. Don't want this fish to shake off the effect of the drug before we get the belts around it. Maybe more of . . . oh, wait, here comes Jason, and he's swimming like he's in one helluva hurry. Look, we'll talk to you later. Over and out."

Just as Davenport was about to open the door for Kromyer, the huge great white suddenly bumped the bottom of the cage so hard that its two occupants were tossed violently against the bars. However, Bill managed to hang on to the camera and continue shooting. They saw Kromyer change direction and swim toward the shark as though he was going to attempt to do what Talanski had done, make physical contact. By this time, Joe had just entered the area. The next bit of action happened so suddenly that no counteraction could've stopped it. The shark, its mouth fully opened, headed straight for Kromyer. Without so much as a trickle of blood, the diver disappeared down the great white's gullet. Compared to larger food items, this one did not require chewing. There was another morsel available, but, for whatever reason, the shark, as it had once before, eased up to the other diver and lightly brushed against him. Then, with a slight tail movement, the mighty engine of destruction gracefully left the scene.

7

There was a lot of confusion on board the *Sea Gull* that evening. With the deaths of two crewmen came mixed feelings as to whether the overall mission should be continued. Dr. Compton had already called Ocean World concerning the tragedies and the surrounding circumstances. He had witnessed fatal situations on explorations before but never anything so uncanny as these. However, the pictures that Bill Zeigler took did not color the truth in any way, and the entire crew was allowed to view those shots repeatedly. The three divers, Talanski, Davenport, and Zeigler, were quizzed heavily about what they had seen.

Although there were no eager new persons who wanted to go on the next day's dive, scientific curiosity gripped them tightly enough to keep interest in capturing the shark. So, at the strategy meeting, various ideas were batted around. The one that seemed to garner the most support was the idea of having the fish follow the boat back to Miami.

"Are you sure it'll stay with us?" queried someone of Dr. Compton.

"At this point, I think we all are convinced," he answered, "that this particular shark has not attacked Joe because of something presently unknown to us or him. Yes, I'm pretty sure we can count on the shark's staying with us as long as this man's on board. However, the hunch is going to be tested tomorrow morning. Joe, do you want to take it from there?"

"Sure, Doc," he answered. "Gentlemen, it's not a complicated plan. What we want to do first in the morning is make sure the shark is still in the vicinity. And, when we've established that, keep him, sorry, I mean *her,* interested by tossing a lot of bait into the water."

"Sounds simple enough to me," said biologist Marvin Hoyt, "but how're we going to know if our shark is the one that'll be eating the bait?"

"Now, here comes the clincher," Dr. Compton said as he put his arm around Joe's shoulder. "Joe is willing to go out in one of the rowboats and ... "

"You mean serve as live bait, Harry?" someone asked.

"That's right," interjected Talanski as he stood up, "serve as live bait. I know this might sound stupid to most of you, but I think I know what I'm getting into here. Look, gentlemen, if that great white shark, the most awesome creature between heaven and hell,

228

hasn't gobbled me down by now, then it's my guess that . . . that . . . I don't know why."

"Maybe she loves you," quipped somebody else. "I understand it's a female."

"Maybe she does," Joe said in a rather pensive tone, "maybe she does."

The room erupted into laughter. However, there was one person who found no humor, and that was Mark Davenport. He shouted, "You people seem to be forgetting that we lost Jason and Matsu to the same goddamn fish you're trying to romanticize here! I was down there also, remember? And I want you to know that I agree with you. It *should* be brought back to Ocean World—with its carcass on the end of a hoisting hook!"

Murmurings of agreement and disagreement began to circulate throughout the room. Suddenly, Davenport, surprised by his own words, took on the role of rabble-rouser. He laid aside his scientific background, and dealt with what he viewed as supernatural evil.

"I'm telling you, gentlemen, and Bill can bear me out on this, that particular great white shark is not only the biggest one we ever saw, its behavior is totally unlike anything I have ever learned about *carcharodon carcharias,* right, Bill?"

"Absolutely. Mark is right, and all of you saw what he's talking about as seen on film. Look, I've been doing underwater photography for over fifteen years now, but, I'll tell you something, until this morning, I had never witnessed such a phenomenon."

Dr. Compton felt uneasy about what was being said, because he could visualize the crowning glory of his long career being destroyed. Therefore, he knew he had to say something that would regain the crew's total cooperation. After quiet was restored to the room, Compton tapping the smoldering ashes out of his ever-present pipe, slowly stood up and addressed the group.

"Practically every person in this room has spent time studying *chondrichthyes* or cartilaginous fishes. And we know they come in all shapes and sizes, from the gigantic whale shark to the smallest of the rays. Now, in between, you have all kinds of vicious sharks, *carcharodon carcharias.* . . ."

"What the hell is he doing?" whispered Davenport to those sitting nearby. "If the old man's going to give us a refresher course in marine biology, then I know he's flipped out."

Dr. Compton continued. "And, as many of you know, man knows less about the great white than any of the other species. However, there are a few commonly known facts that serve us: growth can be anywhere from, say, eight feet to within a few inches of forty; it's extremely aggressive; lives fifteen to twenty years; its range is worldwide inshore and off; devours everything—nature's garbage disposal; always travels alone, never in schools; it must swim continuously or sink; and whether you care to believe it or not, this kind is definitely capable of reasoning.

"So, what is my point? Gentlemen, we have a golden opportunity to make marine history here! Yes, we've lost a couple of damn good colleagues in trying to make our mission a success. But what exploration hasn't? Ever since man was introduced to fire, he's been curious and explorative. So what the hell are we doing that's different? Lives, hundreds of lives have been lost on various quests, and many more will be lost as long as we possess our inquisitive nature.

"There's not a man on this ship who didn't know that the primary mission of this venture was to bring back a great white shark—alive! And, for the past couple of days, we've had a big one right here under our noses! Now, are we willing to throw away the opportunity of a lifetime to even outdo what has been done by the National Geographic Society, Jacques Cousteau, or even the group that captured and killed a thirty-eight-footer off the Hawaiian Islands back in the late thirties?"

Suffice to say, by the time Harry Compton finished talking, even Mark Davenport was convinced that killing and bringing back just the carcass of the great white would by no comparison advance the knowledge of marine biology as much as a real live specimen. But, perhaps more than that, the anticipated glory surrounding such a feat was the thought most prominent among the crew.

8

Weatherwise, the day was shaping up to be another hot one. At just eleven o'clock in the morning, it was evident that the already reached seventy-six-degree temperature and bright sunny sky were welcomed by the five divers, Joe being the leader of this group.

The ship's twenty-foot motorized launch was lowered into the water, and each of its five occupants was filled with nervous anticipation. Even though the launch was made of steel and two high-powered rifles were available, there was still a subtle fear that hung over the morning's venture.

"Mark, you and Bill know how important it is for you guys to keep those cameras rolling all the time," Talanski said as the launch headed away from the mother ship. "We don't want to miss any kind of shot, especially close-ups. I'm going to try to stay on the surface as much as possible after I make contact with her, okay?"

"No problem, Joe," replied Bill. "I'll make sure that we catch everything. But I still don't think it's a good idea for you to dive alone even though you're connected to that cord."

"Yeah," Mark said as he checked Talanski's oxygen tanks. "I still believe there must be a better way of getting that shark to stick around other than offering yourself as bait. But we went through all this at the briefing, so good luck anyhow, kid."

"Thanks, Mark. Hell, you know I don't have any logical reasoning to back any of this—everything's a hunch. And, so far, my hunches about the shark haven't hurt me yet, but . . . well . . . here goes nothing!"

Talanski tumbled backward into the beautiful coral water and leveled off at a depth of thirty feet. Nothing unusual was happening down there. Myriad of brightly colored tropical fish zipped around nibbling at the quarter-pound chunks of squid and tuna that were being tossed from the launch. Then, as if they had responded on cue, seven large mako sharks appeared. Joe gave a hard jerk on his cord, and within less than thirty seconds, he was back on board.

"Suppose we hold up feeding for awhile until they decide to go away," Mark said. "We certainly don't want *them* in the area!"

"Ha, ha," laughed Bill adjusting his camera. "Yeah, especially since old Joe here hasn't declared them to be harmless. Right, big guy?"

Talanski also joked about things with his reply. "Ha, that's right, Billy boy, because the invitation list damnsight didn't include those party crashers."

The five launch occupants were still laughing when one of them noticed a dorsal fin coming in the distance. All eyes and attention focused on it.

231

"That's her," said Joe in a calm voice. "That's her—I can feel it. Okay, Mark, check my tanks; I'm going down right now."

"This is crazy," the biologist replied, "but I've seen it work twice already. Just hope you're not superstitious about three's."

"Well, if I am, it's a little late for that now. Turn the valves up a bit, Mark. I might be under water a little longer on this one. Okay, you guys, here goes nothing!"

Splash!

"I certainly hope Talanski's right about his hunches," Chuck said, "because if he's not . . ."

"Don't even think about it," interrupted Mark as he watched the dorsal fin suddenly submerge about fifty feet from the launch.

"Christ!" Jerry exclaimed. "Did you feel it? That shark brushed our bottom! I hope this thing is heavy enough not to be capsized!"

During the next thirty seconds, four men in the boat witnessed quite a scene. No sooner had Jerry spoken when the great white surfaced within a couple of feet and rolled slightly on her side so as to get a full view of the startled crew. Then she disappeared and moved in fast circles around the craft, causing it to do several complete whirls.

"Hang on, men!" Mark yelled. "I think it's trying to dump us into the water! Crank the engine and let's get the hell outta here before we're swamped!"

"Hey, what about Joe?" someone shouted as the boat sped away.

"We can't do anything about him now," Mark responded. "Besides, we don't even have grenades out here! I tried to tell 'em last night, but nobody listened! Old Harry's in charge, so let his ass handle this one, too!"

From the deck of the *Sea Gull,* everyone watched the launch speeding back on maximum throttle. When it became apparent that only four were on board, it was naturally assumed that the missing man was Talanski. Immediately Dr. Compton grabbed a pair of binoculars and began a visual sweep of the area just below the horizon. As luck would have it, he saw an arm waving in the distance.

"There he is!" yelled Compton. "I *knew* he was alive! Hurry up, signal the launch to go back and get him!"

However, the smaller craft had already pulled alongside and the four divers were coming aboard.

"Keep that motor running!" Compton shouted to the attendants as he practically stumbled down the metal steps. "I'm going out there!"

Davenport, although he and the other divers had been scared by their recent experience, joined the veteran biologist when it was established that Talanski was alive. Three men jumped into the launch and sped toward the figure that was bobbing up and down like a cork.

"I must be crazy to be coming back out here with you guys," Zeigler said over the top of the noisy motor. "But if this is going to mean some more good footage, what the hell, right?"

When the craft was about forty yards away from Talanski, he frantically waved and shouted for the rescuers to come no further. Of course, this was quite puzzling to them, but their puzzlement turned into catatonia when all of a sudden Talanski began to slice through the water like a motorboat while holding on to a tall dorsal fin!

"Jesus Christ Almighty!" came the subdued sound of Mark's voice. "I see it, but I don't believe it!"

There was nothing for the men to do except watch the water show as the thirty-four foot great white shark came close enough to the launch for the occupants to get an unobstructed view of her tremendous size. Joe was treading water forty feet away and making no motions as though he wanted to be picked up.

When the shark disappeared, Joe seized the moment to yell, "Hey, guys, I'm all right! Don't make any rescue moves toward me! Got a feeling that the shark would interpret actions as aggression, and that might prove disastrous for all of us!"

"Joe," shouted Dr. Compton, "are you sure you're all right? How're the oxygen tanks holding up?"

"No problem, Doc! You guys just cut your engine and stay where you are. Little by little, I'm going to ease alongside, then we got to move fast after you pull me on board."

"Okay, Joe, we understand," responded Davenport. "Although I don't like the idea of cutting off the engine, because. . . ."

Whosh!!

"Holy mackerel, look at that!" Zeigler shouted as he aimed his camera.

The great white had broken surface not more than twenty yards away. Her enormously thick body leaped completely out of the water while her jaws held a huge sea turtle. As the shark came down tail first on a forty-five-degree angle, her upper body remained above water, and the audience heard the loud cracking of shell and saw the gobbling down of the five hundred pound turtle in less than ten seconds. After that, the men saw the great white's head submerge and the familiar dorsal fin move slowly in Talanski's direction. When it came within arm's length, he grabbed it. Immediately, the mighty engine of the deep headed away from the launch.

"Look at that! Look at that!" exclaimed Zeigler while continuously aiming his camera. "This footage will astound the whole world! And damn it, I'm the photographer, William Franz Zeigler! Ha, ha, now how do you like them apples!!"

"Very good," Chuck said as he also continued shooting with his camera, "because ole Charles Creighton Landsbury will be right up there with you!"

"Hey, while you two world famous snapshot artists are already enjoying your glory," Dr. Davenport said as he started the motor and headed after shark, "Joe is probably on his way to who knows where on the back of that fish!"

"Steady as she goes, Mark," said Dr. Compton in a rather calm tone. "Don't get too close. I have a feeling that Joe's not in any danger. Let's just lay back a little and see what happens."

At about a hundred and fifty yards away, Talanski let go of the dorsal fin as the great white submerged to deeper depths. When the surface showed no turbulence, Joe waved for the launch to approach. Quickly and silently the men pulled him aboard. It wasn't until the launch pulled alongside of the *Sea Gull* that someone spoke.

"Damn, fellas," said Joe laughingly, "thanks for the smooth ride. At least it was smoother than a Pittsburgh trolley. Come on, I'm not dead, okay?"

"In all the years I've been going on marine expeditions," said Dr. Compton, "never—and I mean never—had I seen *anything* that ever came close to what I saw today! Joe, without a doubt, you've made history!"

"That's for sure," joined Chuck Landsbury, "and we got it all on film, right, Bill?"

"Right," he answered, "but it's too bad we can't get any more footage. Could've turned this into one helluva documentary."

"Well, unless I miss my guess," Davenport added as the launch was being hoisted aboard, "we haven't seen the last of that shark, not as long as Joe's around."

The main discussion of the afternoon meeting was how to make sure that the great white trailed the ship to Miami and the kinds of precautionary measures to be taken so as to prevent danger coming to people or the fish. It wasn't long after the many scientific minds began cranking out all sorts of suggestions that Talanski began to wonder whether he should go along with some of them or none of them.

"Doc, can I talk to you, I mean *really* talk to you?" asked Joe when the session was over.

Even amid the excitement of the day, Dr. Compton remained very much in tune with his young friend, and he was skeptical about many of the things that now surrounded the exploration's mission. Although the old marine biologist would've loved to retire while enjoying the spotlight of the scientific world, he had mixed feelings about doing it at the expense of compromising certain ideals.

"Sure, Joe," he replied. "Suppose we grab a couple of these coffees and go down to my cabin."

Once inside, Compton began, "Joe, you and I haven't been friends for a thousand years, but I guess I'm wise enough to know that longevity doesn't always assure a kind of high quality relationship. So, before you even say anything, I want you to know that I intend to honor your wishes concerning this entire matter, and I know that's what you want to talk about."

"Thanks a lot, Doc, for at least listening to me, because what I'm going to say doesn't make one bit of sense to anybody except me."

"Well, suppose you try me and let's see what happens."

Joe, feeling a little more at ease, began. "Ever since I encountered that shark three days ago, my life has changed. Don't ask me how or why, because I don't know other than the fact that I definitely don't want anything to happen to her. Doc, I've been as close to that fish as any other living thing and survived. Remember the other day I told you a peaceful feeling came over me when I rubbed the shark's nose? Well, I wasn't kidding. I felt—no, feel—as safe and comfortable around that particular shark as I would around a close friend. Does that make any sense, Doc?"

"At this point, who am I to sit in judgment on this thing, Joe? Look, you've actually done something that no other known human being has ever done. Even the thought of your recent adventures scrambles the hell out of my marine biological data base. It's mind boggling for me to think of all the new information that man could compile from this particular great white shark. And I haven't even mentioned the fame and fortune that you, Joseph Bernard Talanski, would amass by just being around to let people see you. Joe, your name would be mentioned in every spoken language!"

Until Dr. Compton said the last sentence, our hero was only mildly interested. However, the thought of having the name *Talanski* rise in international stature appealed greatly.

"I'd like that more than anything, Doc. You couldn't even begin to imagine how important it is for me. But I'm telling you right now, I'm not doing anything—and I mean anything—that'll bring any kind of harm to . . ."

"Wait a minute! Hold on, kid! I wouldn't let anything damage our friendship. You're like . . . like a son to me, Joe. No way would I let that thought evaporate, not even for the sake of scientific advancement.

"Ha, ha, it's funny how I'm talking like this. There once was a time when I would've ridden roughshod over anybody whom I even suspected of trying to tamper with my prestige as a great explorer. Undoubtedly, I had a lot of good people on many of those past expeditions. I thought I didn't need or want anybody around me who wasn't thinking my way. Well, I'll tell you, I destroyed just about every meaningful relationship I had over the years, Joe. I'm talking about not only colleagues at Ocean World but also my wife. I don't know, maybe that's why I reached out for you when you came to work there. It had gotten to the point where I was despised and had outlasted any general respect from my co-workers.

"As you know, this particular exploration in search of a great white shark was reluctantly granted by Ocean World. Fortunately, I still have a few contacts in high places, and they brought a lot of pressure to bear. But I guess I should've known that I'm too damn old to head up a project of this significance. Well, to hell with it. I'm tired, Joe, just plain worn out. Hell, there was once a time when I would've taken whatever measures I thought necessary to accomplish this mission, regardless of your feelings. Now, I just don't have the energy or desire to fight. Besides, we picked up enough to replenish the aquarium. And, as quiet as it's kept, I don't think there're too many people who actually believe that this old man could pull off the greatest catch in the history of marine biology.

"So, Joe m'boy, don't worry about it, and, above all, don't make the same mistake I did so many times, namely, compromise your principles when . . ."

"All right, all right, Doc," Joe interrupted laughingly. "Christ, you've made your point! What you'd *really* like for us to do is bring that shark in alive!"

"Well . . . hrumph . . . the thought did occur to me, but . . . thirty-four. . . ."

"Ha, ha, ha. Come on, Doc, stop trying to bullshit me! Now do you want this shark or not?"

The crafty old veteran, with a twinkle in his eye, looked impishly at his young friend. He broke into a broad grin and answered, "Damn right! I'd like to bring that baby straight up the fucking intracoastal waterway!"

"Okay, Doc," replied Joe as they held up their coffee cups, "we'll do it! Here's to the three of us!"

"Three? Who's the other person?"

"Aw, c'mon, Doc, where're your manners? I'm talking about the most important lady in our lives now!"

"Here, here, I'll drink to that! What're we going to call her? Can't refer to a lady of her magnitude as 'Sharkie,' right?"

Then a very serious look came over Joe's face. He stared momentarily out of the porthole, taking a slow sip of coffee and said, "She has a name, Doc, one that's going to be known all over the friggin' world—Talanski!"

Six

On Stage

1

For the first time in almost two years, every member of Ocean World's board of directors showed up for a meeting. The president, Dr. Wesley Prescott, after receiving the ship-to-shore call from Harry Compton, knew the circumstances surrounding the bringing in of the great white shark were much too intricate for one person to make all of the decisions. Therefore, an emergency meeting was called on very short notice.

Rap, rap, came the sound of the president's gavel on the long, heavy oak table. The buzzings immediately stopped, and everyone's attention focused on Dr. Prescott.

"I certainly appreciate your responding positively to my request that you meet with me this morning, ladies and gentlemen," came the president's opening remark, "but I certainly would not have called you at such an ungodly hour last night were it not for the fact that we need to map out a plan of operation in terms of bringing in the great white shark that the *Sea Gull* captured alive, and . . . "

"Wait a minute, Wes," interrupted Leonard Cochoran. "I thought you just wanted to brief the board as to what's going on, not to ask us to become involved in helping you, the professionals, to map out a plan of operation."

Prescott replied, "I understand perfectly what you're saying, Mr. Cochoran, but Ocean World is faced with a situation that could either bring in multi-millions of dollars or cause us to pay out multi-millions of dollars. The dangers surrounding everything that we do with this shark are many, and we must be absolutely sure that Ocean World's insurance coverage is better than adequate.

"As you know, two lives, those of Dr. Jason Kromyer and Dr. Matsu Kuromoto, were lost. Heaven knows what other tragedies

238

might occur in the process of getting this shark from the ocean into some kind of special confine at Ocean World."

"Dr. Prescott," began millionairess Martha Van Toland, "is it true that the fish is not presently under any confinement?"

"Yes, that's true, Mrs. Van Toland. However, according to what Dr. Compton told me, the shark has remained close to the ship for several days. The crew keeps it interested by throwing a lot of bait and garbage overboard. Also, from what I understand, one member of the expedition—don't have his name before me at this time—is supposed to be pretty good in holding the shark's attention."

"Holding the shark's attention?" exclaimed oil tycoon Craig Upshaw. "And just how in hell, pardon my French, ladies, is this guy doing that? I mean, you folks here at Ocean World are the experts, but every schoolkid knows about the great white shark! That sucker's awesome!"

"You're right, Craig," added the investment banker Bob Amesley, "and houses all over the country would pay handsomely to see it.

"Speaking of seeing it, Wes, when do you think Harry will be ready to lead the shark in?"

"When he called me yesterday, " Prescott said, "the *Sea Gull* had dropped anchor three miles off the Miami coast, and I told him to stay there until I had a chance to touch base with the Board. But, to answer your question, Bob, Dr. Compton and his crew are ready to lead the shark right up to our docking area. However, it's my understanding that this particular one is well over thirty feet long, and . . ."

"Thirty feet? Do you people realize the kind of money that translates into at the admission gate?" Amesley interjected. "Such an attraction would definitely solve all of Ocean World's financial woes!"

"Yeah, but we all know you got to spend money in order to make money," said land developer Doug Winchester, "and I think, before we decide to put out one penny, the Board members ought to see this shark and also . . ."

"Damn it, Doug," shouted Upshaw, "that's an excellent idea! I'd love to get a view of that shark in its natural setting! Do you think you could make arrangements for us to see it as soon as possible, Wes?"

"Well . . . er . . . I guess we could use our mini-sub," responded the president, "although, including the necessary two crewmen, the sub can hold only twelve people at a time."

"Dr. Prescott," said Mrs. Toland, "you needn't include me, because I have no intention of going out there. I'll defer to these eager gentlemen. How about you, Grace?"

Smilingly, Mrs. Grace Forrestal, wife of one of Miami's leading plastic surgeons, replied, "Hardly, darling! When I voted for this project last spring, I certainly didn't plan to become *that* involved! Besides, from what I've heard about the great white shark, it would take a whole bevy of doctors to try to repair the damage that it can cause in a matter of seconds."

After the laughter had ceased, Prescott apprised the Board of several unforeseen expenses that had to be met in order to move the shark. Although he was somewhat skeptical about having too much leak out concerning the success of the mission, Dr. Prescott could do very little to place a control device on the mounting enthusiasm of several Board members.

"Then it is agreed, ladies and gentlemen," said the president, "that we'll hold off notifying the media about anything until we've had a chance to see the shark tomorrow morning."

2

As the bright-yellow mini-submarine slipped silently below the surface, there was also silence inside. Each man was anticipating the great event.

"Okay up there," said Davenport over the radio, "throw in the bait, and make sure the chunks are large!"

Craig Toland was the first to see some movement through the murky waters. "Hey, what's that back there at about seven o'clock?"

The six passengers didn't have very long to wait, because the huge great white shark appeared almost as soon as the pieces of tuna hit the water. With her mouth only partially opened, the leviathan darted around scooping up the delicious bait.

"There she is, my friends," said Dr. Compton in a tone reflecting accomplishment. "You are looking at the most feared creature in the sea, a creature that cunningly uses its power to overcome situations which require a certain amount of reasoning. That monster you're looking at is a living engine placed in the ocean by mother nature to seek out and destroy everything else in the sea. The great white shark fears nothing, folks. And it doesn't have to be hungry to attack. With or without provocation, it will mount a sustained assault on anything that is captured in those two blank black beads it has for eyes. Unlike other ravenous members of the shark family, this species, *carcharodon cacharias* chooses to travel alone. Perhaps (ha, ha, ha) that's because it's too damn mean and unpredictable even for its own kind."

The president and Board members were awe-struck by the size and quickness of the shark. They chatted amongst themselves but never turned their faces away from the observation windows. While the big shots were totally enraptured by what they saw, Dr. Compton and Mark smugly looked at each other and smiled.

"Well, what do you think, Dr. Davenport?" said Compton as he picked up the microphone. "Are these gentlemen ready to see the *real* show?"

"Umm, I suppose so, Dr. Compton, provided they have strong coronary mechanisms."

"*Minnow One* to *Sea Gull*, do you read me?"

"Loud and clear, *Minnow One*," responded the voice aboard ship. "Should Talanski come down now?"

"Affirmative, *Sea Gull*, affirmative."

"Dr. Compton," asked Toland, "is this the fellow we talked to briefly before diving?"

"Yes, and now I want all of you to make sure you keep your eyes glued to the windows, because you're about to witness something that will completely juggle your brains."

"Harry, this is insane!" shouted Prescott. "Don't have that man go out there! The shark'll eat him alive! Are you crazy? Give me that damn mike!"

"It's too late," Davenport said in a calm tone. "Guess who's coming to dinner? And there he is."

Wearing a black wetsuit and two oxygen tanks strapped to his back, Joe swam up to the sub's observation window and waved to its occupants. No sooner had he turned around, the shark appeared out of the murkiness.

"Oh, my God," uttered Amesley, "we're going to witness a tragedy, and there's nothing we can do about it!"

Dr. Prescott, practically becoming undone at the seams, could hardly catch his breath as he gasped, "You're a . . . a goddamn lunatic, Compton, and that man's death . . . that man's death is going to be on your head!"

In the meantime, the great white, with her mouth opened to about two feet, made several wide circles around the lone, unarmed diver. Then she slowed her speed and eased gently up to Joe. He rubbed the palm of his hand across the rough nose. Since remaining motionless is completely out of the question for this species, she continued moving forward with the diver now holding on to one of her lateral fins. Man and shark disappeared into the murky mist.

Except for the low hum of the submarine's motor, no sound was heard in the cabin as spectators looked on in disbelief. Compton and Davenport silently chuckled. Craig Upshaw was the first to speak.

"I saw it, but I'm not quite sure that I'm ready to believe it. Dr. Compton, what the hell's going on here? Do you think that diver's done for or what? Jesus Christ! I didn't come out here to watch a maneater devour one of . . ."

"Hey, look!" Toland yelled. "He's back! The guy's back! That shark didn't eat him after all!"

Amid cheering and acclamations, Joe swam up to the observation window, gave a thumbs-up victory salute, and headed for the surface.

"I just gotta shake that fella's hand," said Amesley. "That is absolutely terrific! What did you say his name was again?"

"Talanski!" Compton shouted, "Joseph Bernard Talanski!"

During the next three days that the *Sea Gull* was anchored off the coast, Ocean World officials were busily making all kinds of arrangements for confining the shark and also extensive media coverage.

It was decided that leading newspapers from all over the nation should be alerted to what was happening near the Miami Beach strip. Local tabloids frantically rearranged schedules so that they might have their key star reporters ready to participate in what was touted to be the biggest fish story ever.

Since the security cap on Ocean World's greatest find was about to be blown via information leaks caused by crew members, Dr. Prescott and the Board of Directors knew that it would be almost impossible to keep curiosity seekers in small boats out of the area. It was for that reason the *Sea Gull* lifted anchor and went twenty-five miles further into the Atlantic.

Although Talanski still had not left the ship, he wasn't bored. At least once a day, Joe was lowered in the cage, a precautionary measure taken against attacks by other sharks. Our hero and crew people often laughed at how he had to be more concerned about the smaller maneaters than about the most feared of them all, the great white.

One of the stipulations that Ocean World imposed on reporters and photographers prior to their even being allowed aboard the *Sea Gull* was an hour's crash course on *carcharodon cacharias*. The real motive behind this unusual requirement was to make sure that every member of the press could internalize the greatness of the discovery and transmit that feeling to the public. Ocean World realized the futility of trying to put a large number of media people on hold, so it selected ten. These ten reporters represented what Ocean World hoped would be the opening of the floodgate to financial stability, and worldwide fame.

After the orientation, Dr. Davenport led the group of newspaper people to the lower deck where preparations for the mini-sub ride were being made.

"Now we're going to be a little cramped inside, folks," Davenport said, "but I'm positive that these few minutes of discomfiture will be well worth your while.

"Incidentally, I hope you photographers don't need flashes, because the shark might react negatively to all the sudden bursts of bright lights."

"Ha, ha, ha," laughed Walt Meadows of the *New York Times*. "This reminds me of the movie *King Kong* when the reporters' flashing cameras upset the ape so much that he broke the magnesium straps and . . ."

"Hey, young fellow," Dr. Compton interrupted. "In all seriousness, we don't want to do anything that might further endanger the diver's life. Remember, this species is extremely aggressive and unpredictable."

"Don't worry," responded the beautiful Jasmine Renfrow, star reporter with the *Miami Herald*. "I believe all of us brought along some pretty sophisticated equipment that doesn't require a lot of light. Speaking of light, when are you going to take the cover off this Mr. Joseph Talanski and let him talk to us? We've been out here for almost three hours and haven't even met him yet!"

"Yes, yes, I know," said Compton as the hatch on the sub was being secured. "And I must apologize to you people. But, Mr. Talanski is doing things that no other human being has ever done. We have absolutely no idea why the shark has not attacked him. Perhaps later investigations and laboratory tests will reveal some information, but, right now, we, and that includes Talanski himself, don't have any answers. Therefore, we've just been following the practice of leaving him totally alone so that he might focus his entire mental faculties on that particular great white shark."

"Are you suggesting that Talanski is hypnotizing this fish?" asked Marty Eason of the *Chicago Sun*, "because if you are . . . "

"No, I'm not suggesting anything. You'll probably get at least *some* answers to your many questions when we hold the official interview this afternoon, okay? Now, suppose we focus our attention on what's happening underwater. All right, Hank, take her down."

Most of the media were seasoned veterans who had covered front-page events many times during their careers. However, the relatively young ages of these people were perhaps more indicative of their aggressiveness in going right to the heart of newsbreaking stories. They were pushy and impatient about this fish tale, and they wanted to know every detail.

The mini-sub leveled off at thirty-five feet and turned on all six of its bright searchlights. Instead of moving them from side to side, the operator held them stationary so that the entire area around the underwater craft was totally illuminated.

When pieces of chum began appearing, so did various marine animals. Two large green turtles fed casually while schools of multicolored fish darted around snatching tidbits. Then, as if a common signal were heard simultaneously by every creature, the stage was quickly evacuated to allow room for other actors—sharks. Several species appeared: mako, tiger, hammerhead, and blue.

"Wow! Look at 'em gobble the bait!" said Bret Carter of the *Washington Post*. "But where is this great white that we've been hearing a lot about?"

Someone replied, "Maybe he's gone to Hollywood to try out for the starring role in that new movie."

Mild laughter floated through the cabin as people were becoming adjusted to looking at the feeding frenzies created by the man-eaters on the other side of the observation windows. Then, up from the deeper depths, came the most feared fish of all, a great white shark. It sounded as though the reporters gasped in unison.

"Is that the one, Mark?" asked Compton. "We can't afford to make any mistakes."

Dr. Davenport squinted severely as he peered through the murky and bloody water. "We haven't sighted more than one white in several days. But let's wait until we can see the underside, and . . . there . . . there . . . yep, it's a female."

All of the other predators, except a twelve-foot blue, swam away when the great white appeared. Compton radioed the boat to cease throwing bait, since he wanted to be sure that only the white would remain. After about three minutes of circling over and under the mini-sub, the great white disappeared. However, the blue stayed within view of the craft's occupants. Suddenly, like some huge nu-clear-powered engine, the great white's long thick body came streaking out of the darkness toward the blue. With her jaws fully extended and lips curled back over rows of jagged teeth, the great white struck. In one chomp, the blue lost several feet of its tail section.

"Holy shit!" cried Dick Sledge of the *Los Angeles Times*. "Did you see that?"

Before anyone replied, the great white had wheeled around, locked her jaws on the remaining torso, and swam off out of sight.

"Damn, I've seen a lot of things," Carter said, "but that was definitely the most gruesome and . . . "

Dr. Compton smiled as he said, "Hang on to your socks, folks, because you're about to witness another first. Okay, up there, we're ready for Joe."

Discord and disbelief ran through the minds and out of the mouths of the startled media people. Nevertheless, they were eager to see whatever else was scheduled for their entertainment.

"This is absolutely insane, man," uttered one of the photographers as he got his camera ready to take some more shots. "No way in hell can anybody avoid being attacked out there!"

While all kinds of things were being said among the mini-sub's media contingent, the appearance of a scuba diver momentarily went unnoticed until Mark called everyone's attention.

"Oh, my God," came the utterance oozing from Ms. Renfrow's lips as she watched another form loom out of the murk.

Almost simultaneous with the diver's appearance came the reappearance of the gigantic great white shark. By then, the reporters and photographers were pretty much beyond the point of being totally aghast at what they might see next. Nevertheless, they were definitely ready to observe what was surely expected to happen as usually dictated by the laws of nature, namely, a shark attack on a lone diver. However, what the media people saw completely scrambled their brains as they watched in awe.

Talanski, after waving to his audience and armed with nothing, turned to meet the approaching shark. Instead of coming close to the defenseless diver, the powerful eating machine gave a slight flick of her tail and swam in a wide circle around man and submarine. Joe, more or less, remained stationary by slowly moving his arms and flipper-covered feet. Another circle, this time smaller.

"I'm afraid that poor bastard has had it," Carter said as he continued talking into his micro tape recorder. "We're about to witness a fatal shark attack. The monster is huge, a good thirty-to thirty-five feet, but its movements are effortless and graceful."

"Okay, folks," said Dr. Compton, "here she comes on her final approach. Now don't even blink, because you'll miss the wonder of what is about to happen."

The great white slowed her motion and, with a frontal move that gave the audience an unobstructed view of her black eyes and broad mouth, she eased up to the diver. Without hesitating, the diver touched and rubbed her lips back and forth several times, all the time being gently nudged away from the sub. Then Talanski did what he had done many times before, took a firm hold on the fish's pectoral fin. In a flash, shark and man were gone.

"What the hell did we just see?" asked one of the reporters.

"I'll be damned if I know," a photographer replied, "but I sure as hell got it all on film!"

"Dr. Compton," queried the lone female, "is what we just saw supposed to be bordering on the miraculous in marine biology?"

"Ms. Renfrow, not only is this a miracle, it is the first time in recorded history that man has ever made friends with a great white shark, the most feared creature in the sea."

Carter, after listening intently, squinted his eyes and asked, "How can you say that diver made friends with the shark when, even as we speak, he might already be in that fish's belly? And another thing, Dr. Compton, how do you plan to handle this obvious disaster since it's been established that this same shark killed and ate a couple of your colleagues last month?"

At this, several people began to talk skeptically about the whole project. One person even remarked that what he had seen was an obvious delayed attack, and he felt put upon to witness a contrived attempt of Ocean World to force a phony situation.

"As far as I'm concerned," added Joel Blumberg of the *Philadelphia Inquirer*, "I have not seen one shred of evidence that supports the original reason why our papers have sent us down to Florida. And, if you'll pardon the pun, something smells fishy."

In spite of the growing doubt as to the credibility of the exploration, Compton and Davenport did not appear unnerved. As a matter of fact, they smiled and listened patiently to the complainers. It was as though the biologists knew that these doubters would soon become believers.

"Look!" yelled one of the photographers. "There's the diver! Holy shit! The shark's right behind him!"

Mass hysteria erupted in the submarine as Joe repeatedly rubbed the gruesome-looking maneater. He even swam up to the observation window and gave the thumbs-up sign.

Carter spoke into his recorder. "In all my years in journalism, I have never seen anything more spectacular than this . . ."

After a few more minutes of swimming around the lighted area with the shark, Talanski pointed to his watch, waved to the enthralled audience, and headed for the surface. Yes, his huge thirty-four foot friend was with him.

Back aboard the ship, amid congratulations, clicking camera shutters, and interviews, Joe felt quite comfortable. Dr. Compton and the other members of Ocean World were surprisingly pleased with the smoothness that Talanski evidenced in talking to the press. However, what went unnoticed was the subtle slipping of a note into the hero's hand.

4

The brief rain shower was just enough to cool things off and stir up the refreshing breeze that flowed through the opened taxi windows. Joe mused that this was the first time in three days that he was alone to pursue his own personal business. And, for the immediate present, that business involved the writer of the note. He was not so naive as to think that the writer wanted to spend a simple and quiet evening with him, no strings attached. By the time the cab pulled up in front of the beautiful Miami Beach condo building, a silvery full moon had appeared from behind the vanishing rain clouds and caused shimmering reflections to enhance the freshness of the night.

Joe identified himself to the uniformed doorman.

"Ah, yes, Miss Renfrow asked me to send you right up."

Thirty-two-year-old Jasmine Renfrow was a rich native New Yorker who used to come to Florida during her spring break days at Boston College. Being the only daughter of a newspaper magnate, Jasmine not only got early training as to what it takes to get top bylines but she also used her raven-haired beauty to charm reluctant interviewers. Not once during her six years with the local tabloid had the young widow failed to nail down stories that carried a lot of social impact.

This latest assignment fascinated Jasmine in that, unbeknownst to the subject in focus, she had utilized some of her many contacts to secure information about him. And it was only after she had privately familiarized herself with Talanski's background did she slip him the note. Joe was totally unaware that the sexy-looking reporter on whose door he was about to knock was knowledgeable about his life from the George School back in Pennsylvania to the present.

"Come right in, Mr. Talanski," purred the gorgeous creature who opened the door. "I must say, you are punctual. Is that one of your many positive characteristics?"

Although Joe was very impressed with Ms. Renfrow's *savoir faire*, as she and he lightly chatted about the shark discovery while they sipped martinis, he felt sure that before the night was over they would be sharing the same bed. Therefore, the progressively more-personal questions asked by the beautiful reporter were openly handled by the fast-becoming-tipsy guest. Jasmine expertly led him into dealing comfortably with her inquiries.

"Joey . . . oops . . . may I call you Joey?" she asked as she got up from the plush sofa to refresh their drinks.

Joe was totally defenseless in the face of all the warm feelings radiating from Ms. Renfrow, and he responded, "Yeah, I'd like that, Jasmine."

Pretending to know nothing of her guest's likes and dislikes, she continued to say little things that seemed to hit upon positive things in Joe's life. Jasmine even found the occasion to mention how much she enjoyed boxing. Talanski was hooked. However, he was not the only one. As the evening wore on, our scheming reporter found herself not only seriously listening to many of the ramblings about Joe's various experiences but also being captivated by his dark eyes. It seemed ironic that what started out to be a time for shifty footwork became a time for personal revelations on both parts.

Jasmine, surprisingly to herself, talked freely about how she was widowed via the ravages of the Vietnam War. "Even though Chet was in R.O.T.C., he didn't have to go, because he had already gotten his acceptance to Tufts Med School. But no! He had to prove something, whatever the hell it was, to his snobby Beacon Hill friends. You know how it is with you macho guys, always doing things on some stupid dare.

"Shortly after we became engaged that spring of our senior year, we went to a garden party that was hosted by the parents of Chet's roommate. Well, after they loaded up on too much beer and still insisted on arguing with some other people about why our country should support Johnson's Southeast Asia policies, Chet and Arnie decided to enlist! Can you imagine that?"

Joe slightly frowned as he reflectively said, "Yeah, I can understand it. I was in a similar frame of mind back then, too. But . . . that's another story. So what happened?"

"Well," Jasmine continued, "they did all right. But, since Arnie wasn't Rotcy, he and Chet weren't stationed together. Not that I cared, because by then I was ready to break off our engagement. However, after I had set up the backdrop for calling it quits, that handsome devil came home on leave and talked me into eloping. Our parents tried to die when we called them from Elkton, Maryland. A month later, Chet's unit was sent to Vietnam. And, five months after he was there, he stepped on a mine . . . and . . . and . . . and. . . ."

"I understand, Jasmine," Talanski softly said when he saw the tears. "Believe me, I understand—I've been there."

"But to lose Chet like that was so . . . so damn unnecessary!" she sobbed.

Without considering whether the crying woman resented his hugging her, Joe reached forth anyway as he said, "I'm afraid trying to apply logic to everything that we consider necessary or unnecessary is not going to work for us in every situation—too many variables."

Perhaps realizing that her original plan was not working made Jasmine pull away from her would-be comforter and laughingly ask, as she quickly wiped her eyes, "Are you also a psychiatrist, among other things?"

Joe fielded the question like a true trooper, replying, "No, but I don't mind telling you that I've seen enough shrinks to know a few of their stock-in-trade comments."

"Ha, ha, Joseph Talanski, you're quite a guy, you know that? And something tells me you're onto why I invited you over, right?"

Leaning back on the coral-colored couch with his arm resting on one of the long cushions, Joe replied, "No to the first one—yes to the second one. Hey, but that's all right. Don't feel bad. People have been looking at me like I'm some kind of freak for a long time. I'm used to it.

"What d'ya want—an exclusive interview that would take you into the real nitty-gritty life of Joe Talanski? Sure, that's it, right? Well, I don't see that as a problem, since you're just trying to do your job—and I like you."

Jasmine was completely puzzled now. She knew that an exclusive interview of this shark mesmerizer was the whole reason for inviting him to her apartment. And, if it meant going to bed with him, then she was prepared to do that also. After all, the brilliant and enterprising reporter had yet to face an interviewing situation that she did not conquer. But something was beginning to happen here, something over which she seemed to be unable to control. Her eyes and ears were beginning to internalize this openly talkative object that, for the past two hours, sat beside her and thoroughly answered all questions. The micro-cassette tape recorder had long since stopped, but Jasmine was so engrossed in the stream of words that she completely forgot about this bit of modern technology.

"You are indeed a strange and fascinating individual, Joey. Tell me, to what would you specifically attribute your recent success?"

Our hero's face broke into broad grin as he replied, "Stupidity!"

After the two finished laughing heartily, Jasmine said, "Really, Joey, I know you're not a shallow person, and I also know you're just trying to humor me—but that's all right. I like it."

Then, a serious look came over Talanski's face as he asked, "Do you know much about sharks, Jasmine?"

"Nothing more than what I've read up on during the past week, and, oh, yes, the knowledge that I gleaned from that crash orientation course we had last Thursday. Why?"

"Well, because, basically, I don't know that much either. Granted, I had been cleaning tanks at Ocean World for the past couple of years, but, beyond that, I really don't have any expertise in dealing with any of them—and I mean from a porkbeagle to a basking. As a matter of fact, if it weren't for Doc, that's Dr. Compton, I probably would be hosing out some tanks right now."

"If you don't really have a broad base of biological knowledge about sharks," queried the reporter as she curled her legs beneath her, "then how do you account for the fact that you were able to cavort around with a thirty-four-foot great white and not be attacked?"

Joe lit a cigarette and said, "Well, as for the broad base of marine biological knowledge that you spoke of, I don't know if it would've helped me down there. Nobody, I mean nobody, was more of an expert on the great white shark then Dr. Kuromoto. And I also must include Dr. Kromyer. Yet, both of those men were fatally attacked by the same one that you saw the other day. Now I don't want to sound smug or even irreverent in the Temple of Knowledge, but their backgrounds served them damn little when they looked into the shark's pupilless black eyes.

"If you ask me why is it that she hasn't attacked me yet, I must say I don't know. But what I *do* know, Jasmine, is that for some strange reason, I feel quite comfortable around her—no fear whatsoever."

There was a brief pause of silence in the room as the reporter moved a little closer to the interviewee and purred, "Well, there's

one thing for certain, sharkman. That female fish must find something unusually attractive about you, and I'm just dying to find out
what it is.''

Not hesitating any longer, Joe kissed those waiting lips with
such fervor that all Jasmine could do, or wanted to do, was enjoy
the mounting passion as it rushed to every pressure point in her
curvaceous body. While their tongues were still engaged, Joe gently
lifted the woman from the couch and carried her into the bedroom.

Seven

Engines of Vengeance

1

The whirlwinds of publicity were blowing stronger each day, and Talanski was enjoying himself tremendously. Jasmine Renfrow had become not only his constant companion but also his unofficial publicity agent—unofficial because Ocean World had taken on all of the official connections that were precipitated by this unusual and momentous shark discovery.

The National Geographic Society and various marine laboratories throughout the world had already contacted Ocean World and set up observational and interview sessions. Even the military, especially naval personnel, became interested in the discovery. And various foreign maritime companies expressed great interest in trying to find out whether Talanski's body was secreting some kind of fluid that deterred the shark from attacking him.

In short, Joe was beginning to make a lot of money on observational dives, interviews, and guest appearances on television. However, in spite of the tremendous amount of demands that were being placed on his time, he handled the media beautifully. Whenever Joe had a question concerning the way he should respond to the people, he consulted his live-in friend, Jasmine Renfrow. She had grown quite attached to this mysteriously attractive man. And, even though Jasmine had a considerable amount of personal information about Joe, she still did not feel as though she really knew him. Nevertheless, after she and he had dated a couple of times, she responded yes to his asking her to move in with him. Besides, it made things convenient for her to be around when Joe wanted advice that would be to his mental advantage and not just to his monetary advantage.

At first, it was not because of love that Joe and Jasmine decided to stop their verbal sparring with each other. However, feelings other than the sensual began to draw together these two people in such a way that their mutual respect for past relationships was honored without an outward show of jealousy.

As Joe gunned his new white Porsche to a stop in the parking lot of Miami's leading television station, he leaned over and kissed Jasmine on the cheek.

"Hmm, that's what I need for good luck," he said.

"You hardly need luck, Joey, the way you've been handling yourself. Like I told you, you're a natural for the media, and people want you to just be you."

"Yeah, but network television, Jasmine? I get a little nervous every time I think of millions of invisible people staring at me through the camera's eye."

"My that's poetic! Hey, just relax, darling. You'll do fine. Remember, practically every one of those viewers out there will be wondering what kind of unnatural power you have over the most feared and dangerous creature in the sea. On top of that, the movie, *Jaws*, has given everybody one helluva eerie feeling at even the mention of a great white shark."

The host of the talk show made Talanski feel comfortable by asking non-technical questions that primarily dealt with the inexplicable action of the shark. This, plus the showing of film clips, held the undivided attention of practically every viewer, young and old, throughout the country.

2

"Hey, Vinnie, come here quick!" yelled the man to his friend who had gone to the kitchen for a couple of beers. "Look at this!"

The large 285-pound man grabbed two cans and hustled back to the T.V. set. "So what the hell do you have on—some fuckin' gab show? I thought we were gonna watch the movie on Channel . . ."

"Sh, sh, stop talking for a second, and look closely at the guy with his legs crossed."

The big man chuckled as he said, "Damn, Frank, I didn't know you were into watching guys cross their legs."

Without taking his eyes off the set, the smaller man replied, "Vinnie, who, in our entire organization, has the best memory for faces and all kinds of trivia shit?"

"You, Frank, but I don't see how . . . "

"What you don't see would make another world. Now, just test your recall ability, if you have any, and tell me whether that guy's face looks familiar."

Vinnie popped the tops of both cans and sat down while keeping his eyes glued to the set.

Then, after about a minute of intense staring, Frank leaned back and calmly said, "I'll bet you a hundred bucks that's the same punk who was with Paco Sanchez the night he was whacked."

"You mean this is the guy who Mr. Corazon had all of us trying to find for damn near six months?"

"Yep, I'm positive! Hell, I was the cabbie who drove the three of 'em down to Ramon's on the wharf. A broad was with 'em, too. Yeah, Vinnie, that's the sonofabitch." Frank Claymont rubbed his chin while talking, because he also remembered being knocked cold by the guy on video.

"Maybe we should call the boss right now since you're so sure about . . . "

"No, no, not just yet, Vinnie," Frank said as he restrained his partner from getting up and going to the telephone. "Let's watch the rest of the program and get more information."

3

"Ah, Joe, come in," said Dr. Prescott looking up from the blueprints that were sprawled across the conference table. "We're having the builders give us a progress report."

The Ocean World executive was referring to the underwater observation deck that would seat five hundred people. The multimillion dollar project had been hesitantly approved by the Board of Directors, even though a couple of them had reservations about investing so much money on one angle. Perhaps this was the reason why a promotional firm was hired. Ocean World did not intend for any money-making aspect to be overlooked while they had two precious and invaluable objects—one huge great white shark and a man who could handle it.

Talanski knew everyone in the room. During the past three months, he was called upstairs many times to confer with all kinds of people. They represented various marine biological institutes, U.S. Navy, foreign countries, motion picture studios, and, of course, the ever-present press.

Upon looking around the room and not seeing his best friend, Joe asked, "Where's Doc?"

"I don't know," Prescott replied, "but he should've been here by now. At any rate, suppose we get started. Mr. Laventhal, why don't you update us as to promotional publicity."

Barry Laventhal, a real winner when it came to implementing fund-raisers and financial investments, began with, "Okay, folks, it's certainly not coming as a surprise to you that The Great White Shark and Friend Project is in place and ready to go as soon as our underwater deck is completed. The money we've been making so far off fees collected from other marine labs has been very good, but no way is it going to compare to the money that'll come in from the general public when we really commercialize. Folks, I'm talking big bucks. . . ."

Laventhal went on to explain how Ocean World could, after only five months, recover the cost of the deck and begin raking in a substantial profit. When Barry finished his report, Floyd Scott, the architect, was asked to go over various features of the nearly completed underwater deck.

At the conclusion of the meeting, when fresh coffee was brought in and everyone was engaged in idle chit-chat, the president tapped the side of his cup and said, "Ladies and gentlemen, may I have your attention, please? I am sure all of us realize that none of this would be taking place today were it not for the bravery of one man. Although I see his handsome features can be considered an asset with members of the female gender, I am still having a problem with trying to figure out whether that includes female sharks!"

Laughter resounded off the beautifully oak-paneled walls and a few risqué remarks were made.

"However," Prescott continued amid the hilarity, "we're pretty confident that as soon as he finds out whatever this strange—and financially profitable—attraction really is, he'll share it with Ocean World first."

"Hear, hear!" someone shouted.

"But seriously, ladies and gentlemen," Prescott went on, "I know that your feelings are in accord with mine when I say, Joe, we all thank you for your unstinting cooperation in helping us keep the shark interested enough to stay in the area. . . ."

Board member Len Cochoran leaned over and said to another board member, "I just hope to hell that fish doesn't decide to take off before we can corral it."

"Oh, stop being a worrywart," smiled the other. "As long as Talanski's here, the fish'll stay. Besides, with the kind of money that guy's rakin' in, he'll see to it that the shark stays around."

"Yeah, I suppose you're right," said Cochoran. "But I certainly would like to know how Talanski's been able to hold off being attacked. Well, I guess that's basically the intriguing part of this whole project."

"Uh-huh. It's what all of those so-called shark experts are trying to determine."

Dr. Prescott's secretary came briskly into the conference room and whispered to him. The smile on the president's face took a radical change to gloom as he, in turn, quickly said something to Joe. No sooner had Prescott done this when Joe practically jumped up from the table and, without any hesitation, ran out of the room.

"Let me have your attention, everyone," requested the president. "I just received word that Harry Compton suffered a massive coronary less than a half-hour ago, and he's being rushed to Miami Heart Institute on Meridian Avenue.That's all the information we have right now."

Five hours later, Joe was still in the waiting area adjoining the Intensive Care Unit of the large hospital complex. Coffee and cigarettes kept him fueled for whenever the doctors might permit him to see his old friend and mentor.

Jasmine had joined her lover an hour earlier, and she did her best to try to give him positive feelings. Nevertheless, Joe continued to speak rather fatalistically. "I'm afraid Doc's not going to pull out of this, Jasmine. You know why? Because he's given up. We had talked about this a couple times within the past month. I knew his heart was failing, but he wouldn't let me tell anybody at Ocean World about it. He's a proud old coot who. . . ."

At that moment, the attending physician came into the waiting area and informed the couple that Dr. Compton was sinking fast. "I'm going to permit you to go in to see him, Mr. Talanski, because he just came out from under heavy sedation and you're the only person he wants to see."

As soon as Joe left the room, Jasmine asked, "What is his condition now, doctor?"

"Not good, Ms. Renfrow, unless he's given a transplant immediately. The irony is that we do have a compatible organ here in the hospital, but Dr. Compton refused it. Can you imagine that?"

Jasmine calmly sat down again as she replied, "Yes . . . yes, I'm afraid I can, doctor."

Talanski had been silently standing at the bedside for a couple of minutes when Dr. Compton finally opened his eyes. He looked at his young friend and uttered, "Joe . . . I might have known you . . . you'd be here."

Talanski gently touched the old man's hand and said, "Of course, Doc, I'm here, and one of the things I'm going to do is find out how soon you'll be going home."

Although Joe would've given anything for the venerable world-renowned biologist to regain his health, there was hardly a chance of that happening unless the heart transplant were to take place. However, before Joe could raise the topic, Dr. Compton said, "I can tell by the look on your face that they told you about my refusing to undergo the operation, right?"

"Well . . . yeah, now that you mention it, Doc, I think you should have the operation. From what I understand, the Institute happens to have a heart in its organ bank that Dr. Ellensworth believes would be accepted by your system, and if . . ."

"Hold on . . . wait a minute, Joe," said Compton weakly lifting a hand and letting it fall. "There's an old Broadway saying: *When the show's over, leave.* And that's exactly what I want to do now, Joe, leave. For years, I bathed in the spotlight of marine biological explorations. But, at the time you met me, that spotlight had gone out, and I had become nothing more than the old man who was in the way of progress. Then, as fate would have it, you came along, Joe. And somehow I knew from the moment I met you down at the fish tanks that you were going to be good for me. My hunch paid off, kid. You're primarily responsible for all of the tremendous recognition I've gotten with the capture of the largest great white shark on record. That's the mountain top . . . the summit . . . there's nothing more worthy of note, my friend. No one is going to parcel me out to some damn nursing home! No, I intend to go out while I'm on top. Thanks to you and Kristina, for sharing and believing in an old man's dream."

The mention of Kristina's name brought instant tears to Joe's eyes. He tried to suppress them but couldn't prevent a few from falling on the wrinkled and gnarled hand that he was holding.

"Damn it, Doc, I came in here to try to cheer you up and look what happens!"

A faint smile came across the old gentleman's face as he said, "What makes us male bimbos think that we must never cry? There's nothing wrong with it—other than the fact that it's embarrassing as hell."

The remark made Joe laugh, and he said, "Doc, you're truly something else."

"Yeah, I know, kid. Look, I'm getting pretty tired just lying here—must be that damn medication."

"Okay, okay, I can tell when I'm not wanted," Talanski replied, smiling. "But I really don't mind being booted out of a place like this. See you tomorrow, all right?"

"Find. And thanks for everything, Joe."

The smile on the biologist's face slowly disappeared as he watched his young friend leave the room. Although Joe turned and waved, he was too far away to see the tears rising in the old man's eyes.

That night, while the young lovers were dining out, the answering machine recorded the following message: "Mr. Talanski, this is Dr. Ellensworth. I am sorry to inform you that Dr. Compton died. Time of death placed at 10:45 P.M. We did all that we could under the circumstances. Please accept our condolences. We're waiting to hear from you."

4

The drive back to the condo from the cemetery was relatively quiet. Joe was deeply immersed in thoughts about his late friend and mentor. Jasmine fully understood the private feelings of her lover enough to remain quiet as he maneuvered his convertible sports machine expertly through downtown traffic. When they slowed to make a left turn into the parking garage, the sleek black sedan that had been following them pulled to a stop across the street.

"So, now we're back at Mr. Big Shot's place," said the rotund driver who could barely fit behind the steering wheel. "What should we do now, Frank? Maybe we should take this guy before. . . ."

"No, we're not doing anything," came an interruption, "until I check with the boss and find out what he wants us to do next."

"Well, you might be right, but I have a feeling that we should whack this guy right now. All that shark shit has probably made him too big for his britches anyhow."

"Yeah," replied the smaller hood. "He could probably fit into yours now. What'd'ya think?"

"Very freakin' funny, Mr. Smart-Ass. One of these days, you're gonna crack on my weight once too damn often, and . . . "

"Hey, whoa, take it easy, big guy. All in fun! Now stop complaining and drive back to that drugstore we passed. I'm going to call the boss."

"But don't you think one of us should stay here? Talanski might leave."

"No problem with that. He has no idea he's been followed. Hey, this guy's such a celebrity now, he's probably forgotten all about the game he helped Paco run on us."

"Yeah, you're probably right, Frank," Vinnie said while negotiating a U-turn. "Besides, during the past week that we've been shadowin' Talanski, I ain't seen no bodyguards or nothin'—just that foxy broad who's always taggin' along."

As usual, Trailblazer's desk was practically covered with money, and all of it was not from legitimate receipts generated by Club Tropicana's dining and dancing clientele. The cocaine runs that he controlled between Miami and other cities were paying off far greater than they were when Paco was driving for him. In other words, the loss that the Trailblazer suffered had become practically so negligible within six months that a more reasonable businessman would've discounted it—but not Luis Corazon. Although he was dealing in millions of dollars each week and had good interstate police coverage, Corazon's strong feelings of vindictiveness unquestionably took control.

As was his practice, the Trailblazer had five of his most trusted men in the huge plush office to help him monitor disbursement of monies received from drivers who transported his drugs to major metropolitan cities throughout the South and North. During these usually two-hour accounting periods, Corazon always relaxed in the stuffed chair behind his solid teak desk and smoked expensive Cuban cigars. Everyone knew that the ringing of the red phone was to occur only in an emergency. So when it rang, the clicking of automatic weapons could be heard all over the office. Even the Trailblazer had his 9mm pistol in hand as he answered the phone.

"Si, que pasa?"

"Boss, this is Frank. Vinnie and me got Talanski's moves covered perfectly. Right now, he and the broad are up in his apartment. It'd be a cinch for me and Vinnie to hit 'em within the next twenty minutes, and . . . well, ah, I thought you . . . nobody, Mr. Corazon, I know I'm not being paid to think, but . . . yes, boss . . . no, sir . . . ah, yes, sir . . ."

By the time Frank had gotten off the phone, he was sweating bullets. On wobbly legs, he made it back to the sedan.

"What the hell's wrong with you?" asked his partner. "You're as white as a goddamn sheet!"

"You'd be, too, if a crazy sonofabitch threatened to chop off your prick and shove it down your throat if you ever used the wrong phone again!"

"What! You mean that little punk didn't give you credit for trackin' down this Talanski guy?"

"Oh, sure," Frank answered. "Luis appreciated that, and he said he'd either give you and me five grand each or have both of us whacked if we draw a blank on this thing."

"Holy, Christ! What's wrong with that freakin' wetback? Don't he have no regards for his men?"

"Of course he does," responded Frank, "but you ought to know he's a crazy bastard once he starts snorting coke. Shit, don't you remember almost a year ago when he personally shot that broad and her kids?"

"Yeah, how the hell could I forget! Me 'n a couple other guys had to git rid of the bodies for Christ's sakes! What a mess! Yeah, that was Paco's broad, come to think of it. Trailblazer caught the bitch 'n her kids at the airport tryin' to get outta the country."

"Hey, Vinny, if you keep recalling details like that maybe you'll get to be a walking personnel file, ha, ha."

The big guy also laughed as he responded with, "Yeah, I can remember the smile on the boss's face when he came outta the room behind his office after he finished layin' the broad right in front of the kids. Soon as he finished screwin' that cunt, he screwed the silencer on his heater, went back in the room, and whacked all of 'em—each one two times in the head.

"Speaking of cunts," Frank said as he quickly became serious, "look who's pulling out of the garage. Trailblazer wants us to bring in Talanski and the broad, but maybe he'll settle for one half right now. Let's get up there."

Joe had just stepped out of the shower when his intercom buzzed.

"Yes."

"Mr. Talanski, Carlos the doorman here. There're two gentlemen to see you. They say they're from Ocean World."

"Okay, Carlos, send them up."

When Joe answered the door of his lavishly decorated apartment, he stared down the barrels of two silencer-equipped .357 magnums.

"Greetings, sharkman!" said Vinnie as he pushed into the apartment, "Don't try nothin' stupid and you won't get hurt."

Frank, not wanting anything to go wrong, decided to call for more help. He remembered vividly what happened down at Ramon's fish and bait shop on the wharf. Twenty minutes later, another big guy with a big gun joined the group.

Other than telling Talanski that they would kill him on the spot if he made any suspicious moves, the three hoods did not reveal any details as to why they were even in the apartment. Unfortunately for Joe, the doorman was not on station when the three abductors escorted their victim through the empty lobby to a waiting car. As soon as they were in the vehicle, a blindfold was tied tightly around Joe's head, and it wasn't removed even after a car's engine was cut off a half-hour later. His hands and feet were bound behind his back as he lay face down on the damp floor in a warehouse. All kinds of questions raced through Joe's mind, but no concrete answers emerged. Then his thoughts were interrupted by the sound of a door being unlocked and approaching footsteps.

Whomp! Talanski's left side got a tremendous shock. Pain coursed through his body like a surge of electricity. Trailblazer had kicked the helplessly prostrate form. Without saying one word, the drug dealer motioned for Vinnie to roll the aching body onto its back. The first blow was painful; however, the second one was completely beyond pain. Trailblazer placed a well-aimed and powerful kick straight to Joe's testicles which caused him to faint. Even the two helpers automatically winced and grabbed their private parts.

"Bring him to!" snarled Corazon. "I'm just starting to warm up on this sonofabitch!"

Cold water brought poor Joe right back to the center of pain, and his blinking eyes had a hard time.

"So, Mr. Joseph Bernard Talanski," said Corazon to the pained and drooping figure that was propped up in an old chair. "We are finally meeting. Do you know who I am?"

Joe, in too much pain to even utter, looked briefly at him and shook his head in the negative.

"Great!" exclaimed the tormentor as he raised his hands in disgust and walked to the other side of the room. "You—you *gringo* dog, you and Paco ripped me off, along with that bitch and her *niños,* and you got the nerve to sit there and tell me you don't even know me? Well, before this night is over, you'll damnsight know who the hell I am!"

"Let me whack him, boss," Frank said, pulling the hammer of his gun and placing the barrel against Joe's right temple. "It certainly would be a pleasure after what they did to Ramon."

"No, at least not just yet. I want *Señor* Talanski to suffer some more—mentally as well as physically."

A smile came across Vinnie's face as he said, "Maybe sharkman here would like to have his cute little girlfriend keep him company. We can easily get her, boss. She lives with this jerk."

"Sounds like a pretty good idea, Vinnie," replied the leader. "Yes, do that. In the meantime, Frank, I want you and a few other boys to stay here until I come back in a couple of hours. I want to check on some business at the club. When Talanski's head clears, question him some more about his connection with Paco Sanchez and my missing bales."

Vinnie really felt inflated with his own importance as he and another one of Trailblazer's men walked across the lobby to the elevator. It wasn't often that the boss even gave him credit for breathing. This was the very first time that Vinnie was ever given any kind of prime responsibility of leadership in carrying out an assignment. Frank was usually the chosen one whenever Trailblazer needed a Caucasian to do a specific job, and, invariably, Frank tapped Vinnie to come along for strong-arm purposes. Well, this time, Vinnie not only made a suggestion that Trailblazer liked but also eagerly looked forward to enjoying the results. Yes, big Vinnie felt good as he and Blinky, another oafish person, rode the elevator up to Talanski's floor.

"I gotta hand it to you, Vinnie, you really know how to make smart moves. This broad she don't suspect nothin', right?"

"Of course not," replied Vinnie as he and his assistant walked down the hall. "Why should she? Her old man's pretty big shit these days with the television stations. So when I slipped the doorman a fifty to sound convincin' over the intercom, I knew it'd be no problem."

Jasmine was not surprised to find Joe gone when she had returned to the apartment, because he had previously mentioned his desire to look through some things at Dr. Compton's home. And, since Jasmine knew how close Joe and the late biologist were, she assumed that her lover had decided to go there alone. However, she was a little perplexed as to why he didn't drive his car.

When the unsuspecting woman opened the door, she saw two huge, burly individuals. Before Jasmine could even think, Vinnie said, "Look, lady, we don't have a lot of time to waste, so listen up good. Your boyfriend is not here, because he's being held by my men in a place not too far from here. Now, you can do one of two things: scream like some stupid broad, which ain't gonna help Talanski, or invite us in and find out the details for savin' his life."

"Saving his life!" the woman reacted. However, Jasmine, as a reporter, was used to handling sticky situations, so she immediately calmed down and invited the men inside.

"Now you're bein' smart, Miss Renfrow," Vinnie said. "Look, Talanski's held by some of my boys, and, if they don't hear from me by nine o'clock, they got orders to kill him. Bein' that it's nearly quarter of, what d'ya wanna do?''

Although Jasmine was fearful for her own safety, she decided that she had better string along until the police could be contacted without endangering her lover's life.

"Okay, Blinky, keep an eye on her while I call.''

Turning his back on the woman, Vinnie held down the receiver as he said, "Hold up on wastin' the shark expert until we find out if his girlfriend's gonna make arrangements for us to get the money . . . what? Look, meathead, I'm not payin' you to think, but I am payin' you to follow my orders, right? Okay, that's more like it. Miss Renfrow seems to be a pretty smart lady, and I'm sure she's gonna cooperate with us if she wants to see her boyfriend alive again. Besides, fifty thousand dollars is a helluva lot of money. At any rate, just make sure nothin' happens to Talanski, okay.''

When Vinnie finished his little fake telephone call, he continued the game by saying to the frightened, but calm, woman. "Look, lady, the three yo-yos I got watchin' your friend ain't too bright. They might not understand my orders, so I'd better get over there right now. Come on, Blinky, let's go—sure hope them guys don't blow it.''

Just as he had hoped she would, Jasmine insisted that she go along also. The seasoned reporter did not think that getting fifty thousand dollars for these kidnappers would be too difficult, because Talanski had become a very rich man. However, Jasmine figured that it was extremely necessary for Joe to tell her how to get the ransom immediately. Police could be contacted later, but the most pressing issue was to save Joe's life. Therefore, Jasmine cooperated by acting as though nothing terrible was happening as she and her two escorts exited the elevator. Ironically, the doorman smiled and winked at the stranger who had tipped him fifty dollars earlier.

6

As soon as Trailblazer's eyes swept the full length of the gorgeous beauty that Vinnie and Blinky had brought back, he decided to extract revenge in a different manner than what he had previously

265

considered. Jasmine was frightened before, but now she was petrified, because she knew what was coming.

"So, my little pretty," said the drug dealer after he had snorted two of the six thin white columns of pure cocaine that were lined up on the table, "you're here to save your boyfriend's ass, is that right?"

Not only was Jasmine getting progressively nervous but she began to regret having come along in the first place. Never before had she ever been placed in such a perilous position.

"Miss Renfrow," said Frank when he grabbed a handful of her hair, "didn't your mother teach you manners. You're supposed to answer when asked a question. Now the gentleman wants to know if you're here to save that scumbag in the other room?"

"Yes," she replied as tears began to flow, "but please . . . please don't hurt me. I can get you the fifty thousand dollars tonight if you'll just let me find out from Joe what I should do."

"Did you hear that, Frank?" laughed the leader right after snorting another white column. "This *gringo* bitch wants to find out from that thief in there what she should do when I, the best Latin lover in Miami, am right here to answer all of her questions and gently scratch that little itch between her legs. Ain't that right, Vinnie?"

"Damn right, boss!"

"Ahh . . . now you see," as another column disappeared, "(cough-grumph) . . . hey, Frankie baby, (sniff) this is really (kumf) . . . good quality. Maybe the lady would like to join me on these last two. Why don't you ask her—since she (sniff) looks a little pale. Besides, this stuff'll put (sniff) roses in her cheeks—all four of 'em. Ha, ha, ha."

Loud laughter penetrated the walls of the darkened room where Joe was chained to a steel beam. Then he heard voices at the door. "This should be a lot of fun, Vinnie."

"Yeah, I never banged a broad while guys were watchin', but I'm gonna give it my best try. How 'bout you, Blinky? You think you can do it?"

"Just watch me. I can get it going on first sight of a real snatch."

"Yeah, bullshit, but let's hurry up 'n take old sharkman here back to the boss."

Perhaps it was the brief eye contact that Vinnie had with Talanski as the chains were being loosened, or maybe it was just a building

266

up of hatred in general. At any rate, Vinnie stopped short and said, "Wait a minute! Am I crazy or what? This is the same guy who wasted my friend and the same guy who's supposed to be lucky with sharks."

"So what're you saying?" asked Blinky surprisingly.

"So I'm sayin' this bastard's too goddamn lucky! And, if we don't watch ourselves, he might just get away when these chains come down."

"Wow, Vinnie, you're really scared of him, huh?"

The mention of such a thing caused the big man to become very upset. However, instead of Vinnie's venting his rage on the speaker, he kicked Talanski in the stomach and began banging his head against the steel beam.

"Christ, Vinnie, you're killing him!" yelled Blinky as he pulled his enraged partner off the helpless form that lay bleeding from the mouth and writhing with pain.

A few minutes later, Talanski was brought into the room where the Trailblazer had already begun getting himself ready for some entertainment with the reporter. Her wrists and ankles were already tied, even though she offered little or no resistance. How could she? The two remaining columns of cocaine had been forced up her nose plus she had been given an injection of heroin.

As soon as Joe saw the condition in which Jasmine was suffering, he cried out, "Mr. Corazon, please let her go! I'll give you whatever you want! Money—my life—I'll give you anything, but please don't hurt her anymore, please!"

"Good," smiled the leader, "however, I don't think you want nothing else to do with this druggie, Mr. Talanski. Look at her—she's a freaking addict, right, boys?"

Laughter filled the room. Then Trailblazer took on a serious look through his partially-opened eyes and continued. "Neither one of you *gringo* dogs will live to see another sunrise if you don't convince me that you can make good on my lost merchandise, *comprende?*"

"Yes, yes, I understand," Joe replied. "And I want you to know, Mr. Corazon, that those few bales stolen by Paco and me are nothing compared to what's stashed in the *Sea Gull's* hold."

"Keep talking."

The directive from the drug king pin was easier given than taken, but Joe knew that any kind of faltering language at this point would cost both his and Jasmine's lives. It was incumbent upon the helpless victim not only to lie but lie effectively, and putting together a narcotics story for a bunch of experts was not going to be easy. However, each time Joe looked at his drugged girlfriend who was being fondled by Vinnie and Frank, he realized that he also had to include a believable ultimatum.

"Take your greasy paws off her!" Joe shouted to the two men who were about to consummate their desires right there in the room. "So help me, Mr. Corazon, if you let this happen to her, then you fucking assholes might as well kill me too . . . here . . . right now, because I won't tell you shit!"

Silence and surprise.

The drug boss leaned back in his chair and snapped his fingers for all action to cease. No one spoke while Corazon lit a cigar, all the time keeping his eyes on the man who apparently had more nerve than sense. After closely scrutinizing his brash prisoner for almost thirty seconds, he got up, walked over to him, pulled out a .9mm automatic, aimed the barrel at Joe's genital area and said, "Tell me about what you got on . . . on the . . . "

"*Sea Gull,*" said Joe in a calm tone. "The laboratory boat we used."

"Yeah, okay, so tell me why I should be interested. Oh, and, Señor Television Personality, if, at any time, I get the feeling that you're just stalling, first I'm gonna blow away your fucking nuts and pecker, then, not sooner than an hour later, I'm gonna put a couple of rounds in your kneecaps after you've watched us gangbang your broad here. *Comprende?*"

Joe still remained calm as he replied, "Sure, I understand. Like I was about to tell you, me and some real close friends at Ocean World put together a plan to bring fifteen thousand kilos of pure coke to Miami stashed on board the *Sea Gull.*"

"Where did you get it?" Corazon asked. "I know for a fact that the Coast Guard has heavy patrols all along the strait."

"We solved that problem ahead of time," Joe continued. "Certain segments of the local station are in on the deal."

Talanski could see that the Trailblazer's interest in his story was mounting steadily, so he continued to pour on the sauce. "As everybody knows, we were successful in capturing the biggest great white shark on record. I don't have to tell you how much attention that brought worldwide."

"Yeah, yeah, so go on with your story," Frank said impatiently. "I'm still not too sure about this guy, Mr. Corazon. He could be lying in hope of saving his ass—and that one over there."

"I swear on my mother's grave," Joe said convincingly. "We transferred the cargo from the Japanese freighter *Kagasa Maru,* which brought the coke up to a rendezvous point six miles southeast of Andros Island. And, while the rest of the *Sea Gull's* crew was occupied with trying to keep the shark within close proximity, my boys and I used one of the ship's motor launches for going out to meet the *Kagasa's* launch, which had the stuff. After we. . . ."

"Wait a minute," interrupted Frank. "I thought you said you got the shipment directly from the freighter."

Perspiration flowed like a river from Joe's armpits, but he knew any kind of hesitancy would be disastrous. Therefore, with all of the bravado that he could muster under the circumstances, our hero laughed and said, "Really, Mr. Corazon, you should consider surrounding yourself with smarter fellows. . . ."

"You bastard!" shouted Frank as he was physically restrained. "I'll see you dead before this night's over!"

Corazon and the others laughed briefly but quickly returned to seriousness when Talanski said that he could deliver the cocaine to them in three hours.

"Look, don't play games with me, *gringo,*" the leader warned.

"The *Sea Gull,*" continued Joe, "is still anchored four miles off Fowey Rocks, because Ocean World didn't want to chance trying to bring in the shark by force, especially after we found out that we could keep it in the area by constantly throwing tuna chunks and other stuff overboard. Shortly after we got back, Ocean World decided to let just a skeleton crew of nine stay on the ship.

"What I'm saying here, Mr. Corazon, is that I can easily get you and your men on board tonight with no problems. As you probably know, I'm pretty important in Ocean World's future plans of opening up a whole new public attraction, which, of course, features me and the shark. I know exactly where the coke is stashed, and you could easily load it into your boat after we get rid of the crew when . . ."

"Hold on, wait a minute," said the drug dealer, "where do you get the *we?* How the hell do you figure into this take?"

"I told you, boss," Frank said, "this jerk's no good! He'd sell out his own grandmother if . . ."

"Quiet, Frank," Corazon ordered as he turned and winked at him. "I don't think *Señor* Talanski would lie to me now, especially when he knows I would enjoy taking his and his girlfriend's lives on the installment plan—one section at a time." With that, Corazon walked over to the semi-conscious woman, took out a pearl-handled switchblade, and placed the cold cutting edge against the nipple of her exposed right breast. "Like I said, I would take their lives on the installment plan."

"Are you going to waste the night wasting Jasmine and me, or are you going to make an easy picking on something that has a street value of over a hundred and fifty million bucks?"

The fresh air made Talanski feel only fifty percent better as the two sedans sped along Biscayne Boulevard toward the docks. Unfortunately, Jasmine was left back at the warehouse under the watchful eyes of three lustful guards,Vinnie being one of them. Trailblazer had given specific orders concerning what they were and were not to do; however, Vinnie was finding it extremely difficult to keep away from the beautiful drugged woman lying on an old cot a few feet from the table where the three thugs were playing poker.

"Come on, keep your mind on the game," Carlos said to Vinnie as the cards were being shuffled. "There ain't no need of even thinking about it so soon, man."

"*Si,* he's right." added Julio as he took a quick peek at his genuine Rolex. "Luis told us not to touch the bitch before five o'clock, and it's not quite midnight yet."

"Yeah, yeah, I understand all that," said Vinnie disgustedly as he picked up his cards. "I'm not stupid, you know."

Carlos and Julio simply glanced at each other and smiled as the big fellow continued talking as if he had to remind himself of the boss's orders.

"I was payin' attention when he told us he would call Efrain at the club as soon as they're back on shore with the coke. Um, let's see now . . . oh, yeah, and you, Carlos, you're supposed to call Efrain at four and . . . and . . . and . . . oh shit, I wish Frank was here."

"What's wrong, Vinnie?" laughed Julio. "Can't you even think straight?"

"No," answered Carlos. "Frankie even takes him to the bathroom, right, Vinnie?"

"Fuck you guys. Deal the cards."

7

The serenity of the beautiful moonlit night seemed beguiled by the turmoil that Trailblazer and fifteen of his heavily armed men were prepared to create upon reaching the *Sea Gull*. Unfortunately, the nine crewmen on board were not equipped to deal with the onslaught of unexpected violence. The only drugs on board were the various legal ones that were in the dispensary, and, all totaled, they wouldn't have a selling price higher than a hundred bucks. In short, Joe realized the impending danger into which his fabricated story was about to take the unsuspecting crewmen. Meanwhile, the sleek forty-foot craft that carried Joe and his captors was less than ten minutes from the anchored *Sea Gull*. During the entire trip, Trailblazer kept asking him various questions about the whole deal, and Joe consistently put together word combinations that were temporarily acceptable. However, time was running out. Talanski knew that Corazon and his men would slaughter everybody once they discovered the big lie. Joe was thinking hard when he suggested that he and no more than five others cover the last hundred yards in the small ten-foot rowboat, so as not to prompt someone on board into calling the Coast Guard.

"Like I told you, Luis," Joe said, "we have some key Coast Guard personnel involved, and they'd be out here with a couple of gunboats before we could get away. I don't need to convince you that they'd blow us right out of the water, do I?"

The veteran drug dealer took a few moments to consult with a couple of his lieutenants, then said, "All right, Talanski, we'll go along with the idea, but this whole thing had better be worth it. Frank, stay close and don't let him out of your sight for one second. If you see the deal's gone sour, waste him."

"It'd be my pleasure, boss," smiled the suspicious underling.

271

A few minutes later, Joe, Frank, and four others were in the small craft and rowing toward the *Sea Gull.*

"Excuse me, gentlemen," said Joe, "but nature calls—have to piss. May I have permission to do it over the side instead of in my pants?"

A few snickers were heard among the other occupants as Frank replied, "Go the hell on, but just make sure you don't have to do number two, you miserable bastard."

Upon sitting down again, Joe felt a splintery area on one of the oars. Another idea occurred to him, and he proceeded to run the palm of his hand roughly against the jagged handle until he felt a free-flowing liquid. Joe then placed his bleeding hand into the water, and said to himself, "Please, God, let her be around."

The great white's keen sense of smell signaled her that there was something of interest near the surface and not too far from where she was casually feeding on anything that moved. With a simple flick of her powerful tailfin, the mighty engine headed for the source of those odors.

The rowboat was now within fifteen feet of the *Sea Gull,* and Joe had already yelled greetings to three crewmen who were standing by to lower the step so that he and the others might come aboard. Since the men of the *Sea Gull* were so accustomed to seeing Talanski bring media persons and assorted visitors on board, suspicion was out of the question.

"Hey guys!" Joe yelled. "Any sign of the fish tonight?"

"Are you kidding?" responded one of the crewmen. "Just like regular clockwork. The last dumping was less than an hour ago. I'm sure it's out there as usual."

Suddenly Talanski leaped over the side and held himself just below the surface while he quickly took off his shoes, trousers, and shirt.

Although the other mobsters were surprised, Frank wasn't. He reacted with, "That sonofabitch! I knew he couldn't be trusted!"

"What happened? Did he fall overboard?" asked someone.

"Hell no," said Frank. "He's trying to pull a fast one. I'm sure! As soon as his head comes up, blow it away!"

Joe's lungs were bursting for air, but he managed to swim under the rowboat's keel to the other side. The moonlight was just bright enough for him to see a huge form loom up from the depths. He didn't even have time to hope that it was his shark and not some other. Joe grabbed the side of the boat and began rocking it in an attempt to dump its occupants into the water.

"Hold on!" cried someone. "He's trying to turn us over! Shoot him! I can't swim!"

Sounds of gunshots filled the air, and bullets zinged all around the small craft. Being totally confused as to what was happening, the *Sea Gull's* crew turned on all of the ship's powerful floodlights. Daytime brightness covered the waters enough for everyone—and everything—to be seen.

In the midst of the confusion, Joe managed to surface and swim a good fifty yards away. Another idea occurred to him, and he yelled to the men in the rowboat, "Hey, you guys, are you looking for me? I'm over here!"

"What d'ya want to do, Frank? Should we go after the bastard?"

"No, you men grab those oars and let's get outta here! Damn it, I tried to tell the boss that fuckin' guy couldn't be trusted, didn't I?"

"Yeah, but what about the coke on that boat, Frank? Ain't we gonna get it?"

"I don't know. Besides, I'm not too sure about . . . hey, what the hell was that?"

Frank was referring to the sudden appearance and disappearance of an object that bumped hard against the boat. Floodlighting from the *Sea Gull* illuminated the area enough for everyone in the rowboat to get an unobstructed view of the object when it appeared again not more than ten feet away. The great white shark had lifted her head completely out of the water. Immediately, Frank and his men reacted by opening fire. Although the fish was hit by practically every round, it quickly submerged in a wake of white foam.

"Talanski!" yelled Joe as he tread water some distance away. Trying to see anything below the surface at night was too difficult, so our hero couldn't tell whether or not his friend was alive or dead. Nevertheless, Joe started swimming toward the *Sea Gull*. Suddenly, he felt a coarse object rub against his leg. Almost immediately, he knew that it was the great white. However, Joe became fearful for his life because of his not wearing the familiar black wetsuit and oxygen tanks while coming in contact with the shark. And when it began to circle him, he thought it was all over for sure this time.

"I don't know if you can hear me, girl, but I love you! If you have to do what's natural, take me in one bite . . . just don't let me suffer, please. . . ."

Suddenly, the huge fish aimed her powerful body at the little rowboat.

Crash! The four occupants were thrown into the water from their splintered craft. Desperate cries for help echoed through the darkness. Corazon knew something had gone wrong when he first heard gunfire minutes before. Instead of giving the order to lift anchor and take off, the greedy, vengeful drug dealer decided to wait for information from his designated boarding party.

As soon as the frightened and confused mobsters landed in the water, they were attacked immediately. Screaming and thrashing didn't last long, because, in less than sixty seconds, Frank and his three associates disappeared down the insatiable gullet of the great white shark.

"Holy Mary, Mother of God," Corazon uttered as he and his remaining men watched in horror what had happened to the others.

"Boss, I think we'd better get outta here!" shouted someone.

Then, as if he had to set up a more important mission, the drug leader pulled himself together and cooly responded, "That Talanski sonofabitch has crossed me once too damn often, and none of us are leaving until I get full satisfaction!

"First we'll kill his future by killing that shark. Second, we're going to take over the ship and get rid of the crew. And, third, I'm going to make Talanski die four times!"

"Look! There's the shark!" yelled a mobster while firing his M-16 automatic rifle at the tall fin. However, before anyone else could follow suit, it disappeared.

In the meantime, Joe had already boarded the *Sea Gull* and made the confused crew aware of what was going down. Unfortunately, there were no guns on the ship, but it was decided that the high-pressured firehoses would be used to try to keep the gangsters from using the access steps on the side of the vessel.

When the Trailblazer's craft was only thirty yards away, Talanski and his men kept their heads down as they got close enough to the railing to dump several buckets of bloody tuna chunks into the water. The great white responded almost instantaneously—and so did the Trailblazer with, "Shoot at the foam! Claudio, you, Lefty, aim for the railing, and keep those bastards away!"

Something in the great white shark's small brain signaled that the stinging pain was caused by the objects directly above. Therefore, she retaliated by attacking it. The gigantic fish's body broke surface with a tremendous leap and landed across the stern of the streamlined fiberglass boat. Tons of flailing ferocious fish proved to be entirely too much for the craft to bear. The shattered rear end sank, while the bow rose completely out of the water. Amid jaws that repeatedly crashed together over rows of razor-sharp jagged teeth, rapid fire of automatic weapons, and men screaming for sacred salvation, chaos reigned supreme. All but three of the ten, after seeing that the boat was sinking, opted to cling precariously to whatever was available rather than leap into the water. Perhaps it didn't make any difference, because the voracious eating machine was already set in full operation. Blood was everywhere as the great white shark chomped on bodies ravenously, leaving a few severed legs, arms, and heads bobbing about until she scooped them up also.

The Trailblazer, being an excellent swimmer, was strongly stroking toward the *Sea Gull* while at the same time calling for a line to be thrown to him. Talanski, realizing that he needed the drug boss as a bargaining chip for freeing Jasmine, threw him a line.

"Corazon," yelled Joe, "will you let my girl go?"

"*Si*, yes, yes, please, pull me up before that shark gets to me! I'll give you anything you want! Just don't let me die like this! For the love of God, don't let me die like this!"

"Okay, fellas, let's haul him in," Joe said as he and some crewmen began to tug hard on the line. "This is one fish that Metro Dade Police'll be glad to land!"

The Trailblazer had been lifted a good six feet out of the water, and he was certainly beginning to feel relatively safe. Looking around at the pieces of the shattered boat, Luis's heart skipped a beat when he saw the last of his men being dragged below the surface. After uttering a quick prayer for the men's souls and his own, he focused his attention on being hoisted aboard.

Suddenly, under the full bathing of floodlights that were still illuminating the entire area, the drug dealer's life came to an end when the great white broke the surface directly beneath him with a tremendous leap that carried the insatiable fully extended maw upward. Corazon looked down just in time to see the gates of Hell open wide to let him enter. There wasn't even time for a scream. And, had it not been for their quick releasing of the line, Joe and his helpers would've certainly been smashed against the steel railings of the deck.

A half-hour later, the *Sea Gull* was buzzing with Coast Guard personnel who had been called earlier. No sooner had the cutter arrived when Talanski persuaded the captain to speed him back to shore. If Jasmine was going to be rescued, it had to be done before daybreak, and Joe knew it. However, by the time the boat pulled in to dock, he had decided that his girl's life wouldn't be worth a penny if the late Trailblazer's men at the club and warehouse should learn of what happened that night.

Time was of the essence and Joe realized, as the cab sped toward his apartment, that the .22 caliber pistol kept in the nighttable drawer would hardly give him the firepower needed against the artillery carried by the mobsters at the warehouse. Notifying the police was out of the question, because he didn't want to run the risk of having some unknown person, or persons, in the department jeopardize any rescue attempt by contacting Corazon's men. He would have to go it alone.

The distance between Joe's apartment and the warehouse was seven miles of city driving. Even in light traffic, it would've taken the cab at least forty minutes to cover the distance; however, our hero's Porsche gobbled it up in fifteen. The dashboard clock indicated 3:17 A.M. as Joe pulled to a stop near the loading platform.

When Julio, smiling, laid out his full house on the table, the other two players groaned in total disappointment.

"Too rich for my blood, *amigo*," Carlos said, tossing in his hand.

"You guys wanna play some more?" asked the winner as he reached through the heavy cloud of cigarette smoke and raked in the huge pile of money from the center of the table.

"Yeah, I'm good for a couple more hands," replied Carlos. "How 'bout you, Vinnie?"

"Eh, what the hell, okay," the big fellow answered. "Might as well if it'll help me keep my mind off that bitch."

"Ha, ha, ha. Hey, don't sweat it," said Julio. "Because nothing's happening before five o'clock, remember?"

"Yeah, yeah, I know what the boss said," Vinnie replied as he picked up his cards. "Look, it's three-thirty already. So, Carlos, why don't you call the club? Efrain's probably heard from the boss by now."

"Okay, I'll do it right after this hand."

The setting moon afforded just enough light for Joe to see how to climb up a drain pipe to one of the broken pullout windows. He was trying to be as quiet as possible, because even the slightest sound would definitely echo throughout the entire building. Not knowing in which specific location the kidnappers were holding Jasmine, plus trying to listen for tell-tale sounds, caused Talanski's heart to beat wildly as he stealthily made his way along the moonlit corridor of the first floor. Then he heard what sounded like an elevator. Sweat popped out of Joe's body as he tightened his grip on the gun and hid behind a stack of storage cartons. When the freight elevator's doors opened and only one person stepped out, Joe knew that he had to make his move immediately.

Carlos, with a cigarette in one hand and an Uzi in the other, strode briskly toward the office where a telephone was located. As Joe watched the stocky figure pass, thoughts of his old green beret training came to mind. Silence and quickness were remembered as he took off his sweat-soaked shirt and twisted it into a tight garrote. Carlos laid the powerful automatic weapon on the desk while dialing. Joe crept to the opened door. Approximately ten feet separated him from the kidnapper. With absolutely no time to think about a more deceptive plan of attack, Talanski stepped inside and quickly wrapped the shirt around Carlos's neck. Maybe it was the thought of kill or be killed that prompted him to pull the two ends as tightly as he could. At any rate, none of the wild kicking or flailing of arms could shake Joe loose from straining his muscles to hang on to the shirt. Then it occurred to him that he needed this guy to lead him to the others. However, just to make sure of who was in control, Talanski grabbed the Uzi from the desk and jammed its muzzle against Carlos's rib cage.

"You can live or die right now!"

It didn't take the surprised and hurting man forever to figure out his predicament when Talanski tied his hands behind him with a piece of strong rope after stuffing much of the shirt into his mouth. Then Joe made a slipknot with another piece and put it around Carlos's neck. Holding the other end, our hero said, "Okay, pal, take me to your friends."

"What the hell's keepin' him so long?" asked Vinnie, going to the doorway and coming back. "I say we start havin' some fun right now. What about you?"

Julio, sitting at the table and casually shuffling the cards while looking at the still-unconscious girl, replied, "Why not?"

"Hey, now you're talkin'," said Vinnie as he stated loosening his belt. "I've been waitin' for this all night. Ha, ha, ha. Old Carlos's gonna hafta settle for sloppy thirds, right?"

The big fellow had already turned Jasmine over and was preparing to mount her from the rear when Carlos was shoved through the half-glass door.

"Freeze, you bastards!" yelled Joe as he held his prisoner in front of him.

Julio, unfortunately, tried to unholster his .9 millimeter but was fatally hit by a short burst of fire from Talanski's Uzi.

"All right, all right!" Vinnie shouted, making no attempt to go for his .45 on the table.

"You fat sonofabitch," growled Talanski through clenched teeth. "You raped her!"

"No, no, I didn't do nothin' to her, man! I swear on my mother's grave!"

Perspiration began to pour from Vinnie's brow as he tried to talk his way out of being killed on the spot, even though his trousers and shorts were dropped to his ankles.

"I can't let you bastards go," said Talanski while kneeling to raise Jasmine to the sitting position. "Look at her, you freaking animals! She's already one step from dying with all that coke in her system! No, I can't let you guys walk out of here to contact the rest of your late boss's mob."

"*Late?*" queried Carlos. "Is Luis dead? I thought you just happened to escape somehow."

"No, I didn't have to escape, my friend, because all of them are out there right now—in the belly of the great white shark."

"Santa Maria," uttered Carlos, "my kid brother Alfredo was one of them!"

"That's too damn bad," said Joe impassively. "Both of you should've tried making money another way."

In the meantime, while Carlos and Joe were engaged in dialogue, Vinnie was trying to ease close enough to the table so that he could grab his .45. What the big fellow didn't know was that Carlos was eyeing the automatic, too. And, as fate would have it, both men leaped for the gun simultaneously. From the kneeling position with semi-conscious Jasmine leaning against his leg, Talanski, holding the Uzi in one hand, emptied the cartridge on the two mobsters. Blood and bits of bones splattered everywhere. When the shooting ceased, Joe picked up his near-dead girlfriend, stepped across the riddled corpses, and quickly made his exit from the once-again quiet warehouse.

Eight

The Making of Believers

1

It took three weeks in the hospital for Jasmine to begin responding positively to the special care that she was receiving. The trauma of her physical and mental experiences at the hands of the kidnappers generated chronic nightmares. And even though Jasmine's system was completely cleansed of all drug traces, her mind was left in shambles. However, through the help of the best psychiatrist in the area, the shakened woman, after six weeks of care, began to recapture some of her former self.

The afternoon sun beat down so hard that even the asphalt of the hospital's parking lot felt hot and spongy beneath Talanski's feet. He had stopped at the florist's to pick up a dozen long-stem roses for Jasmine. And, as he rode up to the seventh floor on the elevator, he was mentally practicing how he intended to propose marriage. Yes, Talanski had made up his mind that he was not going to let Jasmine slip through his fingers. Although the thought had only grazed him before the kidnapping, Joe had lightly entertained the probability during their living together in his lavishly decorated apartment. Up to that point, love was not the main ingredient in this *potpourri*. Talanski's rocket rise up the financial ladder, plus Jasmine's expertise in helping him make good decisions concerning the many publicity offers, brought the couple together but not close enough for her to consider another marriage or for him to cancel out the prospects of sliding between the sheets with some of the numerous nymphs who were constantly bombarding him with propositions. However, the recent close brushes with death and absence of genuine love caused Joe to take stock of his whole life in terms of permanentizing the name *Talanski* on an international level. And what woman, other than the beautiful and brilliant Jasmine Renfrow, could truly help him to realize his goal?

Joe was so deep in thought that he did not notice how the several other passengers on the elevator were looking at him. Finally, a bold lad of eight couldn't hold back any longer. "Say, mister, I know you," he smiled. "You're the man with the pet shark, right?"

Joe, feeling in such a good mood, answered, "Right, kid. You like sharks?"

"Gee, I don't know 'cause how can you talk to a shark under the water? I got a dog, and my kid sister's got a bunny rabbit, and we talk to 'em all the time. But how do you talk to your shark when you're underwater?"

Although Talanski had not previously thought about that angle, he was beginning to wonder whether such a system could be made to work. This thought, however, was only lightly pondered, because he was turning the corridor and approaching his girlfriend's private room.

Joe saw two men standing near Jasmine's doorway. He recognized one as being Dr. Englehardt, the psychiatrist, but he drew a blank on the other man.

"Ah, Mr. Talanski," came the doctor's greeting, "I was just relating to Mr. Tyler how pleased I am with Jasmine's progress."

A puzzled look came over Joe's face as he eyed the medium-built, distinguished-looking elderly gentleman.

"So I'm finally getting to see you in person," said the stranger. "You and your shark were hot news over the wire service six months ago. Congratulations."

"Oh, I'm sorry," said Dr. Englehardt, "but I thought you had met long . . . "

"That's all right," the stranger interrupted as he reached for Joe's hand. "I'm Shelton Tyler, Jasmine's father."

Talanski was taken aback and felt embarrassed at meeting Mr. Tyler under the present circumstances. As they shook hands, our surprised suitor said, "Jasmine has often spoken to me about you, sir. It's a pleasure to meet you."

"Well, I must run now, gentlemen," said the psychiatrist. "Have a few more patients to see. But, briefly reiterating what I told you, Mr. Tyler, I think the general change of location that you mentioned would probably help Jasmine at this juncture on the road to complete stabilization."

Unfortunately, the afternoon sedative began to render the happy patient somewhat drowsy before Joe had an opportunity to talk about his desire to marry her. Besides, the sudden appearance of Jasmine's father made things a little awkward, to say the least. When her words started to ramble, the two men quietly left the room.

"I know you mentioned that you're picking up Mrs. Tyler this evening at the airport," said Joe as they waited for the elevator, "and that you've already reserved a room at the Hilton. But it certainly would give me great pleasure if I might invite the two of you to dinner."

"Well, we do have a few friends whom we must see after tonight's visiting hours here at the hospital; however, I definitely want to talk to you about Jasmine's future."

For some reason, Joe felt very uncomfortable in the older man's presence; nevertheless, he decided to persevere in his determination to relax the atmosphere.

"Do you have time to join me for a drink?" asked Joe looking Jasmine's father straight in the eye.

Although Mr. Tyler was mildly surprised, he quickly decided that maybe it would be better if his wife were not on the scene when he talked to Jasmine's lover.

"Why, I think that's a splendid idea! I'd be happy to join you."

"Great!" responded Joe as they entered the empty elevator. "I know where there's a *real* tap room, just opened last month, The Brass 'n Sawdust."

"Ha, ha! Sounds like one of those Gay Nineties bars in New York where the beer's served in mugs that take muscles to lift."

"Hey, you got it! It's the same way in the 'Burgh!"

2

Except for a few other afternoon patrons in the saloon, Talanski and Mr. Tyler were the only ones who kept the rather fat handlebar-mustashioed, long white-apron-wearing waiter blazing trails across the sawdust-covered floor. It didn't take long for Jasmine's father to slice through all semblances of reluctance and get right down to the bare bones of his immediate concern.

". . . and even though she's been somewhat of a free spirit for the past five years," continued Mr. Tyler, "Jasmine is basically a good girl who deserves a little more than what life's dealing her now. You know she's our only child, and we've tried to give her all of the guidance and love that can be imagined. But (sigh) as you've probably found out by now, Jasmine is a very aggressive and persuasive woman who can usually turn people around to her way of thinking."

Joe nodded affirmatively, responding, "Yeah, I agree, sir, which brings me to something I want to talk to you about since this is . . . "

"I know how you must feel," interrupted Mr. Tyler. "I'm totally aware of the details surrounding the kidnapping and how you amazingly saved Jasmine's life. For that, I'm fully grateful to you, Joe. However, my many years in journalism have, among other things, taught me to look for the future scenario behind the current one."

"I don't mean to be disrespectful in any way, Mr. Tyler," said our hero as he leaned forward on the table after taking a swallow of cold brew, "but why is it I'm getting the feeling that you don't particularly like me and you want me to stop seeing Jasmine?"

The newspaper magnet, being proficient in the art of verbal confrontation, quickly seized the opportunity to press onward. "Jasmine, as you probably know, was thirty-three last month, she's our only child, was married pretty much against our wishes at an extremely young age, and was widowed before she could even enjoy it or have children. Now, I don't know what your ultimate intentions are concerning any future relationship with Jasmine, but I do know that she's presently up there in the hospital struggling to regain some semblance of mental stability—all because of her close association with you. Please don't misconstrue what I'm saying here, Joe, because I am totally familiar with your background from the time you were living with your aunt in Philadelphia right on through your revived association with a Paco Sanchez, an old army buddy who was killed by the same people who tried to take my daughter's life. I'm even familiar with the pre-war work and activities you did while serving with the green berets in Vietnam plus your rehabilitative year when the Army tried to pretend that certain things never occurred. And, naturally, I know about your brief stint as a professional boxer. In no uncertain terms, Joe, when my daughter first asked me to use my information-gathering sources to check into your background for media hype, I delved all the way. . . ."

The anger that stirred within our hero's brain as he listened to just about every situation that involved his life boiled over and burst through the otherwise tight lips. "So what the hell am I supposed to say at this point, Mr. Tyler—that I'm sorry for being born?"

Jasmine's father, well-seasoned in dealing with all kinds of circumstances, would have ordinarily had the conversation under control—but not this time. Ever since his daughter, almost two months ago on the telephone, had related to him that she was beginning to fall in love with Joe Talanski, Mr. Tyler cautioned her against such a move. He desperately tried to talk her into breaking off the relationship, because, in spite of this new fellow's possession of fame and fortune, there were too many odd things in Talanski's life that made the father doubtful. Even after his headstrong daughter was given newly uncovered information about her lover's year in a psychiatric center, she chose to continue pursuing the relationship. Mr. Tyler knew his progeny well enough to realize that she always did pretty much whatever pleased her, so he backed off and watched from the sidelines.

"Of course not, Joe," answered the perturbed father, "but I certainly do not intend to stand around while my daughter serves as a live-in convenience for . . . "

"*A live-in convenience?* Mr. Tyler, believe it or not, this afternoon I came to the hospital with the intention of asking Jasmine to marry me, but I guess meeting you for the first time sort of took me off course; however, when I go back tomorrow morning, I'm going to do it. Why? Because I love her as much as any man could love a woman, and I know she loves me!"

Perhaps informing Jasmine's father of immediate plans was not exactly the wisest thing for Joe to have done under the circumstances, because the veteran newspaper owner moved with quiet dispatch. After saying so long to Joe for what was supposed to have been until the next day, Mr. Tyler returned to the hospital instead of going to the hotel. He expeditiously conferred with key physicians plus the hospital administrator. By nine o'clock that night, Jasmine's father had made all of the necessary arrangements for her release and special air flight to the family's chalet in Lausanne, Switzerland.

Next morning, Joe was in the midst of shaving when his phone rang. "Hello, Dr. Englehardt, what's wrong?"

"Mr. Talanski, were you aware of Jasmine's removal from the hospital? I have no idea, but . . . hello? Hello?"

Twenty minutes later, Joe's Porsche pulled to an abrupt stop in a no-parking zone at the main entrance. Dr. Englehardt met him at the doorway of the empty room.

"What the hell happened?" came Talanski's question as the two headed for the chief administrator's office.

"Well, since I talked to you, I contacted Ray Ingersoll directly. He's the assistant who was in charge last night. Dr. Ingersoll told me that he okayed the release after receiving a telephone authorization from his superior. Apparently, Jasmine's father knew all of the right buttons to push. A check in an amount that far exceeds this month's services was waiting for me when I arrived."

"And all the time that bastard was talking to me, he never once mentioned taking Jasmine away!" snarled Joe as they waited for the secretary to beep her boss.

"Joe, I fully understand why you're so upset," Dr. Englehardt said placing his arm around the angry young man's shoulder, "and I don't blame you. But permit me to give you just a little advice. I've been a psychiatrist for over twenty years, and very few things ever shock me into numbness, especially when it comes to a parent's protecting the young. Jasmine's father doesn't really know you well enough to trust you with his daughter's future. However, he is totally familiar with the desperate and near-fatal circumstances that his daughter was in recently. I dare say if you were he, you would probably do the same thing. . . ."

By the time the hospital administrator had returned to his office, Dr. Englehardt had calmed Talanski down to the point where reasoning was beginning to supplant emotion.

"I'm afraid that's all I can tell you, Mr. Talanski," said the head of the hospital. "We simply do not make an in-depth probe into why patients sign themselves out of the hospital. If we think it's against better medical judgment, then the patient is so advised. Ms. Renfrow was still under heavy medication when she signed the release at the urging of her father. Incidentally, Mr. Tyler insisted upon her leaving the hospital, so, when my assistant called me at home, I gave the okay for him to accept Mr. Tyler's personal checks. He paid for everything on the spot."

Although our hero tried to cover up his smoldering anger, it was quite apparent to Dr. Englehardt that any further discussion of the matter would only serve to aggravate Joe's feelings. Therefore, the perceptive psychiatrist suggested that the two have a light breakfast in the coffee shop. However, Talanski politely refused and left.

3

A couple of hours later, Joe was in diving gear and headed out to the *Sea Gull.* He had decided to throw all of his energies into concentrating on getting himself mentally prepared for the big opening scheduled to take place in one week. The underwater observation deck was ready and the only major thing remaining to be done was to entice the great white into the lake area. Everyone at Ocean World was pretty nervous about this last phase of the project, because success rested squarely on the shoulders of one person.

"Here comes the motorboat!" said one of the two crewmen leaning on the ship's railing. "Now we'll find out if Joe has enough of whatever the hell it takes to get that shark to go in there."

"Yeah, well, I still think it was a better idea to tranquilize her first," responded the other crewmen. "Suppose she decides to just swim away, like she could've done ever since we've been anchored out here, then Ocean World would be up the proverbial creek without a paddle."

"I know, and don't think they haven't tried to convince Talanski to go along with the idea of at least putting a heavy gauge electrified fence around the closed-in lake area. But would he cooperate? Of course not, because according to what I heard, he's afraid the shark might hurt herself. Can you imagine that? The multi-million-dollar investment in building the underwater observation deck could easily go right down the toilet if just one person, Joe Talanski, decides to screw up."

"You know, being out here all these months, feeding that shark makes me wonder if Talanski is still the only person she won't attack."

"Don, if you're thinking what I think you're thinking, forget it! You would last no longer than the time it would take for that shark to close her jaws around you. Just remember what happened to some of our own guys plus that drug pusher and his men. She ate all of the poor bastards, no exceptions."

"Yeah, but . . ."

"Forget it, fella. Nobody else but Talanski can control that shark, and I'm not too sure what he does down there can really be considered control. But there's one thing for sure: the shark hasn't attacked him yet."

"Nick, I still think it's something in this guy's body chemistry. Oh, I know all about the lab tests and other crap that all those scientists from all over the country have run on him, even had his urine sent to Japan, Australia, and a lot of other places, but nobody's come up with concrete proof of anything, right?"

"Yeah, I suppose you're right since Talanski himself can't pinpoint why."

"Come on, let's get below and find out what the latest plan is for moving this fish."

4

Although Mark Davenport and a few other key Ocean World staffers tried to dissuade the Miami media people from playing up the big move, too many of the Board of Directors members were enchanted with the idea that added publicity would be good for the future business. So, instead of the day of the move being a quiet one, it was replete with all the trappings of a huge brass-band-type hoopla. The U.S. Coast Guard station, plus the harbor police, stood ready to make sure that necessary safety precautions were observed. However, with hundreds of small craft jamming the waterways, it was finally decided that the *Sea Gull* was being placed in a very precarious position.

Bob Amesley, President of the Board of Directors, telephoned Dr. Prescott as soon as he got word that the highly publicized arrival of the *Sea Gull* would have to be delayed.

"I know exactly what you are saying, Bob, and I agree. The arrival of the *Sea Gull* into port would have been worth a million dollars in terms of publicity. As a matter of fact, we're in the process of working out details of a plan that would still excite the public about opening day next week . . . oh, of course I know how important this is to future business. However, at the same time, Bob, we certainly don't want to do anything that might cause the shark to swim away."

"Swim away?" shouted Amesley, almost dropping the receiver. "My God. Wes, don't even *think* about it! It was hard enough convincing the other members of the board that we should just rely on Joe's ability to keep the shark near the *Sea Gull* while the underwater deck was being built."

The two talked about how careful they had to be in moving the shark without involving the *Sea Gull.* Dr. Prescott continued speaking in the positive as he tried to reduce Amesley's anxiety. "I'm supposed to meet with Joe and Dr. Davenport in less than two hours from now, and I'm sure we'll come up with a plan that'll work . . . sure, sure, Bob, as soon as we devise a strategy, I'll call you . . . yes . . . yes . . . Of course. . . ."

Later that afternoon, the Ocean World president along with several other employees went out to the anchored *Sea Gull* to confer with Talanski, who had spent the night aboard. When the company motorboat arrived with its passengers, Joe was in his diving gear and ready to go down for the second time that day.

"Don't let us hold you up, Joe," said the president. "We know how important it is for you to keep contact with the shark."

"Thanks, Dr. Prescott," Talanski responded while two oxygen tanks were being strapped to his back. "It was a little too murky down there this morning. Couldn't see a darn thing beyond ten or so feet, and that's risky business in these waters."

"Yeah, I know what you mean," said Mark Davenport. "Our great white is not the only shark with a keen sense of smell. There're plenty of makos, blue tips, hammers, and God knows what else down there considering all the bloody tuna that . . . "

"Amen to that, Mark," said Joe, "because when I saw a couple of huge shadowy forms I surfaced in a hurry. Gentlemen, one of the many things I've learned about my great white is that she always travels alone."

"Ha, ha, ha," laughed a crewman. "How the hell can you be so sure about her social habits, Joe? Your shark has to get together with some appealing male in order to reproduce, right?"

"Unless, of course, old Joe thinks he's capable of doing the job himself," someone else blurted.

"Now that's really neat of you jerks," Talanski retorted. "Not only do you throw garbage overboard, you also throw it out of your mouths!"

"Okay, okay, that's enough of that," said Dr. Prescott, smiling. "Let's get serious for a moment here. Joe, after your dive, we have to talk about the alternate plan for getting the shark into the lake. As I told you over the phone this morning, the board president wants us to have it inside the fenced area before Saturday."

"Oh, great!" exclaimed Nick, one of the crewman. "I certainly would like to know how we're going to do it without having the fish follow the *Sea Gull,* and the harbor police have already said no to that idea."

Joe, after placing the oxygen tube into his mouth and adjusting the goggles, gave the thumbs-up sign and toppled backward into the water. Unlike earlier that day, the sun was shining brightly, and visibility was even good at sixty feet. The small multi-colored fishes that were curiously darting around the diver suddenly disappeared. Something had frightened them.

Talanski turned just in time to see the broad partly opened mouth of the great white shark. Just as many times before, he couldn't be sure that it was his friend—or his end.

"Oh, God, let this be her!" thought Joe as the wide-bodied eating machine headed straight for him.

Earlier that week, while Talanski and some crew members were checking diving gear, he was casually asked what kind of contingency plan should be set into motion if, on the spur of the moment, the shark were to decide to attack. At the time Joe was asked, he was still trying to hold himself together after Jasmine's departure; therefore, our hero was nonchalant about it with part of his reply being, ". . . I only hope that the old girl would be kind enough to take me out in just one helluva chomp."

The thought of death now loomed prominently as the great white circled. Suddenly, football-sized hunks of tuna drifted down within several feet of the diver. Joe's heart nearly stopped functioning when he realized the imminent danger he was in. The huge shark swiftly snatched every piece while our defenseless diver watched in horrific anticipation of being attacked. Talanski was too afraid to do anything except slowly tread so as to remain in the same location. Meanwhile, on board the *Sea Gull,* all hell broke out.

"Lower the cage!" a crewman shouted. "How the fuck could you be so stupid?"

"Never mind trying to deal with him now!" yelled someone else. "Just get this damn thing over the side in a hurry!"

Mark Davenport and two others were already in the cage. Having no time to put on any diving gear except singular oxygen tanks, the three fully clothed men grabbed spear guns.

Dr. Prescott had already broken out in a cold sweat as he clutched the railing and watched the shark cage disappear below the surface. All he could imagine was Talanski being fatally attacked and Ocean World's tremendous financial loss.

It seems that this terrible situation was caused by a crewman, Clint Olsen, whose duty it was to do the afternoon feeding. Unfortunately, when Olsen came topside, he was completely unaware that Talanski was in the water. It wasn't until after he had dumped five buckets of bloody tuna chunks that anyone noticed what was going on.

"Gee, sir," said Olsen to the ship's captain as they and others anxiously waited at the railing. "I had no idea he was down there! Why the hell didn't somebody tell me before I . . . ."

"Take it easy, kid," interrupted the captain. "Joe's been playing Russian roulette with that shark since day one. Unless I miss my guess, and I sure as hell hope I do, the shark's probably included him with the garbage. So don't blame yourself, kid; we all knew it was risky right from the beginning."

Eight minutes after the cage had submerged, it was raised, and none of the would-be rescuers voiced any belief that Talanski was still alive. Even Mark Davenport thought it was all over. However, before the cage had been secured to the deck, Nick saw a distant arm waving above the gentle swells.

"It's him! It's Joe!" shouted the excited crewman.

"Thank God he's alive," Davenport said as he joined two others in the little outboard motorboat that went out to get Talanski. "Be ready with those guns just in case, men."

The smile on Joe's face was a good sight to the rescuers, and he couldn't wait to tell them about his latest plan.

5

Early next morning, a sleek forty-foot inboard motorboat cut her two powerful engines and eased alongside the *Sea Gull*. Board members Bob Amesley and Craig Upshaw were happily greeted by Prescott, Davenport, and Talanski. The latter three had spent the night aboard the *Sea Gull* and were awaiting the board members' arrival. Over hot coffee down in the *Sea Gull's* galley, the men once again reviewed Talanski's plan for getting the great white shark into Ocean World's lake.

Oil tycoon and sportsman Upshaw said, "When old Bob here called me last night and told me about the plan, I told him I just *have* to be part of it! Hell, I wouldn't miss this for all the goddamn oil in Iran!"

Amid the general laughter and high spirits, Amesley looked at his watch and said, "Well, gentlemen, shall we get started? Time is money."

"Right," responded Dr. Davenport. "If we can get underway within the next hmm . . . hmm . . . say half-hour, we should be able to hit the channel tide just right. Getting through there to the lake might be a little tricky."

"How do you feel, Joe? Ready for this venture?" asked Dr. Prescott.

"Yeah," he answered while picking up the bright orange wetsuit that one of the crewmen brought in. "I'm ready. Remember, watch me at all times, because if anything goes wrong back there, I want you guys to reel me in faster than fast, okay?"

"Gotcha, kid," Upshaw said. "Damn, this is exciting! Hey, Joe, maybe someday you'd like to join me on a safari. I've always wanted to hunt cape buffalo. Now there's a mean son of a gun when he's wounded! While bleeding like crazy, he'll track you until the time is . . ."

"Hey, Craig," interrupted Amesley, "put it on hold! I'm sure Joe's thinking about more important stuff right now."

The mid-morning sunlight glistened on the relatively serene waters as Talanski tumbled backward and quickly began his search for the great white shark. Then again, it could hardly be accurate to say that he was the searcher, because, invariably, the shark always sensed his presence and sought him out. That morning was no different, because within three minutes, Joe saw the enormously thick body coming straight toward him. And, although he had seen this approach many times, getting used to it was difficult, especially that broad partly opened mouth displaying double rows of razor-sharp teeth.

Something different happened. The great white, instead of gently coming right up to her friend, veered off when she was only three feet away from being touched by him. This unexpected action caused Joe instant concern. Could it be that the silent communication between these two creatures had caused the great white to apply her power of limited reasoning and decide that she is about to be led into danger by the familiar object that she sees through those emotionless, jet-black orbs? Has the time come for this engine of destruction to stop making exceptions for this tasty morsel and fully live up to the long-established reputation of her species? Unlike any other time since his first encounter several months ago, pure unadulterated fear gripped Talanski's pounding heart. Could it be because he felt that he was about to violate the inexplicable trust that existed between them? The thirty-four-foot leviathan began to make wide circles around Joe. Around and around she went several times. No one on God's earth could have possibly convinced our hero that his time had not come; that his ticket was not going to be punched. Then something strange happened. Instead of just scooping in this floundering food object, the great white gave a slight flick of her tail, and the huge form gracefully glided away until it was completely out of Joe's sight. Without another second of hesitation, his flipper-covered feet sent him straight to the surface.

"Okay, okay!" Talanski yelled, "pull me in! Quick!"

Of course, the other men on board assumed that something had gone wrong down there and that the multi-million-dollar attraction was gone. They were reluctant to ask for fear of being told what they had suspected. But Dr. Davenport, vividly remembering his own brief encounter with the great white shark, broke the silence.

"What happened, Joe?" he inquired as the others stood by. "Did it try to attack you?"

"I . . . I don't think so. Mark, it was as though she knew I was down there to lead her into captivity. I mean my brain was getting all kinds of vibrations! She knows, Mark! I'm telling you she knows!"

"All right, all right, so she knows!" shouted Upshaw. "Christ! Am I going nuts, too, Wes? How the hell can a goddamn fish think? We've just lost a fortune here, guys, and there's not a friggin' thing we can do about it!"

"I suggest we all calm down," said Dr. Prescott as he wiped the beads of sweat from his bald pate. "Let's try to put the situation into proper perspective by. . . ."

"*Proper perspective?*" Amesley shouted. "You're going to stand here, as President of Ocean World, witness the slipping away of a solid gold proper prospective, and calmly suggest that we calm down?"

Suddenly, the huge motorboat rocked radically as though caused by some unseen force.

"Holy shit! What was that?" yelled Upshaw.

Then everyone saw a thick dorsal fin slice through the water as it disappeared and reappeared several times. While the others had their attention fixed on the fin, Talanski quickly adjusted himself for re-entry.

"Hey, and just what the hell do you think you're doing?" asked Davenport. "Don't push your luck, Joe! I'm telling you! That shark might . . . "

"Save it, Mark! Luck is all we got at this point, so keep your fingers crossed!"

Splash! The diver was out of sight. For almost fifteen minutes, the motorboat occupants did not see any signs of Talanski or the shark.

"Do you think Joe might've jumped the gun on this one?" said Prescott. "That fin could've belonged to a mako, or any other kind. I just hope he's all right."

"Don't worry," Davenport responded. "Joe knows how to take care of himself. Besides, he hasn't jerked that line."

They were still talking when all of a sudden Talanski surfaced and pulled himself aboard at the stern.

"Joe, this is getting to be old hat," smiled Upshaw while helping the diver remove the oxygen tanks.

"Yeah, I know, but there's nothing better than a good repeat performance, especially as long as my luck holds out," Talanski said as he turned his attention to Dr. Davenport.

"Okay, Mark, I'm depending upon you to make sure everything goes along according to our plan, because I can't do a helluva lot from back there in the rowboat. Remember, whenever you see my hand raised, cut the motor . . ."

Within the next ten minutes, Joe's plan was ready to become operational. A ten-foot boat was lowered into the water and secured to one end of a hundred feet of rope. Three buckets of blood-soaked tuna chunks were placed in the boat also.

"There, that should do it," Joe said as he was about to get into the small craft.

"Wait a minute! Hold everything!" exclaimed Upshaw. "I can understand your high level of confidence that this plan can work, Joe, because you've been the only human to have any kind of inter-action with the shark . . . "

"And lived," interrupted Dr. Prescott.

"Yeah, and still living to tell about it," Upshaw continued, "but I haven't really seen, or for that matter, nobody else . . . "

Talanski let out a healthy laugh which sort of perturbed the robust sportsman board member.

"Excuse me, Craig, but you are beginning to have doubts about this? Maybe you think this is some kind of a hoax, but, believe me . . . "

"That's where I have one big helluva problem, mister!" Upshaw shot back. "You want everybody to believe you when you tell us bits and pieces of information concerning your dives. Joe, we've moved a multi-million dollar project on *just* your word. How the hell do we really know that other species haven't been dining six times a day at our expense? Sure, I saw the great white shark once, but that was months ago when we were in the submarine."

"Hold on, Craig," said Amesley. "It's ridiculous for us to get into this kind of discussion. I have confidence in Joe here, and I'm positive that you do too, regardless of . . . "

"No, we can't operate properly under a cloud of doubt now that we have come this far," Dr. Prescott added. "And I say we should get on with the task of getting the shark out of the ocean and into the lake."

"Amen to that," responded Dr. Davenport as he resumed checking the tow line. "Okay, Joe, are you ready?"

"Not quite," came the soft response. "There's something I have to do that's more important than anything else right now."

"What is it?" Prescott asked.

"You'll see in a few minutes, don't worry," and with that, Talanski took a large piece of tuna from one of the buckets and jumped into the water.

In less than sixty seconds, our hero surfaced almost a hundred yards away from the boat. He appeared to be holding on to something that was moving in somewhat of a zig-zag pattern. Suddenly, there was a burst of speed that kicked up a foamy wake as Talanski held on with both hands. The men on board then saw the familiar dorsal fin, and they immediately cheered.

As soon as Joe was helped back into the boat, he said, "Okay, was that proof enough that my shark is still out there, or would you like something in concrete?"

Upshaw's eyes widened with anticipation of greater coming attractions as he asked, "Something more than what we just saw?"

"Damn right, if she'll do it while someone else is around."

"What are you saying, Joe?" Mark queried.

"A couple of weeks ago, I sort of broke a long-standing rule and that is never scuba dive unless somebody's topside to take care of any emergency. Well, I shoved off alone in the *Sea Gull's* launch and went out about three-quarters of a mile. I spent maybe twenty minutes with the shark and called it a day.

"As you marine biologists very well know, sharks also have a keen sense of hearing. They can pick up the slightest sound within a wide radius. Anyway, I banged on the side of the boat just below the water line, and you can imagine what happened."

"What the hell did you do, kid," laughed Upshaw, "knock a hole in it?"

Talanski took the wisecrack lightly, because he had already decided to make his associates firm believers. While smiling, Joe leaned over the low section of the stern and, with the palm of his hand, began to tap a few inches below the waterline. Needless to say, everyone thought this was ridiculous, and Dr. Davenport, feeling embarrassed for his friend, tried to justify this erratic behavior. However, the more Davenport talked, the more Talanski pounded. Then it happened.

Whoosh! Bursting the surface less than a few feet away and in full unobstructed view of everybody, the great white shark lifted her enormous head practically five feet out of the water. By strongly moving her lateral fins and tail, the great white held that position for almost fifteen seconds. The sight was awesome, to say the least.

"God help us now!" shouted Amesley as he stumbled back against the cabin door, almost falling down the stairs.

Fear gripped every heart except Talanski's.

"Watch out!" yelled Upshaw. "It's coming in the boat!"

In the midst of the foamy-white churning water, the great white slipped below the surface. She came to the top again. This time, Joe tossed several chunks of tuna near the massive jaws that snatched everything, including one of the buckets that slid off the deck. The feeding activity of the great white caused such turbulence that the forty-foot cabin cruiser rocked from side to side. In a few minutes, after Talanski had stopped throwing into food, the shark disappeared, and the waters became calm again.

"Damn!" chuckled Upshaw. "Being close to a show like that calls for a helluva lot of toilet paper and a change of clothing! Y'all remind me never to doubt this man again!"

By early afternoon, the cabin cruiser was headed for the lake. And the little rowboat, with Talanski inside periodically tossing over tuna chunks, was being towed as per his plan.

Nine

Best Laid Plans

1

Within eight months after the great white shark was introduced to the general public, Ocean World was making more money than had been previously projected. Joe's four daily performances were not only the most talked-about amusement attraction in Florida but in the entire nation. Just to see a human being in close association with a great white shark continuously boggled the minds of spectators.

One balmy afternoon in October, Dr. Prescott called Talanski into his office to talk to none other than Mario Rosetti, the famous movie producer. Talking to movie people was nothing new for Joe; however, what they were seeking was something other than minor actions. And, to each one, Talanski explained why he was reluctant to try anything new with the shark.

After introductions were made, Rosetti got right down to business with, "Mr. Talanski, I'm interested in shooting a film story that includes a real great white shark, not a fake one. Within the past twenty years, a lot has been done about various animals that can be trained, shall we say, to cooperate with actors. Shamu, the killer whale . . ."

"Ahem," interrupted Dr. Prescott. "We would rather not give recognition to our competition, Mr. Rosetti."

"Please, gentlemen, call me Mario, okay? If we could do a full-length feature film revolving around your great white it would probably double what both releases of *King Kong* did at the box office, to say the least about *Orca*."

"Mario," said Joe as he lit a cigarette, "I'm not going to waste your time. I'll tell you the same thing I told all of the other film producers. There is absolutely no set training mode that I've used when dealing with the shark. I can't really pinpoint why she hasn't attacked me up to now. Each time I go into the lake, I risk being devoured. And for even the slightest variation that's made during the time when I'm down there with her, might cost me my life. . . ."

Rosetti, prior to that afternoon's meeting, had already been made aware of the failures that others had in trying to get Talanski into a contract. However, he had planned to make the story details so appealing that refusal would seem ridiculous. The famous film-maker of Italy had earlier convinced the Ocean World powers that the movie would mean even bigger bucks, and the Board of Directors was depending upon Prescott and Davenport to get Talanski to go along with this one.

While Joe was voicing his polite decline of the offer, Rosetti was closely scrutinizing his general appearance in terms of possibly playing himself in the film. At just forty-one, Mario Rosetti had already established an enviable track record among his peers, and he figured doing a spectacular of this magnitude would catapult him to the top of the heap. Therefore, he decided that it would be better if he were to go one on one with this young American.

"Mr. Talanski, I can plainly see," said the filmmaker, "that you are an up-front gentleman who does not like to waste time in small talk. So I'm going to make you an offer that you . . . "

"Oh, no!" laughed Talanski. "If you finish the sentence, I'll die right here!"

"Hey, did you like *The Godfather* series?" asked Rosetti, laughing. "Now that was truly great filming. I mentioned *King Kong* earlier. Have you seen both versions?"

"Of course," Joe replied. "I don't believe there was a kid back in the 'Burgh who didn't see that old '30s black and white at least ten times."

"Did you like it?"

"Loved it!"

"Why?"

"Oh, I don't know . . . maybe it's the way Kong steals your heart away even in his destructive. . . ."

"Uh huh, and what do you think about the more recent release?"

"Well, there's no doubt that the story's gotten sexier. I mean there're connotations in the color version that . . . "

"Yes, but, Joe, was the monkey real?"

"Was it real? What do you mean? I don't follow you."

"Okay, granted the likelihood of finding a fifty-foot tall gorilla is slim as hell, ha, ha, ha. But what about even a regular size gorilla—mountain or lowland—doesn't matter."

Dr. Prescott, up to that point, had remained silent during the meeting because he thought it would be the same as the others—go nowhere. However, the president's curiosity, being highly stimulated, prompted him to say, "Now you have me somewhat perplexed, Mr. Rosetti. What does all this mean?"

"What I'm saying, my friends, is never has a real gorilla been used in any feature film. Real lions, tigers, elephants, and what have you, are used all the time, because man can control them and even train them to perform on cue. But not so the gorilla. Somebody always has to get into the costume and play the part, right?"

"Darn, you're absolutely right!" exclaimed Prescott. "I hadn't given it much thought, but I do know I've seen other real large primates, such as chimpanzees and orangutans, in the movies but not a real gorilla."

Rosetti smiled as he said, "Now let's go into the sea and consider some of those exotic animals in terms of using them in feature films. It would be no problem in getting real whales, octopus, giant squid, mantas, and a helluva lot of other things on film footage to work into movie stories. Even tiger sharks, hammerheads, makos, blues, and many of the others can be worked in nicely. . . ."

"But not a great white shark," Joe interrupted.

"Exactly!" the filmmaker replied excitedly. "No man has ever trained a real gorilla to perform with human actors, but if it ever happens, and I sure as hell hope I'm the first one to put it on film, theaters around the world will be packed . . . "

Talanski found himself listening intently to Rosetti. Unlike the other movie people who had previously tried to get attention, this one's idea sounded plausible. Rosetti seemed to have all of the right answers and suggestions. Instead of the conference ending within the hour, the three men talked for nearly two and a half hours, plus a couple of board members joined them for a late lunch. By the end of the week, Joe, Ocean World, and Mario Rosetti had entered a contractual agreement to make a feature-length film with a real great white shark in the starring role.

2

"And I don't give a damn if he *is* the leading man!" yelled Talanski as he, Rosetti, and several others headed for the lake, "no one, and I mean no one, except me, is supposed to go into the water with the shark! That was part of our agreement! I'm telling you, if she attacks, you and . . . "

"Calm down, for chrissakes!" Davenport interjected. "Mr. Randolph knows better than to go in, right, Mario?"

"But of course," came the film maker's reply. "Steve has starred in three of my pictures already, and I trust his judgment implicitly. He only wanted to get a real uncluttered look at the shark and show Miss Graylin what they would be working with."

Handsome Steven Randolph, the blond-haired, blue-eyed super macho veteran of numerous high-adventure films, had already let it be known that he wanted to familiarize himself with the reported unusual characteristics of this particular great white shark. People in the movie industry, from Hollywood to Rome, were very much aware of this actor's great accomplishments in mesmerizing all kinds of fierce animals to the extent that he was able to work with them directly and not need someone to double for him. Also, when Randolph was signed to do this picture, he made sure to gather all the information he could about great white sharks. Sources from as far away as Australia fed him all kinds of reported incidents of encounters around the Great Barrier Reef.

There was no adventure in all of the imagination of the film world that stimulated interest more than Mario Rosetti's current project. Perhaps this was why, when Talanski was out of town for two weeks, Rosetti talked Mark Davenport into working closely with Steve Randolph. Besides, being a technical consultant was bringing the much-impressed marine biologist not only more money than he anticipated but also the chance to hob-nob with some absolutely gorgeous actresses, especially Carla Graylin, the raven-haired, green-eyed beauty who was recently signed on as Randolph's leading lady.

From the shoreline, Joe and the others watched the small motorboat with its four occupants pull to dock. Steve and Carla, both wearing diving gear, greeted the docksiders in typical Hollywood fashion.

It became obvious to Joe that a lot of changes occurred during his brief absence, the foremost being the relaxation of rules dealing with the shark. And since he was in no mood to argue about matters over which he had no control, our hero decided not to fight the front office on the issue.

"Joe, I want you to meet Miss Carla Graylin," said Steve. "We were fortunate to persuade her to work in this film."

Randolph was certainly right in saying how fortunate they were, because the much-sought-after actress almost signed a contract with another company to do a movie in Greece. However, Rosetti's description of his film's impact was very convincing to Carla and her agent.

As soon as Joe looked into those flashing light-green eyes, he felt weak in the knees. Wow! Could this be the same beauty who had just three years ago, almost walked away with an Oscar for her lead role in the movie *Fire and Ice*?

"Miss Graylin, I'm happy to meet you."

Rosetti and Randolph had already told her about the probable difficulty they would encounter in getting Joe to accept the idea of helping the stars work directly with the shark. Now, upon seeing the fish's handsome keeper, Carla decided that the task shouldn't be so hard after all.

"Please, I would be a much happier woman if you would call me Carla, Joe. Since we're going to be working so closely together, I think we should really get to know each other, don't you agree?"

"Uh, uh, yes, definitely," Joe smilingly replied as Mario, Steve, and Mark also smiled.

3

The general atmosphere at Ocean World was completely dominated by feelings of unbridled popularity and financial success. It was hard to identify a single employee who was not benefiting from the movie that was being filmed in the area. Thousands of spectators passed through the gates seven days a week to see the great white shark plus many of the customers had hopes of being caught by the movie camera.

Handling the day-to-day operation of Ocean World had grown to be so complex that the Board of Directors decided to appoint someone to act as a liaison person between the company and Vista Studios. Dr. Prescott had no problem accepting this decision, because the person whom he wanted to have the position gained unanimous approval.

It wasn't long after Dr. Mark Davenport's appointment that he and Rosetti became close friends. Mark, being a bachelor, never turned down any of the social affairs to which he was invited. Rosetti always made sure that the much-impressed marine biologist met and spent time with many of the gorgeous lovelies who were part of Vista Studios. And, being relieved of all regular duties concerning laboratory matters, Dr. Davenport found plenty of time to pursue his evening delights. However, Mario Rosetti did have a burning ulterior motive for making sure that all of his people were especially nice to Mark, and, while Talanski was out of town on a two-week vacation, Rosetti's ulterior motive surfaced at an afternoon garden party.

"Promise you won't be long, Mark," pouted the sculptured beauty as she placed her glass of champagne next to the sculptured ice swan. "I want you all to myself for the rest of the day after you come out, okay?"

"Of course, baby," Mark replied, giving her a light kiss. "This shouldn't take more than five minutes. Your boss probably wants to see me about some minor detail that could probably wait until tomorrow. But you know how you movie folks are; everything has to happen yesterday."

Having become quite the ladies' man, Davenport gave his date for the afternoon a gentle pinch and swat on her firm buttocks as she turned to switch her sun-tanned frame back to poolside. While the biologist was momentarily admiring the view through his four-hundred-dollar sunglasses, he was joined by a smiling Rosetti.

"Pretty little thing, isn't she?" he said to Mark.

"Ah, Mario, you movie people really live the life."

"You could also, my friend, if you're smart enough to seize a golden, no not gold, a platinum opportunity when it presents itself."

"Well," said Mark, changing his demeanor to serious attention, "I've never passed up advancement opportunities, Mario, and I don't intend to form the bad habit now. But I sense you didn't call me over here to talk about generalities, right?"

"Umm, you're quite a perceptive gentleman, Mark, so I'm not going to waste time beating around the proverbial bush. You were one of the four original divers who came in contact with the great white shark down in the Bahamas. I understand the other two biologists were fatally attacked by the same shark, right?"

"Why, yes, but what does that have to do with . . . "

"Plenty, Mark, from what I can see. Tell me, since your first encounter with the shark, about how many times did you subsequently make exploration dives?"

Davenport was still not too clear as to why that conversation was taking place, but he was astute enough to know when he was being set up for a favor. And, while the film producer was talking, Mark was wondering whether Mario was going to ask him to go in with the shark for whatever reason. However, the biologist had already made up his mind that it was completely out of the question, regardless of any amount offered.

"Mark, you know the various terms of the contract I have with Ocean World for doing this film, and, I must admit, these first few months working with you people have been simply great. Joe's been very cooperative, and I think he's fantastic. But we can't very well make this picture stupendous if we don't shoot some close-up footage of man and shark together."

"Damn, Mario, how much closer can the man get to that eating machine? As it is, Joe's doing more now than he was before!"

"I know, I know, and I'm grateful. But the fact remains we still can't get the full realistic flavor of the story unless the star himself—not his double—can do at least one true scene with the shark!"

"You can't be serious about that, Mario! Do you have any idea what would happen to your picture within about two freaking seconds? Crunch! Gulp! Gone! Your star's light would be out forever! Aside from this odd situation we're enjoying with our particular great white, there isn't another reported close encounter in which anybody anywhere else in the world has gazed into those two black dots and lived to tell about it! Do you actually know how much danger's involved in. . . ."

303

"Cut! Hold it right there, my friend!" Rosetti exclaimed. "I really don't need a lecture at this time. I need someone who, for twenty-five thousand dollars in cash, would provide me with unimpeded access to the shark during the couple weeks of Joe's absence."

Davenport, looking at Rosetti confusedly, replied, "I don't quite understand what you mean. You already shoot film clips when . . . "

"No, that's not what this picture needs, Mark! Anybody can have stand-ins and doubles. What I want is the real thing. I want the leading man himself down there. Look, Steve Randolph is absolutely no stranger to adventurous exploits, and I'm sure he could work out his own shots if given the chance. We've discussed it extensively with the tech crew and those guys agree. If anybody else can do it, Steve Randolph certainly can. All he needs is to be left alone to work out strategies with our guys, and, I guarantee you, Steve'll have that shark eating out of his hand by the time Joe gets back."

In short, Mario Rosetti persuaded Dr. Davenport to cooperate for the twenty-five grand plus the continuation of including the biologist in on every social activity that involved the many beautiful women associated with Vista Studios.

4

Actors and actresses have a special knack for dealing successfully with fans and the like, so, when Steve and Carla talked briefly to Joe that day at dockside, they immediately smothered him beneath several layers of kindness. Steve even apologized for persuading Dr. Davenport to bend the rules concerning the shark. And, in typical Hollywood style, the much-celebrated screen hero invited Talanski to a party he was throwing that evening at the plush Coral Country Club. Needless to say, Joe accepted the invitation.

A light rain had begun to fall by the time Joe arrived at the 3C's and most of the guests had retreated from the huge veranda to the more intimate disco lounge. Other than selected Vista people, there weren't too many outsiders in attendance. Nevertheless, the light waft of marijuana drifted up Talanski's nose as soon as he entered. Although his host did not appear for awhile, Joe overlooked it when he was starting to have a good time on the dance floor. The pulsating multi-colored lights kept beat with the music.

In another room, Rosetti, Randolph, Davenport, and Carla Graylin were discussing various ways that they might get Talanski to cooperate more freely with the stars.

"I'm convinced, especially after this morning's dive," said Steve as he held back his head and sniffed in a thin column of cocaine, "that the shark, as ominous as she might appear, is attracted to me also, right, Carla?"

Before the beautiful actress could speak, Dr. Davenport who had obviously had too many drinks already, replied, "Attracted as in attracted to food, no doubt."

The laser-beam stare that Rosetti shot at the speaker should have been enough to quiet the wagging tongue—but it wasn't. And when the film magnet lightly admonished Mark for having one too many, all hell broke loose.

"I unequivocally resent, sir, what your words imply," said Davenport. "Let me assure you that I am fully capable of holding my liquor. And, while I'm on the subject of capability, let me inform you people that I didn't get my Ph.D. through some mail order house. I devoted a lot of in-depth study and graduated number four."

"What's with this guy, Mario?" asked Steve. "I thought you paid him to stick with us all the way."

Before the filmmaker could reply, Davenport interjected, "Don't try to make me look small, mister! Just who the hell do . . . "

"All right, all right, how about knocking it off, you two?" Rosetti shouted. "We're ready for some real shots with the shark, so let's not ruin things at this point. We need one another now more than before, because I'm sure that Talanski will do all he can to prevent our shooting Steve down there."

"Yeah," joined the leading man, "because I really believe I'm ready to come out of the cage in the shark's presence, right, Carla?"

"Oh, my goodness," smiled the beauty, "thanks for finally realizing my presence also. Yes, Steve's right, especially after what I saw when the shark approached our cage. Steve actually reached through the bars and rubbed its side many times. Other than just slowly swimming around us, the shark did nothing. Even I was tempted to touch the beast, but I guess I chickened out every time it came within reach. Maybe I'll muster enough nerve tomorrow.

"Now, are we going to join the other guests, or stay cooped up in this room for the rest of the night? Besides, Joe is out there, and, since I just met him recently, I think I'd like to get to know him better."

When Carla didn't see Talanski among the revelers, she asked someone to find him. Five minutes later the movie queen was informed that Joe had left.

The rain had stopped, and a bright full moon dominated a starry sky. Instead of returning to his apartment with one of the girls from the party, Joe decided to stop by the lake. For some reason, unknown to himself, he could not wait until the next morning to see the shark.

It was nearly two A.M. when Joe had checked in with Ocean World security for lake clearance.

"Hi, Mr. Talanski," came the gatekeeper's greeting. "You're not planning to dive alone, are you?"

"No, I think I'll just take one of the boats out, Ricardo, and see how the shark's doing."

"Oh, you don't have to worry about her, Mr. Talanski. She's fine. You know, I've been working this night shift for almost three months now, and sometimes I get the strangest feeling while patrolling the shoreline, especially on bright moonlit nights like this one when you can see just about everything."

"Ha, ha, ha. Hey, don't tell me you've seen ghosts out there, Ricardo!"

"No, not ghosts, but I do get the feeling that the shark's right up at the dock! I mean it's scary, man! As a matter of fact, I don't even walk out there any more. It's only around twelve feet wide, and, from what I've learned about great white sharks, they'll come right out of the water to get you."

Joe wasn't surprised to hear the guard speak that way, because all kinds of rumors and frightening stories had been constantly put together ever since the great white was first lured up the river and into the lake. Even though a steel-reinforced link fence was installed across the neck of the river, workers frequently debated whether or not the shark could, or would, someday attempt and succeed in leaping over it. The submerged portion of the fence was anchored in eighty feet of water, and the razor-wired top was almost seven feet above the water line. Nevertheless, Ocean World did very little to abate these concerns, because they were good for business.

After parking his car near the entrance, Joe casually strolled down to the dock. Rather than take one of the three motorboats, he chose to use a craft which had not been in the water since the great white had arrived. As Joe pushed the metal boat into the gentle surf and jumped aboard, he thought about how long it had been since he was last in a canoe.

The night air stirred mildly, and every gentle stroke of the paddle seem to spread wide shimmering swaths of moonlight. When he had approximately reached the middle of the lake, Joe pulled in his paddle and just drifted. He then, with the handle end of the paddle, began to tap on the inside bottom of the canoe. After doing this several times intermittently, Talanski listened and watched very closely. Nothing. Thinking that it was perhaps a bad idea to come out there on the lake at night, Joe picked up the paddle and started stroking for the shore. Suddenly, the canoe was bumped, almost causing it to tip over.

"Is that you, girl?" he said. "Thought you had retired for the evening, ha, ha."

There was just enough moonlight for Joe to see the familiar huge body of the shark glide effortlessly by. Since it was close enough he gently rubbed the rough form.

"How would you like to have a name? You know, old girl, I've been giving the subject a lot of thought lately. See that? There I go. Now how the heck do I know you're an old girl? You might be a young one, right?"

The great white, while Joe was talking swam slowly around the canoe, frequently lifting her enormous head as if to get a better view of her chosen friend.

"I had thought seriously about naming you Talanski. Ha, ha, ha. Now what kind of a tag would that be! Your friends might have one helluva time spelling it. Besides, I think you should have your own name, don't you? You know, I used to think you were someone, or a combination of many people, who I used to know. But, over the past several months, I've come to believe that you are you and not somebody reincarnated. What do you think?"

Round and round the rocking canoe swam the great white, now and then coming in close to be rubbed.

"Naw, you shouldn't be tagged with a name like mine. You're a star, did you know that? Heck, that's right. You are definitely a star, madame, and you should have a star-sounding name, right? Umm, let's see now. How does *Shara* sound to you? Shara, the Beautiful! And you *are* beautiful. Okay, that's it—Shara! Ha, ha, ha! Yeah, with an *a.* not a *k* after the r! Damn, I wish we could celebrate, Shara! Sorry I didn't bring even a minnow out here tonight. Oh, well, you'll forgive me this time, right? Tell you what, Shara, move that Mae West figure of yours over, and I'll join you, okay? How's the water?"

Joe was really enjoying talking to the great white. It made him feel good all over.

"Sorry I didn't bring along my usual wetsuit and all that other stuff, Shara. You don't mind if I skinny-dip this time, do you? Thanks. Gee, I hope I'm not making the biggest mistake of my life. Well, here goes nothing!"

Joe crossed himself and dropped into the water. It was too late for him to consider whether his naked body would be too much of a temptation for the gigantic eating engine, because he had no sooner entered the chilly water when the tall pectoral fin came close enough for him to catch a hold. Zipping along close to the surface gave our hero a most exhilarating feeling. Joe continued talking to Shara during the half-hour that he was in the water. Unlike any other time, Joe felt closer to his friend.

5

In spite of Talanski's protestations, the powers that be at Ocean World were persuaded to permit Steve and Carla to shoot a scene without him. The meeting in Dr. Prescott's office was reluctantly called, because Joe was the only one who had expressed serious concerns about Vista's filming plans for that day. However, the president apologetically requested Rosetti and his team to attend what was promised to be a very short meeting.

"Dr. Prescott," said Mario, "I would appreciate your getting us underway here, because, as we all know, I want the crew to catch every ray of sunlight. Besides, time is money."

"Surely, Mr. Rosetti, this should take no more than a half-hour. Joe here was pretty upset when we decided to let Vista do some lake filming without him. And, in spite of the many good practical reasons we discussed, he is still not satisfied with our decision. Does that pretty much serve as a practical opening for this discussion, Joe?"

"I guess so, Dr. Prescott, but I still believe you people are making a big mistake, to say the least," Talanski answered, "How much do we *really* know about Shara in spite of her being with us almost a year now? Remember she's still a great white shark that . . "

"Wait a minute! Just hold it right there!" Randolph interrupted. "Why are we covering this again? That angle, along with every other one you could possibly think of, Joe, was discussed at yesterday's meeting. So why are you wasting our valuable time? Unless you have something more substantive to add by way of enlightenment, Vista people are going to leave now, right, Mario?"

"Take it easy, Steve," replied the film producer calmly. "Don't get yourself upset over this thing. I want you to be totally relaxed for this afternoon."

"Okay, okay, so I'm relaxed already. But I want to ask the great Mr. Talanski a question. Are you jealous of the fact that I stand a damn good chance of getting to know Shara as well as, or maybe some day even better than, you?"

"Don't be ridiculous, Mr. Heartthrob of America, why should I be jealous of you in your *papier maché* world? I'd just hate to see you make a mistake about Shara—because I'm sure it would be a fatal one."

"Why, you ungrateful bastard! Is that supposed to be your way of trying to put some kind of hex on me?"

Joe, cool and unperturbed, never rose from his seat while Steve had to be restrained from coming at him. Needless to say, the entire Vista delegation walked out immediately.

Rosetti shouted back something about not wanting Talanski anywhere near the set that afternoon. When the door closed, leaving just the three Ocean World people in the room, Joe casually lit a cigarette, poured himself a cup of coffee, and waited for the president and Dr. Davenport to say something.

"That was a bad scene, Joe," Mark began. "You should've just gone along with . . . "

"Gone along with," Talanski said, "like you, Mark, huh? How much are *you* getting on the side for just going along with? I thought your professional integrity would've carried you above all of this Hollywood glitter crap."

"What are you talking about?" Dr. Prescott asked.

"Never mind," Joe answered with a waving off. "I don't think we can do anything to make up for all the damage that's already done, right, Mark?"

Dr. Davenport's surprise at having been discovered quickly changed to anger, and he lashed out with, "And just who the hell do you think you are, Mr. Know-It-All? When are you going to realize that there are others of us who can also work with Shara? Hah, I'm sure your jealousy is getting the best of you, Joe, especially since you learned of Steve's progress. . . ."

"Mark, take it easy," interrupted the president. "There's no need for us to argue. Really, gentlemen, Ocean World looks primarily to the three of us to take care of its investment in this filming project. And I think we're doing a damn good job, in spite of these little meaningless squabbles. Money is coming in faster than we can count it; we have passed every other marine-life facility in the world in terms of a stellar attraction; and . . . "

"And we're pushing our luck needlessly," Joe added as he stood up and put on his sunglasses. "Look, Mark, you and I have been working together ever since Shara was first sighted. And I'd just hate to see . . . oh, shit . . . let it be, okay?"

Prescott was elated when Davenport and Talanski shook hands. He invited them to lunch.

"Thanks," Joe said as he was leaving the office, "but, since I'm not needed for today's filming, I think I'll call a young lady who I'm pretty sure wouldn't mind having lunch with me on board my new cabin cruiser."

"Oh, well, maybe next time," replied Prescott. "Hey, that's some snazzy craft! I saw it moored in the harbor while you were away."

"How about you, Mark? Are you going to turn me down for a more exciting time also?"

"Not on your life, you old tightwad," Dr. Davenport replied gleefully. "It's not every day that anybody can separate you from a few pennies."

"Am I to interpret that insulting remark as an acceptance?"

"Damn right, boss! I'll meet you at the Half Shell say twoish, okay?"

"Phew!" gasped Dr. Prescott, smiling, "The Half Shell, no less! Boy, you really have come a long way in your choice of eateries, Mark!"

"Hey, weren't you the one who, only a few minutes ago, extolled the fact that a lot of money's being made around here?"

As Dr. Davenport was leaving, the president said, "And, Mark, I think it was nice of you guys to shake hands."

6

The camera crew was all set up and ready to shoot the scene, but Rosetti didn't want to go ahead with it before talking to Dr. Davenport again.

"Damn it, Mario," complained Steve as they were standing on the dock, "why do we have to wait for him? The sun is perfect now, and there's plenty of light all the way down to about fifty feet! Besides, it's almost twelve-thirty!"

The film producer, unlike earlier, was beginning to get nervous about gambling so much on his leading man's confidence. And, although Steve tried to reassure him that there was nothing to worry about, Rosetti preferred having Dr. Davenport with them on this all-important occasion; therefore, he dispatched a couple of people to find him. However, out of sheer curiosity, the marine biologist, upon leaving the main building, decided to drop by the lake and see how things were going. Suffice to say, Rosetti felt better when he saw Mark pull up in his convertible Jaguar. A few minutes later, the boat was headed for the floating equipment platform in the center of the lake.

"Thanks a lot for doing this, Mark," said Rosetti. "It's just that I think I'd feel a little better knowing you're around for the most important scene in the film."

"Jesus Christ!" shouted Steve. "what the hell is this, a goddamn holding-hand session? Mario, how often have you seen me do many of my own stunt scenes in other pictures?"

311

"Many, Steve, but let's not forget the fact that we're dealing with an unstable variable here. No one has ever . . . "

"No one? No one? Do you call Mark no one? Ha, ha, ha, this shark shit gets better as we go along, right, pal?"

Dr. Davenport, also somewhat amused, responded, "I'm afraid I have to agree with Steve, Mario, because I've been down there with Shara several times, always in the cage, of course, and, the last time I looked in the mirror, I saw me."

At that point, everybody had a good laugh, even the director. However, he still insisted upon cautioning Steve against taking any unnecessary chances.

"Okay, Mr. Rosetti," said one of the crew as the motorboat pulled along side of the platform. "Give us a couple of minutes to warm up the cage engine, and we'll be ready to shoot."

"Fine, Eric. The sunlight is certainly cooperating nicely."

Three sequential cameramen, Steve, and Mark entered the cage. The apparatus was then hoisted by strong steel cables and poised over the side just before being lowered into the crystal-clear water. Mario smiled faintly as he gave the thumbs-up sign and adjusted his headphone. The filmmaker made sure that everything was in order before giving the go-ahead signal to the crane operator.

A couple of crewmen, whose job it was to monitor the sonar equipment and let the men in the cage know when the shark was approaching, spoke softly as they sat next to each other at the control board. "But Shara's not typical of your everyday, run-of-the-mill great white shark, Bob, and that's what makes this picture unique."

"*Unique* is definitely the right word to describe her. I understand Vista is trying to get Ocean World to give it exclusive rights to all future filming. Ted, is it true?"

"Well, let's just say that sixty-eight million bucks on the barrelhead for a five-year deal is kind of hard to turn down when you all you have to do is say no to the other companies that are going to be banging on the door after *Shara, Queen of the Deep* shatters all box office records."

"Yeah," Ted joined as he fingered dials and switches, "and with Steve playing the role, how can we miss? He's not only a great star but also one helluva nice guy who . . . "

The operators interrupted their conversation, because the screen showed a large object moving toward them. Bob immediately notified the director and others.

"Okay, men," Rosetti said to the cage forty feet below, "Shara's heading this way. Can you see her yet?"

"No, not yet," answered Steve, "but we're ready. I can hardly wait, Mario! This is definitely going to be a great scene!"

Being a little superstitious, Rosetti crossed his fingers and replied, "If anybody can make it a great one, you can, big guy!"

7

The afternoon breeze blowing through the opened cabin porthole did very little by way of cooling the two entwined perspiring bodies that were in the throes of reaching the climactic summit together. Suddenly, amid powerful thrusts and utterances of joy, one of the bodies ceased moving.

"Oh, my god!" shouted the man as he quickly disengaged himself and jumped up from the bed. "Oh, my god!"

The red-haired woman, in total shock, sprang to the sitting position, pulling sheets to cover her nudity. For nearly ten seconds she speechlessly watched her naked partner frantically dialing the ship-to-shore telephone.

"Come on, somebody, answer, answer!" he exclaimed.

Finally the woman gathered enough composure to ask, "Is something wrong with the boat? Joe, I'm talking to you! What's wrong?"

At that, he turned to the perplexed beauty, while still holding the receiver, and said, "Gosh, I'm sorry, Melanie, but something's gone wrong somewhere, and I have to find out what it is!"

The perplexed beauty quickly dressed as she watched and listened to her lover yell at the person on the other end of the line.

". . . No, I'm not trying to interfere with anything, Dr. Prescott, but I *still* think you should send somebody out there to check. Look, don't ask me to explain how I know . . . I just feel it, that's all! Now are you going to . . . bullshit! I'll do it myself!" Click.

Joe deposited the afternoon date at the dock and aimed his car for the lake.

8

When the long graceful form of the great white shark came into full view, the underwater lights plus the natural sunlight illuminated everything. Cameras began to roll as the veteran actor and crew members began carrying out their roles and assignments.

Steve felt exhilarated while he watched the effortless movements of Shara as she poked around the cage.

You are indeed a beautiful creature, thought Steve. *The public's going to like this scene the best!*

Unhesitatingly, the star exited the cage and began swimming toward Shara. She had briefly gone to the surface, perhaps expecting to find some tasty tid-bit since she now knew better than to crunch on the tasteless steel bars of the cage. When the shark turned and saw the familiar-shaped object swimming in her direction, something signalled her that it might be the same familiar object that she had grown to love. The stiff tail gave a moderate flick which caused the thirty-four-foot leviathan to make a wide turn and head to investigate.

All right, baby, Steve thought, *I look just like your friend, so let's give the cameras some excellent footage in this scene.*

Suddenly, the line of fluid canals that are located in the great white's spine tingled with a new signal, and the signal was a basic one—food! The smaller fish that had been curiously swimming around the lighted area darted out of the way as Shara glided past them.

"How are things going down there?" came the film director's questions over the radio. "Can you get a good angle on the shark yet?"

One of the cameramen, Theo Inge, equipped with special electronic audio headgear that enabled him to keep in contact with the crew above, responded, "Affirmative on both questions, Mr. Rosetti. Right now, Steve is out there approximately twenty-five yards from the cage, and we have both him and the shark in full view. No doubt about it, she's really a beautiful animal—so graceful in her movements!''

As the great white approached, Steve began to get a different feeling, especially as the fish's enormously broad face turned into one big cavernous maw surrounded by jagged teeth. The lone diver had only a fraction of a second to view this grotto from the outside. With a quick angle adjustment, the great white took Steve's entire upper torso into its mouth before making a clean bite that left only two legs clinging precariously to what was left of a pelvic region.

The fatal attack occurred so unexpectedly that the other divers were momentarily shocked. They and their cameras had an unobstructed view of the gruesome sight. While blood began to cover the area, veteran cameraman Cooper kept his lens focused on the scene as the great white shark scooped up and swallowed what was left of Steve Randolph.

All hell broke loose topside. Two female members of the filming crew fainted straightaway when Inge shouted what was happening below. Rosetti, after ordering the immediate raising of all cages, called the marine police. Meanwhile, the great white, after having tasted blood, wanted more.

Shara attacked the three cages, trying to get to the divers. Her jaws gripped the bars so violently that one of the steel lifting cables snapped, sending the cage and its two occupants to the lake bottom. Dr. Davenport and cameraman Luke Cooper remained calm as they stayed well to the middle of their cage and watched the rest of the action happening around them.

The underwater lights continued to illuminate much of the area as the crimson coloring caused by Steve's blood disappeared. The great white was awesome in slamming her body against the other two cages as though she was trying to dislodge the divers who were hanging on for their lives. It seemed like an eternity before the cages finally surfaced. One of the divers couldn't wait for the boom to swing the cage onto the deck. He panicked and tried to make the jump. He didn't make it.

"Grab him!" shouted someone on board.

The poor fellow was almost pulled aboard when Shara's huge head broke surface only twenty feet away.

"Oh my god! Help me! Help!"

The powerful engine of the sea covered the relatively short distance in a split second, keeping her head well out of the water and jaws fully extended.

Chomp!!

Shara's razor-sharp teeth left nothing but a quivering arm which the frightened would-be rescuer dropped. No sooner had the severed appendage made a splash when the great white quickly snatched it.

Dr. Davenport's efforts in trying to restore some semblance of order on board were meeting with nothing but failure. One of the crew produced a large-caliber rifle and frantically ran to the railing. At that moment, Shara skimmed the surface and rolled over so as to get a better view of the floating platform. Perhaps, in her limited reasoning, she expected food to be thrown to her. Instead, something stinging struck just above the eye. Then several more stinging objects hit the shark as she glided by and submerged.

"Sonofabitch!" shouted someone. "I think you got him!"

"Don't be too sure about that," interjected Davenport. "Remember, Shara's a great white, and they're known to attack when injured."

"What the hell do we care about that now?" Rosetti said tearfully. "I've lost not only a star but a friend!"

"Yeah! And what about poor Lenny?" someone else said.

"Gentlemen, gentlemen," the marine biologist continued in spite of loud grumblings. "I think we had better get back to shore as soon as possible! You're tampering with the unstable behavior of a thirty-four-foot monster whose kind have been known to destroy every . . ."

"Forget it, Davenport!" interrupted Cooper. "We're not gonna lose everything because of this. Look, Mr. Rosetti, we have some damn exciting frames in our cameras, even in Quinton's, may his soul rest in peace. So why not turn this tragedy into a sure winner? I say we should continue filming until we kill that bitch!"

"Yeah, yeah, yeah!" came cheers from the crew.

"All right, men," said Rosetti as he stared directly at Mark. "Vista's lost two damn good human beings this afternoon because of Ocean World! So let's think about stuffing the shark and having it travel on display!"

316

"Great god! You're crazy, Mario!" Davenport shouted. "You people can't do that!"

"Oh no?" the moviemaker returned. "Vista has dumped millions into this picture already, and we're going to get one helluva return on our investment!"

Franz Huebner, Rosetti's assistant and budget watcher, chimed in with, "You're absolutely right, Mario. And, if we don't improvise, all of us will financially suffer."

Rosetti half-smiled as he nodded in the affirmative and said to Mark, "My friend, you are a marine biologist who is rightfully thinking about your employer's welfare, and I am a filmmaker who's also thinking about my employer's welfare. Ocean World has already made millions on that shark down there, and Vista Studios, after putting a lot of money already into this picture, has nothing to show for it except some footage that could've been shot anywhere and the fatal losses of a damn excellent actor and a good cameraman. Granted, accidents often happen during the filming of high-adventure stories; besides, I'm certainly no stranger to having to improvise."

"Mario, I'm really sorry about what happened to Steve and the other man," Davenport said, "and I'm sure Ocean World and Vista could work something out that . . ."

"Damn right we're going to work something out on paper later! But right now, I got a film to put together, and your shark is going to cooperate—alive and dead!"

"You're making a big mistake, Mario, and I'll be damned if I'm going to stay out here while you people turn a bad situation into an even worse one!"

"Go on! Your so-called technical advising sucks anyhow!" yelled a crew member. "We don't need him, boss! Maybe it'd be better if he went back to shore while we shoot the rest of this scene."

The remainder of the members voiced general accord. They also felt that the shark should be dealt with on a final note. Some spoke of the probability of the picture's making far more money at the box office because of the real deaths.

Mark Davenport felt helpless in his futile effort to convince the Vista people that they should not pursue their newly hatched plan of killing the great white. Threats of huge lawsuits filed by Ocean

317

World meant absolutely nothing to this psyched-up team. The frustrated biologist, amid jeers, got into one of the small outboard motorboats and headed for shore.

"Okay, folks," shouted Rosetti, "let's get this show on the road here! That's right, Al, dump some more of those chunks overboard! We want that goddamn fish to come right up to the platform! Stand by with the gun and gaffers, men! All right now, get ready with those cameras!"

Shara, while scouring the lake bottom for more food, received a strong signal to head upward. When she broke surface, bullets from the high-powered rifle punctured her tough flank and sent pain coursing through the sleek body. Also, when she snatched a hunk of tuna near the platform, two crewmen struck her with gaffing hooks.

Another signal travelled to the great white sharks brain, a different signal, one that told her to get ready for flight or fight. With limited reasoning, Shara decided that the large shadow was the source of her pain.

"Keep those cameras rolling, boys!" shouted Rosetti, "she'll probably come up again in a minute!"

"Over there!" someone yelled, "there's the fin!"

About sixty-five yards away, Shara had come to the surface and began circling the floating platform. More pieces of tuna were heaved into the water by excited crew members. Visions of having the stuffed carcass of this thirty-four-foot great white shark used on special promotions gave everyone a good feeling. Besides, Mr. Rosetti made a vociferous promise that each person would automatically be given at least a five thousand dollar bonus when the shark was hauled ashore.

"Steady now, boys," Cooper cautioned as he and the other cameramen trained their instruments on the shark. "Try to get all good angles! She's coming in!"

"Hand me some more shells," said the sharpshooter who had positioned himself on one of the several wide, elevated shelves that extended six feet beyond the edge of the platform. "With a few more good hits, I think it'll be all over."

Two stinging bullets lodged behind Shara's left ear. She submerged just a few yards away from the craft.

"That did it!" shouted the rifleman as he stood up on the shelf extension, waving his rifle in the air. "I knew she couldn't last much longer!"

"Nice going, Eric," someone said while tossing the young assistant a cold can of beer. "That was *some* shooting, fella! you deserve this one!"

Instead of coming off the shelf, the beaming hero popped the top, lifted the can in a toast to his cheering fellow crewmen, and began guzzling the refreshing brew. Suddenly, the gates of hell swung wide open.

Up from the depths of the lake and crashing resoundingly through the surface directly below the shelf came the enormous blood-stained head of Shara. Eric didn't even have time to leap off the extension before he was totally surrounded by the great white's powerful jaws. It so happened that the cameras were already focused on Eric when the several splintered pieces of the extension and the rifle were snatched by the hungry and angry shark. The incident happened much too quickly for anyone to even think of trying to save the young sharpshooter.

Maybe it was the general atmosphere of tragedy that caused Rosetti and the rest of his crew to take this latest fatality in stride, or maybe it was the knowledge that every gory event that took place was captured on film. Amid the fast movement of equipment in anticipation of Shara's next appearance, people spoke openly of raking in the big bucks upon release of this picture to the theaters. Already, poor Eric was, for the moment, forgotten.

Unlike previous occasions when she came in contact with the large shadow, Shara, in her rudimentary way, now equated this shadow with pain. However, unlike other kinds of sharks, the *carcharodon cacharias* has the very strong propensity to mount a sustained attack on anything that has hurt it.

Rosetti and his filming crew were definitely not expecting an all-out confrontation with the great white, nor were they ready to handle what was about to take place. At full speed, Shara gunned her powerful body engine upward toward the shadow.

Crash!! The huge, grotesque head of the shark splintered the several layers of the platform's flooring and pushed straight through. Shara's jaws repeatedly snapped at everything that came within reach. Mass hysteria erupted as people tried to hold on to their balance and keep from sliding into the shark.

"God help us all!" screamed a crewman who was trying to untie a small outboard motorboat.

Because of the shark's thrashing about, the entire platform began to tilt under the stress and tonnage. The great white dropped back into the churning water through the enormous hole. Within seconds, the structure began to sink.

"Quick!" yelled Rosetti as he tried to maintain his footing on the tilting platform, "throw that equipment in the launch, and let's get the hell outta here! You three guys grab that stuff, and, for God's sake don't let anything happen to it!"

Within seconds, the boat was loaded with most of the crew members and as much of the equipment that could fit into the twenty-foot craft. However, the film director, his assistant, and one other man remained on the badly listing platform. Rosetti wanted to get one more close-up shot of the shark.

"We're taking a heck of a chance staying on this thing," said one of the crew. "No telling what that monster might do next."

"Exactly!" responded Rosetti as he adjusted a portable camera on his own shoulder. "That's why I'm not taking any chances of somebody else's missing the shot of a lifetime. I've been known in other occasions to grab a camera, right, Phil?"

"Absolutely!" came the assistant's reply. "By the way, Mario, how much longer are we going to stay on this platform?"

"Hell, we'll wait until this thing's about to go under," Rosetti answered. "And it looks as though we won't have to wait long. Make sure the motorboat's line is untied. We certainly don't want to. . . ."

"Holy shit!" cried the crewman, "look at that!"

What he was referring to was the tall fin of the great white shark slicing rapidly toward the launch, which was almost at the dock.

"Oh, my god," Rosetti uttered as he quickly trained his camera in that direction.

When Shara was approximately thirty feet away, she lifted her head completely clear of the surface as she bore down on the craft, which was unsuccessfully trying to outrun its pursuer.

Amidst cries for help, some of the occupants made the mistake of standing up while grabbing for anything that could be used as a weapon. Shara slammed into the boat so hard that the men who were not sitting fell overboard. The impact also caused the engine to conk out.

Rosetti and the others with him watched helplessly from the badly damaged platform. However, the veteran filmmaker kept his eye glued to the viewfinder of the camera that was capturing the scene with cold accuracy as each of the floundering victims was fatally dragged underwater. Then, almost fifteen minutes passed with no further sign of the shark.

Meanwhile, the remaining four men on board the launch were able to start the engine and limp in to dock. So much real horror had occurred that they moved like weary battlefield troops.

'Thank god they made it," Rosetti commented.

"Yes, but what about the other guys who fell in?" asked Franz. "Don't even bother to answer, because we all know they're in that shark's belly."

Dwight Farley shook his head and remarked softly, "It's a bad omen."

"What?" asked the filmmaker.

"I said it's a terrible sign, Mario. We never should've tried to do the shooting without Talanski. Now, all we got this afternoon is death by . . . "

"Shut up, Farley!" Huebner shouted. "What the hell's wrong with you anyhow? You're a veteran technician, and you've certainly seen fatal accidents happen on location before!"

"Yeah, but not designed carnage like this! A thirty-four-foot great white shark has murdered us, man! Can't you understand that? Six lives have been snuffed out by that devil fish down there, and you expect me to be calm? Hell, I'm getting back to shore right now!"

The tilting platform had been taking in a lot of water, and it was beginning to sink even faster when Farley moved toward the outboard motorboat. Rosetti's assistant eagerly threatened to fire the frightened technician, but the usually calm director said, "Easy, men. Let's try to keep cool heads. Maybe we should pack it in anyhow, Phil. The shark hasn't surfaced in almost ten minutes now. Besides, I think we've gotten enough on film to do a good script revision based on what took place out here this afternoon."

"You're probably right, Mario," said Huebner. "It's just that six deaths have us all on edge. Oh, and I'm sorry Dwight for . . ."

"No need to apologize to me, Phil. Let's just get the hell back to shore, okay, Mario?"

Within a couple of minutes, the three men had loaded some of the small items and themselves into the outboard and shoved off from the sinking construction. Understandably, the mood was somber and no one chose to talk over the loud motor. Ordinarily, the relatively short five-minute ride between the dock and the equipment platform would have zipped by, but, that afternoon, it seemed like an eternity. While the motor buzzed along doing its best pushing the cargo, all eyes scanned the water. The men did not speak of what was in the forefront of their minds, namely, the great white and the chance that they were taking in being attacked.

Farley, not being able to take it any longer, shouted above the sound of the motor, "For chrissakes, can't we get more speed out of this thing? Sharks are known to respond to loud noises, so we'd better hurry up and reach the dock before something else happens! Besides, I can't swim!"

"Keep calm, Dwight," Rosetti said. "Chances are we probably won't see Shara again today."

Huebner smiled and said, "By the way, Mario, are you really serious about stuffing that fish and sending it around the country for publicity purposes?"

"Absolutely! And not just around the country but around the whole damn world!"

"I'm pretty sure Vista will be able to negotiate. What with all that happened out here this afternoon, Ocean World will probably come to terms, especially after I build up a lot of negative publicity. What do those small-time laboratory eggheads know?"

"Not a helluva lot, I bet," said Farley who was beginning to feel a little better upon hearing the boss's comforting words. "Ha, they'll probably take the money and run."

Whoosh!!

"Oh, my god!" yelled Huebner.

Not more than twenty-five feet away, Shara's broad head broke surface. She momentarily rolled to the side as if to let her huge black eye get a much better view of the boat and its contents. Then skimming alongside much faster than the struggling craft, Shara outdistanced it.

"What's gonna happen now?" asked Huebner. "Do you think she'll attack the boat?"

"I don't know," Rosetti answered as he and the others watched the fin turn toward them and disappear, "but we'd better not wait to find out. Any gas in that can over there?" the filmmaker asked.

Farley nervously grabbed the container, saying, "Yeah, plenty, but so what?"

"Quick, pour a trail out behind us," directed Rosetti. "We're going to try to discourage the shark from coming near the boat. Hurry up! That's good—now watch this!"

Just as he was about to toss a lighted match, the small craft was roughly bumped on the side, causing Farley to drop the five-gallon gasoline container on the floor. Huebner, who had been kneeling over the side while helping to pour fuel, fell back and struck his head, rendering him unconscious. Mario, unfortunately, dropped the match inside, and it ignited the trickle of fuel that had spilled near Huebner's feet. The threat of a blazing fire caused Mario and Dwight to lose all sense of calmness. While trying to extinguish the flames with their shirts, the steering was momentarily ignored. And that's all it took for the boat to turn out of control.

The zig-zagging shadow above highly stimulated Shara into a fighting frame of mind. Perhaps she thought it was a threatening object that had to be dealt with immediately. At any rate, the great white shark gunned her tremendous body engine upward and struck the motorboat with such force that it literally shattered, tossing objects everywhere. The partially filled gasoline can was scooped in and swallowed. Phil Huebner never regained consciousness, and maybe that was for the best, because Shara snatched the sinking man and ate him while circling and eyeing the flailing appendages of the other two men.

Rosetti tried desperately to retrieve the camera, but, because the men were not wearing life vests, he had his hands full in trying to keep his frantic workman's head above water.

"Gasp . . . spluf . . . Mario . . . gasp . . . please don't let me drown! Oh, god . . . help me!"

"Hang on to this piece of board, Dwight! That's it! Now keep moving your legs!"

"The shark, Mario, the shark! Here it comes again!"

The helpless situation in which Rosetti and Farley found themselves was climaxed within seconds after the familiar and ominous fin was seen slicing toward them.

"Oh, Jesus!"

"Holy Mary, Mother of God, pray for us sinners now and at the time of our death . . . "

Crunch!

Dwight Farley was snatched so fast as Shara attacked that the board onto which he was clinging also disappeared.

Mario never spoke another word, because he was fatally dragged down when the great white made a sharp turn and gulped in the other flailing object.

Ten

Covert Operations

1

Although the air-conditioning system in the Dade County Court House was usually adequate to cool the corridors, it was not doing a very good job in keeping down the heat generated by the well-over-thirty television and newspaper people that jammed the relatively limited space outside the Dade County Prosecutor's Office. They were impatiently awaiting the end of the special hearing that was in progress on the other side of the tall, solid oak double doors. Media photographers and T.V. technicians were constantly checking their equipment, because nobody wanted to miss any part of the hottest news in Florida.

"What a waste of taxpayer's money," said one reporter to a colleague as they lit their cigarettes.

"I'm really puzzled by this one," replied the other. "I mean, how the heck can the prosecutor take action against Ocean World in spite of all those deaths? The way I see it, Tom, Vista Studios opted to take those dangerous chances on its own. Hell, those people constantly take all kinds of chances when they're filming on location. You don't have to be wizard to know that."

"Yeah, you're right. Besides, I heard from a pretty reliable source that what the movie people really want is the shark's carcass."

"The what?"

"You heard me right—the carcass. I understand Vista's been unsuccessful in trying to get Ocean World to give 'em the fish outright in return for . . . "

"Wait a minute! You mean to tell me Vista wants to stuff it and have the damn thing travel around the country on promotionals?"

"Exactly!"

"So what you're saying is that all of this criminal negligence hype is part and parcel of Vista's scheme to get free nationwide publicity for its picture, right?"

"Exactly again! Like I said, those people stand to make an incalculable amount of money if they can get the carcass and . . . "

Just then, the oaken double doors ceremoniously swung open, and all pandemonium broke loose as media people pushed and elbowed one another for better position.

Wanda Finnie, the new county prosecutor, had been in the position less than five weeks when her office was bombarded with pressure to investigate the shark attacks. Vista lawyers had converged on Ocean World to try to convince the company that a quick settlement of the tragic situation would be far better than whipping up a lot of public opinion. However, newly elected board president, Craig Upshaw, would not even entertain the idea. As he put it, "I'd rather we take our chances with the good citizenry of Miami than sell out the one big attraction that has captured the interest of the whole world. So, let those Hollywood moguls do whatever the hell they want to do, but we're not budging!"

The prosecutor, instead of yielding to all the emotional hoopla that was generated, decided to hold a closed investigation. Media people had just about gone crazy while waiting for the word.

"Mrs. Finnie, Mrs. Finnie, over here!" yelled a reporter as he shoved his microphone ahead of about fifteen others. "Are criminal charges going to be filed against anyone?"

Even though she was new to the Dade County position, the strikingly beautiful prosecutor was certainly not new to the practicalities of handling the media.

"After having thoroughly investigated the circumstances surrounding the six deaths caused by the particular great white shark in question," said the prosecutor, "we have concluded that there was no criminal negligence involved; therefore, my office will not seek indictments."

"Ma'am," someone else said, "this shark is considered by many to be extremely dangerous and should be destroyed. Would you care to comment on that?"

"Oh, I'm quite sure there are experts who are far more qualified than I on the subject of sharks."

2

Two months later, after it had become quite apparent to Vista Studios that Ocean World was not going to consider the most recent offer of thirty million dollars for Shara, Vista's president, Conrad Blanton, made a reluctant telephone call to someone with whom he had dealings when Vista was only a struggling back-lot outfit.

"*Paisano,* I am well aware of how much you cared for Mario," Blanton said, "and that's one of the reasons why I'm calling. But I suggest we hold a little meeting rather than discuss things over the phone, all right?"

Raphael Lastoni, seventy-eight years old and in failing health, was once one of the most powerful crime bosses in Southern California. However, on the morning of his forty-third birthday, he began serving a twenty-year prison term for a murder conviction. When Lastoni was paroled after doing twelve, he diversified his approach to making money by setting up a rather sophisticated array of businesses, one of which was securing people to do highly sensitive jobs.

"All right, Conrad," the aging mobster replied, "suppose we meet at the Palermo Restaurant tomorrow afternoon, say twelve-thirty, okay? Good. I'll see you then."

After hanging up, Blanton turned around in the heavily stuffed Corinthian leather chair and remarked to his assistant, "You know, I really hate having to do this, but if there's only one person in the world who can get the desired results, Lastoni's the one."

"You have a lot of confidence in him, don't you, CB?"

"Let's face it, Don, the only way we're going to get that shark is to have at least three members of Ocean World's Board of Directors vote in favor of selling it to us, and we've already tried that without success. So-o-o-o-, I guess there's only one way to get those people into the right frame of mind . . . "

"And that is to scare hell out of them."

"Right!"

Next day, Blanton's chauffeured limousine pulled into the circular driveway of the Palermo, one of Los Angeles's leading Italian eateries. The movie head smiled as he briefly reminisced on the old days when he was trying to push Vista Studios into prominence. Lastoni did a lot toward helping Blanton by secretly using the workings of organized crime to do certain things. Needless to say how

327

grateful he was for the assistance, and, when Lastoni introduced him to a struggling young, aspiring film director, Blanton reluctantly placed the neophyte into a top position with Vista. That later proved to be, much to everyone's surprise, an excellent move, because it wasn't long after he was given his first picture assignment that Lastoni's nephew, Mario Rosetti, became quite a notable in the film industry.

"Good afternoon, Mr. Blanton," said the maitre d'. "Please, this way, sir. Mr. Lastoni is expecting you to join him in the Capri Room."

The opulence of the restaurant impressed Vista's president very much, and he made several complimentary remarks to employees as he admired the heavy Mediterranean decor that tastefully exhibited Old World charm.

After Blanton and Lastoni greeted each other with a fond embrace, they casually exchanged pleasantries while the waiters quickly brought in many delicious dishes. When the meal was over, the bodyguards left the two friends in privacy.

"So, Conrad, tell me what I can do for you," said the elder man as he puffed enjoyingly on the knobby cigar.

Two hours later, Blanton left the Palermo a much happier and satisfied man, because Mr. Lastoni, just like in years gone by, had pledged his help.

3

Arthur Mueller, chief of security at Ocean World, parked his car eight blocks away from the hotel where he was to meet with a Mr. Hagawa Nishi, the Japanese businessman who had spoken to him earlier that week. Mueller, while riding in the cab, reflected on the whirlwind of events that seemed to be carrying him into a much higher economic bracket. He thought about how he could do all of the things that were out of the question on his salary.

"Okay, buddy," said the cabbie as he pulled up to the side entrance of the Royal Palms Hotel.

Mueller paid the driver and quickly entered through a door just off the lobby. He did not bother to use the elevator to the third floor for fear of being seen by someone who might know him.

Knock, knock. The person who answered the door to Room 317 was the same hunch-shouldered little man who had set up this meeting.

"Ah, Mr. Mueller, come right in. We have been anticipating your arrival."

"We?" exclaimed the security chief, "I thought this was supposed to involve just you and me!"

"Please, Mr. Mueller," responded the smiling host as he gently held the reluctant visitor's arm and led him into the large suite. "I assure you that all is well. Kindly come in and meet my associates who had to approve of your fee."

Mueller was introduced to three other well-dressed Japanese men who simultaneously stood up and bowed as he entered. No sooner had everyone sat down when Mr. Nishi motioned to one of his associates to place a black attaché case on the marble-top coffee table in front of the visitor.

"Before we review the proposed plans," said Mr. Nishi, "perhaps you would like to see just a small portion of your reward. You certainly may open the case; it is not locked."

Mueller leaned forward and raised the lid. His eyes practically popped out when he saw stacks of money.

"The case contains exactly three hundred twenty-five thousand dollars, Mr. Mueller," said one of the other gentlemen, "half of which you may take with you this afternoon if you will assure us that you can accommodate just a few modifications in your master plan for delivering the great white shark."

While still smiling, another one said in Japanese, "Hagawa, by all that is holy to our ancestors, I hope we are not making a big mistake in trusting this Yankee pig."

"Don't worry," replied Nishi, "his movements will be shadowed by two of our contacts here in Miami. And, if at any point this fool should try to dupe us, they will kill him immediately."

"Hey, you guys," said Mueller as he watched one hundred sixty-two thousand, five hundred dollars being counted out, "what d'ya say we keep this discussion in English, okay? I get a little nervous when people I'm talking to suddenly break into a foreign language. I have to deal with enough of that crap among some of the Hispanics who work for me."

"Ah so, I am very sorry, Mr. Mueller," Nishi said, smiling, "but my associates wanted only to remind me that the freighter, *Kiska Maru,* will be standing by six miles off shore to hoist the great white shark aboard."

"And you can damn well bank on it that I'll be on time," Mueller replied. "None of you people need to worry about anything. Me and my partners will follow through just like I outlined the plan to Mr. Nishi here. Just have the rest of my money ready—cash on the barrelhead."

"Barrelhead?" asked someone perplexingly. "What does barrelhead mean?"

"Ha, ha, ha! Now you fellas know how I felt when you started talking Japanese!"

As Mueller retraced his steps through the plush lobby to a side exit, his palm began to sweat profusely. Never before had he had so much money in his possession. After quickly putting on sunglasses and switching the loaded attaché case to his dryer hand, he hailed a nearby cab and returned to the parked car eight blocks away.

4

Grace Forrestal, a very active member of Ocean World's Board of Directors, had just finished her morning workout on the tennis court and was about to open the door of her car when she was approached by two strangers. Not until they got closer did she notice that stockings covered their faces. Unfortunately, the surprised woman had no time to yell before she was grabbed and shoved into her vehicle. One man sat up front with her, and the other sat in the rear.

"If you scream, Mrs. Forrestal, your life ends here and now," said the man beside her. "But if you cooperate, no harm will come to you or your family."

He then proceeded to drive the frightened woman's car out of the club's parking lot.

"Oh, my god, please don't hurt me!"

"That depends on how well you do precisely what you're told," said the man in the back seat. "Now try to visualize a few things that will happen if you do not cooperate totally."

"Mrs. Forrestal," added the other abductor, "we know you're a loving mother of two daughters, Terri and Maegin, also the devoted wife of Dr. Robert N. Forrestal, one of the best plastic surgeons in the country."

"We also know that you still keep weekly contact with your parents up north in Rumson, New Jersey. I might add that I think their home at 1411 Highland Avenue is quite beautiful."

"Yeah, I'd certainly hate to see it destroyed—with them inside."

"Shh, don't say anything, Mrs. Forrestal, until we've finished, because it is extremely important that you not take all of this for some kind of joke."

"What he means, in other words, Mrs. Forrestal, is we will kill you, your children, your husband, your mother, and your father if you do not vote the right way at tomorrow morning's special meeting of Ocean World's Board of Directors."

During the half-hour drive, Grace Forrestal was totally convinced that her abductors had not only gathered sufficient data concerning daily movements of her family members but also minute details pertaining to each person's likes and dislikes. There was no question in her mind that the safety of her loved ones hinged solely on whether she would cooperate.

The man sitting beside the horrified woman did not project the image of the typical rough hoodlum. Perhaps that was part of the reason why Mrs. Forrestal listened so intently.

"I assure you, madam, that our organization wishes you and your family no harm, but I also assure you that all of you will die within twenty-four hours after the vote if it is not a favorable one."

"But what about the other members of the board?" she asked, "I can't possibly guarantee their vote on . . ."

"Please do not concern yourself with their actions," interrupted the man in the rear seat. "Even as we speak, they are also being counseled."

"What my associate is intimating, Mrs. Forrestal," said the driver, "is there's no need to explain your vote subsequently since the issue was and still is a legitimate one. Besides, we are positive that none of you will be eager to discuss the real reason that prompted you to vote in the affirmative."

"Yes, especially since our nationwide organization will be monitoring all of you and your families for the next twelve months."

331

When they were convinced that their victim was sufficiently orientated, the driver stopped at a fairly busy North Miami intersection.

"As you've noticed, Mrs. Forrestal," said the driver, "We have not made any advances on your belongings or your body. This is strictly business; therefore, the organization reasonably expects you to cooperate one hundred percent. Might we count on your affirmative vote tomorrow?"

"Absolutely!" came the relieved woman's reply.

"Good," replied the man in the rear. "You may get out here, madam. As for your automobile, walk three blocks straight ahead, and you'll find it parked. The key will be over the driver's sun visor."

5

Dr. Prescott's secretary was astonished to find that at ten o'clock in the morning all but three of the board members had already shown up for the meeting, which was scheduled to begin at ten-thirty. When she brought in the processed mail, Miss Langley felt urged to make a comment to her boss, "I still can't figure this one out, sir. There have been numerous meetings of importance, but never before have I ever known so many members to arrive so early! My goodness, we're usually lucky if we get even a quorum by noon! What's so important today? The agenda is certainly not a very interesting one."

Dr. Prescott was almost oblivious to what his secretary was saying, because he was engrossed in perusing one of several travel brochures.

"Rhoda," said the president as he hunched over the colorful folder on his desk, "did you know that this is the best time of year to go to the Scandinavian countries? There are no ice floes jamming the fjords, and the air is so fresh! Ah, but Mrs. Prescott and I haven't really made up our minds as to where we want to go. All I know right now is next week I'm starting my vacation, and I don't want anything to stand in the way. Now what were you saying about the board members, Rhoda? Boy, I'm really not tuned into Ocean World this morning, am I?"

"Ha, ha, you certainly aren't, sir, but you've been working extremely hard this year, and you should just forget about this place for awhile."

"That's easier said than done, Rhoda, but I'm going to try. Who's the latest to arrive?"

"Mr. Upshaw came in a few minutes ago. Everyone's in the conference room. The caterer set up the breakfast buffet in his delicious style as usual. Want me to bring you a nice hot cup of herbal tea before you go in?"

"Umm, no thanks. I think I'll join the others now. Since the agenda's a light one, maybe these people will get out of here in a hurry today."

"That would be perfect for you," said the efficient secretary as she checked her boss's appointment calendar, "because you're scheduled to meet with a couple of people from Vista Studios at three o'clock."

"Hrumph, now *that* shouldn't take long," Prescott replied while briefly looking over several papers as he placed them into a folder. "You would think that after I made a personal call to Mr. Blanton, Vista would've gotten the clear message—no deal! What's wrong with those people? Don't they talk to one another?"

"Well, sir, you know how those Hollywood characters are—always living in a world of make-believe. Maybe they think the Wizard of Oz will *make* us sell Shara to them."

Dr. Prescott was still chuckling to himself as he approached the door of the conference room. Usually, the board members' voices could be heard, but there was hardly a sound penetrating the oak-paneled walls that day.

"Ah, good morning, everyone," came Prescott's warm greeting as he proceeded to shake each male board member's hand and lightly kiss the two ladies on the cheek.

"Wes," said the Board of Directors' President Upshaw, "we were just commenting on how busy all of us are today, so suppose we get started, okay?"

"Fine, That's fine with me, Craig," smiled Prescott as he took a buttered cinnamon croissant. "Hey, you folks have hardly touched the food! Martha, Grace, you ladies be sure to taste the caviar before you leave. It's not quite Beluga, but what the heck!"

Ordinarily the atmosphere of the meeting would have been filled with jovial tones and loose construction; however, this particular one was not, and Dr. Prescott got the message clearly when Doug Winchester said to Upshaw, "Mr. President, can we begin now? I have several important things that must be done today."

A half-hour later, the Board came to the last item on the agenda after practically racing through the others. Dr. Prescott, although marveling at the rapidity with which the meeting was moving, was eager to get back to the travel brochures before lunch.

"In the matter of Vista Studios wanting to purchase Shara," said Upshaw as he thumbed quickly through the several pages of the offer, "all of us have had ample time to consider whether . . . "

"Excuse me, Craig," Prescott interrupted, "I just want the Board to know that I did follow through on calling Mr. Conrad Blanton over two weeks ago and informed him of the unlikelihood that Ocean World would sell Shara at any price."

Then something suddenly occurred that was most unusual. Grace Forrestal erupted like Mt. Vesuvius did on that balmy summer's afternoon in 79 A.D. She took everyone by surprise, especially Dr. Prescott.

"And just who the hell authorized you to do a stupid thing like that?" she bellowed. "If I recall correctly, and I most certainly do, you were supposed to simply hold up on any further discussion with Vista Studios until this month's meeting, nothing more!"

"Yes, but, Grace, I thought . . . "

"You thought! Dr. Prescott, I am well aware of your competency as Ocean World's chief administrator, but we're not paying you to do *all* of our thinking for us! I mean, my god, couldn't you have at least waited until we make things official before you called that . . . that . . . man?"

To say Prescott was taken somewhat aback would really be an understatement. The man was numbed. Never before had the demure Mrs. Forrestal ever spoken out against any of his statements or actions. She had always supported him on every previous issue during her six years on the Board. What was also surprising to the confused executive was the subsequent lack of elaboration by anyone else. Even Bob Amesley, who usually had a lot to say about everything that involved money, breezed over this outburst with apparent ease.

"Wes," he said, "I know we probably gave you the impression that we weren't interested in selling Shara, but, as you know, Ocean World is already faced with a heck of a lot of lawsuits steming from the many deaths caused by . . ."

"Craig, please," interrupted Martha Van Toland as she nervously lit another cigarette. "Do we have to regurgitate all of the distasteful events surrounding that awful creature? I suggest we just get on with the business at hand, namely, the vote."

"Okay, okay, everybody," Board President Craig Upshaw interjected. "There's no need to come down on Wes's butt. Hell, I was the one who unofficially told him to call those people. But . . . er . . . ahem . . . at the time, I didn't project that . . . er . . . that . . . ahem . . . so much more money would have to be paid out for . . ."

"Wait a minute!" shouted Prescott. "What's come over you people all of a sudden? Bob, you yourself checked into our accounting division, and you saw that what Shara and Talanski could bring in during the next year alone could more than triple what Vista's offering!"

Amesley shot out with, "Damn it, Wes, why can't you just shut up, and let the Board do its work? Besides, what I did was all unofficial anyhow! This is the time for real action!"

"I couldn't agree with you more," said Doug Winchester. "So why don't we just do what Martha suggested, and vote the sale up or down right now?"

Silence followed Winchester's words while everyone, except Prescott, seemed to be avoiding one another's eyes and needlessly shuffling through papers. What subsequently took place was undoubtedly the most meaningful action that the Board had ever undertaken.

"All right, members of the Board of Ocean World, I, your president," said Upshaw in a manner which Prescott noticed was entirely out of character, "am now ready to entertain a motion."

Grace Forrestal, after being recognized by the chair, said, "Mr. President, I make a motion that Ocean World, for the sum of thirty million dollars, as stated in the offer, immediately, and I do mean immediately, accept Vista Studio's proposal to purchase Shara, our great white shark."

Eye contact and warmth were absent. Dr. Prescott's blood pressure was trying to burst through the top of his head.

"I second the motion," Doug Winchester followed.

Even though Prescott knew that he was not supposed to take part in the Board's voting on various matters, he felt the itching urgency to speak up, regardless.

"Please," the perspiring executive began, "I beg of you! Don't make this terrible mistake! We'd be throwing away the best money-generating source we could ever expect to . . ."

"Dr. Prescott," interrupted millionairess Martha Van Toland, "you know full well that this Board has, in the past, always valued your suggestions; however, the money Vista Studios is going to pay us for that fish represents . . ."

"Come on, Craig," Amesley interjected, "there's a motion on the floor, and we're wasting time."

"All right, all right," came the president's response. "You've heard the motion, people. Those in favor, please your hands."

Immediately, and without any apparent hesitation, every Board member's hand shot upward. The deed was done. The final agenda item was resolved, and, within the next sixty seconds, the meeting room was emptied of all persons other than the surprised and confused executive. When his secretary entered and saw him leaning against the wall while staring blankly out of the large picture window, she was startled.

"Dr. Prescott, are you feeling ill?"

Instead of responding to the question, he motioned her to join him at the window.

"Rhoda, what we're looking at out there is one heck of a beautiful complex, wouldn't you say?"

"Why . . . er . . . yes, it certainly is."

"And would you also say that I've played at least some minor role in making Ocean World financially successful?"

"Oh, definitely, sir."

"Rhoda, have you ever known me to make illogical recommendations to this Board or misfire on zeroing in on enterprises that could enhance our ability to bring in more revenue?"

"Of course not, sir!"

"Then why in the name of all that's holy did the Board, not more than five minutes ago, decide to throw away the greatest single revenue source Ocean World has ever had?"

"I don't quite understand, sir."

"And that's the exact point—because neither do I! Rhoda, the Board has decided to accept Vista's offer to buy Shara."

"Oh, no! How could they! Everybody knows what a stupid move that would be! Besides, Mr. Talanski's going to have a fit when he learns of this!"

"That could very easily be the understatement of the year, Rhoda."

Prescott put his arm around the secretary's shoulder as they slowly left the meeting room. When she began to sniffle, he said, "There, there now, young lady," giving her his handkerchief, "no time for that. We have to take care of a few unexpected matters before this workday is over.

"First thing I want you to do is to connect me with Blanton in California; then I want you to set up a two o'clock meeting in my office with the head of our legal department. Old Horace might be a little reluctant to cut short his usual three-martini lunch, but tell him this is of the utmost urgency. Oh, and suggest he bring along two of his sharpest assistants. We certainly don't want anything to slip between the cracks. Phew, now comes the most unkindest cut of all. Call Joe over at the lake, and ask him to see me right after his four o'clock show ends."

"Should I call Mrs. Prescott, sir? It looks like you're going to be a little late today."

"Umm, no, that's all right, Rhoda. I'll wait until later this afternoon. You know, I can't, for the life of me, figure out why the Board did a complete about-face on this Vista offer. It's the strangest darn thing, because every member voted affirmative. I'm telling you Rhoda, it was as though I didn't even know those people in there this morning!"

6

The boat, equipped with heavy-duty hoisting gear, cut its engine and dropped anchor just a little over twenty yards outside of the lake that contained Shara. Even though the two men on board had thoroughly reviewed the plan, they were still somewhat nervous about carrying it out.

"Sure hope to hell nothing goes wrong," one said as he and the other man placed several buckets of bloody tuna near the railing.

"Jeff, you worry too much, you know that? Besides, with the ten grand apiece Art gave us last night and ten more coming when we deliver the shark, you can take the little woman on that European tour you've been talking about for a million years."

"Yeah, I guess so. But I still think we should've gotten a bigger slice of the ninety grand Art told us he had got in advance. And the more I think about it, Mel, the more I think Art . . ."

"Jeff, how long have you, Art, and me been friends?"

"I know what you're gonna say, but friendship has a way of taking a back seat when a lot of money's involved. Damn, it just seems to me that with Art being the pretty smart fellow we know him to be, he would've gotten more than just ninety grand deposit from those Japs."

So far, Mueller's plan was working very well, and he made sure that the other security guards saw him in the area.

"Good afternoon, Mr. Mueller," said the guard whose job it was to watch the electronic control panel that monitored everything from the oxygen level in the underwater observation deck to the reinforced steel chain-link gate.

"Hi, Walt," returned the security chief. "How're things going? Pretty dull, huh?"

"Yes, sir, especially since Shara's last performance three days ago. I still can't understand why we're selling her to that movie outfit. Damn, boss, it seems stupid as hell for Ocean World to let go of a gold mine like that! And poor Mr. Talanski—I really feel sorry for him. You know, he's been out there in the lake since yesterday morning. I guess the thought of losing Shara is too much for him."

Mueller, upon learning of Joe's presence, worried about whether the plan should be executed regardless. However, if the security chief had known that our hero was sleeping off the effects of a two-day drinking binge, there would've been no cause for any great concern.

"No one should be in the observation deck!" Mueller said as he casually eased over to the control console. "Rules pertaining to maximum security are for everybody, even him! Let me see today's log sheet, Walt. I want to check something."

When the young guard momentarily left his seat to get the clipboard, Mueller quickly pressed the button that raised the underwater gate. As per the plan, the security chief positioned himself in such a way that the other man did not notice what had happened.

"Okay, Jeff, it's four-thirty on the dot. Should we start dumping the buckets?"

"Yeah, just like Art planned it—now unless something's gone wrong," Jeff replied as they began emptying the bloody contents over the side, "but he's such a stickler for preciseness that I can't imagine any kind of goof up."

The hpyersensitive fluid canals in Shara's back signaled her that something worthwhile investigating was in the area, and she geared her gigantic body to cover the mile and a half distance to the fence very quickly.

"Bingo!" shouted Mel pointing to the fin he saw slicing through the water toward them. "Here she comes, good buddy, right on time!"

"Great! Just keep dumping those buckets while I check the hoisting harness. Don't want anything to go wrong at this stage of the game, right?"

Meanwhile, back at the security station, Mueller was doing a fine job in keeping his subordinate's attention away from the console. ". . . so that's the kind of crap all of us had to do twenty years ago, Walt. I mean there was no such thing as a union shop. The old man ran this place with an iron fist, and, when he told you to jump, you never dared ask why—but instead how high!"

"Ha, ha, ha, wow! You guys really had some rough times! Do you think those days might be returning, chief?"

The veteran just smiled as he looked at his watch and replied, "I doubt it, kid. Things are much better all around now. What entry level guards get these days took damn near five years for me to work up to."

Mueller subtly pressed another button that closed the gate.

"Christ, look at the time!" he said. "I didn't intend to stay so long and bore you."

"Oh, not at all," came the subordinate's reply. "I enjoyed your company, sir. Thanks for stopping by."

When his boss left, Walt cursorily looked over the control console as he turned on the transistor radio to a rock station and settled down to phone his girlfriend.

A half-hour later, Mueller's little outboard was being tied alongside as the co-conspirators hurriedly prepared for the next and most difficult phase of their plan. Jeff and Mel had already put on their diving gear and were ready to move when told.

"Like I said, Art," Jeff remarked, "she's been nothing but cooperative. Me and Mel have been timing the dumpings so as to keep her interested. There! There she is again! And we thought this was gonna be real hard!"

"Don't cheer too soon," cautioned Mueller while lowering the leather harness into the water. "Remember, we have to move very fast and with extreme care once the tranquilizer has knocked her out."

As she had done hundreds of times before, Shara frequently rolled over on her side while gulping huge chunks of blood-covered tuna. The black pupilless eye of indifference surveyed the long object from which food was being thrown.

Pow!

The feathered tranquilizer dart found its mark several inches in front of the great white's gill slits.

"Good shot, boss!" Mel shouted.

The security chief kept his eyes riveted to his watch and said, "Okay, now it's touch 'n go, fellas. Tell me when she surfaces again, because we want to be sure about the effectiveness of this stuff before we even *think* about going in."

More tuna was tossed overboard while the three partners waited for Shara to reappear.

"Damn, I hope the dosage wasn't too much," Mueller said, "because she'll certainly die if she stops swimming."

"In that case," replied Mel, "it's too bad we don't have a deal going with the movie outfit."

"Shut up, asshole!" snapped Jeff. 'Now's not the time for crumby jokes or any of . . . all right, there she is, boss!"

"Forty-eight seconds," Mueller uttered as he lifted the rifle to his shoulder again. "She was down forty-eight seconds, so this one should do it. Easy now, just a little closer, sweetheart, and . . ."

Pow!

"Hurry up, guys! Get your oxygen valves adjusted. Okay, when my hands drops, go in," came Mueller's directions as he again checked his watch.

When one minute and fifteen seconds elapsed, the security chief dropped his hand. Jeff and Mel, equipped with grappling hooks, submarine searchlights, a couple of powerful dart guns, and various other items clasped to their utility belts, toppled backward into the water.

The depth of the channel where the boat was anchored was just under seventy feet. And, just as Mueller had predicted, Shara was found on the bottom. Although her mouth was still partially open as she lay tilted to one side, the great white appeared to be having difficulty breathing.

Mel and Jeff, knowing that their quarry was suffocating because of her not moving forward, quickly went to work. They placed the several big leather straps around the shark's thick body. Then Jeff surfaced to tell Mueller how much lift should be applied to the winch.

In his partner's absence, Mel could not pass up the temptation to get a nice three-inch tooth for a souvenir. He took out his knife and approached the dangerous head from above. However, the diver could not reach the desired angle from that position, so he decided to go at it from the front. Stopping momentarily to view this enormously broad face, the excited souvenir-seeker thought about how chic it would look to have the tooth on an eighteen-karat-gold chain around his neck. With one hand pushing upwards against the great white's rough nose, Mel reached toward the mouth which was still only partially cracked. Suddenly, the orifice opened to nearly three feet. The rapidity with which this was done created such a back force of inrushing water that poor Mel was sucked right into the black hole. Only a few crimson streams of blood drifted from the area; otherwise, no sign of the hopeless diver was discernable. In spite of the split-second action, Shara still remained tilted on the sandy bottom and semi-sedated.

A few minutes later, the slack ropes became taut as they began straining to raise the listing shark.

"I'm sure Mel is all right," said Mueller while operating the hoisting mechanism.

"Yeah, but the jerk should've come up by now!" Jeff exclaimed. "He was supposed to follow me up in two minutes! I even printed it on the tablet and showed it to him!"

"According to the footage I've winched in," Mueller said, "the fish is now forty-six feet off the bottom, and we're ready to shove off."

"But, chief. . . ."

"No *buts,* Jeff! If we don't move soon, she's either gonna come from under the tranquilizer or die on us before we can get her to the Jap ship! Now, I don't know about you, but I'm damn tired of grubbing for peanuts—we're talking money here, Jeff! Look, let me put it another way. Those people've already given us a fat deposit which we're gonna have to give back if we don't make the delivery."

"Okay, okay, I understand all of that, but it would only take a few minutes for us to check on Mel—that stupid sonofabitch."

As soon as Mueller had hurriedly stripped to his shorts and put on a couple of oxygen tanks, the two men went down to inspect the harnessed shark and look for their missing partner. Since the brief search of the area did not reveal any indications of Mel's whereabouts, the divers returned to deck and got the boat underway.

It took almost an hour and a half for the two Ocean World security guards to reach the waiting freighter, *Kiska Maru.* The setting sun looked like a large Florida orange as it was about to touch the horizon. Once, during the towing, they stopped and shot another tranquilizer dart into the great white, because the other two were beginning to wear off. Within ninety seconds after the smaller vessel was secured near the freighter, Mr.Nishi, accompanied by three scuba divers, came down the ladder to greet the Americans.

"Ah, Mr. Mueller," said the well-dressed negotiator, smiling. "I trust you have delivered the merchandise in good condition."

Without waiting for a reply, Mr. Nishi motioned his hand, and the three divers proceeded to the rear of the boat and jumped into the water. Moments later, they were back on board and speaking in Japanese.

"For some reason," whispered Jeff to Mueller, "I'm beginning to get a real uneasy feeling about this deal. Look at those guys up there on the railing. Come on, Art. Let's pick up the rest of our dough and get the hell outta here."

"Take it easy. For crying out loud, Jeff, where're your manners? You just don't grab a handful of money and run. We're dealing with businessmen, not a bunch of Miami druggies. Just keep your mouth shut, and let me do all of the talking, okay?"

342

Mr. Nishi, still smiling, re-joined the two Americans after conferring with his divers. "I am assured that the shark is secured in the harness and that she is still under the effects of tranquilizers. Congratulations on successfully executing your obligations, Mr. Mueller. Now if you and . . . ah . . . Mr. . . . ah . . ."

"Fenwick, Jeff Fenwick," Ocean World's security chief said.

"Splendid. Please accompany me to the captain's quarters, gentlemen. While the shark is being placed into a specially constructed underwater cage, we must drink a *sake* toast for good luck. As you probably know, great white sharks die quickly in totally restricted captivity, so that is why we decided to put Shara into a steel cage that measures sixteen feet wide and forty-five feet in length."

When the Americans boarded the freighter, they saw not only the cage but also the huge submersible pontoon on which the cage would rest while being towed. Undoubtedly, extensive preparation had been taken for that moment, and no concern that might assure a safe and uninterrupted voyage back to Japan was overlooked.

As soon as Jeff saw the contents of the black attaché case, he almost cried out with joy. Never before had he seen so much money. However, silent anger began to overtake his mind when he heard Mr. Nishi say, "As per our agreement, Mr. Mueller, this one hundred sixty-two thousand, five hundred dollars represents the remaining half of the balance that we owe you."

Being a shrewd businessman, whose ability to pick up even the slightest vibration, was one of Mr. Nishi's strongest assets. He immediately detected the change in Jeff's general demeanor and said, "Gentlemen, please excuse me for a moment. I want to say a word to our loading supervisor. I should not be long. Oh, also please do not feel offended because of my having these three crew members remain here in the room. Even though the money is yours, Mr. Mueller, I would deeply appreciate your not touching it until I return. Then we shall count it together, yes?"

"Er . . . sure thing, Mr. Nishi," replied Mueller in a voice like that of a politician who got caught with his hand in the cookie jar.

"Oh, by the way," the smiling Oriental remarked, "these men do not speak English. I certainly hope that you will not have a problem with this."

Neither Mueller nor Jeff uttered a single word for nearly fifteen seconds after Mr. Nishi left the room They both just sat staring at the contents of the case. Then, without taking his eyes off the money, Jeff leaned back in his seat and calmly said, "Art, you're a no good sonofabitch."

In an equally calm tone, the security head replied, "I know. I also know that with only you and me to divvy up this bundle, I'm more than willing to split it with you fifty-fifty, okay, big guy?"

"Mel, may his soul rest in peace, was not exactly the smartest man in the world, but he was my friend, you slick bastard."

Then a broad smile radiated across Jeff's face as he continued looking only at the neatly stacked 100s and 50s and said, "Okay, Art, we'll chop this right down the middle as soon as your Jap friend gets back—and no more fuckin' bullshit."

Meanwhile, Mr. Nishi was finalizing an agreement with two crewmen as they headed toward the room where the two Americans were impatiently waiting. "Absolutely no mistakes can be made at this juncture, do you understand? It must be done in an atmosphere of total surprise."

One of the crewmen grinned as he replied, "Just like Pearl Harbor."

Five minutes later, Mueller and Jeff were officially given the money. Needless to say the two men, although now being very apprehensive of each other, wanted only to take their leave of this scene and get back to port. However, while sitting at the table and sipping warm *sake* with Mr. Nishi, Mueller and his partner did not notice how closely behind their chairs two deck hands were standing. Suddenly, six shots rapidly came from silencer-equipped pistols. So, within a matter of seconds, visions of financial security had evaporated for the ambitious duo from Ocean World. Upon carefully examining the slumping bodies, Mr. Nishi was quite satisfied that they were dead.

Perhaps in their enthusiasm to get the great white shark positioned just right for cage entry, the scuba divers did not think that another tranquilizer dart was necessary. At any rate, when the four tons of revived flesh started thrashing around while being hoisted out of the water, smoke began spewing from the breaking mechanism on the hoist as it strained to hold the load in check.

Snap!!

The harness broke, and Shara, now being totally free, made a couple of stiff tail movements that propelled her completely away from the *Kiska Maru*.

When Mr. Nishi learned of this terrible twist of fortune, he remarked to the captain, "Within my grasp, I had the opportunity to give Japan something of great value. Now, I give nothing but dishonor.

"My friend, you know what I must do. Please provide me with the ceremonial items. At this juncture, there is no other honorable exit for me."

Suffice to say, Mr. Nishi did what he thought he had to do. That same night, the disappointed arranger of high-level business deals arranged and successfully followed through on his last act—hari-kari.

Eleven

Realignment of Priorities

1

"How can you be so damn nonchalant about this, Joe?" asked Mark Davenport as they sat in Dr. Prescott's office. "We've lost the biggest money-maker conceivable, and all you can say is you hope she's all right!"

The three men were continuing their discussion concerning the missing great white shark. During the five days since the discovery, an Ocean World search team, headed by Dr. Davenport, spent many hours following through on any and all leads pertaining to reported great white sightings. Divers, clad in chain-mesh outfits, even encountered a few great whites, but none of them were Shara's size. It was originally believed that she would return to the lake area since this was where plenty of food, plus her human friend, was found.

As for Mueller and his two accomplices, no connection whatever linked them to the missing shark. Suffice to say, the *Kiska Maru's* captain had tied up all loose ends most efficiently. Not only were the bodies of the two Americans dismembered and incinerated but their boat was towed further out to sea and scuttled in three thousand feet of water.

"That's right," returned Joe. "My greatest wish at this time is for Shara to be safe. Earlier this week, I had some misgivings about the whole idea of trying to find her, but now I'm pretty sure that she's gone. You know, every time I think of how Shara must have leaped over the gate, I have to laugh. Plus every time I think of how you people around here believe that I had something to do with Shara's disappearance, I have to laugh even harder."

"Hrumph . . . well . . . er . . . Joe," Prescott began as he shifted uneasily in his cushioned swivel chair, "you must admit that for her

346

to be missing a few days after you and I talked about the Vista deal is rather suspect. A great deal of money was riding on that agreement."

Mark could see the anger rising in Talanski's face, so he tried to soften Prescott's innuendo with, "Joe, you and I came a long way with Shara. We go back to the first sighting, and our lives haven't been the same since then. But I think it's accurate to say that all of us here at Ocean World are a damnsight better off financially because of her. Yes, there've been some tragedies along the way, but they were bound to occur considering the unknown and unstable factors involved. Oh, and what about the strange things that happened to three members of our Board of Directors?"

Mark was referring to the massive heart attacks suffered by Bob Amesley and Grace Forrestal. Both of them were still in intensive care units. Also, one day after the shark was discovered missing, Martha Van Toland and her husband left the country without a trace.

"(Sigh) I've had it with everything," said Joe in a tone barely over a whisper.

"What did you say?" asked Dr. Prescott.

"I said I'm leaving, gentlemen, as in going through that door and never looking back."

'You can't desert us now, Joe!" the president exclaimed, "There are too many questions to be answered about . . ."

"Aw, cut it, Wes! How the hell can I give the kind of answers that will satisfy the press and everybody else? Remember, I'm the same guy who, after you people decided to sell Shara to Vista, was actually out of a job! Ocean World didn't need me anymore, and you know it! The only reason why they kept me on the payroll is because you and Mark here spoke up on my behalf. Otherwise, I would've been out on my ass the same day the show closed.

"Look, I'm grateful to you gentlemen for what you did, but, as old Harry would've probably said, the show's over. Besides, believe it or not, I'm anxious to get out to sea. Ha, ha, can you imagine that! I'm going to load up the rig and set sail for wherever."

Davenport, while listening to Joe, decided that it would serve no benefit to Ocean World to persuade him to remain. However, the marine biologist wanted to talk to Talanski in an entirely different atmosphere. That's why, when Dr. Prescott's secretary buzzed the president for an important phone call, Davenport seized the opportunity to say, "Sounds like Wes is going to be tied up for awhile, Joe. What d'ya say you and I retreat to a watering hole for a couple of cool ones. That is, if you're not planning to hoist anchor right now and sail into the sunset."

Joe laughed as they waved to Prescott and left the office.

At two o'clock in the afternoon, there weren't many patrons in Cavanaugh's. After their second round of beers, Mark began to talk about his suppressed desire to be more adventuresome. ". . . . you might say I was programmed for academic success right from day one. Hell, man, I couldn't have failed if I'd tried! Top honors at Canterbury up in Connecticut, *cum laude* out of Tufts at twenty, and accepted that same year into med school."

Joe always considered himself to be a good listener, but when his drinking buddy left him hanging on the med school thing, he became impatient with, "So?"

"So what?"

"So what the hell happened with med school?"

"Damn! You were listening after all, weren't you?"

Joe just smiled and said, as he signaled for the bartender to refill their mugs, "Of course I was listening; even though you're boring as hell."

"Ah ha!" Mark shouted, lightly punching his friend on the shoulder. "That's exactly what's wrong with me, Joseph! I am definitely boring. Hell, I've known it for years! What else could I be while ploughing the fields of academia? Oh, yeah, you want to know about med school, right?"

Joe nodded affirmatively while hunched over and resting both elbows on the bar.

"Well, my dad, he's still a practicing physician back home in Fall River, was proud as hell that . . . hey, what's so damn funny?"

"Oh, nothing much, Mark. I was just thinking about my stepfather back in the 'Burgh. He's a doctor, too."

"Well, well! I didn't know you were a chosen one also!"

"Ha, ha. No, my friend, I would hardly consider myself a chosen one. But that's another story. Go on with yours."

Mark waved his hand saying, "Hey, Don, how 'bout two more up this end! Well, let's see, where was I? Oh, yeah, I had been accepted to Harvard Medical School. Went one year, Joe. Got As and the rest Bs in all courses. But you know what?"

"What?"

"Met this gorgeous redhead at a Fourth of July party. She was from Palm Beach and visiting relatives in Boston. Heather stole my heart that summer, Joe, but I guess she wasn't as serious as I was about marriage. At any rate, I just had to be near her, know what I mean? So the proverbial feces struck the proverbial fan when I informed my parents that I was taking a leave from med school and going down to Florida for a year. Well, my mother tried to die and dad threatened to disown me for disgracing the family, as he put it. At any rate, I got a part-time job as a lab assistant in the grad school here at University of Miami."

"How did things work out between you and Heather?"

"You had to ask, didn't you?"

"Gee, Mark, I'm sorry to . . ."

"Hey, no problem! I can talk about everything! Wouldn't have been able to do it fifteen years ago, but I'm okay now. You asked about Heather. First of all, I should've told you that she was an obedient child, as it were. Hell, Heather did what her bourbon-'n-branch-water-drinking old pappy wanted her to do—she dumped me and married Roger Crestwood, heir apparent to Crestwood Stables, the polo pony people. After I stopped feeling sorry for myself, I decided to have some fun with every skirt in Florida. That was also when I enrolled for a Ph.D. in marine biology at the University of Florida. Joe, I'm telling you, I used to have so many broads that all of my buddies wondered how I could stay out practically every night and still pull top grades. Shit! What they didn't know was that I was cursed with a brain that damn near works independently of . . . am I boring you yet?"

"No, Mark, not at all. I find all of this very interesting."

"Liar. But that's okay. I'm damn near immune to having my feelings hurt. So, anyway, I breezed through the doctorate program and graduated with honors, naturally."

"Hmm, nice going, Mark. Hey, Don, two more!"

"Nice, you say? Then why the hell didn't my dad come down for graduation? Mom and my sister were there—offered all kinds of lame excuses for him. But here I am, Joe, making more money than I'll ever spend and at the head of the line for ole Wes's job.

349

So why am I so fucking unhappy? I'll tell you why I'm so fucking unhappy. Next month, I'll be forty-two, pal, and I'd like to do something real adventurous. Hell, I'm still a bachelor, no real responsibilities outside of Ocean World, and I'd like to sail with you."

Joe, almost choking on the pretzels he had been munching, exclaimed, "What?!"

"Look, I can easily get a year's leave of absence to do extended marine research, and . . ."

"Forget it, Mark! I don't need any more burdens at this point in my life. You say you'll be forty-two soon? Well, then stay the hell away from me if you'd like to reach forty-three. Take a good look at me, man! I'm not even thirty yet, but already I've seen and been through more tragedies than you could ever imagine. Too many people I grew to love either had their lives seriously hurt or snuffed out completely. You spoke of being cursed with a good brain? Well, buddy, I'm cursed with being bad news for anybody who becomes my close friend. Case in point, Mark, look what happened to Shara. She probably would've been a helluva lot better off if we had never met. Look what happened to her!"

"Don't blame yourself for Shara's disappearance, Joe. She's gone, and we're all richer because of her."

"You know, I've had this strange feeling, Mark, that she is out there waiting for me, and I have to go to her. Nothing else matters."

Davenport understood his friend's feelings very well. Perhaps that's why he said, "A year and a half ago, I would've called you crazy. But I saw you and Shara together, Joe, from day one. And her apparent love for you transcended all instincts and drives possessed by her kind."

"Listen to yourself," Talanski said while lighting another cigarette. "You're talking about Shara as though she's a human being, a woman who's in love."

"Damn! You're right, Joe! I must be off my rocker—or too many beers here."

"No, neither of the above. If Shara is alive, and I believe she is, she'll come looking for me. I don't know whether our relationship will remain as it was, or whether she'll attack this thing that has caused her to be out of character. At any rate, Mark, I have to go out there—alone."

2

The deck of Captain Eddie's party boat was crowded with Saturday morning fishermen who were eagerly looking forward to catching some of the blues that were running heavily in the area. Shortly before seven-thirty, the Miami-based vessel idled her engines, and the chatty, beer-guzzling passengers cast their lines over the side. Suddenly a crewman saw a fin slicing through the water.

"Well, I'll be damned! Hey, Lefty, how would you like to hook a nice big mako?"

"Where?"

"Look closely off starboard stern. See it? There—there—right there!"

"Okay, okay, yeah, I see him! He's coming on fast! Quick, Norm, tell the captain before one of these freakin' weekend warriors gets the same idea!"

Seconds later, two blasts of the boat's horn signaled the raising of all fishing poles. The shark swam around the boat several times. And when it came close enough to the surface, even Captain Eddie became reluctant to pursue his previous thoughts.

"My god!" he uttered. "That's no mako! That's a great white!"

"Let's go for it, Eddie!" shouted one of the fishermen. "Maybe it's the same shark that escaped from Ocean World!"

The huge head broke surface, and the people on deck saw the black orb looking at them for almost eight seconds before the full thirty-four-foot length of Shara skimmed the top and disappeared.

"Did you see that?" said a crewman. "It was as though the shark was looking for somebody in particular!"

3

Talanski had already stocked and serviced his boat. So, when he heard about that morning's sighting, he headed through the channel and into the open sea. For three days our hero, miles away from land, sailed and dove randomly in hope of finding Shara—or being found by her.

Shortly before sunrise on the fourth day, Joe was jolted out of a light slumber.

Thud!

"Holy shit! What the hell was that! Oh, God, don't tell me I've hit something!"

Thud!

He flung open the hatch and began checking for damage.

Whoosh!

Up from the water, and within ten feet of the boat, rose the gigantic head of a great white shark. Joe stood paralyzed for a moment as he gazed at the form. Then it disappeared below the surface.

"No! Shara, don't leave me!! Please don't leave me!!"

With no equipment, or hesitation, Joe plunged head first into the brine. Suddenly, the tremendously thick body of the great white smoothly glided by, its rough skin brushing against Talanski's legs. In a quick, effortless turn, Shara's broad face moved closer. Joe's lungs were practically bursting when he came up for air. Then Shara rose directly beneath him, and she felt something pleasant touch her dorsal fin. Immediately, just as she had done so many times in the past, the great white accelerated with Joe hanging on. When he finally let go, our happy hero, although nearly two hundred yards from his boat, was crying tears of joy.

Shara surfaced several times nearby as her friend swam back to his boat. Finally, Joe mustered enough energy to pull himself aboard. He was not only extremely tired but extremely happy. While lying flat on his back and resting, Talanski took time to think about the present state of affairs. One of the things he decided was that he would never again jeopardize the safety of his great white shark. Joe also decided that he would set sail for the Caribbean immediately—meaning there was no need to ever go back to Miami.

After he had rested somewhat, Talanski stood up and watched the periodic appearance of his friend. Then, in a voice that fanned out over the wide expanse, he yelled, "I love you, Shara!"